THE
BUCCANEERS

By Edith Wharton

THE
BUCCANEERS

A Novel by

Edith Wharton

COMPLETED BY MARION MAINWARING

VIKING

VIKING
Published by the Penguin Group
Penguin Books USA Inc., 375 Hudson Street,
New York, New York 10014, U.S.A.
Penguin Books Ltd, 27 Wrights Lane, London W8 5TZ, England
Penguin Books Australia Ltd, Ringwood, Victoria, Australia
Penguin Books Canada Ltd, 10 Alcorn Avenue,
Toronto, Ontario, Canada M4V 3B2
Penguin Books (N.Z.) Ltd, 182–190 Wairau Road,
Auckland 10, New Zealand

Penguin Books Ltd, Registered Offices:
Harmondsworth, Middlesex, England

First published in 1993 by Viking Penguin,
a division of Penguin Books USA Inc.

1 3 5 7 9 10 8 6 4 2

The Buccaneers, by Edith Wharton, was first published in 1938 by
D. Appleton-Century Company, Inc.

LIBRARY OF CONGRESS CATALOGING-IN-PUBLICATION DATA
Wharton, Edith, 1862–1937.
The buccaneers: a novel/by Edith Wharton; completed by Marion Mainwaring.
p.   cm.
ISBN 0-670-85219-8
1. Man-woman relationships—England—Fiction.   2. Young women—
New York (N.Y.)—Fiction.
3. Americans—England—Fiction.   I. Mainwaring, Marion.   II. Title.
PS3546.H16B83   1993
813'.52—dc20   93-13901

Printed in the United States of America
Set in Sabon
Designed by Ann Gold

This presentation of The Buccaneers *is dedicated
to the memory of Edith Wharton*

and

to Matthew Imrie

*with special thanks
to Mary Pitlick, who identified the buccaneers,
to Nan Graham, to Christina Ward, and to David and
Dorothy Mainwaring.*

M.M.

BOOK ONE

I.

It was the height of the racing season in Saratoga.

The thermometer stood over ninety, and a haze of sun-powdered dust hung in the elms along the street facing the Grand Union Hotel, and over the scant triangular lawns planted with young firs and protected by a low white rail from the depredations of dogs and children.

Mrs. St. George, whose husband was one of the gentlemen most interested in the racing, sat on the wide hotel verandah, a jug of iced lemonade at her elbow and a palmetto fan in one small hand, and looked out between the immensely tall white columns of the portico, which so often reminded cultured travellers of the Parthenon at Athens (Greece). On Sunday afternoons this verandah was crowded with gentlemen in tall hats and frock-coats, enjoying cool drinks and Havana cigars, and surveying the long country street planted with spindling elms; but today the gentlemen were racing, and the rows of chairs were occupied by ladies and young girls listlessly waiting their return, in a drowsy atmosphere of swayed fans and iced refreshments.

Mrs. St. George eyed most of these ladies with a melancholy disfavour, and sighed to think how times had changed since she had first—some ten years earlier—trailed her crinolined skirts up and down that same verandah.

Mrs. St. George's vacant hours, which were many, were filled by such wistful reflexions. Life had never been easy, but it had certainly been easier when Colonel St. George devoted less time to poker, and to Wall Street; when the children were little, crinolines were still worn, and Newport had not yet eclipsed all rival watering-places. What, for instance, could be prettier, or more suitable for a lady, than a black alpaca skirt looped up like a window-drapery above a scarlet serge underskirt, the whole surmounted by a wide-sleeved black poplin jacket with ruffled muslin undersleeves, and a flat "pork-pie" hat like the one the Empress Eugénie was represented as wearing on the beach at Biarritz? But now there seemed to be no definite fashions. Everybody wore what they pleased, and it was as difficult to look like a lady in those tight perpendicular polonaises bunched up at the back that the Paris dress-makers were sending over as in the outrageously low square-cut evening-gowns which Mrs. St. George had viewed with disapproval at the Opera in New York. The fact was, you could hardly tell a lady now from an actress, or—er—the other kind of woman; and society at Saratoga, now that all the best people were going to Newport, had grown as mixed and confusing as the fashions.

Everything was changed since crinolines had gone out and bustles come in. Who, for instance, was that new woman, a Mrs. Closson, or some such name, who had such a dusky skin for her auburn hair, such a fat body for her small uncertain feet, and who, when she wasn't strumming on the hotel piano, was credibly reported by the domestics to lie for hours on her bedroom sofa smoking—yes, *smoking*—big Havana cigars? The gentlemen, Mrs. St. George believed, treated the story as a good joke; to a woman of refinement it could be only a subject for painful meditation.

Mrs. St. George had always been rather distant in her manner to the big and exuberant Mrs. Elmsworth who was seated at this moment nearby on the verandah. (Mrs. Elmsworth was always "edging up.") Mrs. St. George was instinctively distrustful of the advantages of ladies who had daughters of the age of her own, and Lizzy Elmsworth, the eldest of her neighbour's family, was just about the age of Virginia St. George, and might by some (those who preferred the brunette to the very blonde type) be thought as handsome. And besides, where did the Elmsworths come from, as Mrs. St. George had often asked her husband, an irreverent jovial man who invariably replied: "If you were to begin by telling me where *we* do!" . . . so absurd on the part of a gentleman as well known as Colonel St. George in some unspecified district of what Mrs. St. George called the Sa-outh.

But at the thought of that new dusky Closson woman with the queer-looking girl who was so ugly now, but might suddenly turn into a beauty (Mrs. St. George had seen such cases), the instinct of organized defence awoke in her vague bosom, and she felt herself drawn to Mrs. Elmsworth, and to the two Elmsworth girls, as to whom one already knew just how good-looking they were going to be.

A good many hours of Mrs. St. George's days were spent in mentally cataloguing and appraising the physical attributes of the young ladies in whose company her daughters trailed up and down the verandahs, and waltzed and polka-ed for hours every night in the long bare hotel parlours, so conveniently divided by sliding doors which slipped into the wall and made the two rooms into one. Mrs. St. George remembered the day when she had been agreeably awestruck by this vista, with its expectant lines of bent-wood chairs against the walls, and its row of windows draped in crimson brocatelle heavily festooned from overhanging gilt cornices. In those days the hotel ball-room had been her idea of a throne-room in a palace; but since her husband had taken her to a ball at the Seventh Regiment Armoury in New York her standards had changed, and she regarded the splendours of the Grand Union almost as contemptuously as the arrogant Mrs. Eglinton of New York, who had arrived there the previous summer on her way to Lake George, and, after being shown into the yellow damask "bridal suite" by the obsequious landlord, had said she supposed it would do well enough for one night.

Mrs. St. George, in those earlier years, had even been fluttered by an introduction to Mrs. Elmsworth, who was an older habituée of Saratoga than herself, and had a big showy affable husband with lustrous black whiskers, who was reported to have made a handsome fortune on the New York Stock Exchange. But that was in the days when Mrs. Elmsworth drove daily to the races in a high barouche sent from New York, which attracted perhaps too much attention. Since then Mr. Elmsworth's losses in Wall Street had obliged his wife to put down her barouche, and stay at home on the hotel verandah with the other ladies, and she now no longer inspired Mrs. St. George with awe or envy. Indeed, had it not been for this new Closson danger Mrs. Elmsworth in her present situation would have been negligible; but now that Virginia St. George and Lizzy Elmsworth were "out" (as Mrs. St. George persisted in calling it, though the girls could not see much difference in their lives)—now that Lizzy Elmsworth's looks seemed to Mrs. St. George at once more to be admired and less to be feared, and Mabel, the second Elmsworth girl, who was a year older than her own youngest, to be too bony and lantern-jawed for future danger, Mrs. St. George began to wonder whether she and her neighbour might not organize some sort of joint defence against new women with daughters. Later it would not so much matter, for Mrs. St. George's youngest, Nan, though certainly not a beauty like Virginia, was going to be what was called fascinating and by the time her hair was put up the St. George girls need fear no rivalry.

Week after week, day after day, the anxious mother had gone over Miss Elmsworth's points, comparing them one by one with Virginia's. As regards hair and complexion, there could be no doubt; Virginia, all rose and pearl, with sheaves of full fair hair heaped above her low forehead, was as pure and luminous as an apple-blossom. But Lizzy's waist was certainly at least an inch smaller (some said two), Lizzy's dark eyebrows had a bolder curve, and Lizzy's foot—ah, where in the world did an upstart Elmsworth get that arrogant instep? Yes; but it was some comfort to note that Lizzy's complexion was opaque and lifeless compared to Virginia's, and that her fine eyes showed temper, and would be likely to frighten the young men away. Still, she had to an alarming degree what was called "style," and Mrs. St. George suspected that in the circles to which she longed to introduce her daughters style was valued even more highly than beauty.

These were the problems among which her thoughts moved during the endless sweltering afternoon hours, like torpid fish turning about between the weary walls of a too-small aquarium. But now a new presence had invaded that sluggish element. Mrs. St. George no longer compared her eldest daughter and Lizzy Elmsworth with each other; she began to compare them both with the newcomer, the daughter of the unknown Mrs. Closson. It was small comfort to Mrs. St. George (though she repeated it to herself so often) that the Clossons were utterly unknown, that though Colonel St. George played poker with Mr. Closson, and had what the family called "business connections" with him, they were nowhere near the stage when it becomes a pleasing duty for a man to introduce a colleague to his family. Neither did it matter that Mrs. Closson's own past was if anything obscurer than her husband's, and that those who said she was a poor Brazilian widow when Closson had picked her up on a business trip to Rio were smiled at and corrected by others, presumably better informed, who suggested that *divorcée* was the word, and not "widow." Even the fact that the Closson girl (so called) was known not to be Closson's daughter, but to bear a queer exotic name like Santos-Dios ("the Colonel says that's not swearing, it's the language," Mrs. St. George explained to Mrs. Elmsworth when they talked the newcomers over)—even this was not enough to calm Mrs. St. George. The girl, whatever her real name, was known as Conchita Closson; she addressed as "Father" the non-committal pepper-and-salt-looking man who joined his family over Sundays at the Grand Union; and it was of no use for Mrs. St. George to say to herself that Conchita was plain and therefore negligible, for she had the precise kind of plainness which, as mothers of rival daughters know, may suddenly blaze into irresistible beauty. At present Miss Closson's head was too small, her neck was too long, she was too tall and thin, and her hair—well, her hair (oh, horror!) was nearly red. And her skin was dark, under the powder which (yes, my dear—at eighteen!) Mrs. St. George was sure she applied to it; and the combination of red hair and sallow complexion would have put off anybody who had heard a description of them, instead of seeing them triumphantly embodied in Conchita Closson. Mrs. St. George shivered under her dotted muslin ruffled with Valenciennes, and drew a tippet edged with swansdown over her shoulders. At that moment her own daughters, Virginia and Nan, wandered by, one after the other; and the sight somehow increased Mrs. St. George's irritation.

"Virginia!" she called. Virginia halted, seemed to hesitate as to whether the summons were worth heeding, and then sauntered across the verandah toward her mother.

"Virginia, I don't want you should go round any more with that strange girl," Mrs. St. George began.

Virginia's sapphire eyes rested with a remote indifferent gaze on the speaker's tightly buttoned bronze kid boots, and Mrs. St. George suddenly wondered if she had burst a buttonhole.

"What girl?" Virginia drawled.

"How do I know? Goodness knows who they are. Your pa says she was a widow from one of those South American countries when she married Mr. Closson—the mother was, I mean."

"Well, if he says so, I suppose she was."

"But some people say she was just divorced. And I don't want my daughters associating with that kind of people."

Virginia removed her blue gaze from her mother's boots to the little mantle trimmed with swansdown. "I should think you'd roast with that thing on," she remarked.

"Jinny! Now you listen to what I say," her mother ineffectually called after her.

Nan St. George had taken no part in the conversation; at

first she had hardly heeded what was said. Such wrangles between
mother and daughter were of daily, almost hourly, occurrence;
Mrs. St. George's only way of guiding her children was to be
always crying out to them not to do this or that. Nan St. George,
at sixteen, was at the culminating phase of a passionate admiration for her elder sister. Virginia was all that her junior
longed to be: perfectly beautiful, completely self-possessed, calm
and sure of herself. Nan, whose whole life was a series of waves
of the blood, hot rushes of enthusiasm, icy chills of embarrassment and self-depreciation, looked with envy and admiration at
her goddess-like elder. The only thing she did not quite like about
Virginia was the latter's tone of superiority with her mother; to
get the better of Mrs. St. George was too easy, too much like
what Colonel St. George called "shooting a bird sitting." Yet so
strong was Virginia's influence that in her presence Nan always
took the same tone with their mother, in the secret hope of at-
tracting her sister's favourable notice. She had even gone so far
as to mime for Virginia (who was no mimic) Mrs. St. George
looking shocked at an untidy stocking ("Mother wondering
where we were brought up"), Mrs. St. George smiling in her sleep
in church ("Mother listening to the angels"), or Mrs. St. George
doubtfully mustering new arrivals ("Mother smelling a drain").
But Virginia took such demonstrations for granted, and when
poor Nan afterward, in an agony of remorse, stole back alone to
her mother, and whispered through penitent kisses: "I didn't
mean to be naughty to you, Mamma," Mrs. St. George, raising
a nervous hand to her crimped *bandeaux,* would usually reply
apprehensively: "I'm sure you didn't, darling, only don't get my
hair all in a muss again."

Expiation unresponded to embitters the blood, and something within Nan shrank and hardened with each of these rebuffs.
But she now seldom exposed herself to them, finding it easier to
follow Virginia's lead and ignore their parent's admonitions. At
the moment, however, she was actually wavering in her allegiance
to Virginia. Since she had seen Conchita Closson she was no

longer sure that features and complexion were woman's crowning glory. Long before Mrs. St. George and Mrs. Elmsworth had agreed on a valuation of the newcomer, Nan had fallen under her spell. From the day when she had first seen her come whistling around the corner of the verandah, her restless little head crowned by a flapping Leghorn hat with a rose under the brim, and dragging after her a reluctant poodle with a large red bow, Nan had felt the girl's careless power. What would Mrs. St. George have said if one of her daughters had strolled along the verandah whistling, and dragging a grotesque-looking toy-shop animal at her heels? Miss Closson seemed troubled by no such considerations. She sat down on the upper step of the verandah, pulled a lump of molasses candy from her pocket, and invited the poodle to "get up and waltz for it": which the uncanny animal did by rising on his hind legs and performing a series of unsteady circles before his mistress while she licked the molasses from her fingers. Every rocking-chair on the verandah stopped creaking as its occupant sat upright to view the show. "Circus performance!" Mrs. St. George commented to Mrs. Elmsworth; and the latter retorted with her vulgar laugh: "Looks as if the two of 'em were used to showing off, don't it?"

Nan overheard the comments, and felt sure the two mothers were mistaken. The Closson girl was obviously unaware that anyone was looking at her and her absurd dog; it was that absence of self-consciousness which fascinated Nan. Virginia was intensely self-conscious; she really thought just as much as her mother of "what people would say"; and even Lizzy Elmsworth, though she was so much cleverer at concealing her thoughts, was not really simple and natural; she merely affected unaffectedness. It frightened Nan a little to find herself thinking these things, but they forced themselves upon her; and when Mrs. St. George issued the order that her daughters were not to associate with "the strange girl" (as if they didn't all know her name!) Nan felt a rush of anger. Virginia sauntered on, probably content to have shaken her mother's confidence in the details of her dress (a matter of much anxious thought to Mrs. St. George); but Nan stopped short.

"Why can't I go with Conchita if she wants me to?"

Mrs. St. George's faintly withered pink turned pale. "If she *wants you to*? Annabel St. George, what *do* you mean by talking to me that way? What on earth do you care for what a girl like that *wants*?"

Nan ground her heels into the crack between the verandah boards. "I think she's lovely."

Mrs. St. George's small nose was wrinkled with disdain. The small mouth under it drooped disgustedly. She was "Mother smelling a drain."

"Well, when that new governess comes next week, I guess you'll find she feels just the way I do about those people. And you'll have to do what *she* tells you, anyhow," Mrs. St. George helplessly concluded.

A chill of dismay rushed over Nan. The new governess! She had never really believed in that remote bogey. She had an idea that Mrs. St. George and Virginia had cooked up the legend between them, in order to be able to say "Annabel's governess"; as they had once heard that tall proud Mrs. Eglinton from New York, who had stayed only one night at the hotel, say to the landlord: "You must be sure to put my daughter's governess in the room next to her." Nan had never believed that the affair of the governess would go beyond talking; but now she seemed to hear the snap of the hand-cuffs on her wrist.

"A governess—me?"

Mrs. St. George moistened her lips nervously. "All stylish girls have governesses the year before they come out."

"I'm not coming out next year—I'm only sixteen," Nan protested.

"Well, they have them for two years before. That Eglinton girl had."

"Oh, that Eglinton girl! She looked at us all as if we weren't there."

"Well, that's the way for a lady to look at strangers," said Mrs. St. George heroically.

Nan's heart grew black within her. "I'll kill her if she tries to interfere with me."

"You'll drive down to the station on Monday to meet her," Mrs. St. George shrilled back, defiant. Nan turned on her heel and walked away.

II.

The Closson girl had already disappeared with her dog, and Nan suspected that she had taken him for a game of ball in the rough field adjoining the meagre grounds of the hotel. Nan went down the steps of the porch and, crossing the drive, espied the slim Conchita whirling a ball high overhead while the dog spun about frantically at her feet. Nan had so far exchanged only a few shy words with her, and in ordinary circumstances would hardly have dared to join her now. But she had reached an acute crisis in her life, and her need for sympathy and help overcame her shyness. She vaulted over the fence into the field and went up to Miss Closson.

"That's a lovely dog," she said.

Miss Closson flung the ball for her poodle, and turned with a smile to Nan. "Isn't he a real darling?"

Nan stood twisting one foot about the other. "Have you ever had a governess?" she asked abruptly.

Miss Closson opened with a stare of wonder the darkly fringed eyes which shone like pale aquamarines on her small dusky face. "Me? A governess? Mercy, no—what for?"

"That's what I say! My mother and Virginia have cooked it up between them. I'm going to have one next week."

"Land's sake! You're not? She's coming here?"

Nan nodded sulkily.

"*Well*—" Conchita murmured.

"What'll I do about it—what would you?" Nan burst out, on the brink of tears.

Miss Closson drew her lids together meditatively; then she stooped with deliberation to the poodle, and threw the ball for him again.

"I said I'd kill her," broke from Nan in a hoarse whisper.

The other laughed. "I wouldn't do that; not right off, anyhow. I'd get round her first."

"Get round her? How can I? I've got to do whatever she wants."

"No, you haven't. Make her want whatever you want."

"How can I? Oh, can I call you Conchita? It's such a lovely name. Mine's Annabel, really, but everybody calls me Nan. . . . Well, but how can I get round that governess? She'll try to make me learn lists of dates—that's what she's paid for."

Conchita's expressive face became one grimace of disapproval. "Well, I should hate that like castor-oil. But perhaps she won't. I knew a girl at Rio who had a governess, and she was hardly any older than the girl, and she used to . . . well, carry messages and letters for her, the governess did . . . and in the evening she used to slip out to . . . to see a friend . . . and she and the girl knew all each other's secrets; so you see they couldn't tell on each other, neither one of them couldn't. . . ."

"Oh, I see," said Nan, with a feigned air of knowingness. But she was suddenly conscious of a queer sensation in her throat, almost of physical sickness. Conchita's laughing eyes seemed whispering to her through half-drawn lids. She admired Conchita as much as ever—but she was not sure she liked her at that moment.

Conchita was obviously not aware of having produced an unfavourable impression. "Out in Rio I knew a girl who got married that way. The governess carried her notes for her. . . . Do you want to get married?" she asked abruptly.

Nan flushed and stared. Getting married was an inexhaustible theme of confidential talk between her sister and the Elmsworth girls; but she felt herself too young and inexperienced to take part in their discussions. Once, at one of the hotel dances, a young fellow called Roy Gilling had picked up her handkerchief, and refused to give it back. She had seen him raise it meaningly to his young moustache before he slipped it into his pocket; but the incident had left her annoyed and bewildered rather than excited, and she had not been sorry when, soon afterward, he rather pointedly transferred his attentions to Mabel Elmsworth. She knew Mabel Elmsworth had already been kissed behind a door; and Nan's own sister, Virginia, had too, Nan suspected. She herself had no definite prejudices in the matter; she simply felt unprepared as yet to consider matrimonial plans. She stooped to stroke the poodle, and answered, without looking up: "Not to anybody I've seen yet."

The other considered her curiously. "I suppose you like love-making better, eh?" She spoke in a soft drawl, with a languid rippling of the "r"s.

Nan felt her blood mounting again; one of her quick blushes steeped her in distress. Did she—didn't she—like "love-making," as this girl crudely called it (the others always spoke of it as flirting)? Nan had not been subjected to any warmer advances than Mr. Gilling's, and the obvious answer was that she didn't know, having had no experience of such matters; but she had the reluctance of youth to confess to its youthfulness, and she also felt that her likes and dislikes were no business of this strange girl's. She gave a vague laugh and said loftily: "I think it's silly."

Conchita laughed too—a low deliberate laugh, full of repressed and tantalizing mystery. Once more she flung the ball for her intently watching poodle; then she thrust a hand into a fold of her dress, and pulled out a crumpled packet of cigarettes. "Here—have one! Nobody'll see us out here," she suggested amicably.

Nan's heart gave an excited leap. Her own sister and the Elmsworth girls already smoked in secret, removing the traces of

their indiscretion by consuming little highly perfumed pink lozenges furtively acquired from the hotel barber; but they had never
offered to induct Nan into these forbidden rites, which, by awful
oaths, they bound her not to reveal to their parents. It was Nan's
first cigarette, and while her fingers twitched for it she asked herself in terror: "Suppose it should make me sick right before her?"

But Nan, in spite of her tremors, was not the girl to refuse
what looked like a dare, nor even to ask if in this open field they
were really safe from unwanted eyes. There was a clump of low
shrubby trees at the farther end, and Conchita strolled there and
mounted the fence-rail, from which her slender uncovered ankles
dangled gracefully. Nan swung up beside her, took a cigarette,
and bent toward the match which her companion proffered.
There was an awful silence while she put the forbidden object to
her lips and drew a frightened breath; the acrid taste of the to-
bacco struck her palate sharply, but in another moment a pleasant
fragrance filled her nose and throat. She puffed again, and knew
she was going to like it. Instantly her mood passed from timidity
to triumph, and she wrinkled her nose critically and threw back
her head, as her father did when he was tasting a new brand of
cigar. "These are all right—where do you get them?" she enquired
with a careless air; and then, suddenly forgetful of the experience
her tone implied, she rushed on in a breathless little-girl voice:
"Oh, Conchita, won't you show me how you make those lovely
rings? Jinny doesn't really do them right, nor the Elmsworth girls
either."

Miss Closson in turn threw back her head with a smile. She
drew a deep breath and, removing the cigarette from her lips,
curved them to a rosy circle through which she sent a wreath of
misty smoke-rings. "That's how," she laughed, and pushed the
packet into Nan's hands. "You can practise at night," she said
good-humouredly, as she jumped from the rail.

Nan wandered back to the hotel, so much elated by her success as a smoker that her dread of the governess grew fainter. On
the hotel steps she was further reassured by the glimpse, through

the lobby doors, of a tall broad-shouldered man in a Panama hat and light-gray suit who, his linen duster over his arm, his portmanteaux at his feet, had paused to light a big cigar and shake hands with the clerk. Nan gave a start of joy. She had not known that her father was arriving that afternoon, and the mere sight of him banished all her cares. Nan had a blind faith in her father's faculty for helping people out of difficulties—a faith based not on actual experience (for Colonel St. George usually dealt with difficulties by a wave of dismissal which swept them into somebody else's lap), but on his easy contempt for feminine fusses, and his way of saying to his youngest daughter: "You just call on me, child, when things want straightening out." Perhaps he would straighten out even this nonsense about the governess; and meanwhile the mere thought of his large powerful presence, his big cologne-scented hands, his splendid yellow moustache and easy rolling gait, cleared the air of the cobwebs in which Mrs. St. George was always enveloped.

"Hullo, daughter! What's the news?" The Colonel greeted Nan with a resounding kiss, and stood with one arm about her, scrutinizing her lifted face.

"I'm glad you've come, Father," she said, and then shrank back a little, fearful lest a whiff of cigarette smoke should betray her.

"Your mother taking her afternoon nap, I suppose?" the Colonel continued jovially. "Well, come along with me. See here, Charlie" (to the clerk), "send those things right along to my room, will you? There's something in them of interest to this young lady."

The clerk signalled to a black porter, and, preceded by his bags, the Colonel mounted the stairs with Nan.

"Oh, Father! It's lovely to have you! What I want to ask you is—"

But the Colonel was digging into the depths of one of the portmanteaux and scattering over the bed various parts of a showy but somewhat crumpled wardrobe. "Here now; you wait," he puffed, pausing to mop his broad white forehead with a fine cambric handkerchief. He pulled out two parcels, and beckoned to Nan. "Here's some fancy notions for you and Jinny; the girl in the store said it was what the Newport belles are wearing this summer. And this is for your mother, when she wakes up." He took the tissue-paper wrappings from a small red morocco case and pressed the spring of the lid. Before Nan's dazzled eyes lay a diamond brooch formed of a spray of briar-roses. She gave an admiring gasp. "Well, how's that for style?" laughed her father.

"Oh, Father—" She paused, and looked at him with a faint touch of apprehension.

"Well?" the Colonel repeated. His laugh had an emptiness under it, like the hollow under a loud wave; Nan knew the sound. "Is it a present for Mother?" she asked doubtfully.

"Why, who'd you think it was for—not you?" he joked, his voice slightly less assured.

Nan twisted one foot about the other. "It's terribly expensive, isn't it?"

"Why, you critical imp, you—what's the matter if it is?"

"Well, the last time you brought Mother a piece of jewelry there was an all-night row after it, about cards or something," said Nan judicially.

The Colonel burst out laughing, and pinched her chin. "Well, well! You fear the Greeks, eh, do you? How does it go? *Timeo Danaos . . .*"

"What Greeks?"

Her father raised his handsome ironic eyebrows. Nan knew he was proud of his far-off smattering of college culture, and wished she could have understood the allusion. "Haven't they even taught you that much Latin at your school? Well, I guess your mother's right; you *do* need a governess."

Nan paled, and forgot the Greeks. "Oh, Father; that's what I wanted to speak to you about—"

"What about?"

"That governess. I'm going to hate her, you know. She's

going to make me learn lists of dates, the way the Eglinton girl had to. And Mother'll fill her up with silly stories about us, and tell her we mustn't do this and we mustn't say that. I don't believe she'll even let me go with Conchita Closson, because Mother says Mrs. Closson's divorced."

The Colonel looked up sharply. "Oh, your mother says that, does she? She's down on the Clossons? I suppose she would be." He picked up the morocco case and examined the brooch critically. "Yes, that's a good piece; Black, Starr and Frost. And I don't mind telling you that you're right: it cost me a pretty penny. But I've got to persuade your mother to be polite to Mrs. Closson—see?" He wrinkled up his face in the funny way he had and took his daughter by the shoulders. "Business matter, you understand—strictly between ourselves. I need Closson; got to have him. And he's fretted to death about the way all the women cold-shoulder his wife. . . . I'll tell you what, Nan; suppose you and I form a league, defensive and offensive? You help me to talk round your mother, and get her to be decent to Mrs. Closson, and persuade the others to be, and to let the girl go round with all of you; and I'll fix it up with the governess so you don't have to learn too many dates."

Nan uttered a cry of joy. Already the clouds were lifting. "Oh, Father, you're perfectly grand! I knew everything would be all right as soon as you got here! I'll do all I can about Mother— and you'll tell the governess I'm to go round all I like with Conchita?" She flung herself into the Colonel's comforting embrace.

III.

Mrs. St. George, had she looked back far enough, could have recalled a time when she had all of Nan's faith in the Colonel's restorative powers; when to carry her difficulties to him seemed the natural thing, and his way of laughing at them gave her the illusion that they were solved. Those days were past; she had long been aware that most of her difficulties came from the Colonel instead of being solved by him. But she admired him as much as ever—thought him in fact even handsomer than when, before the Civil War, he had dawned on her dazzled sight at a White Sulphur Springs ball, in the uniform of a captain of militia; and now that he had become prominent in Wall Street, where life seemed to grow more feverish every day, it was only natural that he should require a little relaxation, though she deplored its always meaning poker and whisky, and sometimes, she feared, the third element celebrated in the song. Though Mrs. St. George was now a worried middle-aged woman with grown-up daughters, it cost her as much to resign herself to this as when she had first found in her husband's pocket a letter she was not meant to read. But there was nothing to be done about it, or about the whisky and poker, and the visits to establishments where game and champagne were served at all hours, and gentlemen who had won at roulette or the races supped in meretricious company. All this had long since been part of Mrs. St. George's consciousness, yet she was half consoled, when the Colonel joined his family at Long Branch or Saratoga, by the knowledge that all the other worried and middle-aged wives in the long hotel dining-room envied her her splendid husband.

And small wonder, thought Mrs. St. George, contemptuously picturing the gentlemen those ladies had to put up with: that loud red-faced Elmsworth, who hadn't yet found out that big lumps of black whisker were no longer worn except by undertakers, or the poor dyspeptic Closson, who spent such resigned and yawning hours beside the South American woman to whom he was per-haps not married at all. Closson was particularly obnoxious to Mrs. St. George; much as she despised Mrs. Closson, she could almost have pitied her for having nothing better to show as a husband—even if he was that, as Mrs. St. George would add in her confidential exchanges with Mrs. Elmsworth.

Even now, though of late the Colonel had been so evasive and unsatisfactory, and though she wasn't yet sure if he would turn up for the morrow's races, Mrs. St. George reflected thank-fully that if he *did* she wouldn't have to appear in the hotel dining-room with a man about whom a lady need feel apologetic. But when, after her siesta, as she was re-arranging her hair before going back to the verandah, she heard his laugh outside of her door, her slumbering apprehensions started up. "He's too cheer-ful," she thought, nervously folding away her dressing-gown and slippers; for when the Colonel was worried he was always in the highest spirits.

"Well, my dear! Thought I'd surprise the family, and see what you were all up to. Nan's given me a fairly good report, but I haven't run down Jinny yet." He laid a hand on his wife's gray-ing blond hair, and brushed her care-worn forehead with the tip of his moustache—a ritual gesture which convinced him that he had kissed her, and Mrs. St. George that she had been kissed. She looked up at him with admiring eyes.

"That governess is coming on Monday," she began. At the moment of his last successful "turn-over," a few months earlier, his wife had wrung from him the permission to engage a governess; but now she feared a renewal of the discussion about the governess's salary, and yet she knew the girls, and Nan especially, must have some kind of social discipline. "We've got to have her," Mrs. St. George added.

The Colonel was obviously not listening. "Of course, of course," he agreed, measuring the room with his large strides (his inability to remain seated was another trial to his sedentary wife). Suddenly he paused before her and fumbled in his pocket, but produced nothing from it. Mrs. St. George noted the gesture, and thought: "It's the coal bill! But he *knew* I couldn't get it down any lower. . . ."

"Well, well, my dear," the Colonel continued, "I don't know what you've all been up to, but I've had a big stroke of luck, and it's only fair you three girls should share in it." He jerked the morocco case out of another pocket. "Oh, Colonel," his wife gasped as he pressed the spring. "Well, take it—it's for you!" he joked.

Mrs. St. George gazed blankly at the glittering spray; then her eyes filled, and her lip began to tremble. "Tracy . . ." she stammered. It was years since she had called him by his name. "But you oughtn't to," she protested, "with all our expenses. . . . It's too grand—it's like a wedding present. . . ."

"Well, we're married, ain't we?" The Colonel laughed resonantly. "There's the first result of my turn-over, madam. And I brought the girls some gimcracks too. I gave Nan the parcel; but I haven't seen Jinny. I suppose she's off with some of the other girls."

Mrs. St. George detached herself from ecstatic contemplation of the jewel. "You mustn't spoil the girls, Colonel. I've got my hands full with them. I want you to talk to them seriously about not going with that Closson girl. . . ."

Colonel St. George blew a faint whistle through his moustache, and threw himself into the rocking-chair facing his wife's. "Going with the Closson girl? Why, what's the matter with the Closson girl? She's as pretty as a peach, anyhow."

"I guess your own daughters are pretty enough without having to demean themselves running after that girl. I can't keep Nan away from her." Mrs. St. George knew that Nan was the Colonel's favourite, and she spoke with an inward tremor. But it would never do to have this fashionable new governess (who had been with the Russell Parmores of Tarrytown, and with the Duchess of Tintagel in England) imagine that her new charges were hand in glove with the Clossons.

Colonel St. George tilted himself back in his chair, felt for a cigar, and lit it thoughtfully. (He had long since taught Mrs. St. George that smoking in her bedroom was included among his marital rights.) "Well," he said, "what's wrong with the Clossons, my dear?"

Mrs. St. George felt weak and empty inside. When he looked at her in that way, half laughing, half condescending, all her reasons turned to a puff of mist. And there lay the jewel on the dressing-table—and timorously she began to understand. But the girls must be rescued, and a flicker of maternal ardour stirred in her. Perhaps, in his large careless way, her husband had simply brushed by the Clossons without heeding them.

"I don't know any of the particulars, naturally. People *do* say . . . But Mrs. Closson (if that's her name) is not a woman I could ever associate with, so I haven't any means of knowing. . . ."

The Colonel gave his all-effacing laugh. "Oh, well—if you haven't any means of knowing, we'll fix that up all right. But I've got business reasons for wanting you to make friends with Mrs. Closson first; we'll investigate her history afterward."

Make friends with Mrs. Closson! Mrs. St. George looked at her husband with dismay. He wanted her to do the thing that would most humiliate her; and it was so important to him that he had probably spent his last dollar on this diamond bribe. Mrs. St. George was not unused to such situations; she knew that a gentleman's financial situation might at any moment necessitate compromises and concessions. All the ladies of her acquaintance were inured to them: up one day, down the next, as the secret gods of Wall Street decreed. She measured her husband's present need by the cost of the probably unpaid-for jewel, and her heart grew like water.

"But, Colonel—"

"Well, what's wrong with the Clossons, anyhow? I've done business with Closson off and on for some years now, and I don't know a squarer fellow. He's just put me on to a big thing, and if you're going to wreck the whole business by turning up your nose at his wife . . ."

Mrs. St. George gathered strength to reply: "But, Colonel, the talk is that they're not even married. . . ."

Her husband jumped up and stood before her with flushed face and irritated eyes. "If you think I'm going to let my making a big rake-off depend on whether the Clossons had a parson to tie the knot, or only the town-clerk . . ."

"I've got the girls to think of," his wife faltered.

"It's the girls I'm thinking of too. D'you suppose I'd sweat and slave down town the way I do if it wasn't for the girls?"

"But I've got to think of the girls they go with, if they're to marry nice young men."

"The nice young men'll show up in larger numbers if I can put this deal through. And what's the matter with the Closson girl? She's as pretty as a picture."

Mrs. St. George marvelled once more at the obtuseness of the most brilliant men. Wasn't that one of the very reasons for not encouraging the Closson girl?

"She powders her face, and smokes cigarettes. . . ."

"Well, don't our girls and the two Elmsworths do as much? I'll swear I caught a wiff of smoke when Nan kissed me just now."

Mrs. St. George grew pale with horror. "If you'll say that of your daughters you'll say anything!" she protested.

There was a knock at the door, and without waiting for it to be answered Virginia flew into her father's arms. "Oh, Father, how sweet of you! Nan gave me the locket. It's too lovely; with my monogram on it—and in diamonds!"

She lifted her radiant lips, and he bent to them with a smile.

"What's that new scent you're using, Miss St. George? Or have you been stealing one of your papa's lozenges?" He sniffed and then held her at arm's length, watching her quick flush of alarm, and the way in which her deeply fringed eyes pleaded with his.

"See here, Jinny. Your mother says she don't want you to go with the Closson girl because she smokes. But I tell her I'll answer for it that you and Nan would never follow such a bad example—eh?"

Their eyes and their laugh met. Mrs. St. George turned from the sight with a sense of helplessness. "If he's going to let them smoke now . . ."

"I don't think your mother's fair to the Closson girl, and I've told her so. I want she should be friends with Mrs. Closson. I want her to begin right off. Oh, here's Nan," he added, as the door opened again. "Come along, Nan; I want you to stick up for your friend Conchita. You like her, don't you?"

But Mrs. St. George's resentment was stiffening. She could fight for her daughters, helpless as she was for herself. "If you're going to rely on the girls to choose who they associate with! They say the girl's name isn't Closson at all. Nobody knows what it is, or who any of them are. And the brother travels round with a guitar tied with ribbons. No nice girls will go with your daughters if you want them seen everywhere with those people."

The Colonel stood frowning before his wife. When he frowned she suddenly forgot all her reasons for opposing him, but the blind instinct of opposition remained. "You wouldn't invite the Clossons to join us at supper tonight?" he suggested.

Mrs. St. George moistened her dry lips with her tongue. "Colonel—"

"You won't?"

"Girls, your father's joking," she stammered, turning with a tremulous gesture to her daughters. She saw Nan's eyes darken, but Virginia laughed—a laugh of complicity with her father. He joined in it.

"Girls, I see your mother's not satisfied with the present I've

brought her. She's not as easily pleased as you young simpletons."
He waved his hand to the dressing-table, and Virginia caught up
the morocco box. "Oh, Mother—is this for *you?* Oh, I never saw
anything so beautiful! You must invite Mrs. Closson, just to see
how envious it makes her. I guess that's what Father wants you
to do—isn't it?"

The Colonel looked at her sympathetically. "I've told your
mother the plain truth. Closson's put me on to a good thing, and
the only return he wants is for you ladies to be a little humane
to his women-folk. Is that too unreasonable? He's coming today,
by the afternoon train, and he's bringing two young fellows with
him, by the way—his step-son and a young Englishman who's
been working out in Brazil on Mrs. Closson's *estancia.* The son
of an earl, or something. How about that, girls? Two new
dancing-partners! And you ain't any too well off in that line, are
you?" This was a burning question, for it was common knowledge that, if their dancing-partners were obscure and few, it was
because all the smart and eligible young men of whom Virginia
and the Elmsworths read in the "society columns" of the newspapers had deserted Saratoga for Newport.

"Mother knows we generally have to dance with each
other," Virginia murmured sulkily.

"Yes—or with the beaux from Buffalo!" Nan laughed.

"Well, I call that mortifying; but of course, if your mother
disapproves of Mrs. Closson, I guess the young fellows that Closson's bringing'll have to dance with the Elmsworth girls instead
of you."

Mrs. St. George stood trembling beside the dressing-table.
Virginia had put down the box, and the diamonds sparkled in a
sunset ray that came through the slats of the shutters.

Mrs. St. George did not own many jewels, but it suddenly
occurred to her that each one marked the date of a similar episode. Either a woman, or a business deal—something she had to
be indulgent about. She liked trinkets as well as any woman, but
at that moment she wished that all of hers were at the bottom of

the sea. For each time she had yielded—as she knew she was going to yield now. And her husband would always think that it was because he had bribed her. . . .

The readjustment of seats necessary to bring together the St. George and Closson parties at the long hotel supper-table caused a flutter in the room. Mrs. St. George was too conscious of it not to avoid Mrs. Elmsworth's glance of surprise; but she could not deafen herself to Mrs. Elmsworth's laugh. She had always thought the woman had an underbred laugh. And to think that, so few seasons ago, she had held her chin high in passing Mrs. Elmsworth on the verandah, just as she had done till this very afternoon—and how much higher!—in passing Mrs. Closson. Now Mrs. Elmsworth, who did not possess the art of the lifted chin, but whispered and nudged and giggled where a "lady" would have sailed by—now it would be in her power to practise on Mrs. St. George these vulgar means of reprisal. The diamond spray burned like hot lead on Mrs. St. George's breast; yet through all her misery there pierced the old thrill of pride as the Colonel entered the dining-room in her wake, and she saw him reflected in the other women's eyes. Ah, poor Mrs. Elmsworth, with her black-whiskered undertaker, and Mrs. Closson, with her cipher of a husband—and all the other ladies, young or elderly, of whom not one could boast a man of Colonel St. George's quality! Evidently, like Mrs. St. George's diamonds, he was a costly possession, but (unlike the diamonds, she suspected) he had been paid for—oh, how dearly!—and she had a right to wear him with her head high.

But in the eyes of the other guests it was not only the Colonel's entrance that was reflected. Mrs. St. George saw there also the excitement and curiosity occasioned by the re-grouping of seats, and the appearance, behind Mrs. Closson—who came in with her usual somnambulist's walk and thick-lashed stare—of two young men, two authentic new dancers for the hotel beauties.

Mrs. St. George knew all about them. The little olive-faced velvet-eyed fellow, with the impudently curly black hair, was Teddy de Santos-Dios, Mr. Closson's Brazilian step-son, over on his annual visit to the States; the other, the short heavy-looking young man with a low forehead pressed down by a shock of drab hair, an uncertain mouth under a thick drab moustache, and small eyes, slow, puzzled, not unkindly yet not reliable, was Lord Richard Marable, the impecunious younger son of an English marquess, who had picked up a job on the Closson *estancia,* and had come over for his holiday with Santos-Dios. Two "foreigners," and certainly ineligible ones, especially the little black popinjay who travelled with his guitar—but, after all, dancers for the girls, and therefore not wholly unwelcome even to Mrs. St. George, whose heart often ached at the thought of the Newport ball-rooms, where black coat-tails were said to jam every doorway, while at Saratoga the poor girls—

Ah, but there they were, the girls!—the privileged few whom she grouped under that designation. The fancy had taken them to come in late, and to arrive all together, and now, arm in arm, a blushing bevy, they swayed across the threshold of the dining-room like a branch hung with blossoms, drawing the dull middle-aged eyes of the other guests from lobster salad and fried chicken, and eclipsing even the refulgent Colonel—happy girls, with two new dancers for the week-end, they had celebrated the unwonted wind-fall by extra touches of adornment: a red rose in the fold of a fichu, a loose curl on a white shoulder, a pair of new satin slippers, a fresh *moiré* ribbon.

Seeing them through the eyes of the new young men, Mrs. St. George felt their collective grace with a vividness almost exempt from envy. To her, as to those two foreigners, they embodied "the American girl," the world's highest achievement; and she was as ready to enjoy Lizzy Elmsworth's brilliant darkness, and that dry sparkle of Mab's, as much as her own Virginia's roses and Nan's alternating frowns and dimples. She was even able to recognize that the Closson girl's incongruous hair gilded the whole group like a sunburst. Could Newport show anything lovelier, she wondered half-bitterly, as she seated herself between Mr. Closson and young Santos-Dios.

Mrs. Closson, from the Colonel's right, leaned across the table with her soft ambiguous smile. "What lovely diamonds, Mrs. St. George! I wish I hadn't left all mine in the safe at New York!"

Mrs. St. George thought: "She means the place isn't worth bringing jewels to. As if she ever went out anywhere in New York!" But her eyes wandered beyond Mrs. Closson to Lord Richard Marable; it was the first time she had ever sat at table with anyone even remotely related to a British nobleman, and she fancied the young man was ironically observing the way in which she held her fork. But she saw that his eyes, which were sand-coloured like his face, and sandy-lashed, had found another occupation. They were fixed on Conchita Closson, who sat opposite to him; they rested on her unblinkingly, immovably, as if she had been a natural object, a landscape or a cathedral, that one had travelled far to see, and had the right to look at as long as one chose. "He's drinking her up like blotting-paper. I thought they were better brought up over in England!" Mrs. St. George said to herself, austerely thankful that he was not taking such liberties with *her* daughters ("but men always know the difference," she reflected), and suddenly not worrying any longer about how she held her fork.

IV.

Miss Laura Testvalley stood on the wooden platform of the railway station at Saratoga Springs, N.Y., and looked about her. It was not an inspiriting scene; but she had not expected that it would be, and would not have greatly cared if it had. She had been in America for eighteen months, and it was not for its architectural or civic beauties that she had risked herself so far. Miss Testvalley had small means, and a derelict family to assist; and her successful career as a governess in the households of the English aristocracy had been curtailed by the need to earn more money. English governesses were at a premium in the United States, and one of Miss Testvalley's former pupils, whose husband was attached to the British Legation in Washington, had recommended her to Mrs. Russell Parmore, a cousin of the Eglintons and the van der Luydens—the best, in short, that New York had to offer. The salary was not as high as Miss Testvalley had hoped for, but her ex-pupil at the Legation had assured her that among the "new" coal and steel people, who could pay more, she would certainly be too wretched. Miss Testvalley was not sure of this. She had not come to America in search of distinguished manners any more than of well-kept railway stations; but she decided on reflection that the Parmore household might be a useful springboard, and so it proved. Mrs. Russell Parmore was certainly very distinguished, and so were her pallid daughter and her utterly rubbed-out husband; and how could they know that to Miss Test-valley they represented at best a *milieu* of retired colonels at Cheltenham, or the household of a minor canon in a cathedral town? Miss Testvalley had been used to a more vivid setting, and accustomed to social dramas and emotions which Mrs. Russell Parmore had only seen hinted at in fiction; and as the pay was low, and the domestic economies were painful (Mrs. Russell Parmore would have thought it ostentatious and vulgar to live largely), Miss Testvalley, after conscientiously "finishing" Miss Parmore (a young lady whom Nature seemed scarcely to have begun), decided to seek, in a different field, ampler opportunities of action. She consulted a New York governesses' agency, and learned that the "new people" would give "almost anything" for such social training as an accomplished European governess could impart. Miss Testvalley fixed a maximum wage, and in a few days was notified by the agency that Mrs. Tracy St. George was ready to engage her. "It was Mrs. Russell Parmore's reference that did it," said the black-wigged lady at the desk as they exchanged fees and congratulations. "In New York she counts more than all your duchesses"; and Miss Testvalley again had reason to rate her own good sense at its just value. Life at the Parmores', on poor pay and a scanty diet, had been a weary business; but it had been worth while. Now she had in her pocket the promise of eighty dollars a month, and the possibility of a more exciting task; for she understood that the St. Georges were very "new," and the prospect of comparing the manners and customs of the new and the not-new might be amusing. "I wonder," she thought ironically, "if the Duchess would see the slightest difference"—the Duchess meaning always *hers*, the puissant lady of Tintagel, where Miss Testvalley had spent so many months shivering with cold, and bandaging the chilblains of the younger girls, while the other daughters, with their particular "finishing" duenna, accompanied their parents from one ducal residence to another. The Duchess of Tintagel, who had beaten Miss Testvalley's salary well-nigh down to the level of an upper house-maid's, who had so often paid it after an embarrassingly long delay, who had been surprised that a governess should want a fire in her room, or a hot soup for her school-room dinner—the Duchess was now (all unknown to herself) making up for her arrears toward Miss Testvalley. By giving Mrs. Parmore the chance to say, when she had friends to dine, "I happen to know, for instance, that at Tintagel Castle there are only open fires, and the halls and corridors are not heated at all," Miss Testvalley had gained several small favours from her parsimonious employer; and by telling her, in the strictest confidence, that Their Graces had at one time felt a good deal of anxiety about their only son—oh, a simple sweet-natured young man if ever there was one; but, then, the temptations which beset a marquess who was heir to a dukedom!—Miss Testvalley had obtained from Mrs. Parmore a letter of recommendation which placed her at the head of the educational sisterhood in the United States.

Miss Testvalley needed this, and every other form of assistance she could obtain. It would have been difficult for either Mrs. Parmore or the Duchess of Tintagel to imagine how poor she was, or how many people had (or so she thought) a lien on her pitiful savings. It was the penalty of the family glory. Miss Testvalley's grandfather was the illustrious patriot Gennaro Testavaglia of Modena, fomenter of insurrections, hero of the Risorgimento, author of those once famous historical novels *Arnaldo da Brescia* and *La Donna della Fortezza,* but whose fame lingered in England chiefly because he was the cousin of the old Gabriele Rossetti, father of the decried and illustrious Dante Gabriel. The Testavaglias, fleeing from the Austrian inquisition, had come to England at the same time as the Rossettis, and, contracting their impossible name to the scope of English lips, had intermarried with other exiled revolutionaries and anti-Papists, producing sons who were artists and agnostics, and daughters who were evangelicals of the strictest pattern, and governesses in the highest families. Laura Testvalley had obediently followed the family tradition; but she had come after the heroic days of evangelical great ladies who required governesses to match; competition was more active, there was less demand for drawing-room Italian and prayerful considerations on the Collects, and more for German and the natural sciences, in neither of which Miss Testvalley excelled. And in the intervening years the mothers and aunts of the family had grown rheumatic and impotent, the heroic old men lingered on in their robust senility, and the drain on the younger generation grew heavier with every year. By the time she reached her late thirties, Laura had found it impossible, on her English earnings, to keep the grandmother (wife of the Risorgimento hero), and to aid her own infirm mother in supporting an invalid brother and a married sister with six children, whose husband had disappeared in the wilds of Australia. Laura was sure that it was not her vocation to minister to others, but she had been forced into the task early, and continued in it from family pride—and because, after all, she belonged to the group, and the Risorgimento and the Pre-Raphaelites were her chief credentials. And so she had come to America.

At the Parmores' she had learned a good deal about one phase of American life, and she had written home some droll letters on the subject; but she had suspected from the first that the real America was elsewhere, and had been tempted and amused by the idea that among the Wall Street *parvenus* she might discover it. She had an unspoiled taste for oddities and contrasts, and nothing could have been more alien to her private sentiments than the family combination of revolutionary radicalism, Exeter Hall piety, and awestruck reverence for the aristocratic households in which the Testvalley governesses earned the keep of their ex-*carbonari*. "If I'd been a man," she sometimes thought, "Dante Gabriel might not have been the only cross in the family." And the idea obscurely comforted her when she was correcting her pupils' compositions, or picking up the dropped stitches in their knitting.

She was used to waiting in strange railway stations, her old black beaded "dolman" over her arm, her modest horsehair box at her feet. Servants often forget to order the fly which is to fetch the governess, and the lady herself, though she may have meant to come to the station, is not infrequently detained by shopping or calling. So Miss Testvalley, without impatience, watched the other travellers drive off in the spidery high-wheeled vehicles in which people bounced across the humps and ruts of the American country roads. It was the eve of the great race-week, and she was amused by the showy garb of the gentlemen and the much-flounced elegance of their ladies, though she felt sure Mrs. Parmore would have disdained them.

One by one the travellers scattered, their huge "Saratogas" (she knew that expression also) were hoisted into broken-down express-carts that crawled off in the wake of the owners; and at last a new dust-cloud formed down the road and floated slowly nearer, till there emerged from it a lumbering vehicle of the kind which Miss Testvalley knew to be classed as hotel hacks. As it drew up she was struck by the fact that the driver, a small dusky fellow in a white linen jacket and a hat-brim of exotic width, had an orange bow tied to his whip, and a beruffled white poodle with a bigger orange bow perched between himself and the shabby young man in overalls who shared his seat; while from within she felt herself laughingly surveyed by two tiers of bright young eyes. The driver pulled up with a queer guttural cry to his horses, the poodle leapt down and began to dance on his hind legs, and out of the hack poured a spring torrent of muslins, sash-ends, and bright cheeks under swaying hat-brims. Miss Testvalley found herself in a circle of nymphs shaken by hysterical laughter, and as she stood there, small, brown, interrogative, there swept through her mind a shred of verse which Dante Gabriel used to be fond of reciting:

Whence came ye, merry damsels, whence came ye,
So many and so many, and such glee?

and she smiled at the idea that Endymion should greet her at the Saratoga railway station. For it was clearly in search of her that the rabble rout had come. The dancing nymphs hailed her with joyful giggles, the poodle sprang on her with dusty paws, and then turned a somersault in her honour, and from the driver's box came the twang of a guitar and the familiar wail of: "*Nita, Juanita, ask thy soul if we must part?*"

"No, certainly not!" cried Miss Testvalley, tossing up her head toward the driver, who responded with doffed sombrero and hand on heart. "That is to say," she added, "if my future pupil is one of the young ladies who have joined in this very flattering welcome."

The enchanted circle broke, and the nymphs, still hand in hand, stretched a straight line of loveliness before her. "Guess which!" chimed simultaneously from five pairs of lips, while five deep curtsies swept the platform; and Miss Testvalley drew back a step and scanned them thoughtfully.

Her first thought was that she had never seen five prettier girls in a row; her second (tinged with joy) that Mrs. Russell Parmore would have been scandalized by such an exhibition, on the Saratoga railway platform, in full view of departing travellers, gazing employés, and delighted station-loafers; her third that, whichever of the beauties was to fall to her lot, life in such company would be infinitely more amusing than with the Parmores. And still smiling she continued to examine the mirthful mocking faces.

No dominant beauty, was her first impression; no proud angelic heads, ready for coronets or halos, such as she was used to in England; unless indeed the tall fair girl with such heaps of wheat-colored hair and such gentian-blue eyes—or the very dark one, who was too pale for her black hair, but had the small imperious nose of a Roman empress. . . . Yes, those two were undoubtedly beautiful, yet they were not beauties. They seemed rather to have reached the last height of prettiness, and to be perched on that sunny lower slope, below the cold divinities. And with the other three, taken one by one, fault might have been found on various counts; for the one in the striped pink-and-white organdy, though she looked cleverer than the others, had a sharp nose, and her laugh showed too many teeth; and the one in white, with a big orange-coloured sash the colour of the poodle's bow (no doubt she was his mistress), was sallow and red-haired, and you had to look into her pale starry eyes to forget that she was too tall, and stooped a little. And as for the fifth, who seemed so much younger—hardly more than a child—her small face was such a flurry of frowns and dimples that Miss Testvalley did not know how to define her.

"Well, young ladies, my first idea is that I wish you were all to be my pupils; and the second"—she paused, weighed the possibilities, and met the eyes—"the second is that this is Miss Annabel St. George, who is, I believe, to be my special charge." She put her hand on Nan's arm.

"How did you know?" burst from Nan, on the shrill note of a netted bird; and the others broke into laughter.

"Why, you silly, we told you so! Anybody can tell you're nothing but a baby!"

Nan faced about, blazing and quivering. "Well, if I'm a baby, what I want is a nurse, and not a beastly English governess!"

Her companions laughed again and nudged each other; then, abashed, they glanced at the newcomer, as if trying to read in her face what would come next.

Miss Testvalley laughed also. "Oh, I'm used to both jobs," she rejoined briskly. "But, meanwhile, hadn't we better be getting off to the hotel? Get into the carriage, please, Annabel," she said with sudden authority.

She turned to look for her trunk; but it had already been shouldered by the nondescript young man in overalls, who hoisted it to the roof of the carriage, and then, jumping down, brushed the soot and dust off his hands. As he did so, Miss Testvalley confronted him, and her hand dropped from Nan's arm.

"Why—Lord Richard!" she exclaimed; and the young man in overalls gave a sheepish laugh. "I suppose at home they all think I'm in Brazil," he said in an uncertain voice.

"I know nothing of what they think," retorted Miss Testvalley drily, following the girls into the carriage. As they drove off, Nan, who was crowded in between Mab Elmsworth and Conchita, burst into sudden tears. "I didn't mean to call you 'beastly,' " she whispered, stealing a hand toward the new governess; and the new governess, clasping the hand, answered with her undaunted smile: "I didn't hear you call me so, my dear."

V.

Mrs. St. George had gone to the races with her husband—an ordeal she always dreaded and yet prayed for. Colonel St. George, on these occasions, was so handsome, and so splendid in his light racing-suit and gray top hat, that she enjoyed a larger repetition of her triumph in the hotel dining-room; but when this had been tasted to the full there remained her dread of the mysterious men with whom he was hail-fellow-well-met in the paddock, and the dreadful painted women in open carriages who leered and beckoned (didn't she see them?) under the fringes of their sunshades.

She soon wearied of the show, and would have been glad to be back rocking and sipping lemonade on the hotel verandah; yet, when the Colonel helped her into the carriage, suggesting that if she wanted to meet the new governess it was time to be off, she instantly concluded that the rich widow at the Congress Springs Hotel, about whom there was so much gossip, had made him a secret sign, and was going to carry him off to the gambling-rooms for supper—if not worse. But, when the Colonel chose, his arts were irresistible, and in another moment Mrs. St. George was driving away alone, her heart heavy with this new anxiety superposed on so many others.

When she reached the hotel all the frequenters of the verandah, gathered between the columns of the porch, were greeting with hysterical laughter a motley group who were pouring out of the familiar vehicle from which Mrs. St. George had expected to see Nan descend with the dreaded and longed-for governess. The party was headed by Teddy de Santos-Dios, grotesquely accoutred in a hotel waiter's white jacket, and twanging his guitar to the antics of Conchita's poodle, while Conchita herself, the Elmsworth sisters, and Mrs. St. George's own two girls danced up the steps surrounding a small soberly garbed figure, whom Mrs. St. George instantly identified as the governess. Mrs. Elmsworth and Mrs. Closson stood on the upper step, smothering their laughter in lace handkerchiefs; but Mrs. St. George sailed past them with set lips, pushing aside a shabby-looking young man in overalls who seemed to form part of the company.

"Virginia—Annabel," she gasped, "what is the meaning . . . Oh, Miss Testvalley—what *must* you think?" she faltered with trembling lips.

"I think it very kind of Annabel's young friends to have come with her to meet me," said Miss Testvalley; and Mrs. St. George noted with bewilderment and relief that she was actually smiling, and that she had slipped her arm through Nan's.

For a moment Mrs. St. George thought it might be easier to deal with a governess who was already on such easy terms with her pupil; but by the time Miss Testvalley, having removed the dust of travel, had knocked at her employer's door, the latter had been assailed by new apprehensions. It would have been comparatively simple to receive, with what Mrs. St. George imagined to be the dignity of a duchess, a governess used to such ceremonial; but the disconcerting circumstances of Miss Testvalley's arrival, and the composure with which she had met them, had left Mrs. St. George with her dignity on her hands. Could it be—? But no; Mrs. Russell Parmore, as well as the Duchess, answered for Miss Testvalley's unquestionable respectability. Mrs. St. George fanned herself nervously.

"Oh, come in. Do sit down, Miss Testvalley." (Mrs. St. George had expected someone taller, more majestic. She would have thought Miss Testvalley insignificant, could the term be applied to anyone coming from Mrs. Parmore.) "I don't know how my daughters can have been induced to do anything so—so undignified. Unfortunately, the Closson girl—" She broke off, embarrassed by the recollection of the Colonel's injunctions.

"The tall young girl with auburn hair? I understand that one of the masqueraders was her brother."

"Yes; her half-brother. Mrs. Closson is a Brazilian"—but again Mrs. St. George checked the note of disparagement. "Brazilian" was bad enough, without adding anything pejorative. "The Colonel—Colonel St. George—has business relations with Mr. Closson. I never met them before. . . ."

"Ah," said Miss Testvalley.

"And I'm sure my girls and the Elmsworths would never . . ."

"Oh, quite so; I understand. I've no doubt the idea was Lord Richard's."

She uttered the name as though it were familiar to her, and Mrs. St. George caught at Lord Richard. "You knew him already? He appears to be a friend of the Clossons."

"I knew him in England; yes. I was with Lady Brightlingsea for two years—as his sisters' governess."

Mrs. St. George gazed awestruck down this new and resonant perspective. "Lady Brittlesey?" (It was thus that Miss Testvalley had pronounced the name.)

"The Marchioness of Brightlingsea; his mother. It's a very large family. I was with two of the younger daughters, Lady Honoria and Lady Ulrica Marable. I think Lord Richard is the third son. But one saw him at home so very seldom. . . ."

Mrs. St. George drew a deep breath. She had not bargained for this glimpse into the labyrinth of the peerage, and she felt a little dizzy, as though all the Brightlingseas and the Marables were in the room, and she ought to make the proper gestures, and didn't even know what to call them without her husband's being there to tell her. She wondered whether the experiment of an English governess might not after all make life too complicated. And this one's eyebrows were so black and ironical.

"Lord Richard," continued Miss Testvalley, "always has to have his little joke." Her tone seemed to dismiss him, and all his titled relations with him. Mrs. St. George was relieved. "But your daughter Annabel—perhaps," Miss Testvalley continued, "you would like to give me some general idea of the stage she has reached in her different studies?" Her manner was now distinctly professional, and Mrs. St. George's spirits drooped again. If only the Colonel had been there—as he would have been, but for that woman! Or even Nan herself . . . Mrs. St. George looked helplessly at the governess. But suddenly an inspiration came to her. "I have always left these things to the girls' teachers," she said with majesty.

"Oh, quite," Miss Testvalley assented.

"And their father; their father takes a great interest in their studies—when time permits . . ." Mrs. St. George continued. "But of course his business interests . . . which are enormous . . ."

"I think I understand," Miss Testvalley softly agreed.

Mrs. St. George again sighed her relief. A governess who understood without the need of tiresome explanations—was it not more than she had hoped for? Certainly Miss Testvalley looked insignificant; but the eyes under her expressive eyebrows were splendid, and she had an air of firmness. And the miracle was that Nan should already have taken a fancy to her. If only the other girls didn't laugh her out of it! "Of course," Mrs. St. George began again, "what I attach most importance to is that my girls should be taught to—to behave like ladies."

Miss Testvalley murmured: "Oh, yes. Drawing-room accomplishments."

"I may as well tell you that I don't care very much for the girls they associate with here. Saratoga is not what it used to be. In New York, of course, it will be different. I hope you can persuade Annabel to study."

She could not think of anything else to say, and the governess, who seemed singularly discerning, rose with a slight bow, and murmured: "If you will allow me . . ."

Miss Testvalley's room was narrow and bare; but she had already discovered that the rooms of summer hotels in the States were all like that; the luxury and gilding were reserved for the public parlours. She did not much mind; she had never been used to comfort, and her Italian nature did not crave it. To her mind the chief difference between the governess's room at Tintagel, or at Allfriars, the Brightlingsea seat, and those she had occupied since her arrival in America, was that the former were larger (and therefore harder to heat) and were furnished with threadbare relics of former splendour, and carpets in which you caught your heel; whereas at Mrs. Parmore's, and in this big hotel, though the governess's quarters were cramped, they were neat and the furniture was in good repair. But this afternoon Miss Testvalley was perhaps tired, or oppressed by the heat, or perhaps only by an unwonted sense of loneliness. Certainly it was odd to find one's self at the orders of people who wished their daughters to be taught to "behave like ladies." (The alternative being—what, she wondered? Perhaps a disturbing apparition like Conchita Closson.)

At any rate, Miss Testvalley was suddenly aware of a sense of far-away-ness, of a quite unreasonable yearning for the dining-room at the back of a certain shabby house at Denmark Hill, where her mother, in a widow's cap of white crape, sat on one side of the scantily filled grate, turning with rheumatic fingers the pages of the Reverend Frederick Maurice's sermons, while, facing her across the hearth, old Gennaro Testavaglia, still heavy and powerful in his extreme age, brooded with fixed eyes in a big parchment-coloured face, and repeated over and over some forgotten verse of his own revolutionary poems. In that room, with its chronic smell of cold coffee and smouldering coals, of Elliman's liniment and human old age, Miss Testvalley had spent some of the most disheartening hours of her life. *"La mia prigione,"* she had once called it; yet was it not for that detested room that she was homesick!

Only fifteen minutes in which to prepare for supper! (She

had been warned that late dinners were still unknown in American hotels.) Miss Testvalley, setting her teeth against the vision of the Denmark Hill dining-room, went up to the chest of drawers on which she had already laid out her modest toilet appointments; and there she saw, between her yellowish-backed brush and faded pincushion, a bunch of freshly gathered geraniums and mignonette. The flowers had certainly not been there when she had smoothed her hair before waiting on Mrs. St. George; nor had they, she was sure, been sent by that lady. They were not bought flowers, but flowers lovingly gathered; and someone else must have entered in Miss Testvalley's absence, and hastily deposited the humble posy.

The governess sat down on the hard chair beside the bed, and her eyes filled with tears. Flowers, she had noticed, did not abound in the States; at least not in summer. In winter, in New York, you could see them banked up in tiers in the damp heat of the florists' windows: plumy ferns, forced lilac, and those giant roses, red and pink, which rich people offered to each other so lavishly in long white card-board boxes. It was very odd; the same ladies who exchanged these costly tributes in mid-winter lived through the summer without a flower, or with nothing but a stiff bed of dwarf foliage plants before the door, or a tub or two of the inevitable hydrangeas. Yet someone had apparently managed to snatch these flowers from the meagre border before the hotel porch, and had put them there to fill Miss Testvalley's bedroom with scent and colour. And who could have done it but her new pupil?

Quarter of an hour later Miss Testvalley, her thick hair re-braided and glossed with brilliantine, her black merino exchanged for a plum-coloured silk with a crochet lace collar, and lace mittens on her small worn hands, knocked at the door of the Misses St. George. It opened, and the governess gave a little "Oh!" of surprise. Virginia stood there, a shimmer of ruffled white drooping away from her young throat and shoulders. On her heaped-up wheat-coloured hair lay a wreath of corn-flowers; and a black velvet ribbon with a locket hanging from it intensified her fairness like the black stripe on a ring-dove's throat.

"What elegance for a public dining-room!" thought Miss Testvalley; and then reflected: "But no doubt it's her only chance of showing it."

Virginia opened wondering blue eyes, and the governess explained: "The supper-bell has rung, and I thought you and your sister might like me to go down with you."

"Oh—" Virginia murmured; and added: "Nan's lost her slipper. She's hunting for it."

"Very well; shall I help her? And you'll go down and excuse us to your mamma?"

Virginia's eyes grew wider. "Well, I guess Mother's used to waiting," she said, as she sauntered along the corridor to the staircase.

Nan St. George lay face downward on the floor, poking with a silk parasol under the wardrobe. At the sound of Miss Testvalley's voice she raised herself sulkily. Her small face was flushed and frowning. ("None of her sister's beauty," Miss Testvalley thought.) "It's there, but I can't get at it," Nan proclaimed.

"My dear, you'll tumble your lovely frock—"

"Oh, it's not lovely. It's one of Jinny's last-year's organdies."

"Well, it won't improve it to crawl about on the floor. Is your shoe under the wardrobe? Let me try to get it. My silk won't be damaged."

Miss Testvalley put out her hand for the sunshade, and Nan scrambled to her feet. "You can't reach it," she said, still sulkily. But Miss Testvalley, prostrate on the floor, had managed to push a thin arm under the wardrobe, and the parasol presently reappeared with a little bronze slipper on its tip. Nan gave a laugh.

"Well, you *are* handy!" she said.

Miss Testvalley echoed the laugh. "Put it on quickly, and let me help you to tidy your dress. And, oh dear, your sash is untied—" She spun the girl about, re-tied the sash, and smoothed the skirt with airy touches; for all of which, she noticed, Nan uttered no word of thanks.

"And your handkerchief, Annabel?" In Miss Testvalley's opinion no lady should appear in the evening without a scrap of lace-edged cambric, folded into a triangle and held between gloved or mittened finger-tips. Nan shrugged. "I never know where my handkerchiefs are—I guess they get lost in the wash, wandering round in hotels the way we do."

Miss Testvalley sighed at this nomadic wastefulness. Perhaps because she had always been a wanderer herself, she loved orderly drawers and shelves, and bunches of lavender between delicately fluted under-garments.

"Do you always live in hotels, my dear?"

"We did when I was little. But Father's bought a house in New York now. Mother made him do it, because the Elmsworths did. She thought maybe, if we had one, Jinny'd be invited out more; but I don't see much difference."

"Well, I shall have to help you to go over your linen," the governess continued; but Nan showed no interest in the offer. Miss Testvalley saw before her a cold impatient little face— and yet . . .

"Annabel," she said, slipping her hand through the girl's thin arm, "how did you guess I was fond of flowers?"

The blood rose from Nan's shoulders to her cheeks, and a half-guilty smile set the dimples racing across her face. "Mother said we'd acted like a lot of savages, getting up that circus at the station—and what on earth would you think of us?"

"I think that I shall like you all very much; and you especially, because of those flowers."

Nan gave a shy laugh. "Lord Richard said you'd like them."

"Lord Richard?"

"Yes. He says in England everybody has a garden, with lots of flowers that smell sweet. And so I stole them from the hotel border. . . . He's crazy about Conchita, you know. Do you think she'll catch him?"

Miss Testvalley stiffened. She felt her upper lip lengthen,

though she tried to smile. "I don't think it's a question that need concern us, do you?"

Nan stared. "Well, she's my greatest friend—after Jinny, I mean."

"Then we must wish her something better than Lord Richard. Come, my dear, or those wonderful American griddle-cakes will all be gone."

Early in her career Miss Testvalley had had to learn the difficult art of finding her way about—not only as concerned the tastes and temper of the people she lived with, but the topography of their houses. In those old winding English dwellings, half fortress, half palace, where suites and galleries of stately proportions abruptly tapered off into narrow twists and turns, leading to unexpected rooms tucked away in unaccountable corners, and where school-room and nurseries were usually at the far end of the labyrinth, it behoved the governess to blaze her trail by a series of private aids to memory. It was important, in such houses, not only to know the way you were meant to take, but the many you were expected to avoid, and a young governess turning too often down the passage leading to the young gentlemen's wing, or getting into the way of the master of the house in his dignified descent to the breakfast-room, might suddenly have her services dispensed with. To anyone thus trained, the simple plan of an American summer hotel offered no mysteries; and when supper was over and after a sultry hour or two in the red-and-gold ballroom the St. George ladies ascended to their apartments, Miss Testvalley had no difficulty in finding her way up another flight to her own room. She was already aware that it was in the wing of the hotel, and had noted that from its window she could look across into that from which, before supper, she had seen Miss Closson signal to her brother and Lord Richard, who were smoking on the gravel below.

It was no business of Miss Testvalley's to keep watch on

what went on in the Closson rooms—or would not have been, she corrected herself, had Nan St. George not spoken of Conchita as her dearest friend. Such a tie did seem to the governess to require vigilance. Miss Closson was herself an unknown quantity, and Lord Richard was only too well known to Miss Testvalley. It was therefore not unnatural that, after silence had fallen on the long corridors of the hotel, the governess, finding sleep impossible in her small suffocating room, should put out her candle and gaze across from her window at that from which she had seen Conchita lean.

Light still streamed from it, though midnight was past, and presently came laughter, and the twang of Santos-Dios's guitar, and a burst of youthful voices joining in song. Was her pupil's among them? Miss Testvalley could not be sure; but soon, detaching itself from Teddy de Santos-Dios's reedy tenor, she caught the hoarse barytone of another voice.

Imprudent children! It was bad enough to be gathered at that hour in a room with a young man and a guitar; but at least the young man was Miss Closson's brother, and Miss Testvalley had noticed, at the supper-table, much exchange of civilities between the St. Georges and the Clossons. But Richard Marable—that was inexcusable, that was scandalous! The hotel would be ringing with it tomorrow. . . .

Ought not Miss Testvalley to find some pretext for knocking at Conchita's door, gathering her charges back to safety, and putting it in their power to say that their governess had assisted at the little party? Her first impulse was to go; but governesses who act on first impulses seldom keep their places. "As long as there's so much noise," she thought, "there can't be any mischief . . ." and at that moment, in a pause of the singing, she caught Nan's trill of little-girl laughter. Miss Testvalley started up and went to her door; but once more she drew back. Better wait and see— interfering might do more harm than good. If only some exasperated neighbour did not ring to have the rejoicings stopped!

At length music and laughter subsided. Silence followed.

Miss Testvalley, drawing an austere purple flannel garment over her night-dress, unbolted her door and stole out into the passage. Where it joined the main corridor she paused and waited. A door had opened half way down the corridor—Conchita's door—and the governess saw a flutter of light dresses, and heard subdued laughter and good nights. Both the St. George and Elmsworth families were lodged below, and in the weak glimmer of gas she made sure of four girls hurrying toward her wing. She drew back hastily. Glued to her door, she listened, and heard a heavy but cautious step passing by, and a throaty voice humming "Champagne Charlie." She drew a breath of relief, relit her candle, and sat down before her glass to finish her toilet for the night.

Her hair carefully waved on its pins, her evening prayer recited, she slipped into bed and blew out the light. But sleep did not come, and she lay in the sultry darkness and listened, she hardly knew for what. At last she heard the same heavy step returning cautiously, passing her door, gaining once more the main corridor—the step she would have known in a thousand, the way she used to listen for at Allfriars after midnight, groping down the long passage to the governess's room.

She started up. Forgetful of crimping-pins and bare feet, she opened her door again. The last flicker of gas had gone out, and, secure in the blackness, she crept after the heavy step to the corner. It sounded ahead of her half way down the long row of doors; then it stopped, a door opened . . . and Miss Testvalley turned back on leaden feet. . . .

Nothing of that fugitive adventure at Allfriars had ever been known. Of that she was certain. An ill-conditioned youth, the boon companion of his father's grooms, and a small brown governess, ten years his elder, and known to be somewhat curt and distant with everyone except her pupils and their parents—who would ever have thought of associating the one with the other? The episode had been brief; the peril was soon over; and when, the very same year, Lord Richard was solemnly banished from his father's house, it was not because of his having once or twice stolen down the school-room passage at undue hours, but for reasons so far more deplorable that poor Lady Brightlingsea, her reserve utterly broken down, had sobbed out on Miss Testvalley's breast: "Anything, anything else I know his father would have forgiven." (Miss Testvalley wondered. . . .)

VI.

When Colonel St. George bought his house in Madison Avenue it seemed to him fit to satisfy the ambitions of any budding millionaire. That it had been built and decorated by one of the Tweed ring who had come to grief earlier than his more famous fellow-criminals, was to Colonel St. George convincing proof that it was a suitable setting for wealth and elegance. But social education is acquired rapidly in New York, even by those who have to absorb it through the cracks of the sacred edifice; and Mrs. St. George had already found out that no one lived in Madison Avenue, that the front hall should have been painted Pompeian red with a stencilled frieze, and not with naked Cupids and humming-birds on a sky-blue ground, and that basement dining-rooms were unknown to the fashionable. So much she had picked up almost at once from Jinny and Jinny's school-friends; and when she called on Mrs. Parmore to enquire about the English governess, the sight of the Parmore house, small and simple as it was, completed her disillusionment.

But it was too late to change. The Colonel, who was insensitive to details, continued to be proud of his house; even when the Elmsworths, suddenly migrating from Brooklyn, had settled themselves in Fifth Avenue, he would not admit his mistake, or feel the humiliation of the contrast. And yet what a difference it made to a lady to be able to say "Fifth Avenue" in giving her address to Black, Starr and Frost, or to Mrs. Connelly, the fashionable dress-maker! In establishments like that they classed their customers at once, and "Madison Avenue" stood at best for a decent mediocrity.

Mrs. St. George at first ascribed to this unfortunate locality her failure to make a social situation for her girls; yet after the Elmsworths had come to Fifth Avenue she noted with satisfaction that Lizzy and Mabel were not asked out much more than Virginia. Of course, Mr. Elmsworth was an obstacle; and so was Mrs. Elmsworth's laugh. It was difficult—it was even painful—to picture the Elmsworths dining at the Parmores' or the Eglintons'. But the St. Georges did not dine there either. And the question of ball-going was almost as discouraging. One of the young men whom the girls had met at Saratoga had suggested to Virginia that he might get her a card for the first Assembly; but Mrs. St. George, when sounded, declined indignantly, for she knew that in the best society girls did not go to balls without their parents.

These subscription balls were a peculiar source of bitterness to Mrs. St. George. She could not understand how her daughters could be excluded from entertainment for which one could buy a ticket. She knew all about the balls from her hair-dresser, the celebrated Katie Wood. Katie did everybody's hair, and innocently planted dagger after dagger in Mrs. St. George's anxious breast by saying: "If you and Jinny want me next Wednesday week for the first Assembly you'd better say so right off, because I've got every minute bespoke already from three o'clock on," or: "If you're invited to the opening night of the Opera, I might try the new chignon with the bunch of curls on the left shoulder," or, worse still: "I suppose Jinny belongs to the Thursday Evening Dances, don't she? The débutantes are going to wear wreaths of apple-blossom or rose-buds a good deal this winter—or forget-me-nots would look lovely, with her eyes."

Lovely, indeed. But if Virginia had not been asked to belong, and if Mrs. St. George had vainly tried to have her own name added to the list of the Assembly balls, or to get a box for the opening night of the Opera, what was there to do but to say indifferently: "Oh, I don't know if we shall be here—the Colonel's thinking a little of carrying us off to Florida if he can get away"—knowing all the while how much the hair-dresser believed of that excuse, and also aware that, in speaking of Miss Eglinton and Miss Parmore, Katie did not call them by their Christian names. . . .

Mrs. St. George could not understand why she was subjected to this cruel ostracism. The Colonel knew everybody—that is, all the gentlemen he met down town, or at his clubs, and he belonged to many clubs. Their dues were always having to be paid, even when the butcher and the grocer were clamouring. He often brought gentlemen home to dine, and gave them the best champagne and Madeira in the cellar; and they invited him back, but never included Mrs. St. George and Virginia in their invitations.

It was small comfort to learn one day that Jinny and Nan had been invited to act as Conchita Closson's bridesmaids. She thought it unnatural that the Clossons, who were strangers in New York, and still camping at the Fifth Avenue Hotel, should be marrying their daughter before Virginia was led to the altar. And then the bridegroom!—well, everybody knew that he was only a younger son, and that in England, even in the great aristocratic families, younger sons were of small account unless they were clever enough to make their own way—an ambition which seemed never to have troubled Dick Marable. Moreover, there were dark rumours about him, reports of warnings discreetly transmitted through the British Legation in Washington, and cruder tales among the clubs. Still, nothing could alter the fact that Lord Richard Marable was the son of the Marquess of Brightlingsea, and that his mother had been a duke's daughter—and who knows whether the Eglintons and Parmores, though they thanked heaven their dear girls would never be exposed to such risks, were not half envious of the Clossons? But then there was the indecent haste of it. The young people had met for the first time in August; and they were to be married in November! In good society it was usual for a betrothal to last at least a year; and among the Eglintons and Parmores even that time-allowance was thought to betray an undue haste. "The young people should be given time to get to know each other," the mothers of Fifth Avenue decreed; and Mrs. Parmore told Miss Testvalley, when the latter called to pay her respects to her former employer, that she for her part hoped her daughter would never consent to an engagement of less than two years. "But I suppose, dear Miss Testvalley, that among the people you're with now there are no social traditions."

"None except those they are making for themselves," Miss Testvalley was tempted to rejoin; but that would not have been what she called a "governess's answer," and she knew a governess should never be more on her guard than when conversing with a former employer. Especially, Miss Testvalley thought, when the employer had a long nose with a slight droop, and pale lips like Mrs. Parmore's. She murmured that there were business reasons, she understood; Mr. Closson was leaving shortly for Brazil.

"Ah, so they say. But, of course, the rumours one hears about this young man . . . a son of Lord Brightlingsea's, I understand? But, Miss Testvalley, you were with the Brightlingseas; you must have known him?"

"It's a very big family, and when I went there the sons were already scattered. I usually remained at Allfriars with the younger girls."

Mrs. Parmore nodded softly. "Quite so. And by that time this unfortunate young man had already begun his career of dissipation in London. He *has* been dissipated, I believe?"

"Lately I think he's been trying to earn his living on Mr. Closson's plantation in Brazil."

"Poor young man! Do his family realize what a deplorable choice he has made? Whatever his past may have been, it's a pity he should marry in New York, and leave it again, without having any idea of it beyond what can be had in the Closson set. If he'd come in different circumstances, we should all have been so

happy. . . . Mr. Parmore would have put him down at his
clubs . . . he would have been invited everywhere. . . . Yes, it does
seem unfortunate. . . . But of course no one knows the Clossons."

"I suppose the young couple will go back to Brazil after the
marriage," said Miss Testvalley evasively.

Mrs. Parmore gave an ironic smile. "I don't imagine Miss
Closson is marrying the son of a marquess to go and live on a
plantation in Brazil. When I took Alida to Mrs. Connelly's to
order her dress for the Assembly, Mrs. Connelly told me she'd
heard from Mrs. Closson's maid that Mr. Closson meant to give
the young couple a house in London. Do you suppose this is
likely? They can't keep up any sort of establishment in London
without a fairly large income; and I hear Mr. Closson's position
in Wall Street is rather shaky."

Miss Testvalley took refuge in one of her Italian gestures of
conjecture. "Governesses, you know, Mrs. Parmore, hear so much
less gossip than dress-makers and ladies' maids; and I am not Miss
Closson's governess."

"No; fortunately for you! For I believe there were rather
unpleasant rumours at Saratoga. People were bound to find a
reason for such a hurried marriage. . . . But your pupils have been
asked to be bridesmaids, I understand?"

"The girls got to know each other last summer. And you
know how exciting it is, especially for a child of Annabel St.
George's age, to figure for the first time in a wedding procession."

"Yes. I suppose they haven't many chances. . . . But
shouldn't you like to come upstairs and see Alida's Assembly
dress? Mrs. Connelly has just sent it home, and your pupils might
like to hear about it. White tulle, of course—nothing will ever
replace white tulle for a débutante, will it?"

Miss Testvalley, after that visit, felt that she had cast in her lot
once for all with the usurpers and the adventurers. Perhaps because she herself had been born in exile, her sympathies were with

the social as well as the political outcasts—with the weepers by the waters of Babylon rather than those who barred the doors of the Assembly against them. Describe Miss Parmore's white tulle to her pupils, indeed! What she meant—but how accomplish it?—was to get cards for the Assembly for Mrs. St. George and Virginia, and to see to it that the latter's dress outdid Miss Parmore's as much as her beauty over-shadowed that young woman's.

But how? Through Lord Richard Marable? Well, that was perhaps not impossible. . . . Miss Testvalley had detected, in Mrs. Parmore, a faint but definite desire to make the young man's acquaintance, even to have him on the list of her next dinner. She would like to show him, poor young fellow, her manner implied, that there are houses in New York where a scion of the English aristocracy may feel himself at home, and discover (though, alas, too late!) that there are American girls comparable to his own sisters in education and breeding.

Since the announcement of Conchita's engagement, and the return of the two families to New York, there had been a good deal of coming and going between the St. George and Closson households—rather too much to suit Miss Testvalley. But she had early learned to adapt herself to her pupils' whims while maintaining her authority over them, and she preferred to accompany Nan to the Fifth Avenue Hotel rather than let her go there without her. Virginia, being "out," could come and go as she pleased; but among the Parmores and Eglintons, in whose code Mrs. St. George was profoundly versed, girls in the school-room did not walk about New York alone, much less call at hotels, and Nan, fuming yet resigned—for she had already grown unaccountably attached to her governess—had to submit to Miss Testvalley's conducting her to the Closson apartment, and waiting below when she was to be fetched. Sometimes, at Mrs. Closson's request, the governess went in with her charge. Mrs. Closson was almost always in her dressing-room, since leaving it necessitated encasing her soft frame in stays and a heavily whale-boned dress; and she preferred sitting at her piano, or lying on the sofa with a novel and a cigarette, in an atmosphere of steam-heat and heavily scented flowers, and amid a litter of wedding-presents and bridal finery. She was a good-natured woman, friendly and even confidential with everybody who came her way, and, when she caught sight of Miss Testvalley behind her charge, often called to her to come in and take a look at the lovely dress Mrs. Connelly had just sent home, or the embossed soup-tureen of Baltimore silver offered by Mr. Closson's business friends. Miss Testvalley did not always accept; but sometimes she divined that Mrs. Closson wished to consult her, or to confide in her, and while her pupil joined the other girls, she would clear the finery from a chair and prepare to receive Mrs. Closson's confidences—which were usually connected with points of social etiquette, indifferent to the lady herself, but preoccupying to Mr. Closson.

"He thinks it's funny that Dick's family haven't cabled, or even written. Do they generally do so in England? I tell Mr. Closson there hasn't been time yet—I'm so bad at answering letters myself that I can't blame anybody else for not writing! But Mr. Closson seems to think it's meant for a slight. Why should it be? If Dick's family are not satisfied with Conchita, they will be when they see her, don't you think so?" Yes, certainly, Miss Testvalley thought so. "Well, then—what's the use of worrying? But Mr. Closson is a business man and expects everybody to have business habits. I don't suppose the Marquess is in business, is he?"

Miss Testvalley said no, she thought not; and for a moment there flickered up in Mrs. Closson a languid curiosity to know more of her daughter's future relations. "It's a big family, isn't it? Dick says he can never remember how many brothers and sisters he has; but I suppose that's one of his jokes. . . . He's a great joker, isn't he; like my Ted! Those two are always playing tricks on everybody. But how many brothers and sisters are there, really?"

Miss Testvalley, after a moment's calculation, gave the number as eight; Lord Seadown, the heir, Lord John, Lord Richard—and five girls; yes, there were five girls. Only one married as yet,

the Lady Camilla. Her own charges, the Ladies Honoria and Ulrica, were now out; the other two were still in the school-room.
Yes; it was a large family—but not so very large, as English families went. Large enough, however to preoccupy Lady Brightlingsea a good deal—especially as concerned the future of her
daughters.

Mrs. Closson listened with her dreamy smile. Her attention
had none of the painful precision with which Mrs. St. George
tried to master the details of social life in the higher spheres, nor
of the eager curiosity gleaming under Mrs. Parmore's pale eye-
lashes. Mrs. Closson really could not see that there was much
difference between one human being and another, except that
some had been favoured with more leisure than others—and leisure was her idea of heaven.

"I should think Lady Brightlingsea would be worn out, with
all those girls to look after. I don't suppose she's had much time
to think about the boys."

"Well, of course she's devoted to her sons too."

"Oh, I suppose so. And you say the other two sons are not
married?" No, not as yet, Miss Testvalley repeated.

A flicker of interest was again perceptible between Mrs.
Closson's drowsy lids. "If they don't either of them marry, Dick
will be the Marquess some day, won't he?"

Miss Testvalley could not restrain a faint amusement. "But
Lord Seadown is certain to marry. In those great houses it's a
family obligation for the heir to marry."

Mrs. Closson's head sank back contentedly. "Mercy! How
many obligations they all seem to have. I guess Conchita'll be
happier just making a love-match with Lord Richard. He's passionately in love with her, isn't he?" Mrs. Closson pursued with
her confidential smile.

"It would appear so, certainly," Miss Testvalley rejoined.

"All I want is that she should be happy; and he will make
her happy, won't he?" the indulgent mother concluded, as though
Miss Testvalley's words had completely reassured her.

At that moment the door was flung open, and the bride herself whirled into the room. "Oh, Mother!" Conchita paused to greet Miss Testvalley; her manner, like her mother's, was always considerate and friendly. "You're not coming to take Nan away already, are you?" Reassured by Miss Testvalley, she put her hands on her hips and spun lightly around in front of the two ladies.

"Mother! Isn't it a marvel?—It's my Assembly dress," she explained, laughing, to the governess.

It was indeed a marvel; the money these American mothers spent on their daughters' clothes never ceased to astonish Miss Testvalley; but while her appreciative eyes registered every costly detail her mind was busy with the incredible fact that Conchita Closson—"the Closson girl" in Mrs. Parmore's vocabulary—had contrived to get an invitation to the Assembly, while her own charges, who were so much lovelier and more loveable . . . But here they were, Virginia, Nan, and Lizzy Elmsworth, all circling gaily about the future bride, applauding, criticizing, twitching as critically at her ruffles and ribbons as though these were to form a part of their own adornment. Miss Testvalley, looking closely, saw no trace of envy in their radiant faces, though Virginia's was perhaps a trifle sad. "So they've not been invited to the ball, and Conchita *has*," she reflected, and felt a sudden irritation against Miss Closson.

But the irritation did not last. This was Mrs. Parmore's doing, the governess was sure; to secure Lord Richard, she had no doubt persuaded the patronesses of the Assembly—that stern tribunal—to include his fiancée among their guests. Only—how had she, or the others, managed to accept the idea of introducing the fiancée's mother into their hallowed circle? The riddle was answered by Mrs. Closson herself. "First I was afraid I'd have to take Conchita—just imagine it! Get up out of my warm bed in the middle of the night, and rig myself up in satin and whalebones, and feathers on my head—they say I'd have had to wear feathers!" Mrs. Closson laughed luxuriously over this plumed and armoured vision. "But luckily they didn't even invite me.

They invited my son instead—it seems in New York a girl can go to a ball with her brother, even to an Assembly ball . . . and Conchita was so crazy to accept that Mr. Closson said we'd better let her. . . ."

Conchita spun around again, her flexible arms floating like a dancer's on her outspread flounces. "Oh, girls, it's a perfect shame you're not coming too! They ought to have invited all my bridesmaids, oughtn't they, Miss Testvalley?" She spoke with evident good will, and the governess reflected how different Miss Parmore's view would have been, had she been invited to an exclusive entertainment from which her best friends were omitted. But, then, no New York entertainment excluded Miss Parmore's friends.

Miss Testvalley, as she descended the stairs, turned the problem over in her mind. She had never liked her girls (as she already called them) as much as she did at that moment. Nan, of course, was a child, and could comfort herself with the thought that her time for ball-going had not yet come; but Virginia—well, Virginia, whom Miss Testvalley had not altogether learned to like, was behaving as generously as her sister. Her quick hands had displaced the rose-garland on Conchita's shoulder, re-arranging it in a more becoming way. Conchita was careless about her toilet, and had there been any malice in Virginia she might have spoilt her friend's dress instead of improving it. No act of generosity appealed in vain to Miss Testvalley, and as she went down the stairs to the hotel entrance she muttered to herself: "If I only could—if I only knew how!"

VII.

She was so busy with her thoughts that she was startled by the appearance, at the foot of the stairs, of a young man who stood there visibly waiting.

"Lord Richard!" she exclaimed, almost as surprised as when she had first recognized him, disguised in grimy overalls, at the Saratoga station.

Since then she had, of necessity, run across him now and then, at the St. Georges' as well as at Mrs. Closson's; but if he had not perceptibly avoided her, neither had he sought her out, and for that she was thankful. The Lord Richard chapter was a closed one, and she had no wish to re-open it. She had paid its cost in some brief fears and joys, and one night of agonizing tears; but perhaps her Italian blood had saved her from ever, then or after, regarding it as a moral issue. In her busy life there was no room for dead love-affairs; and besides, did the word "love" apply to such passing follies? Fatalistically, she had registered the episode and pigeon-holed it. If ever she were to know an abiding grief it must be caused by one that engaged the soul.

Lord Richard stood before her awkwardly. He was always either sullen or too hearty, and she hoped he was not going to be hearty. But perhaps since those days life had formed him. . . .

"I saw you go upstairs just now—and I waited."

"You waited? For me?"

"Yes," he muttered, still more awkwardly. "Could I speak to you?"

Miss Testvalley reflected. She could not imagine what he wanted, but experience told her that it would almost certainly be something disagreeable. However, it was not her way to avoid issues—and perhaps he only wanted to borrow money. She could not give him much, of course . . . but if it were only that, so much the better. "We can go in there, I suppose," she said, pointing to the door of the public sitting-room. She lifted the *portière* and, finding the room empty, led the way to a ponderous rosewood sofa. Lord Richard shambled after her, and seated himself on the other side of the table before the sofa.

"You'd better be quick—there are always people here receiving visitors."

The young man, thus admonished, was still silent. He sat sideways on his chair, as though to avoid facing Miss Testvalley. A frown drew the shock of drab hair still lower over his low forehead, and he pulled nervously at his drab moustache.

"Well?" said Miss Testvalley.

"I— Look here. I'm no hand at explaining . . . never was . . . but you were always a friend of mine. . . ."

"I've no wish to be otherwise."

His frown relaxed slightly. "I never know how to say things. . . ."

"What is it you wish to say?"

"I— Well, Mr. Closson asked me yesterday if there was any reason why I shouldn't marry Conchita."

His eyes still avoided her, but she kept hers resolutely on his face. "Do you know what made him ask?"

"Well, you see—there's been no word from home. I rather fancy he expected the governor to write, or even to cable. They seem to do such a lot of cabling in this country, don't they?"

Miss Testvalley reflected. "How long ago did you write? Has there been time enough for an answer to come? It's not likely that your family would cable."

Lord Richard looked embarrassed; which meant, she suspected, that his letter had not been sent as promptly as he had let the Clossons believe. Sheer dilatoriness might even have kept him from sending it at all. "You have written, I suppose?" she enquired sternly.

"Oh, yes, I've written."

"And told them everything—I mean about Miss Closson's family?"

"Of course," he repeated, rather sulkily. "I haven't got much of a head for that kind of thing; but I got Santos-Dios to write it all out for me."

"Then you'll certainly have an answer. No doubt it's on the way now."

"It ought to be. But Mr. Closson's always in such a devil of a hurry. Everybody's in a hurry in America. He asked me if there was any reason why my people shouldn't write."

"Well—is there?"

Lord Richard turned in his chair, and glanced at her with an uncomfortable laugh. "You must see now what I'm driving at."

"No, I don't. Unless you count on me to reassure the Clossons?"

"No. Only, if they should take it into their heads to question you . . ."

She felt a faint shiver of apprehension. To question her—about what? Did he imagine that anyone, at this hour, and at this far end of the world, would disinter that old unhappy episode? If this was what he feared, it meant her career to begin all over again, those poor old ancestors of Denmark Hill without support or comfort, and no one on earth to help her to her feet. . . . She lifted her head sternly. "Nonsense, Lord Richard—speak out."

"Well, the fact is, I know my mother blurted out all that stupid business to you before I left Allfriars—I mean about the cheque," he muttered half-audibly.

Miss Testvalley suddenly became aware that her heart had stopped beating by the violent plunge of relief it now gave. Her whole future, for a moment, had hung there in the balance. And after all, it was only the cheque he was thinking of. Now she didn't care what happened! She even saw, in a flash, that she had him at a disadvantage, and her past fear nerved her to use her opportunity.

"Yes, your mother did, as you say, blurt out something. . . ."

The young man, his elbows on the table, had crossed his hands and rested his chin on them. She knew what he was waiting for—but she let him wait.

"I was a poor young fool—I didn't half know what I was doing. . . . My father was damned hard on me, you know."

"I think he was," said Miss Testvalley.

Lord Richard lifted his head and looked at her. He hardly ever smiled, but when he did his face cleared, and became almost boyish again, as though a mask had been removed from it. "You're a brick, Laura—you always were."

"We're not here to discuss my merits, Lord Richard. Indeed, you seem to have doubted them a moment ago." He stared, and she remembered that subtlety was always lost on him. "You imagined, knowing that I was in your mother's confidence, that I might betray it. Was that it?"

His look of embarrassment returned. "I— You're so hard on a fellow. . . ."

"I don't want to be hard on you. But since you suspected I might tell your secrets, you must excuse my suspecting *you*—"

"Me? Of what?"

Miss Testvalley was silent. A hundred thoughts rushed through her brain—preoccupations both grave and trivial. It had always been thus with her, and she could never see that it was otherwise with life itself, where unimportant trifles and grave anxieties so often darkened the way with their joint shadows. At Nan St. George's age, Miss Testvalley, though already burdened with the care and responsibilities of middle life, had longed with all Nan's longing to wear white tulle and be invited to a ball. She had never been invited to a ball, had never worn white tulle; and now, at nearly forty, and scarred by hardships and disappointments, she still felt that early pang, still wondered what, in life, ought to be classed as trifling, and what as grave. She looked again at Lord Richard. "No," she said, "I've only one stipulation to make."

He cleared his throat. "Er—yes?"

"Lord Richard—are you truly and sincerely in love with Conchita?"

The young man's sallow face crimsoned to the roots of his hair, and even his freckled hands, with their short square fingers, grew red. "In love with her?" he stammered. "I . . . I never saw a girl that could touch her. . . ."

There was something curiously familiar about the phrase; and she reflected that the young man had not renewed his vocabulary. Miss Testvalley smiled faintly. "Conchita's very charming," she continued. "I wouldn't for the world have anything—anything that I could prevent—endanger her happiness."

Lord Richard's flush turned to a sudden pallor. "I—I swear to you I'd shoot myself sooner than let anything harm a hair of her head."

Miss Testvalley was silent again. Lord Richard stirred uneasily in his chair, and she saw that he was trying to interpret her meaning. She stood up and gathered her old beaded dolman about her shoulders. "I mean to believe you, Lord Richard," she announced abruptly. "I hope I'm not wrong."

"Wrong? God bless you, Laura." He held out his blunt hand. "I'll never forget—never."

"Never forget your promise about Conchita. That's all I ask." She began to move toward the door, and slowly, awkwardly, he moved at her side. On the threshold she turned back to him. "No, it's not all—there's something else." His face clouded again, and his look of alarm moved her. Poor blundering boy that he still was! Perhaps his father *had* been too hard on him.

"What I'm going to ask is a trifle . . . yet at that age nothing is a trifle. . . . Lord Richard, I'll back you up through thick and thin if you'll manage to get Miss Closson's bridesmaids invited to the Assembly ball next week."

He looked at her in bewilderment. "The Assembly ball?"

"Yes. They've invited you, I know; and your fiancée. In New York, it's considered a great honour—almost" (she smiled) "like being invited to Court in England."

"Oh, come," he interjected. "There's nothing like a Court here."

"No, but this is the nearest approach. And my two girls, the St. Georges, and their friends the Elmsworths are not very well known in the fashionable set which manages the Assemblies. Of course they can't all be invited; and indeed Nan is too young for balls. But Virginia St. George and Lizzy Elmsworth ought not to be left out. Such things hurt young people cruelly. They've just been helping Conchita to arrange her dress, knowing all the while they were not going themselves. I thought it charming of them. . . ."

Lord Richard stood before her in perplexity. "I'm dreadfully sorry. It is hard on them, certainly. I'd forgotten all about that ball. But can't their parents—?"

"Their parents, I'm afraid, are the obstacle."

He bent his puzzled eyes on the ground, but at length light seemed to break on him. "Oh, I see. They're not in the right set? They seem to think a lot about sets in the States, don't they?"

"Enormously. But as you've been invited—through Mrs. Parmore, I understand—and Mr. Santos-Dios also, you two, between you, can certainly get invitations for Virginia and Lizzy. You can count on me, Lord Richard, and I shall count on you. I've never asked you a favour before, have I?"

"Oh, but I say—I'd do anything, of course. But how the devil can I, when I'm a stranger here?"

"Because you're a stranger—because you're Lord Richard Marable. I should think you need only ask one of the patronesses. Or that clever monkey Santos-Dios will help you, as he has with your correspondence." Lord Richard reddened. "In any case," Miss Testvalley continued, "I don't wish to know how you do it; and of course you must not say that it's my suggestion. Any mention of that would ruin everything. But you must get those invitations, Lord Richard."

She held him for a second with her quick decisive smile, just touched his hand, and walked out of the room.

New York society in the 'seventies was a nursery of young beauties, and Mrs. Parmore and Mrs. Eglinton would have told any newcomer from the old world that he would see at an Assembly ball faces to outrival all the Court beauties of Europe. There were rumours, now and then, that others even surpassing the Assembly standard had been seen at the Opera (on off-nights, when the fashionable let, or gave away, their boxes, or at such promiscuous annual entertainments as the Charity ball, the Seventh Regiment ball, and so on). And of late, more particularly, people had been talking of a Miss Closson, daughter or step-daughter of a Mr. Closson, who was a stock-broker or railway-director—or was he a coffee-planter in South America? The facts about Mr. Closson were few and vague, but he had a certain notoriety in Wall Street and on the fashionable race-courses, and had now come into newspaper prominence through the engagement of his daughter (or step-daughter) to Lord Richard Marable, a younger son of the Marquess of Brightlingsea (no, my dear, you must pronounce it Brittlesey). Some of the fashionable young men had met Miss Closson, and spoken favourably, even enthusiastically, of her charms; but, then, young men are always attracted by novelty, and by a slight flavour of, shall we say, fastness, or anything just a trifle off-colour?

The Assembly ladies felt it would be surprising if any Miss Closson could compete in loveliness with Miss Alida Parmore, Miss Julia Vandercamp, or, among the married, with the radiant Mrs. Casimir Dulac, or Mrs. Fred Alston, who had been a van der Luyden. They were not afraid, as they gathered on the shining floor of Delmonico's ball-room, of any challenge to the supremacy of these beauties.

Miss Closson's arrival was, nevertheless, awaited with a certain curiosity. Mrs. Parmore had been very clever about her invitation. It was impossible to invite Lord Richard without his fiancée, since their wedding was to take place the following week; and the ladies were eager to let a scion of the British nobility see what a New York Assembly had to show. But to invite the Closson parents was obviously impossible. No one knew who they were, or where they came from (beyond the vague tropical background), and Mrs. Closson was said to be a *divorcée,* and to lie in bed all day smoking enormous cigars. But Mrs. Parmore, whose daughter's former governess was now with a family who knew the Clossons, had learned that there was a Closson stepson, a clever little fellow with a Spanish name, who was a great friend of Lord Richard's, and was to be his best man; and of course it was perfectly proper to invite Miss Closson with her own brother. One or two of the more conservative patronesses had indeed wavered, and asked what further concessions this might lead to; but Mrs. Parmore's party gained the day, and rich was their reward, for at the eleventh hour Mrs. Parmore was able to announce that Lord Richard's sisters, the Ladies Ulrica and Honoria, had unexpectedly arrived for their brother's wedding, and were anxious, they too—could anything be more gratifying?—to accompany him to the ball.

Their appearance, for a moment, over-shadowed Miss Closson's; yet perhaps (or so some of the young men said afterward) each of the three girls was set off by the charms of the others. They were so complementary in their graces, each seemed to have been so especially created by Providence, and adorned by coiffeur and dress-maker, to make part of that matchless trio, that their entrance was a sight long remembered, not only by the young men thronging about them to be introduced but by the elderly gentlemen who surveyed them from a distance with critical and reminiscent eyes. The patronesses, whose own daughters risked a momentary eclipse, were torn between fears and admiration; but, after all, those lovely English girls, one so dazzlingly fair, the other so darkly vivid, who framed Miss Closson in their contrasting beauty, were only transient visitors; and Miss Closson was herself soon to re-join them in England, and might some day, as the daughter-in-law of a marquess, remember gratefully that New York had set its social seal on her.

No such calculations troubled the dancing men. They had found three new beauties to waltz with—and how they waltzed! The rumour that London dancing was far below the New York standard was not likely to find credit with anyone who had danced with the Ladies Marable. The tall fair one—was she the Lady Honoria?—was perhaps the more harmonious in her movements; but the Lady Ulrica, as befitted her flashing good looks, was as nimble as a gypsy; and if Conchita Closson polka-ed and waltzed as well as the English girls, these surpassed her in the gliding elegance of the square dance, which they performed, it was observed, with such enjoyment, such innocent *abandon,* that they had little to say to their partners beyond a smiling "yes," a laughing "no," or a blushing "thank you."

At supper they were as bewitching as on the floor—and as conspicuously silent. Nowhere in the big supper-room, about the flower-decked tables, was the talk merrier, the laughter louder (a shade too loud, perhaps?—but that was the fault of the young men), than in the corner where the three girls, enclosed in a dense body-guard of admirers, feasted on champagne and terrapin. As Mrs. Eglinton, with some bitterness, afterward remarked to Mrs. Parmore, the allegation that English girls had no conversation must be true; but theirs was a *speaking* silence. Their eyes and smiles were eloquent! She hoped it would teach their own girls that they need not chatter like magpies.

In the small hours of the same night a knock at her door waked Miss Testvalley out of an uneasy sleep. She sat up with a start and, lighting her candle, beheld a doleful little figure in a beribboned pink wrapper.

"Why, Annabel—aren't you well?" she exclaimed, setting down her candle beside the Book of Common Prayer and two other books which always lay together on her night-table.

"Oh, don't call me Annabel, please! I can't sleep, and I feel so lonely. . . ."

"My poor Nan! Come and sit on the bed. What's the matter, child? You're half frozen!" Miss Testvalley, thankful that before going to bed she had wound her white net scarf over her crimping-pins, sat up and drew the quilt around her pupil.

"I'm not frozen; I'm just lonely. I *did* want to go that ball," Nan confessed, throwing her arms about her governess.

"Well, my dear, there'll be plenty of other balls for you when the time comes."

"Oh, but will there? I'm not a bit sure; and Jinny's not either. She only got asked to this one because Lord Richard fixed it up. I don't know how he did it; but I suppose those old Assembly scare-crows are such snobs—"

"Annabel!"

"Oh, bother! When you know they are. If they hadn't been, wouldn't they have invited Jinny and Lizzy long ago to all their parties?"

"I don't think that question need trouble us. Now that your sister and Lizzy Elmsworth have been seen, they're sure to be invited again; and when your turn comes . . ."

Suddenly she felt herself pushed back against her pillows by her pupil's firm young hands. "Miss Testvalley! How can you talk like that, when you know the only way they got invited—"

Miss Testvalley, rearing herself up severely, shook off Nan's clutch. "Annabel! I've no idea how they were invited; I can't imagine what you mean. And I must ask you not to be impertinent."

Nan gazed at her for a moment, and then buried her face among the pillows in a wild rush of laughter.

"Annabel!" the governess repeated, still more severely; but Nan's shoulders continued to shake with mirth.

"My dear, you told me you'd waked me up because you felt

lonely. If all you wanted was someone to giggle with, you'd better go back to bed, and wait for your sister to come home."

Nan lifted a penitent countenance to her governess. "Oh, she won't be home for hours. And I promise I won't laugh any more. Only it *is* so funny! But do let me stay a little longer; please! Read aloud to me, there's a darling; read me some poetry, won't you?"

She wriggled down under the bed-quilt and, crossing her arms behind her, laid her head back against them, so that her brown curls overflowed on the pillow. Her face had gone wistful again, and her eyes were full of entreaty.

Miss Testvalley reached out for *Hymns Ancient and Modern*. But after a moment's hesitation she put it back beside the prayer-book, and took up instead the volume of poetry which always accompanied her on her travels.

"Now, listen very quietly, or I won't go on." Almost solemnly, she began to read.

> *"The blessèd damozel leaned out*
> *From the gold bar of Heaven;*
> *Her eyes were deeper than the depth*
> *Of waters stilled at even;*
> *She had three lilies in her hand,*
> *And the stars in her hair were seven."*

Miss Testvalley read slowly, chantingly, with a rich murmur of vowels, and a lingering stress on the last word of the last line, as though it symbolized something grave and mysterious. Seven . . .

"That's lovely," Nan sighed. She lay motionless, her eyes wide, her lips a little parted.

> *"Her robe, ungirt from clasp to hem,*
> *No wrought flowers did adorn,*
> *But a white rose of Mary's gift. . . ."*

"I shouldn't have cared much for that kind of dress, should you? I suppose it had angel sleeves, if she was in heaven. When I go to my first ball I want to have a dress that *fits*; and I'd like it to be pale-blue velvet, embroidered all over with seed-pearls, like I saw. . . ."

"My dear, if you want to talk about ball-dresses, I should advise you to go to the sewing-room and get the maid's copy of *Butterick's Magazine*," said Miss Testvalley icily.

"No, no! I want to hear the poem—I do! Please read it to me, Miss Testvalley. See how good I am."

Miss Testvalley resumed her reading. The harmonious syllables flowed on, weaving their passes about the impatient young head on the pillow. Presently Miss Testvalley laid the book aside, and folding her hands continued her murmur of recital.

> *"And still she bowed herself and stooped*
> *Out of the circling charm;*
> *Until her bosom must have made*
> *The bar she leaned on warm. . . ."*

She paused, hesitating for the next line, and Nan's drowsy eyes drifted to her face. "How heavenly! But you know it all by heart."

"Oh, yes; I know it by heart."

"I never heard anything so lovely. Who wrote it?"

"My cousin Dante Gabriel."

"Your own cousin?" Nan's eyes woke up.

"Yes, dear. Listen:

> *"And the lilies lay as if asleep*
> *Along her bended arm. . . .*
> *"The sun was gone now; the curled moon*
> *Was like a little feather. . . ."*

"Do you mean to say he's your very own cousin? Aren't you madly in love with him, Miss Testvalley?"

"Poor Dante Gabriel! My dear, he's a widower, and very stout—and has caused all the family a good deal of trouble."

Nan's face fell. "Oh—a widower? What a pity . . . If I had a cousin who was a poet I should be madly in love with him. And I should desert my marble palace to flee with him to the isles of Greece."

"Ah—and when are you going to live in a marble palace?"

"When I'm an ambassadress, of course. Lord Richard says that ambassadresses . . . Oh, darling, don't stop! I do long to hear the rest. . . . I do, really. . . ."

Miss Testvalley resumed her recital, sinking her voice as she saw Nan's lids gradually sink over her questioning eyes till at last the long lashes touched her cheeks. Miss Testvalley murmured on, ever more softly, to the end; then, blowing out the candle, she slid down to Nan's side so softly that the sleeper did not move. "She might have been my own daughter," the governess thought, composing her narrow frame to rest, and listening in the darkness to Nan's peaceful breathing.

Miss Testvalley did not fall asleep herself. She was speculating rather nervously over the meaning of her pupil's hysterical burst of giggling. She was delighted that Lord Richard had succeeded in getting invitations to the ball for Virginia and Lizzy Elmsworth; but she could not understand why Nan regarded his having done so as particularly droll. Probably, she reflected, it was because the invitations had been asked for and obtained without Mrs. St. George's knowledge. Everything was food for giggles when that light-hearted company were together, and nothing amused them more than to play a successful trick on Mrs. St. George. In any case, the girls had had their evening—and a long evening it must have been, since the late-November dawn was chilling the windows when Miss Testvalley at length heard Virginia on the stairs.

Lord Richard Marable, as it turned out, had underrated his family's interest in his projected marriage. No doubt, as Miss Testvalley had surmised, his announcement of the event had been late in reaching them; but the day before the wedding a cable came. It was not, however, addressed to Lord Richard, or to his bride, but to Miss Testvalley, who, having opened it with surprise (for she had never before received a cable), read it in speechless perplexity.

IS SHE BLACK HIS ANGUISHED MOTHER SELINA BRIGHTLINGSEA

For some time the governess pored in vain over this cryptic communication; but at last light came to her, and she leaned her head back against her chair and laughed. She understood just what must have happened. Though there were two splendid globes, terrestrial and celestial, at opposite ends of the Allfriars library, no one in the house had ever been known to consult them; and Lady Brightlingsea's geographical notions, even measured by the family standard, were notoriously hazy. She could not imagine why anyone should ever want to leave England, and her idea of the continent was one enormous fog from which two places called Paris and Rome indistinctly emerged; while the whole Western Hemisphere was little more clear to her than to the forerunners of Columbus. But Miss Testvalley remembered that on one wall of the Vandyke saloon, where the family sometimes sat after dinner, there hung a great tapestry, brilliant in colour, rich and elaborate in design, in the foreground of which a shapely young Negress flanked by ruddy savages and attended by parakeets and monkeys was seen offering a tribute of tropical fruits to a lolling divinity. The housekeeper, Miss Testvalley also remembered, in showing this tapestry to visitors, on the day when Allfriars was open to the public, always designated it as "The Spanish Main and the Americas"—and what could be more natural than that poor bewildered Lady Brightlingsea should connect her son's halting explanations with this instructive scene?

Miss Testvalley pondered for a long time over her reply; then, for once forgetting to make a "governess's answer," she cabled back to Lady Brightlingsea: NO, BUT COMELY.

BOOK TWO

VIII.

On a June afternoon of the year 1875, one of the biggest carriages in London drew up before one of the smallest houses in Mayfair—the very smallest in that exclusive quarter, its occupant, Miss Jacqueline March, always modestly averred.

The tiny dwelling, a mere two-windowed wedge, with a bulging balcony under a striped awning, had been newly painted a pale buff, and freshly festooned with hanging pink geraniums and intensely blue lobelias. The carriage, on the contrary, a vast old-fashioned barouche of faded yellow, with impressive armorial bearings, and coachmen and footmen to scale, showed no signs of recent renovation; and the lady who descended from it was, like her conveyance, large and rather shabby though undeniably impressive.

A freshly starched parlour-maid let her in with a curtsey of recognition. "Miss March is in the drawing-room, my lady." She led the visitor up the narrow stairs and announced from the threshold: "Please, miss, Lady Brightlingsea."

Two ladies sat in the drawing-room in earnest talk. One of the two was vaguely perceived by Lady Brightlingsea to be small and brown, with burning black eyes which did not seem to go with her stiff purple poplin and old-fashioned beaded dolman.

The other lady was also very small, but extremely fair and elegant, with natural blond curls touched with gray, and a delicate complexion. She hurried hospitably forward.

"Dearest Lady Brightlingsea! What a delightful surprise!—You're not going to leave us, Laura?"

It was clear that the dark lady addressed as Laura was meant to do exactly what her hostess suggested she should not. She pressed the latter's hand in a resolute brown kid glove, bestowed a bow and a slanting curtsey on the Marchioness of Brightlingsea, and was out of the room with the ease and promptness of a person long practised in self-effacement.

Lady Brightlingsea sent a vague glance after the retreating figure. "Now, who was that, my dear? I seem to know. . . ."

Miss March, who had a touch of firmness under her deprecating exterior, replied without hesitation: "An old friend, dear Lady Brightlingsea, Miss Testvalley, who used to be governess to the Duchess's younger girls at Tintagel."

Lady Brightlingsea's long pale face grew vaguer. "At Longlands? Oh, but of course. It was I who recommended her to Blanche Tintagel. . . . Testvalley? The name is so odd. She was with us, you know; she was with Honoria and Ulrica before Madame Championnet finished them."

"Yes, I remember you used to think well of her. I believe it was at Allfriars I first met her."

Lady Brightlingsea looked plaintively at Miss March. Her face always grew plaintive when she was asked to squeeze one more fact—even one already familiar—into her weary and overcrowded memory. "Oh, yes . . . oh, yes!"

Miss March, glancing brightly at her guest, as though to reanimate the latter's failing energy, added: "I wish she could have stayed. You might have been interested in her experiences in America. . . ."

"In America?" Lady Brightlingsea's vagueness was streaked by a gleam of interest. "She's been in America?"

"In the States. In fact, I think she was governess to that new beauty who's being talked about a good deal just now. A Miss St. George—Virginia St. George. You may have heard of her?"

Lady Brightlingsea drew herself up and said testily: "But of course she was in America . . . and with some people called St. George. How else would I have known where to send my cable?"

"You—cabled Miss Testvalley?"

"When we learned of my son Richard's engagement, I asked Testvalley if the young woman was black, and I received such an odd reply. 'No but comely.' Such a strange expression."

"The Psalms . . . ?" Miss March suggested gently. "The Song of Songs . . . 'My love is black but comely'? But do tell me if you have heard of Virginia St. George—the beauty?"

Lady Brightlingsea sighed at this new call upon her powers of concentration. "I hear of nothing but Americans. My son's house is always full of them."

"Oh, yes; and I believe that Miss St. George is a particular friend of Lady Richard's."

"Very likely. Is she from the same part of the States—from Brazil?"

Miss March, who was herself a native of the States, had in her youth been astonished at enquiries of this kind, and slightly resentful of them; but long residence in England, and a desire to appear at home in her adopted country, had accustomed her to such geography as Lady Brightlingsea's. "Slightly farther north, I think," she said.

"Ah? But they make nothing of distances in those countries, do they? Is this new young woman rich?" asked Lady Brightlingsea abruptly.

Miss March reflected, and then decided to say: "According to Miss Testvalley, the St. Georges appear to live in great luxury."

Lady Brightlingsea sank back wearily. "That means nothing. My daughter-in-law's people do that too. But the man has never paid her settlements. Her step-father, I mean—I never can remember any of their names. I don't see how they can tell each other apart, all herded together, without any titles or distinctions. It's unfortunate that Richard did nothing about settlements; and now, not even two years after their marriage, the man says he can't go on paying his step-daughter's allowance. And I'm afraid the young people owe a great deal of money."

Miss March heaved a deep sigh of sympathy. "A bad coffee-year, I suppose."

"That's what he says. But how can one tell? Do you suppose those other people would lend them the money?"

Miss March counted it as one of the many privileges of living in London that two or three times a year her friend Lady Bright-lingsea came to see her. In Miss March's youth a great tragedy had befallen her—a sorrow which had darkened all her days. It had befallen her in London, and all her American friends—and they were many—had urged her to return at once to her home in New York. A proper sense of dignity, they insisted, should make it impossible for her to remain in a society where she had been so cruelly, so publicly offended. Miss March listened, hesitated—and finally remained in London. "They simply don't know," she explained to an American friend who also lived there, "what they're asking me to give up." And the friend sighed her assent.

"The first years will be difficult," Miss March had continued courageously, "but I think in the end I shan't be sorry." And she was right. At first she had been only a poor little pretty American who had been jilted by an eminent nobleman; yes, and after the wedding-dress was ordered—the countermanding of that wedding-dress had long been one of her most agonizing memories. But since the unhappy date over thirty years had slipped by; and gradually, as they passed, and as people found out how friendly and obliging she was, and what a sweet little house she lived in, she had become the centre of a circle of warm friends, and the oracle of transatlantic pilgrims in quest of a social opening. These pilgrims had learned that Jacky March's narrow front door led straight into the London world, and a number had already slipped in through it. Miss March had a kind heart, and could never resist doing a friend a good turn; and if her services were sometimes rewarded by a cheque, or a new drawing-room carpet, or a chinchilla tippet and muff, she saw no harm in this way of keeping herself and her house in good shape. "After all, if my friends are kind enough to come here, I want my house and myself, tiny as we both are, to be presentable."

All this passed through Miss March's active mind while she sat listening to Lady Brightlingsea. Even should friendship so incline them, she doubted if the St. George family would be able to come to the aid of the young Dick Marables, but there might be combinations, arrangements—who could tell? Laura Testvalley might enlighten her. It was never Miss March's policy to oppose a direct refusal to a friend.

"Dear Lady Brightlingsea, I'm so dreadfully distressed at what you tell me."

"Yes. It's certainly very unlucky. And most trying for my husband. And I'm afraid poor Dick's not behaving as well as he might. After all, as he says, he's been deceived."

Miss March knew that this applied to Lady Richard's money and not to her morals, and she sighed again. "Mr. St. George was a business associate of Mr. Closson's at one time, I believe. Those people generally back each other up. But of course they all have their ups and downs. At any rate, I'll see, I'll make enquiries. . . ."

"Their ways are so odd, you know," Lady Brightlingsea pursued. It never seemed to occur to her that Miss March was one of "them," and Miss March emitted a murmur of sympathy, for these new people seemed as alien to her as to her visitor. "So very odd. And they speak so fast—I can't understand them. But I suppose one would get used to that. What I *cannot* see is their beauty—the young girls, I mean. They toss about so—they're never still. And they don't know how to carry themselves." She paused to add in a lower tone: "I believe my daughter-in-law dances to some odd instrument—quite like a ballet dancer. I hope her skirts are not as short. And sings in Spanish. Is Spanish their native language still?"

Miss March, despairing of making it clear to Lady Brightlingsea that Brazil was not one of the original Thirteen States, evaded this by saying: "You must remember they've not had the social training which only a Court can give. But some of them seem to learn very quickly."

"Oh, I hope so," Lady Brightlingsea exclaimed, as if clutching at a floating spar. Slowly she drew herself up from the sofacorner. She was so tall that the ostrich plumes on her bonnet might have brushed Miss March's ceiling had they not drooped instead of towering. Miss March had often wondered how her friend managed to have such an air of majesty when everything about her flopped and dangled. "Ah—it's their secret," she thought, and rejoiced that at least she could recognize and admire the attribute in her noble English friends. So many of her travelling compatriots seemed not to understand, or even to perceive, the difference. They were the ones who could not see what she "got out" of her little London house, and her little London life.

Lady Brightlingsea stood in the middle of the room, looking uncertainly about her. At last she said: "We're going out of town in a fortnight. You must come down to Allfriars later, you know."

Miss March's heart leapt up under her trim black satin bodice. (She wore black often, to set off her still fair complexion.) She could never quite master the excitement of an invitation to Allfriars. In London she did not expect even to be offered a meal; the Brightlingseas always made a short season, and there were so many important people whom they had to invite. Besides, being asked down to stay in the country, *en famille,* was really much more flattering—more intimate. Miss March felt herself blushing to the roots of her fair curls. "It's so kind of you, dear Lady Brightlingsea. Of course, you know there's nothing I should like better. I'm never as happy anywhere as at Allfriars."

Lady Brightlingsea gave a mirthless laugh. "You're not like my daughter-in-law. She says she'd as soon spend a month in the family vault. In fact, she'd never be with us at all if they hadn't had to let their house for the season."

Miss March's murmur of horror was inarticulate. Words failed her. These dreadful new Americans—would London ever be able to educate them? In her confusion she followed Lady

Brightlingsea to the landing without speaking. There her visitor suddenly turned toward her. "I wish we could marry Seadown," she said.

This allusion to the heir of the Brightlingseas was a fresh surprise to Miss March. "But surely—in Lord Seadown's case it will be only too easy," she suggested with a playful smile.

Lady Brightlingsea produced no answering smile. "You must have heard, I suppose, of his wretched entanglement with Lady Churt. It's much worse, you know, than if she were a disreputable woman. She costs him a great deal more, I mean. And we've tried everything. . . . But he won't look at a nice girl. . . ." She paused, her wistful eyes bent entreatingly on Miss March's responsive face. "And so, in sheer despair, I thought perhaps, if this friend of my daughter-in-law's is rich, really rich, it might be better to try. . . . There's something about these foreigners that seems to attract the young men."

Yes—there was, as Jacky March had reason to know. Her own charm had been subtler and more discreet, and in the end it had failed her, but the knowledge that she had possessed it gave her a feeling of affinity with this new band of marauders, social aliens though they were: the wild gypsy who had captured Dick Marable, and her young friends who, two years later, had come out to look over the ground, and do their own capturing.

Miss March, who was always on her watch-tower, had already sighted and classified them: the serenely lovely Virginia St. George, whom Lady Brightlingsea had singled out for Lord Seadown, and her younger sister, Nan, negligible as yet compared with Virginia, but odd and interesting too, as her sharp little observer perceived. It was a novel kind of invasion, and Miss March was a-flutter with curiosity, and with an irrepressible sympathy. In Lady Brightlingsea's company she had quite honestly blushed for the crude intruders; but, freed from the shadow of the peerage, she felt herself mysteriously akin to them, eager to know more of their plans, and even to play a secret part in the adventure.

Miss Testvalley was an old friend, and her arrival in London with a family of obscure but wealthy Americans had stirred the depths of Miss March's social curiosity. She knew from experience that Miss Testvalley would never make imprudent revelations concerning her employers, much less betray their confidence; but her shrewd eye and keen ear must have harvested, in the transatlantic field, much that would be of burning interest to Miss March, and the latter was impatient to resume their talk. So far, she knew only that the St. George girls were beautiful, and their parents rich, yet that fashionable New York had rejected them. There was much more to learn, and there was also this strange outbreak of Lady Brightlingsea's to hint at, if not reveal, to Miss Testvalley.

It was certainly a pity that their talk had been interrupted by Lady Brightlingsea; yet Miss March would not for the world have missed the latter's visit and, above all, her unexpected allusion to her eldest son. For years Miss March had carried in her bosom the heavy weight of the Marable affairs, and this reference to Seadown had thrown her into such agitation that she sat down on the sofa and clasped her small wrinkled hands over her anxious heart. Seadown to marry an American—what news to communicate to Laura Testvalley!

Miss March rose and went quickly to her miniature writing-desk. She wrote a hurried note in her pretty flowing script, sealed it with silver-gray wax, and rang for the beruffled parlour-maid. Then she turned back into the room. It was crowded with velvet-covered tables and quaint corner-shelves all laden with photographs in heavy silver or morocco frames, surmounted by coronets, from the baronial to the ducal—one, even, royal (in a place of honour by itself, on the mantel). Most of these photographs were of young or middle-aged women, with long necks and calm imperious faces, crowned with diadems or nodded over by Court feathers. "Selina Brightlingsea," "Blanche Tintagel, "Elfrida Marable," they were signed in tall slanting hands. The handwriting was as uniform as the features, and nothing but the signatures seemed to differentiate these carven images. But in a corner by itself (pushed behind a lamp at Lady Brightlingsea's arrival) was one, "To Jacky from her friend Idina Churt," which Miss March now drew forth and studied with a furtive interest. What chance had an untaught transatlantic beauty against this reprehensible creature, with her tilted nose and impertinent dark fringe? Yet, after studying the portrait for a while, Miss March, as she set it down, simply murmured: "Poor Idina."

IX.

Mrs. St. George had been bitterly disappointed in her attempt to launch her daughters in New York. Scandalized though she was by Virginia's joining in the wretched practical joke played on the Assembly patronesses by Lord Richard Marable and his future brother-in-law, she could not think that such a prank would have lasting consequences. The difficulty, she believed, lay with Colonel St. George. He was too free-and-easy, too much disposed to behave as if Fifth Avenue and Wall Street were one. As a social figure no one took him seriously (except certain women she could have named, had it not demeaned her even to think of them), and by taking up with the Clossons, and forcing her to associate publicly with that divorced foreigner, he had deprived her girls of all chance of social recognition. Miss Testvalley had seen it from the first. She too was terribly upset about the ball; but she did not share Mrs. St. George's view that Virginia and Nan, by acting as bridesmaids to Conchita Closson, had increased the mischief. At the wedding their beauty had been much remarked; and, as Miss Testvalley pointed out, Conchita had married into one of the greatest English families, and if ever the girls wanted to do a London season, knowing the Brightlingseas would certainly be a great help.

"A London season?" Mrs. St. George gasped, in a tone implying that her burdens and bewilderments were heavy enough already.

Miss Testvalley laughed. "Why not? It might be much easier

than New York; you ought to try," that intrepid woman declared.

Mrs. St. George, in her bewilderment, repeated this to her eldest daughter; and Virginia, who was a thoughtful girl, turned the matter over in her mind. The New York experiment, though her mother regarded it as a failure, had not been without its compensations; especially the second winter, when Nan emerged from the school-room. There was no doubt that Nan supplemented her sister usefully; she could always think of something funny or original to say, whereas there were moments when Virginia had to rely on the length of her eyelashes and the lustre of her lips, and trust to them to plead for her. Certainly the two sisters made an irresistible pair. The Assembly ladies might ignore their existence, but the young men did not; and there were jolly little dinners and gay theatre-parties in plenty to console the exiled beauties. Still, it was bitter to be left out of all the most exclusive entertainments, to have not a single invitation to Newport, to be unbidden to the Opera on the fashionable nights. With Mrs. St. George it rankled more than with her daughters. With the approach of the second summer she had thought of hiring a house at Newport; but she simply didn't dare—and it was then that Miss Testvalley made her bold suggestion.

"But I've never been to England. I wouldn't know how to get to know people. And I couldn't face a strange country all alone."

"You'd soon make friends, you know. It's easier sometimes in foreign countries."

Virginia here joined in. "Why shouldn't we try, Mother? I'm sure Conchita'd be glad to get us invitations. She's awfully good-natured."

"Your father would think we'd gone crazy."

Perhaps Mrs. St. George hoped he would; it was always an added cause for anxiety when her husband approved of holiday plans in which he was not to share. And that summer she knew he intended to see the Cup Races off Newport, with a vulgar drinking crowd, Elmsworth and Closson among them, who had joined him in chartering a steam-yacht for the occasion.

Colonel St. George's business association with Mr. Closson

had turned out to be an exceptionally fruitful one, and he had not failed to remind his wife that its pecuniary results had already justified him in asking her to be kind to Mrs. Closson. "If you hadn't, how would I have paid for this European trip, I'd like to know, and all the finery for the girls' London season?" he had playfully reminded her, as he pressed the steamer-tickets and a letter of credit into her reluctant hand.

Mrs. St. George knew then that the time for further argument was over. The letter of credit, a vaguely understood instrument which she handled as though it were an explosive, proved that his decision was irrevocable. The pact with Mr. Closson had paid for the projected European tour, and would also, Mrs. St. George bitterly reflected, help to pay for the charter of the steam-yacht, and the champagne orgies on board, with ladies in pink bonnets. All this was final, unchangeable, and she could only exhale her anguish to her daughters and their governess.

"Now your father's rich, his first idea is to get rid of us, and have a good time by himself."

Nan flushed up, longing to find words in defence of the Colonel; and Virginia spoke for her. "How silly, Mother! Father feels it's only fair to give us a chance in London. You know perfectly well that if we get on there we'll be invited everywhere when we get back to New York. That's why Father wants us to go."

"But I simply couldn't go to England all alone with you girls," Mrs. St. George despairingly repeated.

"But we won't be alone. Of course Miss Testvalley'll come too!" Nan interrupted.

"Take care, Nan! If I do, it will be to try to get you on with your Italian," said the governess. But they were all aware that by this time she was less necessary to her pupils than to their mother.

X.

In the long summer twilight a father and son were pacing the terrace of an old house called Honourslove, on the edge of the Cotswolds. The irregular silver-gray building, when approached from the village by a drive winding under ancient beech-trees, seemed, like so many old dwellings in England, to lie almost in a hollow, screened to the north by hanging woods, and surveying from its many windows only its own lawns and trees; but the terrace on the other front overlooked an immensity of hill and vale, with huddled village roofs and floating spires. Now, in the twilight, though the sky curved above so clear and luminous, everything below was blurred, and the spires were hardly distinguishable from the tree-trunks; but to the two men strolling up and down before the house long familiarity made every fold of the landscape visible.

The Cotswolds were in the blood of the Thwartes, and their rule at Honourslove reached back so far that the present baronet, Sir Helmsley Thwarte, had persuaded himself that only by accident (or treachery—he was given to suspecting treachery) had their title to the estate dropped out of Domesday.

His only son, Guy, was not so sure; but, as Sir Helmsley said, the young respect nothing and believe in nothing, least of all in the validity of tradition. Guy did, however, believe in Honourslove, the beautiful old place which had come to be the first and last article of the family creed. Tradition, as embodied in the ancient walls and the ancient trees of Honourslove, seemed to him as priceless a quality as it did to Sir Helmsley; and, indeed, he sometimes said to himself that if ever he succeeded to the baronetcy he would be a safer and more vigilant guardian than his father, who loved the place and yet had so often betrayed it.

"I'd have shot myself rather than sell the Titian," Guy used to think in moments of bitterness. "What's the Holbein, by comparison? But then my father's sure to outlive me—so what's the odds?"

As they moved side by side that summer evening, it would have been hard for a looker-on to decide which had the greater chance of longevity: the heavy vigorous man approaching the sixties, a little flushed after his dinner and his bottle of Burgundy, but obliged to curb his quick stride to match his son's more leisurely gait; or the son, tall and lean, and full of the balanced energy of the hard rider and quick thinker.

"You don't adapt yourself to the scene, sir. It's an insult to Honourslove to treat the terrace as if it were the platform at Euston, and you were racing for your train."

Sir Helmsley was secretly proud of his own activity, and nothing pleased him better than his son's disrespectful banter on his over-youthfulness. He slackened his pace with a gruff laugh.

"I suppose you young fellows expect the gray-beards to drag their gouty feet and lean on staves, as they do in *Oedipe-roi* at the Français."

"Well, sir, as your beard's bright auburn, that strikes me as irrelevant." Guy knew this would not be unwelcome either; but a moment later he wondered if he had not overshot the mark. His father stopped short and faced him. "Bright auburn, indeed? Look here, my dear fellow, what is there behind this indecent flattery?" His voice hardened. "Not another bill to be met—eh?"

Guy gave a short laugh. He *had* wanted something, and had perhaps resorted to flattery in the hope of getting it; but his admiration for his brilliant and impetuous parent, even when not disinterested, was sincere.

"A bill—?" He laughed again. That would have been easier—though it was never easy to confess a lapse to Sir Helmsley. Guy had never learned to take his father's tropical fits of rage without wincing. But to make him angry about money would have been less dangerous; and, at any rate, the young man was familiar with the result. It always left him seared, but still upright; whereas . . .

"Well?"

"Nothing, sir."

The father gave one of his angry "foreign" shrugs (reminiscent of far-off Bohemian days in the Quartier Latin), and the two men walked on in silence.

There were moments during their talks—and this was one —when the young man felt that, if each could have read the other's secret mind, they would have found little to unite them except a joint love of their house and the land it stood on. But that love was so strong, and went so deep, that it sometimes seemed to embrace all the divergences. Would it now, Guy wondered? "How the devil shall I tell him?" he thought.

The two had paused, and stood looking out over the lower terraces to the indistinct blue reaches beyond. Lights were beginning to prick the dusk, and every roof which they revealed had a name and a meaning to Guy Thwarte. Red Farm, where the famous hazel copse was, Ausprey with its decaying Norman church, Little Ausprey with the old heronry at the Hall, Odcote, Sudcote, Lowdon, the ancient borough with its market-cross and its rich minster—all were thick with webs of memory for the youth whose people had so long been rooted in their soil. And those frail innumerable webs tightened about him like chains at the thought that in a few weeks he was to say goodbye to it all, probably for many months.

After preparing for a diplomatic career, and going through a first stage at the Foreign Office, and a secretaryship in Brazil, Guy Thwarte had suddenly decided that he was not made for diplomacy, and, braving his father's wrath at this unaccountable defection, had settled down to a period of hard drudgery with an eminent firm of civil engineers who specialized in railway building. Though he had a natural bent for the work, he would probably never have chosen it had he not hoped it would be a quick way to wealth. The firm employing him had big contracts out for building railways in Far Eastern and South American lands, and Guy's experience in Brazil had shown him that in those regions there were fortunes to be made by energetic men with a practical knowledge of the conditions. He preferred making a fortune to marrying one, and it was clear that sooner or later a great deal of money would be needed to save Honourslove and keep it going. Sir Helmsley's financial ventures had been even costlier than his other follies, and the great Titian which was the glory of the house had been sold to cover the loss of part of the fortune which Guy had inherited from his mother, and which, during his minority, had been in Sir Helmsley's imprudent hands. The subject was one never touched upon between father and son, but it had imperceptibly altered their relations, though not the tie of affection between them.

The truth was that the son's case was hardly less perplexing than the father's. Contradictory impulses strove in both. Each had the same love for the ancient habitation of their race, which enchanted but could not satisfy them, each was anxious to play the part fate had allotted to him, and each was dimly conscious of an inability to remain confined in it, and painfully aware that their secret problems would have been unintelligible to most men of their own class and kind. Sir Helmsley had been a grievous disappointment to the county, and it was expected that Guy should make up for his father's short-comings by conforming to the expected standards, should be a hard rider, a good shot, a conscientious landlord and magistrate, and should in due time (and as soon as possible) marry a wife whose settlement would save Honourslove from the consequences of Sir Helmsley's follies.

The county was not conscious of anything incomprehensible about Guy. Sir Helmsley had dabbled dangerously in forbidden things; but Guy had a decent reputation about women, and it was incredible that a man so tall and well set up, and such a brilliant point-to-point rider, should mess about with poetry or painting. Guy knew what was expected of him, and secretly agreed with his observers that the path they would have him follow was the right one for a man in his situation. But since Honourslove had to be saved, he would rather try to save it by his own labour than with a rich woman's money.

Guy's stage of drudgery as an engineer was now over, and he had been chosen to accompany one of the members of the firm on a big railway-building expedition in South America. His knowledge of the country, and the fact that his diplomatic training had included the mastering of two or three foreign languages, qualified him for the job, which promised to be lucrative as well as adventurous and might, he hoped, lead to big things. Sir Helmsley accused him of undergoing the work only for the sake of adventure; but, aggrieved though he was by his son's decision, he respected him for sticking to it. "I've been only a brilliant failure myself," he had grumbled at the end of their discussion; and Guy had laughed back: "Then I'll try to be a dingy success."

The memory of this talk passed through the young man's mind; and with it the new impulse which, for the last week, had never been long out of his thoughts, and now threatened to absorb them. Struggle as he would, there it was, fighting in him for control. "As if my father would ever listen to reason!" But was this reason? He leaned on the balustrade, and let his mind wander over the rich darkness of the countryside.

Though he was not yet thirty, his life had been full of dramatic disturbances; indeed, to be the only son of Sir Helmsley Thwarte was in itself a potential drama. Sir Helmsley had been born with the passionate desire to be an accomplished example of his class, the ideal English squire; but a contrary streak in his nature was perpetually driving him toward art and poetry and travel, odd intimacies with a group of painters and decorators of socialistic tendencies, reckless dalliance with ladies, and a loud contempt for the mental inferiority of his county neighbours.

Against these tendencies he waged a spasmodic and unavailing war, accusing and excusing himself in the same breath, and expecting his son to justify his vagaries, and to rescue him from their results. During Lady Thwarte's life the task had been less difficult; she had always, as Guy now understood, kept a sort of cold power over her husband. To Guy himself she remained an enigma; the boy had never found a crack through which to penetrate beyond the porcelain-like surface of her face and mind. But while she lived things had gone more smoothly at Honourslove. Her husband's oddest experiments had been tried away from home, and had never lasted long; her presence, her power, her clear conception of what the master of Honourslove ought to be, always drew him back to her and to conformity.

Guy summed it up by saying to himself: "If she'd lived, the Titian never would have gone." But she had died, and left the two men and their conflicting tendencies alone in the old house. . . . Yes; she had been the right mistress for such a house. Guy was thinking of that now, and knew that the same thought was in his father's mind, and that his own words had roused it to the pitch of apprehension. Who was to come after her? father and son were both thinking.

"Well, out with it!" Sir Helmsley broke forth abruptly.

Guy straightened himself with a laugh. "You seem to expect a confession of bankruptcy or murder. I'm afraid I shall disappoint you. All I want is to have you ask some people to tea."

"Ah—? Some 'people'?" Sir Helmsley puffed dubiously at his cigar. "I suppose they've got names and a local habitation?"

"The former, certainly. I can't say as to the rest. I ran across them the other day in London, and as I know they're going to spend next Sunday at Allfriars I thought—"

Sir Helmsley Thwarte drew the cigar from his lips, and looked along it as if it were a telescope at the end of which he saw an enemy approaching.

"Americans?" he queried, in a shrill voice so unlike his usual impressive barytone that it had been known to startle servants and trespassers almost out of their senses, and even in his family to cause a painful perturbation.

"Well—yes."

"Ah—" said Sir Helmsley again. Guy proffered no remark, and his father broke out irritably: "I suppose it's because you know how I hate the whole spitting tobacco-chewing crew, the dressed-up pushing women dragging their reluctant backwoodsmen after them, that you suggest polluting my house, and desecrating our last few days together, by this barbarian invasion—eh?"

There had been a time when his father's outbursts, even when purely rhetorical, were so irritating to Guy that he could meet them only with silence. But the victory of choosing his career had given him a lasting advantage. He smiled, and said: "I don't seem to recognize my friends from your description."

"Your friends—your friends? How many of them are there?"

"Only two sisters—the Miss St. Georges. Lady Richard would drive them over, I imagine."

"Lady Richard? What's she? Some sort of West Indian octoroon, I believe?"

"She's very handsome, and has auburn hair."

Sir Helmsley gave an angry laugh. "I suppose you think the similarity in our colouring will be a tie between us."

"Well, sir, I think she'll amuse you."

"I hate women who try to amuse me."

"Oh, she won't try—she's too lazy."

"But what about the sisters?"

Guy hesitated. "Well, the rumour is that the oldest is going to marry Seadown."

"Seadown—marry Seadown? Good God, are the Brightlingseas out of their minds? It was well enough to get rid of Dick Marable at any price. There wasn't a girl in the village safe from him, and his father was forever buying people off. But Seadown—

Seadown marry an American? There won't be a family left in England without that poison in their veins."

Sir Helmsley walked away a few paces and then returned to where his son was standing. "Why do you want these people asked here?"

"I—I like them," Guy stammered, suddenly feeling as shamefaced as a guilty school-boy.

"Like them!" In the darkness, the young man felt his father's nervous clutch on his arm. "Look here, my boy—you know all the plans I had for you. Plans—dreams, they turned out to be! I wanted you to be all I'd meant to be myself. The enlightened landlord, the successful ambassador, the model M.P., the ideal M.F.H. The range was wide enough—or ought to have been. Above all, I wanted you to have a steady career on an even keel. Just the reverse of the crazy example I've set you."

"You've set me the example of having too many talents to keep any man on an even keel. There's not much danger of my following you in that."

"Let's drop compliments, Guy. You're a gifted fellow; too much so, probably, for your job. But you've more persistency than I ever had, and I haven't dared to fight your ideas, because I could see they were more definite than mine. And now—"

"Well, sir?" his son queried, forcing a laugh.

"And now—are you going to wreck everything, as I've done so often?" He paused, as if waiting for an answer; but none came. "Guy, why do you want those women here? Is it because you've lost your head over one of them? I've a right to an answer, I think."

Guy Thwarte appeared to have none ready. Too many thoughts were crowding through his mind. The first was: "How like my father to corner me when anybody with a lighter hand would have let the thing pass unnoticed! But he's always thrown himself against life head foremost. . . ." The second: "Well, and isn't that what I'm doing now? It's the family folly, I suppose. . . . Only, if he'd said nothing . . . When I spoke I really hadn't got beyond . . . well, just wanting to see her again . . . and now . . ."

Through the summer dark he could almost feel the stir of his father's impatience. "Am I to take your silence as an answer?" Sir Helmsley challenged him.

Guy relieved the tension with a laugh. "What nonsense! I ask you to let me invite some friends and neighbours to tea. . . ."

"To begin with, I hate these new-fangled intermediate meals. Why can't people eat enough at luncheon to last till dinner?"

"Well, sir, to dine and sleep, if you prefer."

"Dine and sleep? A pack of strange women under my roof?" Sir Helmsley gave a grim laugh. "I should like to see Mrs. Bolt's face if she were suddenly told to get their rooms ready! Everything's a foot deep in dust and moths, I imagine."

"Well, it might be a good excuse for a clean-up," rejoined his son good-humouredly. But Sir Helmsley ignored this.

"For God's sake, Guy—you're not going to bring an American wife to Honourslove? I shan't shut an eye tonight unless you tell me."

"And you won't shut an eye if I tell you 'yes'?"

"Damn it, man—don't fence."

"I'm not fencing, sir; I'm laughing at your way of jumping at conclusions. I shan't take any wife till I get back from South America; and there's not much chance that this one would wait for me till then—even if I happened to want her to."

"Ah, well. I suppose, this last week, if you were to ask me invite the devil I should have to do it."

From her post of observation in the window of the housekeeper's room, Mrs. Bolt saw the two red cigar-tips pass along the front of the house and disappear. The gentlemen were going in, and she could ring to have the front door locked, and the lights put out everywhere but in the baronet's study and on the stairs.

Guy followed his father across the hall, and into the study. The lamp on the littered writing-table cast a circle of light on crowded book-shelves, on Sienese predellas, and on bold unsteady water-colours and charcoal-sketches by Sir Helmsley himself.

Over the desk hung a small jewel-like picture in a heavy frame, with "D. G. Rossetti" inscribed beneath. Sir Helmsley glanced about him, selected a pipe from the rack, and filled and lit it. Then he lifted up the lamp.

"Well, Guy, I'm going to assume that you mean to have a good night's sleep."

"The soundest, sir."

Lamp in hand, Sir Helmsley moved toward the door. He paused—was it voluntarily?—half way across the room, and the lamplight touched the old yellow marble of the carved mantel, and struck upward to a picture above it, set in elaborate stucco scrolls. It was the portrait of a tall thin woman in white, her fair hair looped under a narrow diadem. As she looked forth from the dim background, expressionless, motionless, white, so her son remembered her in their brief years together. She had died, still young, during his last year at Eton—long ago, in another age, as it now seemed. Sir Helmsley, still holding the lifted lamp, looked up too. "She was the most beautiful woman I ever saw," he said abruptly—and added, as if in spite of himself: "But utterly unpaintable; even Millais found her so."

Guy offered no comment, but went up the stairs in silence after his father.

XI.

The St. George girls had never seen anything as big as the house at Allfriars except a public building, and as they drove toward it down the long avenue, and had their first glimpse of Inigo Jones's most triumphant expression of the Palladian dream, Virginia said with a little shiver: "Mercy—it's just like a gaol."

"Oh, no—a palace," Nan corrected.

Virginia gave an impatient laugh. "I'd like to know where you've ever seen a palace."

"Why, hundreds of times, I have, in my dreams."

"You mustn't tell your dreams. Miss Testvalley says nothing bores people so much as being told other people's dreams."

Nan said nothing, but an iron gate seemed to clang shut in her—the gate that was so often slammed by careless hands. As if anyone could be bored by such dreams as hers!

"Oh," said Virginia, "I never saw anything so colossal. Do you suppose they live all over it? I guess our clothes aren't half dressy enough. I told Mother we ought to have something better for the afternoon than those mauve organdies."

Nan shot a side-glance at the perfect curve of her sister's cheek. "Mauve's the one colour that simply murders me. But nobody who sees *you* will bother to notice what you've got on."

"You little silly, you, shut up. . . . Look, there's Conchita and the poodle!" cried Virginia in a burst of reassurance. For there, on the edge of the drive, stood their friend, in a crumpled but picturesque yellow muslin and flapping garden-hat, and a first glance at her smiling waving figure assured the two girls of her welcome. They sprang out, leaving the brougham to be driven on with maid and luggage, and instantly the trio were in each other's arms.

"Oh, girls, girls—I've been simply pining for you! I can't believe you're really here!" Lady Richard cried, with a tremor of emotion in her rich Creole voice.

"Conchita! Are you really glad?" Virginia drew back and scanned her anxiously. "You're lovelier than ever; but you look terribly tired. Don't she look tired, Nan?"

"Don't talk about me. I've looked a fright ever since the baby was born. But he's a grand baby, and they say I'll be all right soon. Jinny, darling, you can't think how I've missed you both! Little Nan, let me have a good look at you. How big your eyes have grown. . . . Jinny, you and I must be careful, or this child will crowd us out of the running. . . ."

Linked arm in arm, the three loitered along the drive, the poodle caracoling ahead. As they approached the great gateway, Conchita checked their advance. "Look, girls! It *is* a grand house, isn't it?"

"Yes; but I'm not a bit afraid any more," Nan laughed, pressing her arm.

"Afraid? What were you afraid of?"

"Virginia said you'd be as grand as the house. She didn't believe you'd be really glad to see us. We were scared blue of coming."

"Nan—you little idiot!"

"Well, you did say so, Jinny. You said we must expect her to be completely taken up with her lords and ladies."

Conchita gave a dry little laugh. "Well, you wait," she said.

Nan stood still, gazing up at the noble façade of the great house. "It *is* grand. I'm so glad I'm not afraid of it," she murmured, following the other two up the steps between the mighty urns and columns of the doorway.

It was a relief to the girls—though somewhat of a surprise —that there was no one to welcome them when they entered the big domed hall hung with tall family portraits and moth-eaten trophies of the chase. Conchita, seeing that they hesitated, said: "Come along to your room—you won't see any of the in-laws till dinner"; and they went with her up the stairs, and down a succession of long corridors, glad that the dread encounter was postponed. Miss Jacky March, to whom they had been introduced by Miss Testvalley, had assured them that Lady Brightlingsea was the sweetest and kindest of women; but this did not appear to be Conchita's view, and they felt eager to hear more of her august relatives before facing them at dinner.

In the room with dark heavy bed-curtains and worn chintz armchairs which had been assigned to the sisters, the lady's-maid was already shaking out their evening toilets. Nan had wanted to take Miss Testvalley to Allfriars, and had given way to a burst of childish weeping when it was explained to her that girls who were "out" did not go visiting with their governesses. Maids were a new feature in the St. George household, and when, with Miss Jacky March's aid, Laura Testvalley had run down a paragon, and introduced her into the family, Mrs. St. George was even more terrified than the girls. But Miss Testvalley laughed. "You were afraid of me once," she said to Virginia. "You and Nan must get used to being waited on, and having your clothes kept in order. And don't let the woman see that you're not used to it. Behave as if you'd never combed your own hair or rummaged for your stockings. Try and feel that you're as good as any of these people you're going about with," the dauntless governess ordained.

"I guess we're as good as anybody," Virginia replied haughtily. "But they act differently from us, and we're not used to them yet."

"Well, act in your own way, as you call it—that will amuse them much more than if you try to copy them."

After deliberating with the maid and Conchita over the choice of dinner-dresses, they followed their friend along the corridor to her own bedroom. It was too late to disturb the baby, who was in the night-nursery in the other wing; but in Conchita's big shabby room, after inspecting everything it contained, the sisters settled themselves down happily on a wide sofa with broken springs. Dinner at Allfriars was not till eight, and they had an hour ahead of them before the dressing-gong. "Tell us about everything, Conchita darling," Virginia commanded.

"Well, you'll find only a family party, you know. They don't have many visitors here, because they have to bleed themselves white to keep the place going, and there's not much left for entertaining. They're terribly proud of it—they couldn't imagine living in any other way. At least my father-in-law couldn't. He thinks God made Allfriars for him to live in, and Frenshaw—the other place, in Essex; but he doesn't understand why God gave him so little money to do it on. He's so busy thinking about that, that he doesn't take much notice of anybody. You mustn't mind. My mother-in-law's good-natured enough; only she never can think of anything to say to people she isn't used to. Dick talks a little when he's here; but he so seldom is, what with racing and fishing and shooting. I believe he's at Newmarket now, but he seldom keeps me informed of his movements." Her aquamarine eyes darkened as she spoke her husband's name.

"But aren't your sisters-in-law here?" Virginia asked.

Conchita smiled. "Oh, yes, poor dears; there's nowhere else for them to go. But they're too shy to speak when my mother-in-law doesn't; sometimes they open their mouths to begin, but they never get as far as the first sentence. You must get used to an ocean of silence, and just swim about in it as well as you can. I haven't drowned yet, and you won't. Oh—and Seadown's here this week. I think you'll like him; only he doesn't say much either."

"Who does talk, then?" Nan broke in, her spirits sinking at this picture of an Allfriars evening.

"Well, I do; too much so, my mother-in-law says. But this evening you two will have to help me out. Oh, and the Rector thinks of something to say every now and then; and so does Jacky March. She's just arrived, by the way. You know her, don't you?"

"That little Miss March with the funny curls, that Miss Test-valley took us to see?"

"Yes. She's an American, you know—but she's lived in England for years and years. I'll tell you something funny—only you must swear not to let on. She was madly in love with Lord Brightlingsea—with my father-in-law. Isn't that a good one?" said Conchita with her easy laugh.

"Mercy! In love? But she must be sixty," cried Virginia, scandalized.

"Well," said Nan gravely. "I can imagine being in love at sixty."

"There's nothing crazy you can't imagine," her sister retorted. "But can you imagine being in love with Miss March?"

"Oh, she wasn't sixty when it happened," Conchita continued. "It was ages and ages ago. She *says* they were actually engaged, and that he jilted her after the wedding-dress was ordered; and I believe he doesn't deny it. But of course he forgot all about her years ago; and after a time she became a great friend of Lady Brightlingsea's, and comes here often, and gives all the children the loveliest presents. Don't you call that funny?"

Virginia drew herself up. "I call it demeaning herself; it shows she hasn't any proper pride. I'm sorry she's an American."

Nan sat brooding in her corner. "I think it just shows she loves him better than she does her pride."

The two elder girls laughed, and she hung her head with a sudden blush. "Well," said Virginia, "if Mother heard that she'd lock you up."

The dressing-gong boomed through the passages, and the sisters sprang up and raced back to their room.

The Marquess of Brightlingsea stood with his coat-tails to the monumental mantelpiece of the red drawing-room, and looked

severely at his watch. He was still, at sixty, a splendid figure of a
man, firm-muscled, well set up, with the sloping profile and coldly
benevolent air associated, in ancestral portraits, with a tie-wig and
ruffles crossed by an Order. Lord Brightlingsea was a just man,
and having assured himself that it still lacked five minutes to eight
he pocketed his watch with a milder look, and began to turn
about busily in the empty shell of his own mind. His universe was
a brilliantly illuminated circle extending from himself at its centre
to the exact limit of his occupations and interests. These com-
prised his dealings with his tenantry and his man of business, his
local duties as Lord Lieutenant of the County and Master of Fox-
hounds, and participation in the manly sports suitable to his rank
and age. The persons ministering to these pursuits were necessarily in the foreground, and the local clergy and magistracy in the
middle distance, while his family clung in a precarious half-light
on the periphery, and all beyond was blackness. Lady Brightlingsea considered it her duty to fish out of this outer darkness,
and drag for a moment into the light, any person or obligation
entitled to fix her husband's attention; but they always faded back
into night as soon as they had served their purpose.

Lord Brightlingsea had learned from his valet that several
guests had arrived that afternoon, his own eldest son among
them. Lord Seadown was seldom at Allfriars except in the
hunting-season, and his father's first thought was that if he had
come at so unlikely a time it was probably to ask for money. The
thought was excessively unpleasant, and Lord Brightlingsea was
eager to be rid of it, or at least to share it with his wife, who was
more used to such burdens. He looked about him impatiently, but
Lady Brightlingsea was not in the drawing-room, nor in the Vandyke saloon beyond. Lord Brightlingsea, as he glanced down the
length of the saloon, said to himself: "Those tapestries ought to
be taken down and mended"—but that too was an unpleasant
thought, associated with much trouble and expense, and therefore
belonging distinctly to his wife's province. Lord Brightlingsea was
well aware of the immense value of the tapestries, and knew that

if he put them up for sale all the big London dealers would compete for them; but he would have kicked out of the house anyone who approached him with an offer. "I'm not sunk as low as Thwarte," he muttered to himself, shuddering at the sacrilege of the Titian carried off from Honourslove to the auction-room.

"Where the devil's your mother?" he asked, as a big-boned girl in a faded dinner-dress entered the drawing-room.

"Mamma's talking with Seadown, I think; I saw him go into her dressing-room," Lady Honoria Marable replied.

Lord Brightlingsea cast an unfavourable glance on his daughter. ("If her upper teeth had been straightened when she was a child we might have had her married by this time," he thought. But that, again, was Lady Brightlingsea's affair.)

"It's an odd time for your mother to be talking in her dressing-room. Dinner'll be on the table in a minute."

"Oh, I'm sure Mamma will be down before the others. And Conchita's always late, you know."

"Conchita knows that I won't eat my soup cold on her account. Who are the others?"

"No one in particular. Two American girls who are friends of Conchita's."

"H'm. And why were they invited, may I ask?"

Honoria Marable hesitated. All the girls feared their father less than they did their mother, because she sometimes remembered things and he did not. Lord Brightlingsea was swept through life on a steady amnesiac flow; his wife's forgetfulness was interrupted by occasional jerks forward, as if she were jolted in her side-saddle by an unruly mount. Honoria feared him least of all, and when Lady Brightlingsea was not present was almost at her ease with him. "Mamma told Conchita to ask them down, I think. She says they're very rich. I believe their father's in the American army. They call him 'Colonel.'"

"The American army? There isn't any. And they call dentists 'Colonel' in the States." But Lord Brightlingsea's countenance had softened. "Seadown . . ." he thought. If that were the reason for his son's visit, it altered the situation, of course. And, much as he disliked to admit such considerations to his mind, he repeated carelessly: "You say these Americans are very rich?"

"Mamma has heard so. I think Miss March knows them, and she'll be able to tell her more about them. Miss March is here too, you know."

"Miss March?" Lord Brightlingsea's sloping brow was wrinkled in an effort of memory. He repeated: "March—March. Now, that's a name I know."

Lady Honoria smiled. "I should think so, Papa!"

"Now, why? Do you mean that I know her too?"

"Yes. Mamma told me to be sure to remind you."

"Remind me of what?"

"Why, that you jilted her, and broke her heart. Don't you remember? You're to be particularly nice to her, Papa; and be sure not to ask her if she's ever seen Allfriars before."

"I—what? Ah, yes, of course . . . That old nonsense! I hope I'm 'nice,' as you call it, to everyone who comes to my house," Lord Brightlingsea rejoined, pulling down the lapels of his dress-coat, and throwing back his head majestically.

At the same moment the drawing-room door opened again, and two girls came into the room. Lord Brightlingsea, gazing at them from the hearth, gave a faint exclamation, and came forward with extended hand. The elder and taller of the two advanced to meet it.

"You're Lord Brightlingsea, aren't you? I'm Miss St. George, and this is my sister, Annabel," the young lady said, in a tone that was fearless without being familiar.

Lord Brightlingsea fixed on her a gaze of undisguised benevolence. It was a long time since his eyes had rested on anything so fresh and fair, and he found the sensation very agreeable. It was a pity, he reflected, that his eldest son lacked his height, and had freckles and white eye-lashes. "Gad," he thought, "if I were Seadown's age . . ."

But before he could give further expression to his approval

another guest had appeared. This time it was someone vaguely known to him: a small elderly lady, dressed with a slightly antiquated elegance, who came toward him reddening under her faint touch of rouge. "Oh, Lord Brightlingsea—" And as he took her trembling little hand he repeated to himself: "My wife's old friend, of course; Miss March. The name's perfectly familiar to me—what the deuce else did Honoria say I was to remember about her?"

XII.

When the St. George girls, following candle in hand the bedward procession headed by Lady Brightlingsea, had reached the door of their room, they could hardly believe that the tall clock ticking so loudly in the corner had not gone back an hour or two.

"Why, is it only half past ten?" Virginia exclaimed.

Conchita, who had followed them in, threw herself on the sofa with a laugh. "That's what I always think when I come down from town. But it's not the clocks at Allfriars that are slow, my father-in-law sees to that. It's the place itself." She sighed. "In London the night's just beginning. And the worst of it is that when I'm here I feel as dead with sleep by ten o'clock as if I'd been up till daylight."

"I suppose it's the struggling to talk," said Nan irrepressibly.

"That, and the awful certainty that when anybody does speak nothing will be said that one hasn't heard a million times before. Poor little Miss March! What a fight she put up; but it's no use. My father-in-law can never think of anything to say to her.—Well, Jinny, what did you think of Seadown?"

Virginia coloured; the challenge was a trifle too direct. "Why, I thought he looked pretty sad too, like all the others."

"Well, he *is* sad, poor old Seedy. The fact is—it's no mystery—he's tangled up with a rapacious lady who can't afford to let him go; and I suspect he's so sick of it that if any nice girl came along and held out her hand . . ."

Virginia, loosening her bright tresses before the mirror, gave them a contemptuous toss. "In America girls don't have to hold out their hands."

"Oh, I mean, just be kind; show him a little sympathy. He isn't easy to amuse; but I saw him laugh once or twice at things Nan said."

Nan sat up in surprise. "Me? Jinny says I always say the wrong thing."

"Well, you know, that rather takes in England. They're so tired of the perfectly behaved Americans who are afraid of using even a wrong word."

Virginia gave a slightly irritated laugh. "You'd better hold your hand out, Nan, if you want to be Conchita's sister-in-law."

"Oh, misery! What I like is just chattering with people I'm not afraid of—like that young man we met the other day in London who said he was a friend of yours. He lives somewhere near here, doesn't he?"

"Oh, Guy Thwarte. Rather! He's one of the most fascinating detrimentals in England."

"What's a detrimental?"

"A young man that all the women are mad about, but who's too poor to marry. The only kind left for the married women, in fact—so hands off, please, my dear. Not that I want Guy for myself," Conchita added with her lazy laugh. "Dick's enough of a detrimental for me. What I'm looking for is a friend with a settled income that he doesn't know how to spend."

"*Conchita!*" Virginia exclaimed, flushed with disapproval.

Lady Richard rose from the sofa. "So sorry! I forgot you little Puritans weren't broken in yet. Good night, dears. Breakfast at nine sharp; and don't forget family prayers." She stopped on the threshold to add in a half-whisper: "Don't forget, either, that the day after tomorrow we're going to drive over to call on him—

the detrimental, I mean. And even if you don't care about him, you'll see the loveliest place in all England."

"Well, it was true enough, what Conchita said about nobody speaking," Virginia remarked when the two sisters were alone. "Did you ever know anything as awful as that dinner? I couldn't think of a word to say. My voice just froze in my throat."

"I didn't mind so much, because it gave me a chance to look," Nan rejoined.

"At what? All I saw was a big room with cracks in the ceiling, and bits of plaster off the walls. And after dinner, when those great bony girls showed us albums with views of the Rhine, I thought I should scream. I wonder they didn't bring out a magic lantern!"

Nan was silent. She knew that Virginia's survey of the world was limited to people, the clothes they wore, and the carriages they drove in. Her own universe was so crammed to bursting with wonderful sights and sounds that, in spite of her sense of Virginia's superiority—her beauty, her ease, her self-confidence—Nan sometimes felt a shamefaced pity for her. It must be cold and lonely, she thought, in such an empty colourless world as her sister's.

"But the house is terribly grand, don't you think it is? I like to imagine all those people on the walls, in their splendid historical dresses, walking about in the big rooms. Don't you believe they come down at night sometimes?"

"Oh, shut up, Nan. You're too old for baby-talk. . . . Be sure you look under the bed before you blow out the candle. . . ."

Virginia's head was already on the pillow, her hair overflowing it in ripples of light.

"Do come to bed, Nan. I hate the way the furniture creaks. Isn't it funny there's no gas? I wish we'd told that maid to sit up for us." She waited a moment, and then went on: "I'm sorry for Lord Seadown. He looks so scared of his father; but I thought

Lord Brightlingsea was very kind, really. Did you see how I made him laugh?"

"I saw they couldn't either of them take their eyes off you."

"Oh, well—if they have nobody to look at but those daughters I don't wonder," Virginia murmured complacently, her lids sinking over her drowsy eyes.

Nan was not drowsy. Unfamiliar scenes and faces always palpitated in her long afterward; but the impact of new scenes usually made itself felt before that of new people. Her soul opened slowly and timidly to her kind, but her imagination rushed out to the beauties of the visible world; and the decaying majesty of Allfriars moved her strangely. Splendour neither frightened her, nor made her self-assertive, as it did Virginia; she never felt herself matched against things greater than herself, but softly merged in them; and she lay awake, thinking of what Miss Testvalley had told her of the history of the ancient Abbey, which Henry VIII had bestowed on an ancestor of Lord Brightlingsea's, and of the tragic vicissitudes following on its desecration. She lay for a long time listening to the mysterious sounds given forth by old houses at night, the undefinable creakings, rustlings, and sighings which would have frightened Virginia had she remained awake, but which sounded to Nan like the long murmur of the past breaking on the shores of a sleeping world.

In a majestic bedroom at the other end of the house the master of Allfriars, in dressing-gown and slippers, appeared from his dressing-room. On his lips was a smile of retrospective satisfaction seldom seen by his wife at that hour.

"Well, those two young women gave us an unexpectedly lively evening—eh, my dear? Remarkably intelligent, that eldest girl; the beauty, I mean. I'm to show her the pictures tomorrow morning. By the way, please send word to the Vicar that I shan't be able to go to the vestry meeting at eleven; he'd better put it off till next week. . . . What are you to tell him? Why—er—

unexpected business. . . . And the little one, who looks such a child, had plenty to say for herself too. She seemed to know the whole history of the place. Now, why can't our girls talk like that?"

"You've never encouraged them to chatter," replied Lady Brightlingsea, settling a weary head on a longed-for pillow; and her lord responded by a growl. As if talk were necessarily chatter! Yet as such Lord Brightlingsea had always regarded it when it issued from the lips of his own family. How little he had ever been understood by those nearest him, he thought; and as he composed himself to slumber in his half of the vast bed, his last conscious act was to murmur over: "The Hobbema's the big black one in the red drawing-room, between the lacquer cabinets; and the portrait of Lady Jane Grey that they were asking about must be the one in the octagon room, over the fireplace." For Lord Brightlingsea was determined to shine as a connaisseur in the eyes of the young ladies for whom he had put off the vestry meeting.

The terrace of Honourslove had never looked more beautiful than on the following Sunday afternoon. The party from Allfriars—Lady Richard Marable, her brother-in-law Lord Seadown, and the two young ladies from America—had been taken through the house by Sir Helmsley and his son and, after a stroll along the shady banks of the Love, murmuring in its little glen far below, had returned by way of the gardens to the chapel hooded with ivy at the gates of the park. In the gardens they had seen the lavender borders, the hundreds of feet of rosy brick hung with peaches and nectarines, the old fig-tree heavy with purple fruit in a sheltered corner; and in the chapel, with its delicately traceried roof and dark oaken stalls, had lingered over kneeling and recumbent Thwartes. Thwartes in cuirass and ruff, in furred robes, in portentous wigs, their stiffly farthingaled ladies at their sides, and baby Thwartes tucked away overhead in little marble cots. And now, turning back to the house, they were looking out from the terrace over the soft reaches of country bathed in afternoon light.

After the shabby vastness of Allfriars, everything about Honourslove seemed to Nan St. George warm, cared for, exquisitely intimate. The stones of the houses, the bricks of the walls, the very flags of the terrace were so full of captured sunshine that in the darkest days they must keep an inner brightness. Nan, though too ignorant to single out the details of all this beauty, found herself suddenly at ease with the soft mellow place, as though some secret thread of destiny attached her to it.

Guy Thwarte, somewhat to her surprise, had kept at her side during the walk and the visit to the chapel. He had not said much, but with him also Nan had felt instantly at ease. In his answers to her questions she had detected a latent passion for every tree and stone of the beautiful old place—a sentiment new to her experience, as a dweller in houses without histories, but exquisitely familiar to her imagination. "Why 'Honourslove'?" Nan asked as they slowly paced the terrace. "I know there's a river Love; but why—?"

"No one really knows."

"It makes me think of that portrait of a Cavalier you showed me, with long curls and a plumed hat and lace collar—raising his sword, ready to die for the King!"

Guy smiled. "We had Roundheads in the family too. But I've always had the same notion. Do you know the poem by Lovelace?" Nan shook her head, her brown eyes eager. "He was leaving his lady to go to 'the warres,' and he ends: 'I could not love thee, dear, so much, Loved I not honour more.' "

They had walked together to the far end of the terrace before Nan noticed that the others, guided by Sir Helmsley, were passing through the glass doors into the hall. Nan turned to follow, but her companion laid his hand on her arm. "Stay," he said quietly.

Without answering, she perched herself on the ledge of the balustrade, and looked up at the long honey-coloured front of the house, with the great carven shield above the door, and the quiet lines of cornice and window-frames.

"I wanted you to see it in this light. It's the magic hour," he explained.

She turned her glance from the house to his face. "I see why Conchita says it's the most beautiful place in England."

He smiled. "I don't know. I suppose, if one were married to a woman one adored, one would soon get beyond her beauty. That's the way I feel about Honourslove. It's in my bones."

"Oh, then you understand!" she exclaimed.

"Understand—?"

Nan coloured a little; the words had slipped out. "I mean about the *beyondness* of things. I know there's no such word."

"There's such a feeling. When two people have reached it together it's—well, they are 'beyond.' " He broke off. "You see now why I wanted you to come to Honourslove," he said in an odd new voice.

She was still looking at him thoughtfully. "You knew I'd understand."

"Oh, everything!"

She sighed for pleasure; but then: "No. There's one thing I don't understand. How you go away and leave it all for so long."

He gave a nervous laugh. "You don't know England. That's part of our sense of beyondness. I'd do more than that for those old stones."

Nan bent her eyes to the worn flags on the terrace. "I see; that was stupid of me."

For no reason at all the quick colour rushed to her temples again; and the young man coloured too. "It's a beautiful view," she stammered, suddenly self-conscious.

"It depends who looks at it," he said.

She dropped to her feet, and turned to gaze away over the shimmering distances. Guy Thwarte said nothing more, and for a long while they stood side by side without speaking, each seeing the other in every line of the landscape.

Sir Helmsley, after fulminating in advance against the foreign intruders, had been all smiles on their arrival. Guy was used to such sudden changes of the paternal mood, and knew that feminine beauty could be counted on to produce them. His father could never, at the moment, hold out against deep lashes and brilliant lips, and no one knew better than Virginia St. George how to make use of such charms.

"That red-haired witch from Brazil has her wits about her," Sir Helmsley mumbled that evening over his after-dinner cigar. "I don't wonder she stirs them up at Allfriars. Gad, I should think Master Richard Marable had found his match. . . . But your St. George girl is a goddess . . . *patuit dea*—I think I like 'em better like that . . . divinely dull . . . just the quiet bearers of their own beauty, like the priestesses in a Panathenaic procession. . . ." He leaned back in his armchair and looked sharply across the table at his son, who sat with bent head, drawing vague arabesques on the mahogany. "Guy, my boy—that kind are about as expensive to acquire as the Venus of Milo; and as difficult to fit into domestic life."

Guy Thwarte looked up with an absent smile. "I daresay that's what Seadown's thinking, sir."

"Seadown?"

"Well, I suppose your classical analogies are meant to apply to the eldest Miss St. George, aren't they?"

Father and son continued to look at each other, the father perplexed, the son privately amused. "What? Isn't it the eldest—?" Sir Helmsley broke out.

Guy shook his head, and his father sank back with a groan. "Good Lord, my boy! I thought I understood you. Sovran beauty . . . and that girl has it."

"I suppose so, sir."

"You *suppose*—?"

Guy held up his head and cleared his throat. "You see, sir, it happens to be the younger one—"

"The younger one? I didn't even notice her. I imagined you

were taking her off my hands so that I could have a better chance with the beauties."

"Perhaps in a way I was," said Guy. "Though I think you might have enjoyed talking to her almost as much as gazing at the goddess."

"H'm. What sort of talk?"

"Well, she came to a dead point before the Rossetti in the study, and at once began to quote 'The Blessed Damozel.' "

"That child? So the Fleshly School has penetrated to the backwoods! Well, I don't know that it's exactly the best food for the family breakfast-table."

"I imagine she came on it by chance. It appears she has a wonderful governess who's a cousin of the Rossettis."

"Ah, yes. One of old Testavaglia's descendants, I suppose. What a queer concatenation of circumstances, to doom an Italian patriot to bring up a little Miss Jonathan!"

"I think it was rather a happy accident to give her someone with whom she could talk of poetry."

"Well—supposing you were to leave that to her governess? Eh? I say, Guy, you don't mean—?"

His son paused before replying. "I've nothing to add to what I told you the other day, sir. My South American job comes first; and God knows what will have become of her when I get back. She's only eighteen and I've only seen her twice. . . ."

"Well, I'm glad you remember that," his father interjected. "I never should have, at your age."

"Oh, I've given it thought enough, I can assure you," Guy rejoined, still with his quiet smile.

Sir Helmsley rose from his chair. "Shall we finish our smoke on the terrace?"

They went out together into the twilight, and strolled up and down, as their habit was, in silence. Guy Thwarte knew that Sir Helmsley's mind was as crowded as his own with urgent passionate thoughts clamouring to be expressed. And there was so little time left in which to utter them! To the young man his father's step and his own sounded as full of mystery as the tread of the coming years. After a while they made one of their wonted pauses, and stood leaning against the balustrade above the darkening landscape.

"Eh, well—what are you thinking of?" Sir Helmsley broke out, with one of his sudden jerks of interrogation.

Guy pondered. "I was thinking how strange and far-off everything here seems to me already. I seem to see it all as sharply as things in a dream."

Sir Helmsley gave a nervous laugh. "H'm. And I was thinking that the strangest thing about it all was to hear common-sense spoken about a young woman under the roof of Honourslove." He pressed his son's arm, and then turned abruptly away, and they resumed their walk in silence; for in truth there was nothing more to be said.

XIII.

A dark-haired girl who was so handsome that the heads nearest her were all turned her way stood impatiently at a crowded London street-corner. It was a radiant afternoon of July; and the crowd which had checked her advance had assembled to see the fine ladies in their state carriages on the way to the last Drawing-room of the season.

"I don't see why they won't let us through. It's worse than a village circus," the beauty grumbled to her companion, a younger girl who would have been pretty save for that dazzling proximity, but who showed her teeth too much when she laughed. She laughed now.

"What's wrong with just staying where we are, Liz? It beats any Barnum show I ever saw, and the people are ever so much more polite. Nobody shoves you. Look at that antique yellow coach coming along now, with the two powdered giants hanging on at the back—oh, Liz!—and the old mummy inside. I guess she dates way back beyond the carriage. But look at her jewels, will you? My goodness—and she's got a real live crown on her head!"

"Shut up, Mab—everybody's looking at you," Lizzy Elmsworth rejoined, still sulkily, though in spite of herself she was beginning to be interested in the scene.

The younger girl laughed again. "They're looking at *you,* you silly. It rests their eyes, after all the scare-crows in those circus-chariots. Liz, why do you suppose they dress up like queens at the waxworks, just to go to an afternoon party?"

"It's not an ordinary party. It's the Queen's Drawing-room."

"Well, I'm sorry for the Queen if she has to feast her eyes for long on some of these beauties. . . . Oh, good; the carriages are moving. Better luck next time. This next carriage isn't half as grand, but maybe it's pleasanter inside. . . . Oh!" Mab Elmsworth suddenly exclaimed, applying a sharp pinch to her sister's arm.

" 'Oh' what? I don't see anything so wonderful—"

"Why, look, Lizzy! Reach up on your tip-toes. In the third carriage—if it isn't the St. George girls! Look, *look*! When they move again they'll see us."

"Nonsense. There are dozens of people between us. Besides, I don't believe it is. . . . How in the world should they be here?"

"Why, I guess Conchita fixed it up. Or don't they present people through our Legation?"

"You have to have letters to the Minister. Who on earth'd have given them to the St. Georges?"

"I don't know; but there they are. Oh, Liz, look at Jinny, will you? She looks like a queen herself—a queen going to her wedding, with that tulle veil and the feathers. . . . Oh, mercy, and there's little Nan! Well, the headdress isn't as becoming to her— she hasn't got the *style,* has she? Now, Liz! The carriages are moving. . . . I'm not tall enough—you reach up and wave. They're sure to see us if you do."

Lizzy Elmsworth did not move. "I can survive not being seen by the St. George girls," she said coldly. "If only we could get out of this crowd."

"Oh, just wait till I squeeze through, and make a sign to them! There—. Oh, thank you so much. . . . Now they see me! Jinny—Nan—do look! It's Mab. . . ."

Lizzy caught her sister by the arm. "You're making a show of us; come away," she whispered angrily.

"Why, Liz . . . just wait a second. I'm sure they saw us. . . ."

"I'm sure they didn't want to see us. Can't you understand?

A girl screaming at the top of her lungs from the side-walk . . . Please come when I tell you to, Mabel."

At that moment Virginia St. George turned her head toward Mab's gesticulating arm. Her face, under its halo of tulle and arching feathers, was so lovely that the eyes in the crowd deserted Lizzy Elmsworth. "Well, they're not *all* mummies going to Court," a man said good-naturedly; and the group about him laughed.

"Come away, Mabel," Miss Elmsworth repeated. She did not know till that moment how much she would dislike seeing the St. George girls in the glory of their Court feathers. She dragged her reluctant sister through a gap in the crowd, and they turned back in the direction of the hotel where they were staying.

"Now I hope you understand that they saw us, *and didn't want to see us!*"

"Why, Liz, what's come over you? A minute ago you said they couldn't possibly see us."

"Now I'm sure they did, and made believe not to. I should have thought you'd have had more pride than to scream at them that way among all those common people."

The two girls walked on in silence.

Mrs. St. George and her two daughters had, they hardly knew how (with Colonel St. George's too-hearty encouragement), drifted, or been whirled, into Miss Testvalley's wild project of a London season; and now, on a hot July afternoon, when Mrs. St. George would have been so happy sipping her lemonade in friendly company on the Grand Union verandah, she sat in the melancholy exile of a London hotel, and wondered when the girls would get back from that awful performance they called a Drawing-room.

There had been times—she remembered ruefully—when she had not been happy at Saratoga, had felt uncomfortable in the company of the dubious Mrs. Closson, and irritated by the vulgar exuberance of Mrs. Elmsworth; but such was her present loneliness that she would have welcomed either with open arms. And it was precisely as this thought crossed her mind that the buttons knocked on the door to ask if she would receive Mrs. Elmsworth.

"Oh, my dear!" cried poor Mrs. St. George, falling on her visitor's breast; and two minutes later the ladies were mingling their loneliness, their perplexities, their mistrust of all things foreign and unfamiliar, in an ecstasy of interchanged confidences.

The confidences lasted so long that Mrs. Elmsworth did not return to her hotel until after her daughters. She found them alone in the dark shiny sitting-room which so exactly resembled the one inhabited by Mrs. St. George, and saw at once that they were out of humour with each other, if not with the world. Mrs. Elmsworth disliked gloomy faces, and on this occasion felt herself entitled to resent them, since it was to please her daughters that she had left her lazy pleasant cure at Bad Ems to give them a glimpse of the London season.

"Well, girls, you look as if you were just home from a funeral," she remarked, breathing heavily from her ascent of the hotel stairs, and restraining the impulse to undo the upper buttons of her strongly whale-boned Paris dress.

"Well, we are. We've just seen all the old corpses in London dressed up for that circus they call a Drawing-room," said her eldest daughter.

"They weren't all corpses, though," Mab interrupted. "What do you think, Mother? We saw Jinny and Nan St. George, rigged out to kill, feathers and all, in the procession!"

Mrs. Elmsworth manifested no surprise. "Yes, I know. I've just been sitting with Mrs. St. George, and she told me the girls had gone to the Drawing-room. She said Conchita Marable fixed it up for them. So you see it's not so difficult, after all."

Lizzy shrugged impatiently. "If Conchita has done it for them we can't ask her to do it again for us. Besides, it's too late;

I saw in the paper it was the last Drawing-room. I told you we ought to have come a month ago."

"Well, I wouldn't worry about that," said her mother good-naturedly. "There was a Miss March came in while I was with Mrs. St. George—such a sweet little woman. An American; but she's lived for years in London, and knows everybody. Well, she said going to a Drawing-room didn't really amount to anything; it just gave the girls a chance to dress up and see a fine show. She says the thing is to be in the Prince of Wales's set. That's what all the smart women are after. And it seems that Miss March's friend Lady Churt is very intimate with the Prince and has introduced Conchita to him, and he's crazy about her Spanish songs. Isn't that funny, girls?"

"It may be very funny. But I don't see how it's going to help us," Lizzy grumbled.

Mrs. Elmsworth gave her easy laugh. "Well, it won't, if you don't help yourselves. If you think everybody's against you, they will be against you. But that Miss March has invited you and Mabel to take tea at her house next week—it seems everybody in England takes tea at five. In the country-houses the women dress up for it, in things they call 'tea-gowns.' I wish we'd known that when we were ordering our clothes in Paris. But Miss March will tell you all about it, and a lot more besides."

Lizzy Elmsworth was not a good-tempered girl, but she was too intelligent to let her temper interfere with her opportunities. She hated the St. George girls for having got ahead of her in their attack on London, but was instantly disposed to profit by the breach they had made. Virginia St. George was not clever, and Lizzy would be able to guide her; they could be of the greatest use to each other, if the St. Georges could be made to enter into the plan. Exactly what plan, Lizzy herself did not know; but she felt instinctively that, like their native country, they could stand only if they were united.

Mrs. St. George, in her loneliness, had besought Mrs. Elmsworth to return the next afternoon. She didn't dare invite Lizzy and Mab, she explained, because her own girls were being taken to see the Tower of London by some of their new friends (Lizzy's resentment stirred again as she listened); but if Mrs. Elmsworth would just drop in and sit with her, Mrs. St. George thought perhaps Miss March would be coming in too, and then they would talk over plans for the rest of the summer. Lizzy understood at once the use to which Mrs. St. George's loneliness might be put. Mrs. Elmsworth was lonely too; but this did not greatly concern her daughter. In the St. George and Elmsworth circles unemployed mothers were the rule; but Lizzy saw that, by pooling their solitudes, the two ladies might become more contented, and therefore more manageable. And, having come to lay siege to London, Miss Elmsworth was determined, at all costs, not to leave till the citadel had fallen.

"I guess I'll go with you," she announced, when her mother rose to put on her bonnet for the call.

"Why, the girls won't be there; she told me so. She says they'll be round to see you tomorrow," said Mrs. Elmsworth, surprised.

"I don't care about the girls; I want to see that Miss March."

"Oh, well," her mother agreed. Lizzy was always doing things Mrs. Elmsworth didn't understand, but Mab usually threw some light on them afterward. And certainly, Mrs. Elmsworth reflected, it became her elder daughter to be in one of her mysterious moods. She had never seen Lizzy look more goddess-like than when they ascended Mrs. St. George's stairs together.

Miss March was not far from sharing Mrs. Elmsworth's opinion. When the Elmsworth ladies were shown in, Miss March was already sitting with Mrs. St. George. She had returned on the pretext of bringing an invitation for the girls to visit Holland House; but in reality she was impatient to see the rival beauty. Miss Testvalley, the day before, had told her all about Lizzy Elmsworth, whom some people thought, in her different way, as handsome as Virginia, and who was certainly cleverer. And here she was, stalking in ahead of her mother, in what appeared to be the new American style, and carrying her slim height and small regal head with an assurance which might well eclipse Virginia's milder light.

Miss March surveyed her with the practised eye of an old frequenter of the marriage-market.

"Very fair girls usually have a better chance here; but Idina Churt is dark—perhaps, for that reason, this girl might be more likely . . ." Miss March lost herself in almost maternal musings. She often said to herself (and sometimes to her most intimate friends) that Lord Seadown seemed to her like her own son; and now, as she looked on Lizzy Elmsworth's dark splendour, she murmured inwardly: "Of course, we must find out first what Mr. Elmsworth would be prepared to do. . . ."

To Mrs. Elmsworth, whom she greeted with her most persuasive smile, she said engagingly: "Mrs. St. George and I have such a delightful plan to suggest to you. Of course, you won't want to stay in London much longer. It's so hot and crowded; and before long it will be a dusty desert. Mrs. St. George tells me that you're both rather wondering where to go next, and I've suggested that you should join her in hiring a lovely little cottage on the Thames belonging to a friend of mine, Lady Churt. It could be had at once, servants and all—the most perfect servants—and I've stayed so often with Lady Churt that I know just how cool and comfortable and lazy one can be there. But I was thinking more especially of your daughters and their friends. . . . The river's a Paradise at their age . . . the punting by moonlight, and all the rest. . . ."

Long-past memories of the river's magic brought a sigh to Miss March's lips; but she turned it into a smile as she raised her forget-me-not eyes to Lizzy Elmsworth's imperial orbs. Lizzy returned the look, and the two immediately understood each other.

"Why, Mother, that sounds perfectly lovely. You'd love it too, Mrs. St. George, wouldn't you?" Lizzy smiled, stooping gracefully to kiss her mother's friend. She had no idea what punting was, but the fact that it was practised by moonlight suggested the exclusion of rheumatic elders, and a free field—or river, rather—for the exercise of youthful arts. And in those she felt confident of excelling.

XIV.

The lawn before Lady Churt's cottage (or bungalow, as the knowing were beginning to say) spread sweetly to the Thames at Runnymede. With its long deck-like verandah, its awnings stretched from every window, it seemed to Nan St. George a fairy galleon making, all sails set, for the river. Swans, as fabulous to Nan as her imaginary galleon, sailed majestically on the silver flood; and boats manned by beautiful bare-armed athletes sped back and forth between the flat grass-banks.

At first Nan was the only one of the party on whom the river was not lost. Virginia's attention travelled barely as far as the circles of calceolarias and lobelias dotting the lawn, and the vases of red geraniums and purple petunias which flanked the door; she liked the well-kept flowers and bright turf, and found it pleasant, on warm afternoons, to sit under an ancient cedar and play at the new-fangled tea-drinking into which they had been initiated by Miss March, with the aid of Lady Churt's accomplished parlour-maid. Lizzy Elmsworth and Mabel also liked the tea-drinking, but were hardly aware of the great blue-green boughs under which the rite was celebrated. They had grown up between city streets and watering-place hotels, and were serenely unconscious of the "beyondness" of which Nan had confided her mysterious sense to Guy Thwarte.

The two mothers, after their first bewildered contact with

Lady Churt's servants, had surrendered themselves to these accomplished guides, and lapsed contentedly into their old watering-
place habits. To Mrs. St. George and Mrs. Elmsworth the cottage
at Runnymede differed from the Grand Union at Saratoga only
in its inferior size, and more restricted opportunities for gossip.
True, Miss March came down often with racy tit-bits from London, but the distinguished persons concerned were too remote to
interest the exiles. Mrs. St. George missed even the things she had
loathed at Saratoga—the familiarity of the black servants, the obnoxious sociability of Mrs. Closson, and the spectacle of the race-
course, with ladies in pink bonnets lying in wait for the Colonel.
Mrs. Elmsworth had never wasted her time in loathing anything.
She would have been perfectly happy at Saratoga and in New
York if her young ladies had been more kindly welcomed there.
She privately thought Lizzy hard to please, and wondered what
her own life would have been like if she had turned up her nose
at Mr. Elmsworth, who was a clerk in the village grocery-store
when they had joined their lot; but the girls had their own ideas,
and since Conchita Closson's marriage (an unhappy affair, as it
turned out) had roused theirs with social ambition, Mrs. Elmsworth was perfectly willing to let them try their lot in England,
where beauty such as Lizzy's (because it was rarer, she supposed)
had been known to raise a girl almost to the throne. It would
certainly be funny, she confided to Mrs. St. George, to see one of
their daughters settled at Windsor Castle (Mrs. St. George
thought it would be exceedingly funny to see one of Mrs. Elmsworth's); and Miss March, to whom the confidence was passed
on, concluded that Mrs. Elmsworth was imperfectly aware of the
difference between the ruler of England and her subjects.

"Unfortunately, Their Royal Highnesses are all married,"
she said with her instructive little laugh; and Mrs. Elmsworth
replied vaguely: "Oh, but aren't there plenty of other dukes?" If
there were, she could trust Lizzy, her tone implied; and Miss
March, whose mind was now bent on uniting the dark beauty to
Lord Seadown, began to wonder if she might not fail again, this

time not as in her own case, but because of the young lady's too-great ambition.

Mrs. Elmsworth also missed the friendly bustle of the Grand Union, the gentlemen coming from New York on Saturdays with the Wall Street news, and the flutter created in the dining-room when it got round that Mr. Elmsworth had made another hit on the market; but she soon resigned herself to the routine of *bésique* with Mrs. St. George. At first she too was chilled by the silent orderliness of the household; but though both ladies found the maid-servants painfully unsociable, and were too much afraid of the cook ever to set foot in the kitchen, they enjoyed the absence of domestic disturbances, and the novel experience of having every wish anticipated.

Meanwhile, the bungalow was becoming even more attractive than when its owner inhabited it. Parliament sat exceptionally late that year, and many were the younger members of both Houses, chafing to escape to Scotland, and the private secretaries and minor government officials, still chained to their desks, who found compensations at the cottage on the Thames. Reinforced by the guardsmen quartered at Windsor, they prolonged the river season in a manner unknown to the oldest inhabitants. The weather that year seemed to be in connivance with the American beauties, and punting by moonlight was only one of the mid-summer distractions to be found at Runnymede.

To Lady Richard Marable the Thames-side cottage offered a happy escape from her little house in London, where there were always duns to be dealt with, and unpaid servants to be coaxed to stay. She came down often, always bringing the right people with her, and combining parties, and inventing amusements, which made invitations to the cottage as sought after as cards to the Royal enclosure. There was not an ounce of jealousy in Conchita's easy nature. She was delighted with the success of her friends, and proud of the admiration they excited. "We've each got our own line," she said to Lizzy Elmsworth, "and if we only back each other up we'll beat all the other women hands down. The men are blissfully happy in a house where nobody chaperons them, and they can smoke in every room, and gaze at you and Virginia, and laugh at my jokes, and join in my Deep South songs. It's too soon yet to know what Nan St. George and Mab will contribute; but they'll probably develop a line of their own, and the show's not a bad one as it is. If we stick to the rules of the game, and don't play any low-down tricks on each other" ("Oh, Conchita," Lizzy protested, with a beautiful pained smile), "we'll have all London in our pocket next year."

No one followed the Runnymede revels with a keener eye than Miss Testvalley. The invasion of England had been her own invention, and from a thousand little signs she already knew it would end in conquest. But from the outset she had put her charges on their guard against a too-easy triumph. The young men were to be allowed as much innocent enjoyment as they chose; but Miss Testvalley saw to it that they remembered the limits of their liberty. It was amusement enough to be with a group of fearless and talkative girls, who said new things in a new language, who were ignorant of tradition and unimpressed by distinctions of rank; but it was soon clear that their young hostesses must be treated with the same respect, if not with the same ceremony, as English girls of good family. When Tony Grant-Johnston, a young man with a candid freckled face and curly ginger hair, asked if he might bring his sister, with whom he was staying while he studied law, Miss Testvalley drew herself up and looked at him in a manner such that, without appearing surprised, he changed colour and murmured unhappily: "I see . . . I'm sorry."

"Miss Testvalley, why were you so stern?" Annabel asked. "I like him."

"He is a very agreeable young man," her governess rejoined; "but he knows he ought not to have suggested bringing his sister, Mrs. Cholmondeley, whose divorce was in the papers last month."

"Mother is death on divorced women," Nan said, "but she never says why."

"I gather that American custom is different," replied Miss

Testvalley, "but the Church of England does not recognize re-marriage by a divorced woman. She may be *legally* married in a Registrar's office, but the marriage is not sacramental."

Miss Testvalley sighed at her pupil's blank face. Annabel had in certain respects the instincts of a noble pagan. Religious doctrine, happily, lay outside the governess's sphere; it was, however, her duty to clarify the social aspects of marriage. "A woman is divorced because she has deserted her husband or has a . . . is in love with another man. Or is alleged to be," she added punctiliously. "A divorced woman is cast out by good society."

"Even when she marries the man she's in love with, and it's legal even if it isn't in a church?"

"Even then. Divorce," Miss Testvalley explained, "is intended to *punish* her, not to make her life pleasanter."

"But that isn't fair," Nan protested.

When Miss Testvalley was young—the liberal Testavaglias imposed no censorship on their daughters' reading—she had followed the debates on the Divorce Act in *The Times*, and she remembered that the House of Lords had badly wanted a clause prohibiting a divorced woman from marrying the "co-respondent" on whose account she was sued. "Nevertheless, Annabel, the *fact* is that a divorced woman is a social outcast."

Further comment seemed unnecessary. It was unlikely that her ingenuous, morally sensitive pupil would ever sink into the mire of the divorce court.

Miss Testvalley, when she persuaded the St. Georges to come to England, had rejoiced at the thought of being once more near her family; but she soon found that her real centre of gravity was in the little house at Runnymede. She performed the weekly pilgrimage to Denmark Hill in the old spirit of filial piety; but the old enthusiasm was lacking. Her venerable relatives (thanks to her earnings in America) were now comfortably provided for; but they had grown too placid, too static, to occupy her. Her natural inclination was for action and conflict, and all her thoughts were engrossed by her young charges. Miss March was an admirable lieutenant, supplying the social experience which Miss Testvalley lacked; and between them they administered the cottage at Runnymede like an outpost in a conquered province.

Miss March, who was without Miss Testvalley's breadth of vision, was slightly alarmed by the audacities of the young ladies, and secretly anxious to improve their social education.

"I don't think they understand *yet* what a duke is," she sighed to Miss Testvalley, after a Sunday when Lord Seadown had unexpectedly appeared at the cottage with his cousin the young Duke of Tintagel.

Miss Testvalley laughed. "So much the better! I hope they never will. Look at the well-brought-up American girls who've got the peerage by heart, and spend their lives trying to be taken for members of the British aristocracy. Don't they always end by marrying curates or army-surgeons—or just not marrying at all?"

A reminiscent pink suffused Miss March's cheek. "Yes . . . sometimes; perhaps you're right. . . . But I don't think I shall ever quite get used to Lady Richard's Spanish dances; or to the peculiar words in some of her songs."

"Lady Richard's married, and needn't concern us," said Miss Testvalley. "What attracts the young men is the girls' naturalness, and their not being afraid to say what they think." Miss March sighed again, and said she supposed that was the new fashion; certainly it gave the girls a better chance. . . .

Lord Seadown's sudden appearance at the cottage seemed in fact to support Miss Testvalley's theory. Miss March remembered Lady Churt's emphatic words when the lease had been concluded. "I'm ever so much obliged to you, Jacky. You've got me out of an awfully tight place by finding tenants for me, and getting such a good rent out of them. I only hope your American beauties will want to come back next year. But I've forbidden Seadown to set foot in the place while they're there, and if Conchita Marable coaxes him down you must swear you'll let me know, and I'll see it doesn't happen again."

Miss March had obediently sworn; but she saw now that she must conceal Lord Seadown's visits instead of denouncing them. Poor Idina's exactions were obviously absurd. If she chose to let her house she could not prevent her tenants from receiving anyone they pleased; and it was clear that the tenants liked Seadown, and that he returned the sentiment, for after his first visit he came often. Lady Churt, luckily, was in Scotland; and Miss March trusted to her remaining there till the lease of the cottage had expired.

The Duke of Tintagel did not again accompany his friend. He was a young man of non-committal appearance and manner, and it was difficult to say what impression the American beauties made on him; but, to Miss March's distress, he had apparently made little if any on them.

"They don't seem in the least to realize that he's the greatest match in England," Miss March said with a shade of impatience. "Not that there would be the least chance . . . I understand the Duchess has already made her choice; and the young Duke is a perfect son. Still, the mere fact of his coming . . ."

"Oh, he came merely out of curiosity. He's always been rather a dull young man, and I daresay all the noise and the nonsense simply bewildered him."

"Oh, but you know him, of course, don't you? You were at Tintagel before you went to America. Is it true that he always does what his mother tells him?"

"I don't know. But the young men about whom that is said usually break out sooner or later," said the governess with a shrug.

About this time she began to wonder if the atmosphere of Runnymede were not a little too stimulating for Nan's tender sensibilities. Since Teddy de Santos-Dios, who had joined his sister in London, had taken to coming down with her for Sundays, the fun had grown fast and furious. Practical jokes were Teddy's chief accomplishment, and their preparations involved rather too much familiarity with the upper ranges of the house, too much popping in and out of bedrooms, and too many screaming midnight pillow-fights. Miss Testvalley saw that Nan, whose feelings always rushed to extremes, was growing restless and excited, and she felt the need of shielding the girl and keeping her apart. That the others were often noisy, and sometimes vulgar, did not disturb Miss Testvalley; they were obviously in pursuit of husbands, and had probably hit on the best way of getting them. Seadown was certainly very much taken by Lizzy Elmsworth; and two or three other young men had fallen victims to Virginia's graces. But it was too early for Nan to enter the matrimonial race, and when she did, Miss Testvalley hoped it would be for different reasons, and in a different manner. She did not want her pupil to engage herself after a night of champagne and song on the river; her sense of artistic fitness rejected the idea of Nan's adopting the same methods as her elders.

Mrs. St. George was slightly bewildered when the governess suggested taking her pupil away from the late hours and the continuous excitements at the cottage. It was not so much the idea of parting from Nan, as of losing the moral support of the governess's presence, that troubled Mrs. St. George. "But, Miss Testvalley, why do you want to go away? I never know how to talk to those servants, and I never can remember the titles of the young men that Conchita brings down, or what I ought to call them."

"I'm sure Miss March will help you with all that. And I do think Nan ought to get away for two or three weeks. Haven't you noticed how thin she's grown? And her eyes are as big as saucers. I know a quiet little place in Cornwall where she could have some bathing, and go to bed every night at nine."

To everyone's surprise, Nan offered no objection. The prospect of seeing new places stirred her imagination, and she seemed to lose all interest in the gay doings at the cottage when Miss Testvalley told her that, on the way, they would stop at Exeter, where there was a very beautiful cathedral.

"And shall we see some beautiful houses too? I love seeing

houses that are so ancient and so lovely that the people who live there have them in their bones."

Miss Testvalley looked at her pupil sharply. "What an odd expression! Did you find it in a book?" she asked, for the promiscuity of Nan's reading sometimes alarmed her.

"Oh, no. It was what that young Mr. Thwarte said to me about Honourslove. It's why he's going away for two years—so that he can make a great deal of money and come back and spend it on Honourslove."

"H'm—from what I've heard, Honourslove could easily swallow a good deal more than he's likely to make in two years, or even ten," said Miss Testvalley. "The father and son are both said to be very extravagant, and the only way for Mr. Guy Thwarte to keep up his ancestral home will be to bring a great heiress back to it."

Nan looked thoughtful. "You mean, even if he doesn't love her?"

"Oh, well, I daresay he'll love her—or be grateful to her, at any rate."

"I shouldn't think gratitude was enough," said Nan with a sigh. She was silent again for a while, and then added: "Mr. Thwarte has read all your cousin's poems—Dante Gabriel's, I mean."

Miss Testvalley gave her a startled glance. "May I ask how you happened to find that out?"

"Why, because there's a perfectly beautiful picture by your cousin in Sir Helmsley's study, and Mr. Thwarte showed it to me. And so we talked of his poetry too. But Mr. Thwarte thinks there are other poems even more wonderful than 'The Blessed Damozel.' Some of the sonnets in *The House of Life*, I mean. Do you think they're more beautiful, Miss Testvalley?"

The governess hesitated; she often found herself hesitating over the answers to Nan's questions. "You told Mr. Thwarte that you'd read some of those poems?"

"Oh, yes; I told him I'd read every one of them."

"And what did he say?"

"He said . . . he said he'd felt from the first that he and I would be certain to like the same things; and he *loved* my liking Dante Gabriel. I told him he was your cousin, and that you were devoted to him."

"Ah—well, I'm glad you told him that, for Sir Helmsley Thwarte is an old friend of my cousin's, and one of his best patrons. But you know, Nan, there are people who don't appreciate his poetry—don't appreciate how beautiful it is—and I'd rather you didn't proclaim in public that you've read it all. Some people are so stupid that they wouldn't exactly understand a young girl's caring for that kind of poetry. You see, don't you, dear?"

"Oh, yes. They'd be shocked, I suppose, because it's all about love. But that's why I like it, you know," said Nan composedly.

Miss Testvalley made no answer, and Nan went on in a thoughtful voice: "Shall we see some other places as beautiful as Honourslove?"

The governess reflected. She had not contemplated a round of sight-seeing for her pupil, and Cornwall did not seem to have many sights to offer. But at length she said: "Well, Trevennick is not so far from Tintagel. If the family are away I might take you there, I suppose. You know the old Tintagel was supposed to have been King Arthur's castle."

Nan's face lit up. "Where the Knights of the Round Table were? Oh, Miss Testvalley, can we see that too? And the mere where he threw his sword Excalibur? Oh, couldn't we start tomorrow, don't you think?"

Miss Testvalley felt relieved. She had been slightly disturbed by Nan's allusion to Honourslove, and the unexpected glimpse it gave of an exchange of confidences between Guy Thwarte and her pupil; but she saw that in another moment the thought of visiting the scenes celebrated in Tennyson's famous poems had swept away all other fancies. *The Idylls of the King* had been one of Nan's magic casements, and Miss Testvalley smiled to herself at the ease with which the girl's mind flitted from one new vision to another.

"A child still, luckily," she thought, sighing, she knew not why, at what the future might hold for Nan when childish things should be put away.

XV.

The Duke of Tintagel was a young man burdened with scruples. This was probably due to the fact that his father, the late Duke, had had none. During all his boyhood and youth the heir had watched the disastrous effects of not considering trifles. It was not that his father had been either irresponsible or negligent. The late Duke had had no vices; but his virtues were excessively costly. His conduct had always been governed by a sense of the over-whelming obligations connected with his great position. One of these obligations, he held, consisted in keeping up his rank; the other, in producing an heir. Unfortunately, the Duchess had given him six daughters before a son was born, and two more afterward in the attempt to provide the heir with a younger brother; and although daughters constitute a relatively small charge on a great estate, still, a duke's daughters cannot (or so their parent thought) be fed, clothed, educated, and married at as low a cost as young women of humbler origin. The Duke's other obligation, that of keeping up his rank, had involved him in even heavier expenditure. Hitherto Longlands, the seat in Somersetshire, had been thought imposing enough even for a duke; but its owner had always been troubled by the fact that the new castle at Tintagel, built for his great-grandfather in the approved Gothic style of the day, and with the avowed intention of surpassing Inveraray, had never been inhabited. The expense of completing it, and living in it in suitable state, appeared to have discouraged its creator; and for years it stood abandoned on its Cornish cliff, a sadder ruin than the other, until it passed to the young Duke's father. To him it became a torment, a reproach, an obsession; the Duke of Tintagel must live at Tintagel as the Duke of Argyll lived at Inveraray, with a splendour befitting the place; and the carrying out of this resolve had been the late Duke's crowning achievement.

His young heir, who had just succeeded him, had as keen a sense as his father of ducal duties. He meant, if possible, to keep up in suitable state both Tintagel and Longlands, as well as Folyat House, his London residence; but he meant to do so without the continued drain on his fortune which his father had been obliged to incur. The new Duke hoped that, by devoting all his time and most of his faculties to the care of his estate and the personal supervision of his budget, he could reduce his cost of living without altering its style; and the indefatigable Duchess, her numerous daughters notwithstanding, found time to second the attempt. She was not the woman to let her son forget the importance of her aid; and though a perfect understanding had always reigned between them, recent symptoms made it appear that the young Duke was beginning to chafe under her regency.

Soon after his visit to Runnymede, he and his mother sat together in the Duchess's boudoir in the London house, a narrow lofty room on whose crowded walls authentic Raphaels were ultimately mingled with water-colours executed by the Duchess's maiden aunts and photographs of shooting-parties at the various ducal estates. The Duchess invariably arranged to have this hour alone with her son, when breakfast was over, and her daughters (of whom death or marriage had claimed all but three) had gone their different ways. The Duchess had always kept her son to herself, and the Ladies Clara, Ermyntrude, and Almina Folyat would never have dreamed of intruding on them.

At present, as it happened, all three were in the country, and Folyat House had put on its summer sack-cloth; but the Duchess lingered on, determined not to forsake her son till he was released from his Parliamentary duties.

"I was hoping," she said, noticing that the Duke had twice glanced at the clock, "that you'd manage to get away to Scotland for a few days. Isn't it possible? The Hopeleighs particularly wanted you to go to them at Loch Skarig. Lady Hopeleigh wrote yesterday to ask me to remind you. . . ."

The Duchess was small of stature, with firm round cheeks, a small mouth, and quick dark eyes under an anxiously wrinkled forehead. She did not often smile, and when, as now, she attempted it, the result was a pucker similar to the wrinkles on her brow. "You know that someone else will be very grieved if you don't go," she insinuated archly.

The Duke's look passed from faint *ennui* to marked severity. He glanced at the ceiling, and made no answer.

"My dear Ushant," said the Duchess, who still called him by the title he had borne before his father's death, "surely you can't be blind to the fact that poor Jean Hopeleigh's future is in your hands. It is a serious thing to have inspired such a deep sentiment. . . ."

The Duke's naturally inexpressive face had become completely expressionless, but his mother continued: "I only fear it may cause you a lasting remorse. . . ."

"I will never marry anyone who hunts me down for the sake of my title," exclaimed the Duke abruptly.

His mother raised her neat dark eyebrows in a reproachful stare. "For your title? But, my dear Ushant, surely Jean Hopeleigh . . ."

"Jean Hopeleigh is like all the others. I'm sick of being tracked like a wild animal," cried the Duke, who looked excessively tame.

The Duchess gave a deep sigh. "Ushant—!"

"Well?"

"You haven't—it's not possible—formed an imprudent attachment? You're not concealing anything from me?"

The Duke's smiles were almost as difficult as his mother's, but his muscles made an effort in that direction. "I shall never form an attachment until I meet a girl who doesn't know what a duke is!"

"Well, my dear, I can't think where one could find a being so totally ignorant of everything on which England's greatness rests," said the Duchess impressively.

"Then I shan't marry."

"Ushant—!"

"I'm sorry, Mother—"

She lifted her sharp eyes to his. "You remember that the roof at Tintagel has still to be paid for?"

"Yes."

"Dear Jean's settlements would make all that so easy. There's nothing the Hopeleighs wouldn't do. . . ."

The Duke interrupted her. "Why not marry me to a Jewess? Some of those people in the City could buy up the Hopeleighs and not feel it."

The Duchess drew herself up. Her lips trembled, but no word came. Her son stalked out of the room. From the threshold he turned to say: "I shall go down to Tintagel on Friday night to go over the books with Blair." His mother could only bend her head; his obstinacy was beginning to frighten her.

The Duke got into the train on the Friday with a feeling of relief. His high and continuous sense of his rank was combined with a secret desire for anonymity. If he could have had himself replaced in the world of fashion and politics by a mechanical effigy of the Duke of Tintagel, while he himself went obscurely about his private business, he would have been a happier man. He was as firmly convinced as his mother that the greatness of England rested largely on her dukes. The Dukes of Tintagel had always had a strong sense of public obligation; and the young Duke was determined not to fall below their standard. But his real tastes were for small matters, for the *minutiae* of a retired and leisurely existence. When he was a little boy his secret longing had been to be a clock-maker; or rather (since their fabrication might have been too delicate a business) a man who sold clocks and sat among them in his little shop, watching them, doctoring them, taking their temperature, feeling their pulse, listening to their chimes, oiling, setting, and regulating them. The then Lord Ushant had never avowed this longing to his parents; even in petticoats he had understood that a future duke can never hope to keep a clock-shop. But often, wandering through the great saloons and interminable galleries of Longlands and Tintagel, he had said to himself with a beating heart: "Some day I'll wind all those clocks myself, every Sunday morning, before breakfast."

Later he felt that he would have been perfectly happy as a country squire, arbitrating in village disputes, adjusting differences between vicar and school-master, sorting fishing-tackle, mending broken furniture, doctoring the dogs, re-arranging his collection of stamps; instead of which, fate had cast him for the centre front of the world's most brilliant social stage.

Undoubtedly his mother had been a great help. She enjoyed equally the hard work and the pompous ceremonial incumbent on conscientious dukes; and the poor young Duke was incorrigibly conscientious. But his conscience could not compel him to accept a marriage arranged by his mother. That part of his life he intended to arrange for himself. His departure for Tintagel was an oblique reply to the Duchess's challenge. She had told him to go to Scotland, and he was going to Cornwall instead. The mere fact of being seated in a train which was hurrying westward was a declaration of independence. The Duke longed above all to be free, to decide for himself; and though he was ostensibly going to Tintagel on estate business, his real purpose was to think over his future in solitude.

If only he might have remained unmarried! Not that he was without the feelings natural to young men; but the kind of marriage he was expected to make took no account of such feelings.

"I won't be hunted—I won't!" the Duke muttered as the train rushed westward, seeing himself as a panting quarry pursued by an implacable pack of would-be Duchesses. Was there no escape? Yes. He would dedicate his public life entirely to his country, but in private he would do as he chose. Valiant words, and easy to speak when no one was listening; but with his mother's small hard eyes on him, his resolves had a way of melting. Was it true that if he did not offer himself to Jean Hopeleigh the world might accuse him of trifling with her? If so, the sooner he married someone else the better. The chief difficulty was that he had not yet met anyone whom he really wanted to marry.

Well, he would give himself at least three days in which to think it all over, out of reach of the Duchess's eyes. . . .

A salt mist was drifting to and fro down the coast as the Duke, the next afternoon, walked along the cliffs toward the ruins of the old Tintagel. Since early morning he had been at work with Mr. Blair, the agent, going into the laborious question of reducing the bills for the roof of the new castle, and examining the other problems presented by the administration of his great domain. After that, with agent and housekeeper, he had inspected every room in the castle, carefully examining floors and ceilings, and seeing to it that Mr. Blair recorded the repairs to be made, but firmly hurrying past the innumerable clocks, large and small, loud and soft, which from writing-table and mantel-shelf and cabinet-top cried out to him for attention. "Have you a good man for the clocks?" he had merely asked, with an affectation of indifference, and when the housekeeper replied, "Oh, yes, Your Grace, Mr. Trelly from Wadebridge comes once a week, the same that His Late Grace always employed," he had passed on with a distinct feeling of disappointment; for probably a man of that sort would resent anyone else's winding the clocks—a sentiment which the Duke could perfectly appreciate.

Finally, wearied by these labours, which were as much out of scale with his real tastes as the immense building itself, he had lunched late and hastily on bread and cheese, to the despair of the housekeeper, who had despatched a groom before daylight to scour Wadebridge for delicacies.

The Duke's afternoon was his own, and, his meagre repast over, he set out for a tramp. The troublesome question of his marriage was still foremost in his mind; for, after inspecting the castle, he felt more than ever the impossibility of escaping from his ducal burdens. Yet how could the simple-hearted girl of whom he was in search be induced to share the weight of these great establishments? It was unlikely that a young woman too ignorant of worldly advantages to covet his title would be attracted by his responsibilities. Why not remain unmarried, as he had threatened, and let the title and the splendours go to the elderly clergyman who was his heir presumptive? But no—that would be a still worse failure in duty. He must marry, have children, play the great part assigned to him.

As he walked along the coast toward the ruined Tintagel, he shook off his momentary cowardice. The westerly wind blew great trails of fog in from the sea, and now and then, between them, showed a mass of molten silver, swaying heavily, as though exhausted by a distant gale. The Duke thought of the stuffy heat of London, and the currents of his blood ran less sedately. He would marry, yes; but he would choose his own wife, and choose her away from the world, in some still backwater of rural England. But here another difficulty lurked. He had once, before his father's death, lit on a girl who fitted ideally into his plan: the daughter of a naval officer's widow, brought up in a remote Norfolk village. The Duke had found a friend to introduce him, had called, had talked happily with the widow of parochial matters, had shown her what was wrong with her clock, and had even contrived to be left alone with the young lady. But the young lady could say no more than "Yes" and "No," and she placed even these monosyllables with so little relevance that, face to face with her, he was struck dumb also. He did not return, and the young lady married a curate.

The memory tormented him now. Perhaps, if he had been

patient, had given her time—but no, he recalled her blank bewildered face, and thought what a depressing sight it would be every morning behind the tea-urn. Though he sought simplicity, he dreaded dulness. Dimly conscious that he was dull himself, he craved the stimulus of a quicker mind; yet he feared a dull wife less than a brilliant one, for with the latter how could he maintain his superiority? He remembered his discomfort among those loud rattling young women whom his cousin Seadown had taken him to see at Runnymede. Very handsome they were, each in her own way; nor was the Duke insensible to beauty. One especially, the fair one, had attracted him. She was less noisy than the others, and would have been an agreeable sight at the breakfast-table; and she carried her head in a way to show off the Tintagel jewels. But marry an American—? The thought was inconceivable. Besides, supposing she should want to surround herself with all those screaming people, and supposing he had to invite the mother—he wasn't sure which of the two elderly ladies with dyed fringes *was* the mother—to Longlands or Tintagel whenever a child was born? From this glimpse into an alien world the Duke's orderly imagination recoiled. What he wanted was an English bride of ancient lineage and Arcadian innocence; and somewhere in the British Isles there must be one awaiting him. . . .

XVI.

After their early swim the morning had turned so damp and foggy that Miss Testvalley said to Nan: "I believe this would be a good day for me to drive over to Polwhelly and call at the vicarage. You can sit in the garden a little while if the sun comes out."

The vicarage at Polwhelly had been Miss Testvalley's chief refuge during her long lonely months at Tintagel with her Folyat pupils, and Nan knew that she wished to visit her old friends. As for Nan herself, after the swim and the morning walk, she preferred to sit in the inn garden, sheltered by a tall fuchsia hedge, and gaze out over the headlands and the sea. She had not even expressed the wish to take the short walk along the cliffs to the ruins of Tintagel; and she had apparently forgotten Miss Testvalley's offer to show her the modern castle of the same name. She seemed neither listless nor unwell, the governess thought, but lulled by the strong air, and steeped in a lazy beatitude; and this was the very mood Miss Testvalley had sought to create in her.

But an hour or two after Trevennick's only fly had carried off Miss Testvalley, the corner where Nan sat became a balcony above a great sea-drama. A twist of the wind had whirled away the fog, and there of a sudden lay the sea in a metallic glitter, with white clouds storming over it, hiding and then revealing the fiery blue sky between. Sit in the shelter of the fuchsia hedge on

such a day? Not Nan! Her feet were already dancing on the sun-
beams, and in another minute the gate had swung behind her,
and she was away to meet the gale on the downs above the village.

When the Duke of Tintagel reached the famous ruin from which
he took his name, another freak of the wind had swept the fog
in again. The sea was no more than a hoarse sound on an invisible
shore, and he climbed the slopes through a cloud filled with the
stormy clash of sea-birds. To some minds the change might have
seemed to befit the desolate place; but the Duke, being a good
landlord, thought only: "More rain, I suppose; and that is certain
to mean a loss on the crops."

But the walk had been exhilarating, and when he reached
the upper platform of the castle, and looked down through a
break in the fog at the savage coast-line, a feeling of pride and
satisfaction crept through him. He liked the idea that a place so
ancient and renowned belonged to him, was a mere milestone in
his race's long descent; and he said to himself: "I owe everything
to England. Perhaps after all I ought to marry as my mother
wishes. . . ."

He had thought he had the wild place to himself, but as he
advanced toward the edge of the platform he perceived that his
solitude was shared by a young lady who, as yet unaware of his
presence, stood wedged in a coign of the ramparts, absorbed in
the struggle between wind and sea.

The Duke gave an embarrassed cough; but, between the
waves and the gulls, the sound did not carry far. The girl remained motionless, her profile turned seaward, and the Duke was
near enough to study it in detail.

She had not the kind of beauty to whirl a man off his feet,
and his eye was free to note that her complexion, though now
warmed by the wind, was naturally pale, that her nose was a trifle
too small, and her hair a tawny uncertain mixture of dark and
fair. Nothing overpowering in all this; but being overpowered was
what the Duke most dreaded. He went in fear of the terrible

beauty that is born and bred for the strawberry leaves, and the face he was studying was so grave yet so happy that he felt somehow reassured and safe. This girl, at any rate, was certainly not thinking of dukes; and in the eyes she presently turned to him he saw not himself but the sea.

He raised his hat, and she looked at him, surprised but not disturbed. "I didn't know you were there," she said simply.

"The grass deadens one's steps . . ." the Duke apologized.

"Yes. And the birds scream so—and the wind."

"I'm afraid I startled you."

"Oh, no. I didn't suppose the place belonged to me. . . ." She continued to scrutinize him gravely, and he wondered whether a certain fearless gravity were not what he liked best in woman. Then suddenly she smiled, and he changed his mind.

"But I've seen you before, haven't I?" she exclaimed. "I'm sure I have. Wasn't it at Runnymede?"

"At Runnymede?" he stammered, his heart sinking. The smile, then, had after all been for the Duke!

"Yes. I'm Nan St. George. My mother and Mrs. Elmsworth have taken a little cottage there—Lady Churt's cottage. A lot of people come down from London to see my sister, Virginia, and Liz Elmsworth, and I have an idea you came one day—didn't you? There are so many of them—crowds of young men; and always changing. I'm afraid I can't remember all their names. But didn't Teddy de Santos-Dios bring you down the day we had that awful pillow-fight? I know—you're a Mr. Robinson."

In an instant the Duke's apprehensive mind registered a succession of terrors. First the dread that he had been recognized and marked down; then the more deadly fear that, though this had actually happened, his quick-witted antagonist was clever enough to affect an impossible ignorance. A Mr. Robinson! For a fleeting second the Duke tried to feel what it would be like to be a Mr. Robinson . . . a man who might wind his own clocks when he chose. It did not feel as agreeable as the Duke had imagined— and he hastily re-became a duke.

Yet would it not be safer to accept the proffered alias? He

wavered. But no; the idea was absurd. If this girl, though he did not remember ever having seen her, had really been at Runnymede the day he had gone there, it was obvious that, though she might not identify him at the moment (a thought not wholly gratifying to his vanity), she could not long remain in ignorance. His face must have betrayed his embarrassment, for she exclaimed: "Oh, then, you're not Mr. Robinson? I'm so sorry! Virginia (that's my sister; I don't believe you've forgotten *her*)—Virginia says I'm always making stupid mistakes. And I know everybody hates being taken for somebody else; and especially for a Mr. Robinson. But won't you tell me your name?"

The Duke's confusion increased. But he was aware that hesitation was ridiculous. There was no help for it; he had to drag himself into the open. "My name's Tintagel."

Nan's eyebrows rose in surprise, and her smile enchanted him again. "Oh, but how perfectly splendid! Then of course you know Miss Testvalley?"

The Duke stared. He had never seen exactly that effect produced by the announcement of his name. "Miss Testvalley?"

"Oh, don't you know her? How funny! But aren't you the brother of those girls whose governess she was? They used to live at Tintagel. I mean Clara and Ermie and Mina. . . ."

"Their governess?" It suddenly dawned on the Duke how little he knew about his sisters. The fact of being regarded as a mere appendage to these unimportant females was a still sharper blow to his vanity; yet it gave him the reassurance that even now the speaker did not know she was addressing a duke. Incredible as such ignorance was, he was constrained to recognize it. "She knows me only as their brother," he thought. "Or else," he added, "she knows who I am and doesn't care."

At first neither alternative was wholly pleasing; but after a moment's reflection he felt a glow of relief. "I remember my sisters had a governess they were devoted to," he said, with a timid affability.

"I should think so! She's perfectly splendid. Did you know

she was Dante Gabriel Rossetti's own cousin?" Nan continued, her enthusiasm rising, as it always did when she spoke of Miss Testvalley.

The Duke's perplexity deepened; and it annoyed him to have to grope for his answers in conversing with this prompt young woman. "I'm afraid I know very few Italians—"

"Oh, well, you wouldn't know *him*; he's very ill, and hardly sees anybody. But don't you love his poetry? Which sonnet do you like best in *The House of Life*? I have a friend whose favourite is the one that begins: 'When do I see thee most, belovéd one?' "

"I—the fact is, I've very little time to read poetry," the Duke faltered.

Nan looked at him incredulously. "It doesn't take much time if you really care for it. But lots of people don't—Virginia doesn't. . . . Are you coming down soon to Runnymede? Miss Testvalley and I are going back next week. They just sent me here for a little while to get a change of air and some bathing, but it was really because they thought Runnymede was too exciting for me."

"Ah," exclaimed the Duke, his interest growing, "you don't care for excitement, then?" (The lovely child!)

Nan pondered the question. "Well, it all depends. . . . Everything's exciting, don't you think so? I mean sunsets and poetry, and swimming out too far in a rough sea. . . . But I don't believe I care as much as the others for practical jokes: frightening old ladies by dressing up as burglars with dark lanterns, or putting wooden rattlesnakes in people's beds—do *you*?"

It was the Duke's turn to hesitate. "I— Well, I must own that such experiences are unfamiliar to me; but I can hardly imagine being amused by them."

His mind revolved uneasily between the alternatives of disguising himself as a burglar or listening to a young lady recite poetry; and to bring the talk back to an easier level he said: "You're staying in the neighbourhood?"

"Yes. At Trevennick, at the inn. I love it here, don't you? You must live somewhere near here, I suppose?"

Yes, the Duke said; his place wasn't above three miles away. He'd just walked over from there. . . . He broke off, at a loss how to go on; but his interlocutor came to the rescue.

"I suppose you must know the vicar at Polwhelly? Miss Testvalley's gone to see him this afternoon. That's why I came up here alone. I promised and swore I wouldn't stir out of the inn garden—but how could I help it, when the sun suddenly came out?"

"How indeed?" echoed the Duke, attempting one of his difficult smiles. "Will your governess be very angry, do you think?"

"Oh, fearfully, at first. But afterward she'll understand. Only I do want to get back before she comes in, or she'll be worried. . . ." She turned back to the rampart for a last look at the sea; but the deepening fog had blotted out everything. "I must really go," she said, "or I'll never find my way down."

The Duke's gaze followed hers. Was this a tentative invitation to guide her back to the inn? Should he offer to do so? Or would the governess disapprove of this even more than of her charge's wandering off alone in the fog? "If you'll allow me— may I see you back to Trevennick?" he suggested.

"Oh, I wish you would. If it's not too far out of your way?"

"It's—it's on my way," the Duke declared, lying hurriedly; and they started down the steep declivity. The slow descent was effected in silence, for the Duke's lie had exhausted his conversational resources, and his companion seemed to have caught the contagion of his shyness. Inwardly he was thinking: "Ought I to offer her a hand? Is it steep enough—or will she think I'm presuming?"

He had never before met a young lady alone in a ruined castle, and his mind, nurtured on precedents, had no rule to guide it. But nature cried aloud in him that he must somehow see her again. He was still turning over the best means of effecting another meeting—an invitation to the castle, a suggestion that he should call on Miss Testvalley?—when, after a slippery descent from the ruins, and an arduous climb up the opposite cliff, they reached the fork of the path where it joined the lane to Trevennick.

"Thank you so much; but you needn't come any further. There's the inn just below," the young lady said, smiling.

"Oh, really? You'd rather—? Mayn't I?"

She shook her head. "No, really," she mimicked him lightly; and with a quick wave of dismissal she started down the lane.

The Duke stood motionless, looking irresolutely after her, and wondering what he ought to have said or done. "I ought to have contrived a way of going as far as the inn with her," he said to himself, exasperated by his own lack of initiative. "It comes of being always hunted, I suppose," he added, as he watched her slight outline lessen down the hill.

Just where the descent took a turn toward the village, Nan encountered a familiar figure panting upward.

"Annabel—I've been hunting for you everywhere!"

Annabel laughed and embraced her duenna. "You weren't expected back so soon."

"You promised me faithfully that you'd stay in the garden. And in this drenching fog—"

"Yes; but the fog blew away after you'd gone, and I thought that let me off my promise. So I scrambled up to the castle—that's all."

"That's all? Over a mile away, and along those dangerous slippery cliffs?"

"Oh, it was all right. There was a gentleman there who brought me back."

"A gentleman—in the ruins?"

"Yes. He says he lives somewhere round here."

"How often have I told you not to let strangers speak to you?"

"He didn't. I spoke to him. But he's not really a stranger, darling; he thinks he knows you."

"Oh, he does, does he?" Miss Testvalley gave a sniff of incredulity.

"I saw he wanted to ask if he could call," Nan continued, "but he was too shy. I never saw anybody so scared. I don't believe he's been around much."

"I daresay he was shocked by your behaviour."

"Oh, no. Why should he have been? He just stayed with me while we were getting up the cliff; after that I said he musn't come any farther. Why, there he is still—at the top of the lane, where I left him. I suppose he's been watching to see that I got home safely. Don't you call that sweet of him?"

Miss Testvalley released herself from her pupil's arm. Her eyes were not only keen but far-sighted. They followed Nan's glance, and rested on the figure of a young man who stood above them on the edge of the cliff. As she looked, he turned slowly away.

"Annabel! Are you sure that was the gentleman?"

"Yes . . . He's funny. He says he has no time to read poetry. What do you suppose he does instead?"

"But it's the Duke of Tintagel!" Miss Testvalley suddenly declared.

"The Duke? That young man?" It was Nan's turn to give an incredulous laugh. "He said his name was Tintagel, and that he was the brother of those girls at the castle; but I thought of course he was a younger son. He never said he was the Duke."

Miss Testvalley gave an impatient shrug. "They don't go about shouting out their titles. The family name is Folyat. And he has no younger brother, as it happens."

"Well, how was I to know all that? Oh, Miss Testvalley," exclaimed Nan, spinning around on her governess, "but if he's the Duke he's the one Miss March wants Jinny to marry!"

"Miss March is full of brilliant ideas."

"I don't call that one particularly brilliant. At least, not if I was Jinny, I shouldn't. I think," said Nan, after a moment's pondering, "that the Duke's one of the stupidest young men I ever met."

"Well," rejoined her governess severely, "I hope he thinks nothing worse than that of you."

XVII.

The Mr. Robinson for whom Nan St. George had mistaken the Duke of Tintagel was a young man much more confident of his gifts, and assured as to his future, than that retiring nobleman. There was nothing within the scope of his understanding which Hector Robinson did not know, and mean at some time to make use of. His grandfather had been first a miner and then a mine-owner in the North; his father, old Sir Downman Robinson, had built up one of the biggest cotton-industries in Lancashire, and been rewarded with a knighthood, and Sir Downman's only son meant to turn the knighthood into a baronetcy, and the baronetcy into a peerage. All in good time.

Meanwhile, as a partner in his father's big company, and director in various City enterprises, and as Conservative M.P. for one of the last rotten boroughs in England, he had his work cut out for him, and could boast that his thirty-five years had not been idle ones.

It was only on the social side that he had hung fire. In coming out against his father as a Conservative, and thus obtaining without difficulty his election to Lord Saltmire's constituency, Mr. Robinson had flattered himself that he would secure a footing in society as readily as in the City. Had he made a miscalculation? Was it true that fashion had turned toward Liberalism, and that a young Liberal M.P. was more likely to find favour in the circles to which Mr. Robinson aspired?

Perhaps it was true; but Mr. Robinson was a Conservative by instinct, by nature, and in his obstinate self-confidence was determined that he would succeed without sacrificing his political convictions. And at any rate, when it came to a marriage, he felt reasonably sure that his Conservatism would recommend him in the families from which he intended to choose his bride.

Mr. Robinson, surveying the world as his oyster, had already (if the figure be allowed) divided it into two halves, each in a different way designed to serve his purpose. The one, which he labelled "Mayfair," held out possibilities of immediate success. In that set, which had already caught the Heir to the Throne in its glittering meshes, there were ladies of the highest fashion who, in return for pecuniary favours, were ready and even eager to promote the ascent of gentlemen with short pedigrees and long purses. As a member of Parliament, he had a status which did away with most of the awkward preliminaries; and he found it easy enough to pick up, among his masculine acquaintances, an introduction to that privileged group beginning to be known as "the Marlborough set."

But it was not in this easy-going world that he meant to marry. Socially as well as politically, Mr. Robinson was a true Conservative, and it was in the duller half of the London world, the half he called "Belgravia," that he intended to seek a partner. But into those uniform cream-coloured houses where dowdy dowagers ruled, and flocks of marriageable daughters pined for a suitor approved by the family, Mr. Robinson had not yet forced his way. The only interior known to him in that world was Lord Saltmire's, and in this he was received on a strictly Parliamentary basis. He had made the immense mistake of not immediately recognizing the fact, and of imagining, for a mad moment, that the Earl of Saltmire, who had been so ready to endow him with a seat in Parliament, would be no less disposed to welcome him as a brother-in-law. But Lady Audrey de Salis, plain, dowdy, and one of five unmarried sisters, had refused him curtly and all too definitely; and the shock had thrown him back into the arms of Mayfair. Obviously he had aspired too high, or been too impatient; but it was in his nature to be aspiring and impatient, and if he was to succeed it must be on the lines of his own character.

So he had told himself as he looked into his glass on the morning of his first visit to the cottage at Runnymede, whither Teddy de Santos-Dios was to conduct him. Mr. Robinson saw in his mirror the energetic reddish features of a young man with a broad short nose, a dense crop of brown hair, and a heavy brown moustache. He had been among the first to recognize that whiskers were going out, and had sacrificed as handsome a pair as the City could show. When Mr. Robinson made up his mind that a change was coming, his principle was always to meet it half way; and so the whiskers went. And it did make him look younger to wear only the fashionable moustache. With that, and a flower in the buttonhole of his Poole coat, he could take his chance with most men, though he was aware that the careless un-self-consciousness of the elect was still beyond him. But in time he would achieve that too.

Certainly he could not have gone to a better school than the bungalow at Runnymede. The young guardsmen, the budding M.P.'s and civil servants, who frequented it were all of the favoured caste whose ease of manner Mr. Robinson envied; and nowhere were they so easy as in the company of the young women already familiar to fashionable London as "the Americans." Mr. Robinson returned from that first visit enchanted and slightly bewildered, but with the fixed resolve to go back as often as he was invited. Before the day was over he had lent fifty pounds to Teddy de Santos-Dios, and lost another fifty at poker to the latter's sister, Lady Richard Marable, thus securing a prompt invitation for the following week; and after that he was confident of keeping the foothold he had gained.

But if the young ladies enchanted him he saw in the young men his immediate opportunity. Lady Richard's brother-in-law, Lord Seadown, was, for instance, one of the golden youths to whom Mr. Robinson had vainly sought an introduction. Lord Richard Marable, Seadown's younger brother, he did know; but

Lord Richard's acquaintance was easy to make, and led nowhere, least of all in the direction of his own family. At Runnymede, Lord Richard was seldom visible; but Lord Seadown, who was always there, treated with brotherly cordiality all who shared the freedom of the cottage. There were others too, younger sons of great houses, officers quartered at Windsor or Aldershot, young Parliamentarians and minor government officials reluctantly detained in town at the season's end, and hailing with joy the novel distractions of Runnymede; there was even—on one memorable day—the young Duke of Tintagel, a shrinking neutral-tinted figure in that highly coloured throng.

"Now if *I* were a Duke—!" Robinson thought, viewing with pity the unhappy nobleman's dull clothes and embarrassed manner; but he contrived an introduction to His Grace, and even a few moments of interesting political talk, in which the Duke took eager refuge from the call to play blindman's-buff with the young ladies. All this was greatly to the good, and Mr. Robinson missed no chance to return to Runnymede.

On a breathless August afternoon he had come down from London, as he did on most Saturdays, and joined the party about the tea-table under the big cedar. The group was smaller than usual. Miss March was away visiting friends in the Lake country. Nan St. George was still in Cornwall with her governess. Mrs. St. George and Mrs. Elmsworth, exhausted by the heat, had retired to the seclusion of their bedrooms, and only Virginia St. George and the two Elmsworth girls, under the doubtful chaperonage of Lady Richard Marable, sat around the table with their usual guests—Lord Seadown, Santos-Dios, Hector Robinson, a couple of young soldiers from Windsor, and a caustic young civil servant, the Honourable Miles Dawnly, who could always be trusted to bring down the latest news from London—or, at that season, from Scotland, Homburg, or Marienbad, as the case might be.

Mr. Robinson by this time felt quite at home among them. He agreed with the others that it was far too hot to play tennis or even croquet, or to go on the river before sunset, and he lay contentedly on the turf under the cedar, thinking his own thoughts, and making his own observations, while he joined in the languid chatter about the tea-table.

Of observations there were always plenty to be made at Runnymede. Robinson, by this time, had in his hands most of the threads running from one to another of these careless smiling young people. It was obvious, for instance, that Miles Dawnly, who had probably never lost his balance before, was head-over-ears in love with Conchita Marable, and that she was "playing" him indolently and amusedly, for want of a bigger fish. But the neuralgic point in the group was the growing rivalry between Lizzy Elmsworth and Virginia St. George. Those two inseparable friends were gradually becoming estranged; and the reason was not far to seek. It was between them now, in the person of Lord Seadown, who lay at their feet, plucking up tufts of clover, and gazing silently skyward through the dark boughs of the cedar. It had for some time been clear to Robinson that the susceptible young man was torn between Virginia St. George's exquisite profile and Lizzy Elmsworth's active wit. He needed the combined stimulus of both to rouse his slow imagination, and Robinson saw that while Virginia had the advantage as yet, it might at any moment slip into Lizzy's quick fingers. And Lizzy saw this too.

Suddenly Mabel Elmsworth, at whose feet no one was lying, jumped up and declared that if she sat still a minute longer she would take root. "Walk down to the river with me, will you, Mr. Robinson? There may be a little more air than under the trees."

Robinson had no particular desire to walk to the river, or anywhere else, with Mab Elmsworth. She was jolly, and conversable enough, but minor luminaries never interested him when stars of the first magnitude were in view. However, he was still tingling with the resentment aroused by the Lady Audrey de Salis's rejection, and in the mood to compare unfavourably that silent and large-limbed young woman with the swift nymphs of Runnymede. At Runnymede they all seemed to live, metaphorically, from hand to mouth. Everything that happened seemed to be improvised, and this suited his own impetuous pace much better than the sluggish *tempo* of the Saltmire circle. He rose, therefore, at Mabel's summons, wondering what the object of the invitation could be. Was she going to ask him to marry her? A little shiver ran down his spine; for all he knew, that might be the way they did it in the States. But her first words dispelled his fear.

"Mr. Robinson, Lord Seadown's a friend of yours, isn't he?"

Robinson hesitated. He was far too intelligent to affect to be more intimate with anyone than he really was, and after a moment he answered: "I haven't known him long; but everybody who comes here appears to be on friendly terms with everybody else."

His companion frowned slightly. "I wish they really were! But what I wanted to ask you was—have you ever noticed anything particular between Lord Seadown and my sister?"

Robinson stopped short. The question took him by surprise. He had already noticed, in these free-mannered young women, a singular reticence about their family concerns, a sort of moral modesty that seemed to constrain them to throw a veil over matters freely enough discussed in aristocratic English circles. He repeated: "Your sister?"

"You probably think it's a peculiar question. Don't imagine I'm trying to pump you. But everybody must have seen that he's tremendously taken with Lizzy, and that Jinny St. George is doing her best to come between them."

Robinson's embarrassment deepened. He did not know where she was trying to lead him. "I should be sorry to think that of Miss St. George, who appears to be so devoted to your sister."

Mabel Elmsworth laughed impatiently. "I suppose that's the proper thing to say. But I'm not asking you to take sides—I'm not even blaming Virginia. Only it's been going on now all summer, and what I say is, it's time he chose between them, if he's ever going to. It's very hard on Lizzy, and it's not fair that he should make two friends quarrel. After all, we're all alone in a strange country, and I daresay our ways are not like yours, and may lead you to make mistakes about us. All I wanted to ask is, if you couldn't drop a hint to Lord Seadown."

Hector Robinson looked curiously at this girl, who might have been pretty in less goddess-like company, and who spoke with such precocious wisdom on subjects delicate to touch. "By Jove, she'd make a good wife for an ambitious man," he thought. He did not mean himself, but he reflected that the man who married her beautiful sister might be glad enough, at times, to have such a counsellor at his elbow.

"I think you're right about one thing, Miss Elmsworth. Your ways are so friendly, so kind, that a fellow, if he wasn't careful, might find himself drawn two ways at once—"

Mabel laughed. "Oh, you mean: we flirt. Well, it's in our blood, I suppose. And no one thinks the worse of a girl for it at home. But over here it may seem undignified; and perhaps Lord Seadown thought he had the right to amuse himself without making up his mind. But in America, when a girl has shown that she really cares, it puts a gentleman on his honour, and he understands that the game has gone on long enough."

"I see."

"Only we've nobody here to say this to Lord Seadown" (Mabel seemed tacitly to assume that neither mother could be counted on for the purpose—not at least in such hot weather), "and so I thought—"

Mr. Robinson murmured, "Yes—yes—" and after a pause went on: "But Lord Seadown is Lady Richard's brother-in-law. Couldn't she—?"

Mabel shrugged. "Oh, Conchita's too lazy to be bothered. And if she took sides, it would be with Jinny St. George, because they're great friends, and she'd want all the money she can get for Seadown. Colonel St. George is a very rich man nowadays."

"I see," Mr. Robinson again murmured. It was out of the question that he should speak on such a matter to Lord Seadown, and he did not know how to say this to anyone as inexperienced as Mabel Elmsworth. "I'll think it over—I'll see what can be done," he pursued, directing his steps toward the group under the cedar in his desire to cut the conversation short.

As he approached he thought what a pretty scene it was: the young women in their light starched dresses and spreading hats, the young men in flannel boating-suits, stretched at their feet on the turf, and the afternoon sunlight filtering through the dark boughs in dapplings of gold.

Mabel Elmsworth walked beside him in silence, clearly aware that her appeal had failed; but suddenly she exclaimed: "There's a lady driving in that I've never seen before. . . . She's stopping the carriage to get out and join Conchita. I suppose it's a friend of hers, don't you?"

Calls from ladies, Mr. Robinson had already noticed, were rare and unexpected at the cottage. If a guardsman had leapt from the station fly, Mabel, whether she knew him or not, would have remained unperturbed; but the sight of an unknown young woman of elegant appearance filled her with excitement and curiosity. "Let's go and see," she exclaimed.

The visitor, who was dark-haired, with an audaciously rouged complexion, and the kind of nose which the Laureate had taught his readers to describe as tip-tilted, was personally unknown to Mr. Robinson also; but, thanks to the Bond Street photographers and the new society journals, her features were as familiar to him as her reputation.

"Why, it's Lady Churt—it's your landlady!" he exclaimed, with a quick glance of enquiry at his companion. The tie between Seadown and Lady Churt had long been notorious in their little world, and Robinson instantly surmised that the appearance of the lady might have a far from favourable bearing on what Mabel Elmsworth had just been telling him. But Mabel hurried forward without responding to his remark, and they joined the party just as Lady Churt was exchanging a cordial hand-clasp with Lady Richard Marable.

"Darling!"

"Darling Idina, what a surprise!"

"Conchita, dearest—I'd no idea I should find you here! Won't you explain me, please, to these young ladies—my tenants, I suppose?" Lady Churt swept the group with her cool amused glance, which paused curiously, and as Robinson thought somewhat anxiously, on Virginia St. George's radiant face.

"She looks older than in her photographs—and hunted, somehow," Robinson reflected, his own gaze resting on Lady Churt.

"I'm Lady Churt—your landlady, you know," the speaker continued affably, addressing herself to Virginia and Lizzy. "Please don't let me interrupt this delightful party. Mayn't I join it instead? What a brilliant idea to have tea out here in hot weather! I always used to have it on the terrace. But you Americans are so clever at arranging things." She looked about her, mustering the group with her fixed metallic smile. With the exception of Hector Robinson, the young men were evidently all known to her, and she found an easy word of greeting for each. Lord Seadown was the last that she named.

"Ah, Seadown—so you're here too? Now I see why you forgot that you were lunching with me in town today. I must say you chose the better part." She dropped into the deep basket-chair which Santos-Dios had pushed forward, and held out her hand for a proffered mint-julep. "No tea, thanks—not when one of Teddy's demoralizing mixtures is available. . . . You see, I know what to expect when I come here. . . . A cigarette, Seadown? I hope you've got my special supply with you, even if you've forgotten our engagement?" She smiled again upon the girls. "He spoils me horribly, you know, by always remembering to carry about my particular brand."

Seadown, with flushed face and lowering brow, produced the packet, and Lady Churt slipped the contents into her cigarette-case. "I do hope I'm not interrupting some delightful plan or other? Perhaps you were all going out on the river? If you were, you mustn't let me delay you, for I must be off again in a few minutes."

Everyone protested that it was much too hot to move, and

Lady Churt continued: "Really, you had no plans? Well, it *is* pleasanter here than anywhere else. But perhaps I'm dreadfully in the way. Seadown's looking at me as if I were. . . ." She turned her glance laughingly toward Virginia St. George. "The fact is, I'm not at all sure that landladies have a right to intrude on their tenants unannounced. I daresay it's really against the law."

"Well, if it is, you must pay the penalty by being detained at our pleasure," said Lady Richard gaily; and after a moment's pause Lizzy Elmsworth came forward. "Won't you let me call my mother and Mrs. St. George, Lady Churt? I'm sure they'd be sorry not to see you. It was so hot after luncheon that they went up to their rooms to rest."

"How very wise of them! I wouldn't disturb them for the world." Lady Churt set down her empty glass, and bent over the lighting of a cigarette. "Only you really mustn't let me interfere for a moment with what you were all going to do. You see," she added, turning about with a smile of challenge, "you see, though my tenants haven't yet done me the honour of inviting me down, I've heard what amusing things are always going on here, and what wonderful ways you've found of cheering up the poor martyrs to duty who can't get away to the grouse and the deer—and I may as well confess that I'm dreadfully keen to learn your secrets."

Robinson saw that this challenge had a slightly startling effect on the three girls, who stood grouped together with an air of mutual defensiveness unlike their usual easy attitude. But Lady Richard met the words promptly. "If your tenants haven't invited you down, Idina dear, I fancy it's only because they were afraid to have you see how rudimentary their arts are compared to their landlady's. So many delightful people had already learnt the way to the cottage that there was nothing to do but to leave the door unlatched. Isn't that your only secret, girls? If there's any other" —she too glanced about her with a smile—"well, perhaps it's *this*; but this, remember, *is* a secret, even from the stern mammas who are taking their siesta upstairs."

As she spoke she turned to her brother. "Come, Teddy—if

everybody's had tea, what about lifting the tray and things on to the grass, and putting this table to its real use?" Two of the young men sprang to her aid; and in a moment tray and tea-cloth had been swept away, and the green baize top of the folding table had declared its original purpose.

"Cards? Oh, how jolly!" cried Lady Churt. She drew a seat up to the table, while Teddy de Santos-Dios, who had disappeared into the house, hurried back with a handful of packs. "But this is glorious! No wonder my poor little cottage has become so popular. What—poker? Oh, by all means. The only game worth playing—I took my first lesson from Seadown last week. . . . Seadown, I had a little *porte-monnaie* somewhere, didn't I? Or did I leave it in the fly? Not that I've much hope of finding anything in it but some powder and a few pawn-tickets. . . . Oh, Seadown, will you come to my rescue? Lend me a fiver, there's a darling—I hope I'm not going to lose more than that."

Lord Seadown, who, since her arrival, had maintained a look of gloomy detachment, drew forth his note-case with an embarrassed air. She received it with a laugh. "What? *Carte blanche?* What munificence! But let me see—" She took up the note-case, ran her fingers through it, and drew out two or three five-pound notes. "Heavens, Seadown, what wealth! How am I ever going to pay you back if I lose? Or even if I win, when I need so desperately every penny I can scrape together?" She slipped the notes into her purse, which the observant Hector Robinson, alert for the chance of making himself known to the newcomer, had hastened to retrieve from the fly. Lady Churt took the purse with a brief nod for the service rendered, and a long and attentive look at the personable Hector; then she handed back Lord Seadown's note-case. "Wish me luck, my dear! Perhaps I may manage to fleece one or two of these hardened gamblers."

The card-players, laughing, settled themselves about the table. Lady Churt and Lady Richard sat on opposite sides. Lord Seadown took a seat next to his sister-in-law, and the other men disposed themselves as they pleased. Robinson, who did not care to play, had casually placed himself behind Lady Churt, and the three girls, resisting a little banter and entreaty, declared that they also preferred to walk about and look on at the players.

The game began in earnest, and Lady Churt opened with the supernaturally brilliant hand which often falls to the lot of the novice. The stakes (the observant Robinson noticed) were higher than usual, the players consequently more intent. It was one of those afternoons when thunder invisibly amasses itself behind the blue, and as the sun dropped slowly westward it seemed as though the card-table under the cedar-boughs were overhung by the same feverish hush as the sultry lawns and airless river.

Lady Churt's luck did not hold. Too quickly elated, she dashed ahead toward disaster. Robinson was not long in discovering that she was too emotional for a game based on dissimulation, and no match for such seasoned players as Lady Richard and Lady Richard's brother. Even the other young men had more experience, or at any rate more self-control, than she could muster; and though her purse had evidently been better supplied than she pretended, the time at length came when it was nearly empty.

But at that very moment her luck turned again. Robinson could not believe his eyes. The hand she held could hardly be surpassed; she understood enough of the game to seize her opportunity and fling her last notes into the jack-pot presided over by Teddy de Santos-Dios's glossy smile and supple gestures. There was more money in the jack-pot than Robinson had ever seen on the Runnymede card-table, and a certain breathlessness pervaded the scene, as if the weight of the thundery sky were in the lungs of the players.

Lady Churt threw down her hand, and leaned back with a sparkle of triumph in eyes and lips. But Miles Dawnly, with an almost apologetic gesture, had spread his cards upon the table.

"Begorra! A royal flush—" a young Irish lieutenant gasped out. The groups about the table stared at each other. It was one of those moments which make even seasoned poker-players gasp. For a short interval of perplexity Lady Churt was silent; then the exclamations of the other players brought home to her the shock of her disaster.

"It's the sort of game that fellows write about in their memoirs," murmured Teddy, almost awestruck; and the lucky winner gave an embarrassed laugh. It was almost incredible to him too.

Lady Churt pushed back her chair, nearly colliding with the attentive Robinson. She tried to laugh. "Well, I've learnt my lesson! Lost Seadown's last copper, as well as my own. Not that he need mind; he's won more than he lent me. But I'm completely ruined—down and out, as I believe you say in the States. I'm afraid you're all too clever for me, and one of the young ladies had better take my place," she added with a drawn smile.

"Oh, come, Idina, don't lose heart!" exclaimed Lady Richard, deep in the game, and annoyed at the interruption.

"Heart, my dear? I assure you I've never minded parting with that organ. It's losing the shillings and pence that I can't afford."

Miles Dawnly glanced across the table at Lizzy Elmsworth, who stood beside Hector Robinson, her keen eyes bent on the game. "Come, Miss Elmsworth, if Lady Churt is really deserting us, won't you replace her?"

"Do, Lizzy," cried Lady Richard; but Lizzy shook her head, declaring that she and her friends were completely ignorant of the game.

"What, even Virginia?" Conchita laughed. "There's no excuse for her, at any rate, for her father is a celebrated poker-player. My respected parent always says he'd rather make Colonel St. George a handsome present than sit down at poker with him."

Virginia coloured at the challenge, but Lizzy, always quicker at the uptake, intervened before she could answer.

"You seem to have forgotten, Conchita, that girls don't play cards for money in America."

Lady Churt turned suddenly toward Virginia St. George, who was standing behind her. "No. I understand the game you young ladies play has fewer risks, and requires only two players," she said, fixing her vivid eyes on the girl's bewildered face. Robinson, who had drawn back a few steps, was still watching her intently. He said to himself that he had never seen a woman so angry, and that certain small viperine heads darting forked tongues behind their glass cases at the Zoo would in future always remind him of Lady Churt.

For a moment Virginia's bewilderment was shared by the others about the table; but Conchita, startled out of her absorption in the game, hastily assumed the air of one who is vainly struggling to repress a burst of ill-timed mirth. "How frightfully funny you are, Idina! I do wish you wouldn't make me laugh so terribly in this hot weather!"

Lady Churt's colour rose angrily. "I'm glad it amuses you to see your friends lose their money," she said. "But unluckily I can't afford to make the fun last much longer."

"Oh, nonsense, darling! Of course your luck will turn. It's been miraculous already. Lend her something to go on with, Seadown, do. . . ."

"I'm afraid Seadown can't go on either. I'm sorry to be a spoil-sport, but I must really carry him off. As he forgot to lunch with me today, it's only fair that he should come back to town for dinner."

Lord Seadown, who had relapsed into an unhappy silence, did not break it in response to this; but Lady Richard once more came to his rescue. "We love your chaff, Idina; and we hope the idea of your carrying off Seadown is only a part of it. You say he was engaged to lunch with you today; but isn't there a mistake about dates? Seedy, in his family character as my brother-in-law, brought me down here for the weekend, and I'm afraid he's got to wait and see me home on Monday. You wouldn't suppose my husband would mind my travelling alone, would you, considering how much he does it himself—or professes to; but as a matter of fact he and my father-in-law, who disagree on so many subjects, are quite agreed that I'm not to have any adventures if they can help it. And so you see . . . But sit down again, darling, do. Why should you hurry away? If you'll only stop and dine you'll have an army of heroes to see you back to town; and Seadown's society at dinner."

The effect of this was to make Lady Churt whiten with anger under her paint. She glanced sharply from Lady Richard to Lord Seadown.

"Yes, do, Idina," the latter at length found voice to say.

Lady Churt threw back her brilliant head with another laugh. "Thanks a lot for your invitation, Conchita darling—and for yours too, Seadown. It's really rather amusing to be asked to dine in one's own house. . . . But today I'm afraid I can't. I've got to carry you back to London with me, Seadown, whoever may have brought you here. The fact is"—she turned another of her challenging glances on Virginia St. George—"the fact is, it's time your hostesses found out that you don't go with the house; at least not when I'm not living in it. That ought to have been explained to them, perhaps—"

"Idina . . ." Lord Seadown muttered in anguish.

"Oh, I'm not blaming anybody! It's such a natural mistake. Lord Seadown comes down so continually when I'm here," Lady Churt pursued, her eyes still on Virginia's burning face, "that I suppose he simply forgot the house was let, and went on coming from the mere force of habit. I do hope, Miss St. George, his being here hasn't inconvenienced you? Come along, Seadown, or we'll miss our train; and please excuse yourself to these young ladies, who may think your visits were made on their account—mayn't they?"

A startled silence followed. Even Conchita's ready tongue seemed to fail her. She cast a look of interrogation at her brother-in-law, but his gaze remained obstinately on the ground, and the other young men had discreetly drawn back from the scene of action.

Virginia St. George stood a little way from her friends. Her head was high, her cheeks burning, her blue eyes dark with indignation. Mr. Robinson, intently following the scene, wondered whether it were possible for a young creature to look more proud and beautiful. But in another moment he found himself reversing his judgment; for Mr. Robinson was all for action, and suddenly, swiftly, the other beauty, Virginia's friend and rival, had flung herself into the fray.

"Virginia! What are you waiting for? Don't you see that Lord Seadown has no right to speak till you do? Why don't you tell him at once that he has your permission to announce your engagement?" Lizzy Elmsworth cried with angry fervour.

Mr. Robinson hung upon this dialogue with the breathless absorption of an experienced play-goer discovering the gifts of an unknown actress. "By Jove—by Jove," he murmured to himself. His talk with Mabel Elmsworth had made clear to him the rivalry he had already suspected between the two beauties, and he could measure the full significance of Lizzy's action.

"By Jove—she knew she hadn't much of a chance with Seadown, and quick as lightning she decided to back up the other girl against the common enemy." His own admiration, which, like Seadown's, had hitherto wavered between the two beauties, was transferred in a flash, and once for all, to Lizzy. "Gad, she looks like an avenging goddess—I can almost hear the arrow whizzing past! What a party-leader she'd make," he thought; and added, with inward satisfaction: "Well, she won't be thrown away on this poor nonentity, at all events."

Virginia St. George still stood uncertain, her blue entreating eyes turned with a sort of terror on Lady Churt.

"Seadown!" the latter repeated with an angry smile.

The sound of his name seemed to rouse the tardy suitor. He lifted his head, and his gaze met Virginia's and detected her tears. He flushed to his pale eyebrows.

"This is all a mistake, a complete mistake. I mean," he stammered, turning to Virginia, "it's just a joke of Lady Churt's—who's such an old friend of mine that I know she'll want to be the first to congratulate me . . . if you'll only tell her that she may."

He went up to Virginia, and took possession of her trembling hand. Virginia left it in his, but with her other hand she drew Lizzy Elmsworth to her.

"Oh, Lizzy," she faltered.

Lizzy bestowed on her a kiss of congratulation, and drew back with a little laugh. Mr. Robinson, from his secret observatory, guessed exactly what was passing through her mind. "She's begun to realize that she's thrown away her last hope of Seadown; and very likely she repents her rashness. But the defence of the clan before everything; and I daresay he wasn't the only string to her bow."

Lady Churt stood staring at the two girls with a hard bright intensity which, as the silence lengthened, made Mr. Robinson conscious of a slight shiver down his spine. At length she too broke into a laugh. "Really—" she said. "Really . . ." She was obviously struggling for the appropriate word. She found it in another moment.

"Engaged? Engaged to Seadown? What a delightful surprise! Almost as great a one, I suspect, to Seadown as to Miss St. George herself. Or is it only another of your American jokes—just a way you've invented of keeping Seadown here over Sunday? Well, for my part you're welcome either way. . . ." She paused, and her quick ironic glance travelled from face to face. "But if it's serious, you know—then of course I congratulate you, Seadown. And you too, Miss St. George." She went up to Virginia, and looked her straight in the eyes. "I congratulate you, my dear, on your cleverness, on your good looks, on your success. But you must excuse me for saying that I know Seadown far too well to congratulate you on having caught him for a husband."

She held out a gloved hand rattling with bracelets, just touched Virginia's shrinking fingers, and stalked past Lord Seadown without seeming to see him.

"Conchita, darling, how cleverly you've staged the whole business. We must really repeat it the next time there are *tableaux vivants* at Stafford House." Her eyes took a rapid survey of the young men. "And now I must be off. Mr. Dawnly, will you see me to my fly?"

Mr. Robinson turned from the group with a faint smile as Miles Dawnly advanced to accompany Lady Churt. "What a tit-bit for Dawnly to carry back to town!" he thought. "Poor woman . . . She'll have another try for Seadown, of course—but the game's up, and she probably knows it. I thought she'd have kept her head better. But what fools the cleverest of them can be. . . ." He had the excited sense of having assisted at a self-revelation such as the polite world seldom offers. Every accent of Lady Churt's stinging voice, every lift of her black eyebrows and tremor of her red lips, seemed to bare her before him in her avidity, her disorder, her social arrogance, and her spiritual poverty. The sight curiously re-adjusted Mr. Robinson's sense of values, and his admiration for Lizzy Elmsworth grew with his pity for her routed opponent.

XVIII.

Under the fixed smile of the Folyat Raphael, the Duchess of Tintagel sat at breakfast opposite two of her many daughters, the Ladies Almina Folyat and Gwendolen de Lurey.

When the Duke was present he reserved to himself the right to glance through the morning paper between his cup of tea and his devilled kidneys; but in his absence his mother exercised the privilege, and had the *Morning Post* placed before her as one of her jealously guarded rights.

She always went straight to the Court Circular, and thence (guided by her mother's heart) to the Fashionable Marriages; and now, after a brief glance at the latter, she threw the journal down with a sudden exclamation.

"Oh, Mamma, what is it?" both daughters cried in alarm. Lady Almina thought wistfully: "Probably somebody else she had hopes of for Ermie or me is engaged," and Lady Gwendolen de Lurey, who had five children, and an invalid husband with a heavily mortgaged estate, reflected, as she always did when she heard of a projected marriage in high life, that when her own engagement had been announced everyone took it for granted that Colonel de Lurey would inherit within the year the immense fortune of a paralyzed uncle—who after all was still alive. "So there's no use planning in advance," Lady Gwendolen concluded wearily, glancing at the clock to make sure it was not yet time to take her second girl to the dentist (the children always had to draw lots for the annual visit to the dentist, as it was too expensive to take more than one a year).

"What is it, Mamma?" the daughters repeated apprehensively.

The Duchess laid down the newspaper, and looked first at one and then at the other. "It is—it is—that I sometimes wonder what we bring you all up for!"

"Mamma!"

"Yes; the time, and the worry, and the money—"

"But what in the world has happened, Mamma?"

"What has happened? Only that Seadown is going to marry an American! That a—what's the name?—a Miss Virginia St. George of New York is going to be première Marchioness of England!" She pushed the paper aside, and looked up indignantly at the imbecile smile of the Raphael Madonna. "And nobody cares," she ended bitterly, as though including that insipid masterpiece in her reproach.

Lady Almina and Lady Gwendolen repeated with astonishment: "Seadown?"

"Yes; your cousin Seadown—who used to be at Longlands so often that at one time I *had* hoped . . ."

Lady Almina flushed at the hint, which she took as a personal reproach, and her married sister, seeing her distress, intervened: "Oh, but, Mamma, you know perfectly well that for years Seadown has been Idina Churt's property, and nobody has had a chance against her."

The Duchess gave her dry laugh. "Nobody? It seems this girl had only to lift a finger—"

"I daresay, Mamma, they use means in the States that a well-bred English girl wouldn't stoop to."

The Duchess stirred her tea angrily. "I wish I knew what they are!" she declared, unconsciously echoing the words of an American President when his most successful general was accused of intemperance.

Lady Gwendolen, who had exhausted her ammunition, again glanced at the clock. "I'm afraid, Mamma, I must ask you to excuse me if I hurry off with Clare to the dentist. It's half past nine—and in this house I'm always sure Ushant keeps the clocks on time."

The Duchess looked at her with unseeing eyes. "Oh, Ushant—!" she exclaimed. "If either of you can tell me where Ushant is—or why he's not in London, when the House has not risen—I shall be much obliged to you!"

Lady Gwendolen had slipped away under cover of this outburst, and the Duchess's unmarried daughter was left alone to weather the storm. She thought: "I don't much mind, if only Mamma lets me alone about Seadown."

Lady Almina Folyat's secret desire was to enter an Anglican Sisterhood, and, next to the grievance of her not marrying, she knew none would be so intolerable to her mother as her joining one of these High Church masquerades, as the evangelical Duchess would have called it. "If you want to dress yourself up, why don't you go to a fancy-ball?" the Duchess had parried her daughter's first approach to the subject; and since then Lady Almina had trembled, and bided her time in silence. She had always thought, she could not tell why, that perhaps when Ushant married he might take her side—or at any rate set her the example of throwing off their mother's tyranny.

"Seadown marrying an American! I pity poor Selina Brightlingsea; but she has never known how to manage her children." The Duchess folded the *Morning Post* and gathered up her correspondence. Her morning duties lay before her, stretching out in a long monotonous perspective to the moment when all Ushant's clocks should simultaneously strike the luncheon hour. She felt a sudden discouragement when she thought of it—she to whom the duties of her station had for over thirty years been what its pleasures would have been to other women. Well—it was a joy, even now, to do it all for Ushant, neglectful and ungrateful as he had lately been, and she meant to go on with the task unflinchingly till the day when she could put the heavy burden into the hands of his wife. And what a burden it seemed to her that morning!

She reviewed it all, as though it lay outlined before her on some vast chart: the treasures, the possessions, the heirlooms: the pictures, the jewels—Raphaels, Correggios, Ruysdaels, Vandykes, and Hobbemas, the Naxos marble, the Folyat rubies, the tiaras, the legendary Ushant diamond, the plate, the great gold service for royal dinners, the priceless porcelain, the gigantic ranges of hot-houses at Longlands; and then the poor, the charities, the immense distribution of coal and blankets, committee-meetings, bazaar-openings, foundation-layings; and last, but not least onerous, the recurring Court duties, inevitable as the turn of the seasons. She had been Mistress of the Robes, and would be so again; and her daughter-in-law, of course, could be no less. The Duchess smiled suddenly at the thought of what Seadown's prospects might have been if he had been a future duke, not merely a future marquess, and obliged to initiate his American wife into the official duties of her station! "It will be bad enough for his poor mother as it is—but fancy having to prepare a Miss St. George of New York for her duties as Mistress of the Robes. But no—the Queen would never consent. The Prime Minister would have to be warned. . . . But what nonsense I'm inventing!" thought the Duchess, pushing back her chair, and ringing to tell the butler that she would see the groom-of-the-chambers that morning before the housekeeper.

"No message from the Duke, I suppose?" she asked, as the butler backed toward the threshold.

"Well, Your Grace, I was about to mention to Your Grace that His Grace's valet has just received a telegram instructing him to take down a couple of portmanteaux to Tintagel, where His Grace is remaining for the present."

The door closed, and the Duchess sat looking ahead of her blindly. She had not noticed that her second daughter had also disappeared, but now a sudden sense of being alone—quite alone and unwanted—overwhelmed her, and her little piercing black eyes grew dim.

"I hope," she murmured to herself, "this marriage will be a

warning to Ushant." But this hope had no power to dispel her sense of having to carry her immense burden alone.

When the Duke finally joined his mother at Longlands, he had surprisingly little to say about his long stay at Tintagel. There had been a good many matters to go into with Blair; and he had thought it better to remain till they were settled. So much he said, and no more; but his mere presence gradually gave the Duchess the comfortable feeling of slipping back with him into the old routine.

The shooting-parties had begun, and, as usual, in response to long-established lists of invitations, the guns were beginning to assemble. The Duchess always made out these lists; her son had never expressed any personal preference in the matter. Though he was a moderately good shot, he took no interest in the sport and, as often as he could, excused himself on the ground of business. His cousins Seadown and Dick Marable, both ardent sportsmen and excellent shots, used often to be asked to replace him on such occasions; and he always took it for granted that Seadown would be invited, though Dick Marable no longer figured in the list.

After a few days, therefore, he said to his mother: "I'm afraid I shall have to go up to town tomorrow morning for a day or two."

"To town? Are you never going to allow yourself a proper holiday?" she protested.

"I shan't be away long. When is Seadown coming? He can replace me."

The Duchess's tight lips grew tighter. "I doubt if Seadown comes. In fact, I've done nothing to remind him. So soon after his engagement, I could hardly suggest it, could I?"

The Duke's passive countenance showed a faint surprise. "But surely, if you invite the young lady—"

"And her mamma? And her sister? I understand there's a sister—" the Duchess rejoined ironically.

"Yes," said the Duke, the slow blood rising to his face, "there's a sister."

"Well, you know how long in advance our shooting-parties are made up; even if I felt like adding three unknown ladies to our list, I can't think where I could put them."

Knowing the vast extent of the house, her son received this in a sceptical silence. At length he said: "Has Seadown brought Miss St. George to see you?"

"No. Selina Brightlingsea simply wrote me a line. I fancy she's not particularly eager to show off the future Marchioness."

"Miss St. George is wonderfully beautiful," the Duke murmured.

"My dear Ushant, nothing will convince me that our English beauties can be surpassed.—But since you're here, will you glance at the seating of tonight's dinner-table. The Hopeleighs, you remember, are arriving. . . ."

"I'm afraid I'm no good at dinner-tables. Hadn't you better consult one of the girls?" replied the Duke, ignoring the mention of the expected guests; and as he turned to leave the room his mother thought, with a sinking heart: "I might better have countermanded the Hopeleighs. He has evidently got wind of their coming, and now he's running away from them."

The cottage at Runnymede stood dumb and deserted-looking as the Duke drove up to it. The two mothers, he knew, were in London, with the prospective bride and her friends Lizzy and Mab, who were of course to be among her bridesmaids. In view of the preparations for her daughter's approaching marriage, Mrs. St. George had decided to take a small house in town for the autumn, and, as the Duke also knew, she had chosen Lady Richard Marable's, chiefly because it was near Miss Jacky March's modest dwelling, and because poor Conchita was more than ever in need of ready money.

The Duke of Tintagel was perfectly aware that he should

find neither Mrs. St. George nor her elder daughter at Runnymede; but he was not in quest of either. If he had not learned,
immediately on his return to Longlands, that Jean Hopeleigh and
her parents were among the guests expected there, he might never
have gone up to London, or taken the afternoon train to Staines.
It took the shock of an imminent duty to accelerate his decisions;
and to run away from Jean Hopeleigh had become his most urgent duty.

He had not returned to the cottage since the hot summer day
when he had avoided playing blindman's-buff with a bevy of
noisy girls only by letting himself be drawn into a tiresome political discussion with a pushing young man whose name had escaped him.

Now the whole aspect of the place was changed. The house
seemed empty; the bright awnings were gone, and a cold gray
mist hung in the cedar-boughs and hid the river. But the Duke
found nothing melancholy in the scene. He had a healthy indifference to the worst vagaries of the British climate, and the mist
reminded him of the day when, in the fog-swept ruins of Tintagel,
he had come on the young lady whom it had been his exquisite
privilege to guide back to Trevennick. He had called at the inn
the next day, to re-introduce himself to the young lady's governess, and to invite them both to the new Tintagel; and for a fortnight his visits to the inn at Trevennick, and theirs to the ducal
seat, had been frequent and protracted. But, though he had spent
with them long hours which had flown like minutes, he had never
got beyond saying to himself: "I shan't rest till I've found an
English girl exactly like her." And to be sure of not mistaking the
copy he had continued his study of the original.

Miss Testvalley was alone in the little upstairs sitting-room at
Runnymede. For some time past she had craved a brief respite
from her arduous responsibilities, but now that it had come she
was too agitated to profit by it.

It was startling enough to be met, on returning home with Nan, by the announcement of Virginia's engagement; and when she had learned of Lady Churt's dramatic incursion she felt that the news she herself had to impart must be postponed—the more so as, for the moment, it was merely a shadowy affair of hints, apprehensions, divinations.

If Miss Testvalley could have guessed the consequences of her proposal to give the St. George girls a season in England, she was not sure she would not have steered Mrs. St. George back to Saratoga. Not that she had lost her taste for battle and adventure; but she had developed a tenderness for Nan St. George, and an odd desire to shelter her from the worldly glories her governess's rash advice had thrust upon the family. Nan was different, and Miss Testvalley could have wished a different future for her; she felt that Belgravia and Mayfair, shooting-parties in great country-houses, and the rest of the fashionable routine to which Virginia and the Elmsworth girls had taken so promptly, would leave Nan bewildered and unsatisfied. What kind of life would satisfy her, Miss Testvalley did not profess to know. The girl, for all her flashes of precocity, was in most ways immature, and the governess had a feeling that she must shape her own fate, and that only unhappiness could come of trying to shape it for her. So it was as well that at present there was no time to deal with Nan.

Virginia's impending marriage had thrown Mrs. St. George into a state of chaotic despair. It was too much for her to cope with—too complete a revenge on the slights of Mrs. Parmore and the cruel rebuff of the Assembly ladies. "We might better have stayed in New York," Mrs. St. George wailed, aghast at the practical consequences of a granted prayer.

Miss Jacky March and Conchita Marable soon laughed her out of this. The trembling awe with which Miss March spoke of Virginia's privilege in entering into one of the greatest families in England woke a secret response in Mrs. St. George. She, who had suffered because her beautiful daughters could never hope to marry into the proud houses of Eglinton or Parmore, was about to become the mother-in-law of an earl, who would one day (in a manner as unintelligible to Mrs. St. George as the development of the embryo) turn into the premier Marquess of England. The fact that it was all so unintelligible made it seem more dazzling. "At last Virginia's beauty will have a worthy setting," Miss March exulted; and when Mrs. St. George anxiously murmured: "But look at poor Conchita. Her husband drinks, and behaves dreadfully with other women, and she never seems to have enough money—" Miss March calmed her with the remark: "Well, you ask her if she'd rather be living in Fifth Avenue, with more money than she'd know how to spend."

Conchita herself confirmed this. "Seadown's always been the good boy of the family. He'll never give Jinny any trouble. After all, that hateful entanglement with Idina Churt shows how quiet and domestic he really is. That was why she held him so long. He likes to sit before the same fire every evening. . . . Of course, with Dick it's different. The family shipped him off to South America because they couldn't keep him out of scrapes. And if I took a sentimental view of marriage I'd sit up crying half the night. . . . But I'll tell you what, Mrs. St. George, even that's worth while in London. In New York, if a girl's unhappily married there's nothing to take her mind off it; whereas here there's never really time to think about it. And of course Jinny won't have my worries, and she'll have a position that Dick couldn't have given me even if he'd been a model son and husband."

Most of this was beyond Mrs. St. George's grasp; but the gist of it was consoling, and even flattering. After all, if it was the kind of life Jinny wanted, and if even poor Conchita, and that wretched Jacky March, who'd been so cruelly treated, agreed that London was worth the price—well, Mrs. St. George supposed it must be; and anyhow Mrs. Parmore and Mrs. Eglinton must be rubbing their eyes at this very moment over the announcement of Virginia's engagement in the New York papers. All that London could give, in rank, in honours, in social glory, was only, to Mrs. St. George, a knife to stab New York with—and that weapon she clutched with feverish glee. "If only her father rubs the Brightling-seas into those people he goes with at Newport," she thought vindictively.

The bell rung by the Duke tinkled languidly and long before a flurried maid appeared; and the Duke, accustomed to seeing double doors fly open on velvet carpets at his approach, thought how pleasant it would be to live in a cottage with too few servants, and have time to notice that the mat was shabby, and the brass knocker needed polishing.

Mrs. St. George and Mrs. Elmsworth were up in town. Yes, he knew that; but might he perhaps see Miss Testvalley? He muttered the name as if it were a term of obloquy, and the dazzled maid curtsied him into the drawing-room and rushed up to tell the governess.

"Did you tell His Grace that Miss Annabel was in London too?" Miss Testvalley asked.

No, the maid replied; but His Grace had not asked for Miss Annabel.

"Ah—" murmured the governess. She knew her man well enough by this time to be aware that this looked serious. "It was me he asked for?" And the maid, evidently sharing her astonishment, declared that it was.

"Oh, Your Grace, there's no fire!" Miss Testvalley exclaimed, as she entered the drawing-room a moment later and found her visitor standing close to the icy grate. "No, I won't ring. I can light a fire at least as well as any house-maid."

"Not for me, please," the Duke protested. "I dislike over-heated rooms." He continued to stand near the hearth. "The—the fact is, I was just noticing, before you came down, that this clock appears to be losing about five minutes a day—that is, supposing it to be wound on Sunday mornings."

"Oh, Your Grace—would you come to our rescue? That

clock has bothered Mrs. St. George and Mrs. Elmsworth ever since we came here—"

But the Duke had already opened the glass case and, with his ear to the dial, was sounding the clock as though it were a human lung. "Ah—I thought so!" he exclaimed in a tone of quiet triumph; and for several minutes he continued his delicate manipulations, watched attentively by Miss Testvalley, who thought: "If ever he nags his wife—and I should think he might be a nagger—she will only have to ask him what's wrong with the drawing-room clock. And how many clocks there must be, at Tintagel and Longlands and Folyat House!"

"There—but I'm afraid it ought to be sent to a professional," said the Duke modestly, taking the seat designated by Miss Testvalley.

"I'm sure it will be all right. Your Grace is so wonderful with clocks." The Duke was silent, and Miss Testvalley concluded that doctoring the time-piece had been prompted less by an irrepressible impulse than by the desire to put off weightier matters. "I'm so sorry," she said, "that there's no one here to receive you. I suppose the maid told you that our two ladies have taken a house in town, to prepare for Miss St. George's wedding."

"Yes, I've heard of that," said the Duke, almost solemnly. He cast an anxious glance about him, as if in search of something; and Miss Testvalley thought it proper to add: "And your young friend Annabel has gone to London with her sister."

"Ah—" said the Duke laboriously.

He stood up, walked back to the hearth, gazed at the passive face of the clock, and for a moment followed the smooth movement of the hands. Then he turned to Miss Testvalley. "The wedding is to take place soon?"

"Very soon; in about a month. Colonel St. George naturally wants to be present, and business will take him back to New York before December. In fact, it was at first intended that the wedding should take place in New York—"

"Oh—" murmured the Duke in the politely incredulous tone

of one who implies: "Why attempt such an unheard-of experiment?"

Miss Testvalley caught his meaning and smiled. "You know Lord and Lady Richard were married in New York. It seems more natural that a girl should be married from her own home."

The Duke looked doubtful. "Have they the necessary churches?" he asked.

"Quite adequate," said Miss Testvalley drily.

There was another and heavier silence before the Duke continued: "And does Mrs. St. George intend to remain in London, or will she take a house in the country?"

"Oh, neither. After the wedding Mrs. St. George will go to her own house in New York. She will sail immediately with the Colonel."

"Immediately—" echoed the Duke. He hesitated. "And Miss Annabel—?"

"Naturally goes home with her parents. They wish her to have a season in New York."

This time the silence closed in so oppressively that it seemed as though it had literally buried her visitor. Miss Testvalley felt an impulse to dig him out, but repressed it.

At length the Duke spoke in a hoarse, unsteady voice. "It would be impossible for me—er—to undertake the journey to New York."

Miss Testvalley gave him an amused glance. "Oh, it's settled that Lord Seadown's wedding is to be in London."

"I—I don't mean Seadown's. I mean—my own," said the Duke. He stood up again, walked the length of the room, and came back to her. "You must have seen, Miss Testvalley . . . It has been a long struggle, but I've decided . . ."

"Yes?"

"To ask Miss Annabel St. George—"

Miss Testvalley stood up also. Her heart was stirred with an odd mixture of curiosity and sympathy. She really liked the Duke—but could Annabel ever be brought to like him?

"And so I came down today, in the hope of consulting with you—"

Miss Testvalley interrupted him. "Duke, I must remind you that arranging marriages for my pupils is not included in my duties. If you wish to speak to Mrs. St. George—"

"But I don't!" exclaimed the Duke. He looked so startled that for a moment she thought he was about to turn and take flight. It would have been a relief to her if he had. But he coughed nervously, cleared his throat, and began again.

"I've always understood that in America it was the custom to speak first to the young lady herself. And, knowing how fond you are of Miss St. George, I merely wished to ask—"

"Yes, I am very fond of her," Miss Testvalley said gravely.

"Quite so. And I wished to ask if you had any idea whether her . . . her feelings in any degree corresponded with mine," faltered the anxious suitor.

Miss Testvalley pondered. What should she say? What could she say? What did she really wish to say? She could not, at the moment, have answered any of these questions; she knew only that, as life suddenly pressed closer to her charge, her impulse was to catch her fast and hold her tight.

"I can't reply to that, Your Grace. I can only say that I don't know."

"You don't know?" repeated the Duke in surprise.

"Nan in some ways is still a child. She judges many things as a child would—"

"Yes! That's what I find so interesting . . . so unusual. . . ."

"Exactly. But it makes your question unanswerable. How can one answer for a child who can't yet answer for herself?"

The Duke looked crestfallen. "But it's her childish innocence, her indifference to money and honours and—er—that kind of thing, that I value so immensely. . . ."

"Yes. But you can hardly regard her as a rare piece for your collection."

"I don't know, Miss Testvalley, why you should accuse me of such ideas. . . ."

"I don't accuse you, Your Grace. I only want you to understand that Nan is one thing now, but may be another, quite different, thing in a year or two. Sensitive natures alter strangely after their first contact with life."

"Ah, but I should make it my business to shield her from every contact with life!"

"I'm sure you would. But what if Nan turned out to be a woman who didn't want to be shielded?"

The Duke's countenance expressed the most genuine dismay. "Not want to be shielded? I thought you were a friend of hers," he stammered.

"I am. A good friend, I hope. That's why I advise you to wait, to give her time to grow up."

The Duke looked at her with a hunted eye, and she suddenly thought: "Poor man! I daresay he's trying to marry her against someone else. Running away from the fatted heiress . . . But Nan's worth too much to be used as an alternative."

"To wait? But you say she's going back to the States immediately."

"Well, to wait till she returns to England. She probably will, you know."

"Oh, but I can't wait!" cried the Duke, in the astonished tone of the one who has never before been obliged to.

Miss Testvalley smiled. "I'm afraid you must say that to Annabel herself, not to me."

"I thought you were my friend. I hoped you'd advise me. . . ."

"You don't want me to advise you, Duke. You want me to agree with you."

The Duke considered this for some time without speaking; then he said: "I suppose you've no objection to giving me the London address?" And the governess wrote it down for him with her same disciplined smile.

XIX.

Longlands House, October 25
To Sir Helmsley Thwarte, Bart.
Honourslove, Lowdon, Glos.

My dear Sir Helmsley:

It seems an age since you have given Ushant and me the pleasure of figuring among the guns at Longlands; but I hope next month you will do us that favour.

You are, as you know, always a welcome guest; but I will not deny that this year I feel a special need for your presence. I suppose you have heard that Selina Brightlingsea's eldest boy is marrying an American—so that there will soon be two daughters-in-law of that nationality in the family. I make no comment beyond saying that I fail to see why the virtue and charms of our English girls are not sufficient to satisfy the hearts of our young men. It is useless, I suppose, to argue such matters with the interested parties; one can only hope that, when experience has tested the more showy attractions of the young ladies from the States, the enduring qualities of our own daughters will re-assert themselves. Meanwhile, I am selfishly glad that it is poor Selina, and not I, on whom such a trial has been imposed.

But to come to the point. You know Ushant's exceptionally high standards, especially in family matters, and will not be surprised to hear that he feels we ought to do our cousinly duty towards the Brightlingseas by inviting Seadown, his fiancée, and the latter's family (a Colonel and Mrs. St. George, and a younger daughter) to Longlands. He says it would not matter half as much if Seadown were marrying one of our own kind; and though I do not quite follow this argument, I respect it, as I do all my dear son's decisions. You see what is before me, therefore; and though you may not share Ushant's view, I hope your own family feeling will prompt you to come and help me out with all these strange people.

The shooting is especially good this year, and if you could manage to be with us from the 10th to the 18th of November, Ushant assures me the sport will be worthy of your gun.

Believe me

> Yours very sincerely
>
> Blanche Tintagel

> Longlands House, November 15

To Guy Thwarte Esqre
Care of the British Consulate General,
Rio Janeiro
(To be forwarded)

My dear Boy,

Look on the above address and marvel! You who know how many years it is since I have allowed myself to be dragged into a Longlands shooting-party will wonder what can have caused me to succomb at last.

Well—queerly enough, a sense of duty! I have, as you know, my (rare) moments of self-examination and remorse. One of these penitential phases coincided with Blanche Tintagel's invitation, and as it was reinforced by a moving appeal to my tribal loyalty, I thought I ought to respond, and I did. After all, Tintagel is our Duke, and Longlands is our Dukery, and we local people ought all to back each other up in subversive times like these.

The reason of Blanche's cry for help will amuse you. Do you remember, one afternoon just before you left for Brazil, having asked me to invite to Honourslove two American young ladies, friends of Lady Dick Marable's, who were staying at Allfriars? You were so urgent that my apprehensions were aroused; and I imagine rightly. But, being soft-hearted, I yielded, and Lady Richard appeared with an enchantress, and the enchantress's younger sister, who seemed to me totally eclipsed by her elder, though you apparently thought otherwise. I've no doubt you will recall the incident.

Well—Seadown is to marry the beauty, a Miss St. George, of New York. Rumours, of course, are rife about the circumstances of the marriage. Seadown is said to have been trapped by a clever manoeuvre; but as this report probably emanates from Lady Churt— the Ariadne in the case—it need not be taken too seriously. We know that American business men are "smart," but we also know that their daughters are beautiful; and, having seen the young lady who has supplanted Ariadne, I have no difficulty in believing that her "beaux yeux" sufficed to let Seadown out of prison—for friends and foes agree that the affair with the relentless Idina had become an imprisonment. They also say that Papa St. George is very wealthy, and that consideration must be not without weight—its weight in gold—to the Brightlingseas. I hope they will not be disappointed, but, as you know, I am no great believer in transatlantic fortunes—though I trust, my dear fellow, that the one you are now amassing is beyond suspicion. Otherwise I should find it hard to forgo your company much longer.

It's an odd chance that finds me in an atmosphere so different from that of our shabby old house, on the date fixed for the despatch of my monthly chronicle. But I don't want to miss the South American post, and it may amuse you to have a change from the ordinary small beer of Honourslove. Certainly the contrast is not without interest; and perhaps it strikes me the more because of my disintegrating habit of seeing things through other people's eyes, so that at this moment I am viewing Longlands, not as a familiar and respected monument, but as the unheard-of and incomprehensible phenomenon that a great English country-seat offers to the unprejudiced gaze of the American backwoodsman and his females. I refer to the St. George party, who arrived the day before yesterday, and are still in the first flush of their bewilderment.

The Duchess and her daughters are of course no less bewildered. They have no conception of a society not based on aristocratic institutions, with Inveraray, Welbeck, Chatsworth, Longlands, and so forth as its main supports; and their guests cannot grasp the meaning of such institutions or understand the hundreds of minute observances forming the texture of an old society. This has caused me, for the first time in my life, to see from the outside at once the absurdity and the impressiveness of our great ducal establishments, the futility of their domestic ceremonial, and their importance as custodians of historical tradition and of high (if narrow) social standards. My poor friend Blanche would faint if she knew that I had actually ventured to imagine what an England without dukes might be, perhaps may soon be; but she would be restored to her senses if she knew that, after weighing the evidence for and against, I have decided that, having been afflicted with dukes, we'd better keep 'em. I need hardly add that such problems do not trouble the St. Georges, who have not yet reached the stage of investigating social origins.

I can't imagine how the Duchess and the other ladies deal with Mrs. St. George and her daughters during the daily absence of the guns; but I have noticed that American young ladies cannot be kept quiet for an indefinite time by being shown views of Vesuvius and albums of family water-colours.

Luckily, it's all right for the men. The shooting has never been better, and Seadown, who is in his element, has had the surprise of finding that his future father-in-law is not precisely out of his. Colonel St. George is a good shot; and it is not the least part of the joke that he is decidedly bored by covert shooting, an institution as new to him as dukedoms, and doesn't understand how a man who respects himself can want to shoot otherwise than over a dog. But he accommodates himself well enough to our effete habits, and is in fact a big good-natured easy-going man, with a kind of florid good looks, too-new clothes, and a collection of funny stories, some of which are not new enough.

As to the ladies, what shall I say? The beauty *is* a beauty, as I discovered (you may remember) the moment she appeared at Honourslove. She is precisely what she was then: the obvious, the finished exemplar, of what she professes to be. And, as you know, I have always had a preference for the icily regular. Her composure is unshakeable; and under a surface of American animation I imagine she is as passive as she looks. She giggles with the rest, and says, "Oh, girls," but on her lips such phrases acquire a classic cadence. I suspect her of having a strong will and knowing all the arts of exaction. She will probably get whatever she wants in life, and will give in return only her beautiful profile. I don't believe her soul has a full face. If I were in Seadown's place I should probably be as much in love with her as he is. As a rule I don't care for interesting women; I mean in the domestic relation. I prefer a fine figure-head embodying in a beautiful form a solid bulk of usage and conformity. But I own that figure-heads lack conversation. . . .

Your little friend is not deficient in this respect; and she is also agreeable to look upon. Not beautiful; but there is a subtler form of loveliness, which the unobservant confuse with beauty, and which this young Annabel is on the way to acquire. I say "on the way" because she is still a bundle of engaging possibilities rather than a finished picture. Of the mother there is nothing to say, for that excellent lady evidently requires familiar surroundings to bring out such small individuality as she possesses. In the unfamiliar she becomes invisible; and Longlands and she will never be visible to each other.

Most amusing of all is to watch our good Blanche, her faithful daughters, and her other guests, struggling with the strange beings suddenly thrust upon them. Your little friend (the only one with whom one can converse, by the way) told me that when Lady Brightlingsea heard of Dick Marable's engagement to the Brazilian beauty she cabled to the St. Georges' governess: "Is she black?" Well, the attitude of Longlands towards its transatlantic guests is not much more enlightened than Selina Brightlingsea's. Their bewilderment is so great that, when one of the girls spoke of archery clubs being fashionable in the States, somebody blurted out: "I suppose the Indians taught you?"; and I am constantly expecting them to ask Mrs. St. George how she heats her wigwam in winter.

The only exceptions are Seadown, who contributes little beyond a mute adoration of the beauty, and—our host, young Tintagel. Strange to say, he seems curiously alert and informed about his American visitors; so much so that I'm wondering if his including them in the party is due only to a cousinly regard for Seadown. My short study of the case has almost convinced me that his motives are more interested. His mother, of course, has no suspicion of this—when did our Blanche ever begin to suspect anything until it was emblazoned across the heavens? The first thing she said to me (in explaining the presence of the St. Georges) was that, since so many of our young eligibles were beginning to make these mad American marriages, she thought that Tintagel should see a few specimens at close quarters. *Sancta simplicitas!* If this is her object, I fear the specimens are not well chosen. I suspect that Tintagel had them invited because he's very nearly, if not quite, in love with the younger girl, and, being a sincere believer in the importance of dukes, wants her family to see what marriage with an English duke means.

How far the St. Georges are aware of all this, I can't say. The only one I suspect of suspecting it is the young Annabel; but these Americans, under their forthcoming manner, their surface-gush, as some might call it, have an odd reticence about what goes on underneath. At any rate, the young lady seems to understand something of her environment, which is a sealed book to the others. She has been better educated than her sister, and has a more receptive mind. It seems as though someone had sown in a bare field a sprinkling of history, poetry, and pictures, and every seed had shot up in a flowery tangle. I fancy the sower is the little brown governess of whom you spoke (her pupil says she is little and brown). Miss Annabel asks so many questions about English life in town and country, about rules, customs, traditions, and their why and wherefore, that I sometimes wonder if she is not preparing for a leading part on the social stage; then a glimpse of utter simplicity dispels the idea, and I remember that all her country-people are merciless questioners, and conclude that she has the national habit, but exercises it more intelligently than the others. She is immensely interested in the history of this house, and has an emotional sense at least of its beauties; perhaps the little governess—that odd descendant of old Testavaglia's—has had a hand in developing this side also of her pupil's intelligence.

Miss Annabel seems to be devoted to this Miss Testvalley, who is staying on with the family though both girls are out, and one on the brink of marriage, and who is apparently their guide in the world of fashion—odd as such a rôle seems for an Italian revolutionary. But I understood she had learned her way about the great world as governess in the Brightlingsea and Tintagel households. Her pupil, by the way, tells me that Miss Testvalley knows all about the circumstances in which my D. G. Rossetti was painted, and knows also the mysterious replica with variants which is still in D.G.'s possession, and which he has never been willing to show me. The girl, the afternoon she came to Honourslove, apparently looked closely enough at my picture to describe it in detail to her governess, who says that in the replica the embroidered border of the cloak is *peach-coloured* instead of blue. . . .

All this has stirred up the old collector in me, and when the St. Georges go to Allfriars, where they have been asked to stay before the wedding, Miss Annabel has promised to try to have the governess invited, and to bring her to Honourslove to see the picture. What a pity you won't be there to welcome them! The girl's account of the Testavaglia and her family excites my curiosity almost as much as this report about the border of the cloak.

After the above, which reads, I flatter myself, not unlike a page of Saint-Simon, the home chronicle will seem tamer than ever. Mrs. Bolt has again upset everything in my study by having it dusted. The chestnut mare has foaled, and we're getting on with the ploughing. We are having too much rain—but when haven't we too much rain in England? The new grocer at Little Ausprey threatens to leave, because he says his wife and the non-conformist minister— But there, you always pretend to hate village scandals, and as I have, for the moment, none of my own to tempt your jaded palate, I will end this confession of an impenitent but blameless parent.

Your aff^{te} H.T.

P.S. The good Blanche asked anxiously about you— your health, plans, and prospects, the probable date of your return—and I told her I would give a good deal to know myself. Do you suppose she has her eye on you for Ermie or Almina? Seadown's defection was a hard blow; and if I'm right about Tintagel, heaven help her!

BOOK THREE

XX.

The windows of the Correggio room at Longlands overlooked what was known as the Duchess's private garden, a floral masterpiece designed by the great Sir Joseph Paxton, of Chatsworth and Crystal Palace fame. Beyond an elaborate cast-iron fountain swarmed over by chaste divinities, and surrounded by stars and crescents of bedding plants, an archway in the wall of yew and holly led down a grass avenue to the autumnal distances of the home park. Mist shrouded the slopes dotted with mighty trees, the bare woodlands, the lake pallidly reflecting a low uncertain sky. Deer flitted spectrally from glade to glade, and on remoter hill-sides blurred clusters of sheep and cattle were faintly visible. It had rained heavily in the morning; it would doubtless rain again before night; and in the Correggio room the drip of water sounded intermittently from the long reaches of roof-gutter and from the creepers against the many-windowed house-front.

The Duchess, at the window, stood gazing out over what seemed a measureless perspective of rain-sodden acres. Then, with a sigh, she turned back to the writing-table and took up her pen. A sheet of paper lay before her, carefully inscribed in a small precise hand:

To a Dowager Duchess.
To a Duchess.

To a Marchioness.

To the wife of a Cabinet Minister who has no rank by birth.

To the wife of a Bishop.

To an Ambassador.

The page was inscribed: "Important," and under each headline was a brief formula for beginning and ending a letter. The Duchess scrutinized this paper attentively; then she glanced over another paper bearing a list of names, and finally, with a sigh, took from a tall mahogany stand a sheet of note-paper with "Longlands House" engraved in gold under a ducal coronet, and began to write.

After each note she struck a pencil line through one of the names on the list, and then began another note. Each was short, but she wrote slowly, almost laboriously, like a conscientious child copying out an exercise; and at the bottom of the sheet she inscribed her name, after assuring herself once more that the formula preceding her signature corresponded with the instructions before her. At length she reached the last note, verified the formula, and for the twentieth time wrote out underneath: "Annabel Tintagel."

There before her, in orderly sequence, lay the invitations to the first big shooting-party of the season at Longlands, and she threw down her pen with another sigh. For a minute or two she sat with her elbows on the desk, her face in her hands; then she uncovered her eyes, and looked again at the note she had just signed.

"Annabel Tintagel," she said slowly: "Who *is* Annabel Tintagel?"

The question was one which she had put to herself more than once during the last months, and the answer was always the same: she did not know. Annabel Tintagel was a strange figure with whom she lived, and whose actions she watched with a cold curiosity, but with whom she had never arrived at terms of intimacy, and never would. Of that she was now sure.

There was another perplexing thing about her situation. She was now, to all appearances, Annabel Tintagel, and had been so for over two years; but before that she had been Annabel St. George, and the figure of Annabel St. George, her face and voice, her likes and dislikes, her memories and moods, all that made up her tremulous little identity, though still at the new Annabel's side, no longer composed the central Annabel, the being with whom this strange new Annabel of the Correggio room at Longlands, and the Duchess's private garden, felt herself really one. There were moments when the vain hunt for her real self became so perplexing and disheartening that she was glad to escape from it into the mechanical duties of her new life. But in the intervals she continued to grope for herself, and to find no one.

To begin with, what had caused Annabel St. George to turn into Annabel Tintagel? That was the central problem! Yet how could she solve it, when she could no longer question that elusive Annabel St. George, who was still so near to her, yet as remote and unapproachable as a plaintive ghost?

Yes—a ghost. That was it. Annabel St. George was dead, and Annabel Tintagel did not know how to question the dead, and would therefore never be able to find out why and how that mysterious change had come about. . . .

"The greatest mistake," she mused, her chin resting on her clasped hands, her eyes fixed unseeingly on the dim reaches of the park, "the greatest mistake is to think that we ever know why we do things. . . . I suppose the nearest we can ever come to it is by getting what old people call 'experience.' But by the time we've got that we're no longer the persons who did the things we no longer understand. The trouble is, I suppose, that we change every moment; and the things we did stay."

Of course, she could have found plenty of external reasons: a succession of incidents, leading, as a trail leads across a desert, from one point to another of the original Annabel's career. But what was the use of recapitulating these points, when she was no longer the Annabel whom they had led to this splendid and lonely room set in the endless acres of Longlands?

The curious thing was that her uncertainty and confusion of mind seemed to have communicated themselves to the new world into which she found herself transplanted—and that she was aware of the fact. "They don't know what to make of me, and why should they, when I don't know what to make of myself?" she had once said, in an unusual burst of confidence, to her sister, Virginia, who had never really understood her confidences, and who had absently rejoined, studying herself while she spoke in her sister's monumental cheval-glass, and critically pinching her waist between thumb and fore-finger: "My dear, I've never yet met an Englishman or an Englishwoman who didn't know what to make of a duchess, if only they had the chance to try. The trouble is, you don't give them the chance."

Yes; Annabel supposed it was that. Fashionable London had assimilated with surprising rapidity the lovely transatlantic invaders. Hostesses who only two years ago would have shuddered at the clink of tall glasses and the rattle of cards, now threw their doors open to poker-parties, and offered intoxicating drinks to those to whom the new-fangled afternoon tea seemed too reminiscent of the school-room. Hands trained to draw from a Broadwood the dulcet cadences of "La Sonnambula" now thrummed the banjo to "Juanita" or "The Swanee River." Girls, and even young matrons, pinned up their skirts to compete with the young men in the new game of lawn-tennis on lordly lawns; smoking was spreading from the precincts reserved for it to dining-room and library (it was even rumoured that "the Americans" took sly whiffs in their bedrooms!); Lady Seadown was said to be getting up an amateur Negro minstrel performance for Christmas, which she and Seadown would spend at Longlands, and as for the wild games introduced into country-house parties, there was no denying that, even after a hard day's hunting or shooting, they could tear the men from their after-dinner torpor.

A blast of outer air had freshened the stagnant atmosphere of Belgravian drawing-rooms, and while some sections of London society still shuddered (or affected to shudder) at "the Americans," others, and the uppermost among them, openly applauded and imitated them. But in both groups the young Duchess of Tintagel remained a figure apart. The Dowager Duchess spoke of her as "my perfect daughter-in-law," but praise from the Dowager Duchess had about as much zest as a Sunday-school diploma. In the circle where the pace was set by Conchita Marable, Virginia Seadown, and Lizzy Elmsworth (now married to the brilliant young Conservative member of Parliament, Mr. Hector Robinson), the circle to which, by kinship and early associations, Annabel belonged, she was as much a stranger as in the straitest fastnesses of the peerage. "Annabel has really managed," Conchita drawled with her slow smile, "to be considered unfashionable among the unfashionable"—and the phrase clung to the young Duchess, and catalogued her once for all.

One side of her loved, as much as the others did, dancing, dressing up, midnight romps, practical jokes played on the pompous and elderly; but the other side, the side which had dominated her since her arrival in England, was passionately in earnest and beset with vague dreams and ambitions, in which a desire to better the world alternated with a longing for solitude and poetry.

If her husband could have kept her company in either of these regions, she might not have given a thought to the rest of mankind. But in the realm of poetry the Duke had never willingly risked himself since he had handed up his *vale* at Eton, and a great English nobleman of his generation could hardly conceive that he had anything to learn regarding the management of his estates from a little American girl whose father appeared to be a cross between a stock-broker and a professional gambler, and whom he had married chiefly because she seemed too young and timid to have any opinions on any subject whatever.

"The great thing is that I shall be able to form her," he had said to his mother, on the dreadful day when he had broken the news of his engagement to the horrified Duchess; and the Duchess had replied, with a flash of unwonted insight: "You're very skilful, Ushant; but women are not quite as simple as clocks."

As simple as clocks. How like a woman to say that! The Duke smiled. "Some clocks are not at all simple," he said with an air of superior knowledge.

"Neither are some women," his mother rejoined; but there both thought it prudent to let the discussion drop.

Annabel stood up and looked about the room. It was large and luxurious, with walls of dark-green velvet framed in heavily carved and gilded oak. Everything about its decoration and furnishings—the towering malachite vases, the ponderous writing-table supported on winged geniuses in ormolu, the heavily foliaged wall-lights, the Landseer portrait, above the monumental chimney-piece, of her husband as a baby, playing with an elder sister in a tartan sash—all testified to a sumptuous "re-doing," doubtless dating from the day when the present Dowager had at last presented her lord with an heir. A stupid, oppressive room—somebody else's room, not Annabel's . . . But on three of the velvet-panelled walls hung the famous Correggios; in the half-dusk of an English November they were like rents in the clouds, tunnels of radiance reaching out to pure sapphire distances. Annabel looked at the golden limbs, the parted lips gleaming with laughter, the abandonment of young bodies under shimmering foliage. On dark days—and there were many—these pictures were her sunlight. She speculated about them, wove stories about them, and hung them with snatches of verse from Miss Testvalley's poet cousin. How was it they went?

Beyond all depth away
The heat lies silent at the brink of day:
Now the hand trails upon the viol-string

That sobs, and the brown faces cease to sing,
Sad with the whole of pleasure.

Were there such beings anywhere, she wondered, save in the dreams of poets and painters, such landscapes, such sunlight? The Correggio room had always been the reigning Duchess's private boudoir, and at first it had surprised Annabel that her mother-in-law should live surrounded by scenes before which Mrs. St. George would have veiled her face. But gradually she understood that, in a world as solidly buttressed as the Dowager Duchess's by precedents, institutions, and traditions, it would have seemed more subversive to displace the pictures than to hear the children's Sunday-school lessons under the laughter of those happy pagans. The Correggio room had always been the Duchess's boudoir, and the Correggios had always hung there. "It has always been like that," was the Dowager's invariable answer to any suggestion of change; and she had conscientiously brought up her son in the same creed.

The Duke (who privately considered that his works of art not only conferred prestige on Longlands but were glorified by being there) told Annabel, "They are a trust," when, accompanied by Mr. Rossiter, his curator, a plump hands-rubbing man nervously eager to please, he first showed her the boudoir. "It is deplorable," he observed to Mr. Rossiter, who groaned assent, "that Sir Helmsley Thwarte sold his Titian, to an American, I fancy. Things should stay where they belong. Now he's left with his Holbein, which I think is inferior?"

"Oh, but it's very, *very* fine, and worth a great deal, Your Grace!—far less than the Titian, to be sure; but the Titian is—was—*hors concours.*"

Though she had been married for over two years, it was for her first big house-party at Longlands that the new Duchess was preparing. The first months after her marriage had been spent at Tintagel, in a solitude deeply disapproved of by the Duke's mother, who for the second time found herself powerless to influence her son. The Duke gave himself up with a sort of dogged abandonment to the long-dreamed-of delights of solitude and domestic bliss. The ducal couple (as the Dowager discovered with horror, on her first visit to them) lived like any middle-class husband and wife, tucked away in a wing of the majestic pile, where two butlers and ten footmen should have been drawn up behind the dinner-table, and a groom-of-the-chambers have received the guests in the great hall. Grooms-of-the-chambers, butlers, and footmen had all been relegated to Longlands, and to his mother's dismay only two or three personal servants supplemented the understudies who had hitherto sufficed for Tintagel's simple needs on his trips to Cornwall.

Even after their return to London and Longlands the young couple continued to disturb the Dowager Duchess's peace of mind. The most careful and patient initiation into the functions of the servants attending on her had not kept Annabel from committing what seemed to her mother-in-law inexcusable, perhaps deliberate blunders; such as asking the groom-of-the-chambers to fetch her a glass of water, or bidding one of the under housemaids to lace up her dinner-dress when her own maid was accidentally out of hearing.

"It's not that she's *stupid*, you know, my dear," the Dowager avowed to her old friend Miss Jacky March, "but she puts one out, asking the reason of things that have nothing to do with reasons—such as why the housekeeper doesn't take her meals with the upper servants, but only comes in for dessert. What would happen next, as I said to her, in a house where the housekeeper *did* take her meals with the upper servants? That sort of possibility never occurs to the poor child; yet I really can't call her stupid. I often find her with a book in her hand. I think she thinks too much about things that oughtn't to be thought about," wailed the bewildered Duchess. "And the worst of it is that dear Ushant doesn't seem to know how to help her"—her tone implying that, in any case, such a task should not have been laid on him. And Miss Jacky March murmured her sympathy.

XXI.

Those quiet months in Cornwall, which already seemed so much more remote from the actual Annabel than her girlhood at Saratoga, had been of her own choosing. She did not admit to herself that her first sight of the ruins of the ancient Tintagel had played a large part in her wooing; that if the Duke had been only the dullest among the amiable but dull young men who came to the bungalow at Runnymede she would hardly have given him a second thought. But the idea of living in that magic castle by the sad western sea had secretly tinged her vision of the castle's owner; and she had thought that he and she might get to know each other more readily there than anywhere else. And now, in looking back, she asked herself if it were not her own fault that the weeks at Tintagel had not brought the expected understanding. Instead, as she now saw, they had only made husband and wife more unintelligible to each other. To Annabel, the Cornish castle spoke with that rich low murmur of the past which she had first heard in its mysterious intensity the night when she had lain awake in the tapestried chamber at Allfriars, beside the sleeping Virginia, who had noticed only that the room was cold and shabby. Though the walls of Tintagel were relatively new, they were built on ancient foundations, and crowded with the treasures of the past; and nearby was the mere of Excalibur, and from her windows she could see the dark-gray sea, and sometimes, at night-fall, the mys-

terious barge with black sails putting out from the ruined castle
to carry the dead King to Avalon.

Of all this, nothing existed for her husband. He saw the new
Tintagel only as a costly folly of his father's which family pride
obliged him to keep up with fitting state, in spite of the unfruitful
acres which made its maintenance so difficult. In shouldering
these cares, however, he did not expect his wife to help him, save
by looking her part as a beautiful and angelically pure young
duchess whose only duties consisted in bestowing her angelic presence on entertainments for the tenantry and agricultural prize-
givings. The Duke had grown up under the iron rod of a mother
who, during his minority, had managed not only his property, but
his very life, and he had no idea of letting her authority pass to
his wife. Much as he dreaded the duties belonging to his great
rank, deeply as he was oppressed by them, he was determined to
perform them himself, were it ever so hesitatingly and painfully,
and not to be guided by anyone else's suggestions.

To his surprise, such suggestions were not slow in coming
from Annabel. She had not yet learned that she was expected to
remain a loving and adoring looker-on, and in her daily drives
over the estate (in the smart pony-chaise, with its burnished trap-
pings and gay piebald ponies) she often, out of sheer loneliness,
stopped for a chat at toll-gates, farm-houses and cottages, made
purchases at the village shops, scattered toys and lollipops among
the children, and tried to find out from their mothers what she
could do to help them. It had filled her with wonder to learn that
for miles around, both at Longlands and Tintagel, all these people
in the quaint damp cottages and the stuffy little shops were her
husband's tenants and dependents; that he had the naming of the
rectors and vicars of a dozen churches, and that even the old men
and women in the mouldy alms-houses were there by virtue of
his bounty. But when she had grasped the extent of his power it
seemed to her that to help and befriend those who depended on
him was the best service she could render him. Nothing in her
early bringing-up had directed her mind towards any kind of or-

ganized beneficence, but she had always been what she called "sorry for people," and it seemed to her that there was a good deal to be sorry about in the lot of these people who depended solely, in health and sickness, on a rich man's whim.

The discovery that her interest in them was distasteful to the Duke came to her as a great shock, and left a wound that did not heal. Coming in one day, a few months after their marriage, from one of her exploring expeditions, she was told that His Grace wished to speak to her in his study, and she went in eagerly, glad to seize the chance of telling him at once about the evidences of neglect and poverty she had come upon that very afternoon.

"Oh, Ushant, I'm so glad you're in! Could you come with me at once to the Linfrys' cottage, down by St. Gildas's; you know, that damp place under the bridge, with the front covered with roses? The eldest boy's down with typhoid, and the drains ought to be seen to at once if all the younger ones are not to get it." She spoke in haste, too much engrossed in what she had to say to notice the Duke's expression. It was his silence that roused her; and when she looked at him she saw that his face wore what she called its bolted look—the look she most disliked to see on it. He sat silent, twisting an ivory paper-cutter between his fingers.

"May I ask who told you this?" he asked at length, in a voice like his mother's when she was rebuking an upper housemaid.

"Why, I found it out myself. I've just come from there."

The Duke stood up, knocking the paper-cutter to the floor.

"You've been there? Yourself? To a house where you tell me there is typhoid fever? In your state of health? I confess, Annabel—" His lips twitched nervously under his scanty blond moustache.

"Oh, bother my state of health! I feel all right, really I do. And you know the doctors have ordered me to walk and drive every day."

"But not go and sit with Mrs. Linfry's sick children, in a house reeking with disease."

"But, Ushant, I just had to! There was no one to see about them. And if the house reeks with disease, whose fault is it but ours? They've no sick-nurse, and nobody to help the mother, or tell her what to do; and the doctor comes only every other day."

"Is it your idea, my dear, that I should provide every cottage on my estates, here and elsewhere, with a hospital nurse?" the Duke asked ironically.

"Well, I wish you would! At least there ought to be a nurse in every village, and two in the bigger ones; and the doctor ought to see his patients every day; and the drains—Ushant, you must come with me *at once* and smell the drains!" cried Nan in a passion of entreaty.

She felt the Duke's inexpressive eyes fixed coldly on her.

"If your intention is to introduce typhoid fever at Tintagel, I can imagine no better way of going about it," he began. "But perhaps you don't realize that, though it may not be as contagious as typhus, the doctors are by no means sure . . ."

"Oh, but they *are* sure; only ask them! Typhoid comes from bad drains and infected milk. It can't hurt you in the least to go down and see what's happening at the Linfrys'; and you ought to, because they're your own tenants. Won't you come with me now? The ponies are not a bit tired, and I told William to wait—"

"I wish you would not call Armson by his Christian name; I've already told you that in England head grooms are called by their surnames."

"Oh, Ushant, what *can* it matter? I call you by your surname, but I never can remember about the others. And the only thing that matters now . . ."

The Duke walked to the hearth, and pulled the embroidered bell-rope beside the chimney. To the footman who appeared he said: "Please tell Armson that Her Grace will not require the pony-chaise any longer this afternoon."

"But—" Annabel burst out; then she stood silent till the door closed on the servant. The Duke remained silent also.

"Is that your answer?" she asked at length, her breath coming quickly.

He lifted a more friendly face. "My dear child, don't look so tragic. I'll see Blair; he shall look into the drains. But do try to remember that these small matters concern my agent more than they do me; and that they don't concern you at all. My mother was very much esteemed and respected at Tintagel, but though she managed my affairs so wisely, it never occurred to her to interfere directly with the agent's business, except as regards Christmas festivities, and the annual school-treat. Her holding herself aloof increased the respect that was felt for her; and my wife could not do better than to follow her example."

Annabel stood staring at her husband without speaking. She was too young to understand the manifold inhibitions, some inherited, some peculiar to his own character, which made it impossible for him to act promptly and spontaneously; but she knew him to be by nature not an unkind man, and this increased her bewilderment.

Suddenly a flood of words burst from her. "You tell me to be careful about my health in the very same breath that you say you can't be bothered about these poor people, and that their child's dying is a small matter, to be looked after by the agent. It's for the sake of your own child that you forbid me to go to see them—but I tell you I don't want a child if he's to be brought up with such ideas, if he's to be taught, as you have been, that it's right and natural to live in a palace with fifty servants, and not care for the people who are slaving for him on his own land, to make his big income bigger! I'd rather be dead than see a child of mind taught to grow up as—as you have!"

She broke down and dropped into a seat, hiding her face in her hands. Her husband looked at her without speaking. Nothing in his past experience had prepared him for such a scene, and the consciousness that he did not know how to deal with it increased his irritation. Had Annabel gone mad—or was it only what the doctors called her "condition"? In either case, he felt equally incapable of resolute and dignified action. Of course, if he were told that it was necessary, owing to her "condition," he would send these Linfrys—a shiftless lot—money and food, would ask the doctor to see the boy oftener; though it went hard with him to swallow his own words, and find himself again under a woman's orders. At any rate, he must try to propitiate Annabel, to get her into a more amenable mood; and as soon as possible must take her back to Longlands, where she would be nearer a London physician, accustomed to bringing dukes into the world.

"Annabel," he said, going up to her, and laying his hand on her bent head.

She started to her feet. "Let me alone," she exclaimed, and brushed past him to the door. He heard her cross the hall and go up the stairs in the direction of her own rooms; then he turned back to his desk. One of the drawing-room clocks stood there before him, disembowelled; and as he began (with hands that still shook a little) to put it cautiously together, he remembered his mother's comment: "Women are not always as simple as clocks." Had she been right?

After a while, he laid aside the works of the clock and sat staring helplessly before him. Then it occurred to him that Annabel, in her present mood, was quite capable of going contrary to his orders, and sending for a carriage to drive her back to the Linfrys'—or heaven knew where. He rang again, and asked for his own servant. When the man came, the Duke confided in him that Her Grace was in a somewhat nervous state, and that the doctors wished her to be kept quiet, and not to drive out again that afternoon. Would Bowman therefore see the head coachman at once, and explain that, even if Her Grace should ask for a carriage, some excuse must be found. . . . They were not, of course, to say anything to implicate the Duke, but it must be so managed that Her Grace should not be able to drive out again that day.

Bowman acquiesced, with the look of respectful compassion which his face often wore when he was charged with his master's involved and embarrassed instructions; and the Duke, left alone, continued to sit idly at his writing-table.

Annabel did not reappear that afternoon; and when the Duke, on his way up to dress for dinner, knocked at her sitting-room door, she was not there. He went on to his own dressing-room, but on the way met his wife's maid, and asked if Her Grace were already dressing.

"Oh, no, Your Grace. I thought the Duchess was with Your Grace. . . ."

A little chill caught him about the heart. It was nearly eight o'clock, for they dined late at Tintagel; and the maid had not yet seen her mistress! The Duke said with affected composure: "Her Grace was tired this afternoon. She may have fallen asleep in the drawing-room"—though he could imagine nothing less like the alert and restless Annabel.

Oh, no, the maid said again; Her Grace had gone out on foot two or three hours ago, and had not yet returned.

"On foot?"

"Yes, Your Grace. Her Grace asked for her pony-carriage; but I understood there were orders—"

The Duke interrupted irritably: "The doctor's orders were that Her Grace should not go out at all today."

The maid lowered her lids as if to hide her incredulous eyes, and he felt that she was probably acquainted with every detail of the day's happenings. The thought sent the blood up to the roots of his pale hair, and he challenged her nervously. "You must at least know which way Her Grace said she was going."

"The Duchess said nothing to me, Your Grace. But I understand she sent to the stables and, finding she could not have a carriage, walked away through the park."

"That will do. . . . There's been some unfortunate misunderstanding about Her Grace's orders," stammered the Duke, turning away to his dressing-room.

The day had been raw and cloudy, and with the dusk rain had begun, and was coming down now in a heavy pour that echoed through the narrow twisting passages of the castle and made their sky-lights rattle. And in this icy down-pour his wife, his Duchess, the expectant mother of future dukes, was wandering somewhere on foot, alone and unprotected. Anger and alarm contended in the Duke. If anyone had told him that marrying a simple unworldly girl, hardly out of the school-room, would add fresh complications to a life already over-burdened with them, he would have scoffed at the idea. Certainly he had done nothing to deserve such a fate. And he wondered now why he had been so eager to bring it upon himself. Though he had married for love only a few months before, he was now far more concerned with Annabel as the mother of his son than for her own sake. The first weeks with her had been very sweet—but since then her presence in his house had seemed only to increase his daily problems and bothers. The Duke rang and ordered Bowman to send to the stables for the station-brougham, and when it arrived he drove down at break-neck speed to the Linfrys' cottage. But Nan was not there. The Duke stared at Mrs. Linfry blankly. He did not know where to go next, and it mortified him to reveal his distress and uncertainty to the coachman. "Home!" he ordered angrily, getting into the carriage again; and the dark drive began once more. He was half way back when the carriage stopped with a jerk, and the coachman, scrambling down from the box, called to him in a queer frightened voice.

The Duke jumped out and saw the man lifting a small dripping figure into the brougham. "By the mercy of God, Your Grace . . . I think the Duchess has fainted."

"Drive like the devil. . . . Stop at the stables to send a groom for the doctor," stammered the Duke, pressing his wife in his arms. The rest of the way back was as indistinct to him as to the girl who lay so white on his breast. Bowed over her in anguish, he remembered nothing till the carriage drove under the echoing gate-tower at Tintagel, and lights and servants pressed confusedly about them. He lifted Annabel out, and she opened her eyes and took a few steps across the hall. "Oh—am I here again?" she said, with a little laugh; then she swayed forward, and he caught her as she fell. . . .

To the Duchess of Tintagel who was signing the last notes of invitation for the Longlands shooting-party, the scene at Tintagel and what had followed now seemed as remote and legendary as the tales that clung about the old ruins of Arthur's castle. Annabel had put herself hopelessly in the wrong. She had understood it without being told, she had acknowledged it and wept over it at the time; but the irremediable had been done, and she knew that never, in her husband's eyes, would any evidence of repentance atone for that night's disaster.

The miscarriage which had resulted from her mad expedition through the storm had robbed the Duke of a son; of that he was convinced. He, the Duke of Tintagel, wanted a son, he had a right to expect a son, he would have had a son, if this woman's criminal folly had not destroyed his hopes. The physicians summoned in consultation spoke of the necessity of many months of repose. . . . Even they did not seem to understand that a duke must have an heir, that it is the purpose for which dukes make the troublesome effort of marrying.

It was now well over a year since that had happened, and after long weeks of illness a new Annabel—a third Annabel—had emerged from the ordeal. Life had somehow, as the months passed, clumsily readjusted itself. As far as words went, the Duke had forgiven his wife; they had left the solitude of Tintagel as soon as the physicians thought it possible for the Duchess to be moved; and now, in their crowded London life, and at Longlands, where the Dowager had seen to it that all the old ceremonial was re-established, the ducal pair were too busy, too deeply involved in the incessant distractions and obligations of their station, to have time to remember what was over and could not be mended.

Yet sometimes unwelcome remembrance forced itself upon them. After the move to Longlands, when Annabel was strong enough to walk a fifth of a mile, the Duke had taken her from the Correggio room to the classical sculpture gallery, again accompanied by Mr. Rossiter, who had pointed out busts of the Emperors Hadrian and Trajan, Roman copies of Greek Athenas and Apollos, and black-and-umber pottery of various periods. Nan was reproaching herself for an ignorance of the "classical" which must explain her tepid response to the exhibits, when, approaching the far end of the gallery, she caught her breath at the sight of a bas-relief in warm, almost breathing, marble. A seated woman had one hand on the shoulder of a young girl who was turning away from her. Both figures were in profile. Their drapery rippled as if the stone were liquid, but in their sad faces was the stillness of eternity.

Annabel stood transfixed. "It is the most beautiful thing I have ever seen. . . . Is it Greek?"

"Yes, Your Grace, from Naxos." Mr. Rossiter spoke instructively. "It represents Demeter, or Ceres, goddess of fields and crops, and her daughter Persephone, or Proserpine, who, as you know, was abducted by Dis, or Pluto, god of the underworld. Ceres, disguised as a peasant woman, sought her everywhere. She neglected the agriculture of men, and her absence brought winter. Jupiter commanded Pluto to restore Ceres' daughter to earth for six months of every year. It is a pre-scientific explanation of the seasons."

"I believe the bas-relief is of considerable artistic importance," said the Duke, "but one cannot take great satisfaction in a fragment."

As Annabel looked a question, Mr. Rossiter explained, "It is one side of a throne which originally had a high back and sides. The other side was described by an eighteenth-century traveller who saw the throne entire. It depicted Hera—Juno—seated with an infant on her knees. She, of course, was the goddess who protected women in childbirth."

Annabel winced, and the Duke stiffened. Mr. Rossiter went on hastily: "Its present whereabouts are unknown."

"It is probably in America," the Duke said dourly.

"Probably, pirates that they are over there! . . . That is . . ."
Mr. Rossiter, having floundered from one gaffe to another, rattled
off more information: "Bonaparte took the sculpture as loot, but
the British captured the ship it was on and rescued it. Unfortunately, by the time Your Grace's great-grandfather Tintagel pur-
chased this, the central part and the other side had vanished."

"It should not have been allowed to leave England," said the
Duke.

"But why," Annabel asked, "should it not be returned to
Naxos?"

The two men smiled indulgently. But the Duke, morose
again, repeated: "There is no satisfaction in owning a fragment."

Since then, Annabel had sometimes gone to look at the relief
by herself, without Mr. Rossiter's well-meaning commentary.
Grave, beyond merriment, it was the antithesis of the Correggios,
yet gave her a sense of happiness. It was like the music for the
Dance of the Blessed Spirits in the opera *Orphée,* which she had
seen in London in the months before Jinny's marriage, sad, calm,
and sweet. . . . Perhaps it was the "beyondness" of the Elysian
Fields.

Annabel gradually learned that it was not only one's self that
changed. The ceaseless, mysterious flow of days wore down and
altered the shape of the people nearest one, so that one seemed
fated to be always a stranger among strangers. The mere fact, for
instance, of Annabel St. George's becoming Annabel Tintagel had
turned her mother-in-law, the Duchess of Tintagel, into a dowager duchess, over whose diminished head the mighty roof of
Longlands had shrunk into the modest shelter of a lovely little
rose-clad dower-house at the gates of the park. And everyone else,
as far as Annabel's world reached, seemed to have changed in the
same way.

That, at times, was the most perplexing part of it. When, for
instance, the new Annabel tried to think herself back onto the
verandah of the Grand Union Hotel, waiting for her father and

his stock-broker friends to return from the races, or in the hotel
ball-room with the red damask curtains, dancing with her sister,
Conchita Closson, and the Elmsworth girls, or with the obscure
and infrequent young men who now and then turned up to partner their wasted loveliness—when she thought, for instance, of
Roy Gilling and the handkerchief she had dropped, and he had
kissed and hidden in his pocket—it was like looking at the flickering figures of the magic lanterns she used to see at children's
parties. What was left, now, of those uncertain apparitions, and
what relation, say, did the Conchita Closson who had once
seemed so ethereal and elusive bear to Lady Dick Marable, beautiful still, though she was growing rather too stout, but who had
lost her lovely indolence and detachment, and was now perpetually preoccupied about money, and immersed in domestic difficulties and clandestine consolations—or to Virginia, her own
sister Virginia, who had seemed to Annabel so secure, so aloof,
so disdainful of everything but her own pleasures, but who, as
Lady Seadown, was enslaved to that dull half-asleep Seadown,
absorbed in questions of rank and precedence, and in awe—actually in awe—of her father-in-law's stupid arrogance, and of
Lady Brightlingsea's bewildered condescensions?

Yes; changed, every one of them, vanished out of recognition, as the lost Annabel of the Grand Union had vanished. As
she looked about her, the only figures which seemed to have pre-
served their former outline were those of her father and his business friends; but that, perhaps, was because she so seldom saw
them, because when they appeared, at long intervals, for a hurried
look at transatlantic daughters and grandchildren, they brought
New York with them, solidly and loudly, remained jovially unconscious of any change of scene and habits greater than that
between the east and west shores of the Hudson, and hurried
away again, leaving behind them cheques and christening-mugs,
and unaware to the last that they had been farther from Wall
Street than across the ferry.

Perhaps Mabel Elmsworth was unchanged; no one knew.

Mabel had gone back to America after Virginia's wedding to Sea-down and almost immediately had married. Mrs. Elmsworth had described Caleb Whittaker as an "older" widower from Magnesia, Illinois, and very rich. He collected "pictures and things." Mabel had stood godmother, by proxy, at the christening of Virginia's first-born son. (Lizzy, Jinny's first choice, had suggested that she ask poor Mabel, to whom it would mean so much, so far away from her friends. . . .) Mabel had sent silver mugs, silver spoons, and a golden bowl. Her rare letters told Lizzy that she was well, sent love to all the girls, and wished they'd come and visit.

Ah, yes—and Laura Testvalley, her darling old Val! She had remained her firm sharp-edged self. But then she too was usually away, she had not suffered the erosion of daily contact. The real break with the vanished Annabel had come, the new Annabel sometimes thought, when Miss Testvalley, her task at the St. Georges' ended, had vanished into the seclusion of another family which required "finishing." Miss Testvalley, since she had kissed the bride after the great Tintagel wedding, had re-appeared only at long intervals, and as it were under protest. It was one of her principles—as she had often told Annabel—that a governess should not hang about her former pupils. Later they might require her—there was no knowing, her subtle smile implied—but, once the school-room was closed, she should vanish with the tattered lesson-books, the dreary school-room food, the cod-liver oil, and the chilblain cures.

Perhaps, Annabel thought, if her beloved Val had remained with her, they might between them have rescued the old Annabel, or at least kept up communication with her ghost—a faint tap now and then against the walls which had built themselves up about the new Duchess. But as it was, there was the new Duchess isolated in her new world, no longer able to reach back to her past, and not having yet learned how to communicate with her present.

"In fact"—the realization came to Annabel—"the Duchess

Ushant has in his possession is only a fragment. And he doesn't value fragments highly."

She roused herself from these vain musings, and took up her pen. A final glance at the list had shown her that one invitation had been forgotten—or, if not forgotten, at least postponed.

Dear Mr. Thwarte,

The Duke tells me that you have lately come back to England, and he hopes so much that you can come to Longlands for our next shooting-party, on the 18th. He asks me to say that he is anxious to have a talk with you about the situation at Lowdon. He hopes you intend to stand if Sir Hercules Loft is obliged to resign, and wishes you to know that you will have his full support.

Yours sincerely,

Annabel Tintagel

Underneath she added: "P.S. Perhaps you'd remember me if I signed Nan St. George." But what was the sense of that, when there was no longer anyone of that name? She tore the note up, and re-wrote it without adding the postscript.

XXII.

Guy Thwarte had not been back at Honourslove long enough to expect a heavy mail beside his breakfast plate. His years in Brazil had cut him off more completely than he had realized from his former life; and he was still in the somewhat painful stage of picking up the threads.

"Only one letter? Lucky devil, I envy you!" grumbled Sir Helmsley, taking his seat at the other end of the table and impatiently pushing aside a stack of newspapers, circulars, and letters.

The young man glanced with a smile at his father's correspondence. He knew so well of what it consisted: innumerable bills, dunning letters, urgent communications from bookmakers, tradesmen, the chairmen of political committees or art-exhibitions, scented notes from enamoured ladies, or letters surmounted by mysterious symbols from astrologers, palmists, or alchemists—for Sir Helmsley had dabbled in most of the arts, and bent above most of the mysteries. But today, as usual, his son observed, the bills and the dunning letters predominated. Guy would have to put some order into that; and probably into the scented letters too.

"Yes, I'm between two worlds yet—'powerless to be born' kind of feeling," he said as he took up the solitary note beside his own plate. The writing was unknown to him, and he opened the envelope with indifference.

"Oh, my dear fellow—don't say that; don't say 'powerless,'" his father rejoined, half-pleadingly, but with a laugh.
"There's such a lot waiting to be done; we all expect you to put
your hand to the plough without losing a minute. I was lunching
at Longlands the other day and had a long talk with Ushant. With
old Sir Hercules Loft in his dotage for the last year, there's likely
to be a vacancy at Lowdon at any minute, and the Duke's anxious
to have you look over the ground without losing any time, especially as that new millionaire from Glasgow is said to have
some chance of getting in."

"Oh, well—" Guy was glancing over his letter while his father spoke. He knew Sir Helmsley's great desire was to see him
in the House of Commons, an ambition hitherto curbed by the
father's reduced fortune, but brought into the foreground again
since the son's return from exile with a substantial bank-account.

Guy looked up from his letter. "Tintagel's been talking to
you about it, I see."

"You see? Why—has he written to you already?"

"No. But she has. The new American Duchess—the little girl
I brought here once, you remember?" He handed the letter to his
father, whose face expressed a growing satisfaction as he read.

"Well—that makes it plain sailing. You'll go to Longlands,
of course?"

"To Longlands?" Guy hesitated. "I don't know. I'm not sure
I want to."

"But if Tintagel wants to see you about the seat? You ought
to look over the ground. There may not be much time to lose."

"Not if I'm going to stand—certainly."

"*If!*" shouted Sir Helmsley, bringing down his fist with a
crash that set the Crown Derby cups dancing. "Is that what
you're not sure of? I thought we were agreed before you went
away that it was time there was a Thwarte again in the House of
Commons."

"Oh—before I went away," Guy murmured. His father's
challenge, calling him back suddenly to his old life, the traditional
life of a Thwarte of Honourslove, had shown him for the first

time how far from it all he had travelled in the last years, how remote had become the old sense of inherited obligations which had once seemed the very marrow of his bones.

"Now you've made your pile, as they say out there," Sir Helmsley continued, attempting a lighter tone, but unable to disguise his pride in the incredible fact of his son's achievement—a Thwarte who had made money!—"now that you've made your pile, isn't it time to think of a career? In my simplicity, I imagined it was one of your principal reasons for exiling yourself."

"Yes; I suppose it was," Guy acquiesced.

After this, for a while, father and son faced one another in silence across the breakfast-table, each, as is the way of the sensitive, over-conscious of the other's thoughts. Guy, knowing so acutely what was expected of him, was vainly struggling to become again the young man who had left England over three years earlier; but, strive as he would, he could not yet fit himself into his place in the old scheme of things. The truth was, he was no longer the Guy Thwarte who had left, and would probably never recover that lost self. The break had been too violent, the disrupting influences too powerful. Those dark rich stormy years of exile lay like a raging channel between himself and his old life, and his father's summons only drove him back upon himself.

"You'll have to give me time, sir—I seem to be on both sides of the globe at once," he muttered at length with bent head.

Sir Helmsley stood up abruptly, and, walking around the table, laid a hand on his son's shoulder. "My dear fellow, I'm so sorry. It seems so natural to have you back that I'd forgotten the roots you've struck over there. . . . I'd forgotten the grave. . . ."

Guy's eyes darkened, and he nodded. "All right, sir. . . ." He stood up also. "I think I'll take a turn about the stables." He put the letter from Longlands into his pocket, and walked out alone onto the terrace. As he stood there, looking out over the bare November landscape, and the soft blue hills fading into a low sky, the sense of kinship between himself and the soil began to creep through him once more. What a power there was in these accumulated associations, all so low-pitched, soft, and unobtrusive, yet which were already insinuating themselves through his stormy Brazilian years, and sapping them of their reality! He felt himself becoming again the school-boy who used to go nutting in the hazel-copses of the Red Farm, who fished and bathed in the dark pools of the Love, stole nectarines from the walled gardens, and went cub-hunting in the autumn dawn with his father, glorying in Sir Helmsley's horsemanship, and racked with laughter at his jokes—the school-boy whose heart used to beat to bursting at that bend of the road from the station where you first sighted the fluted chimney-stacks of Honourslove.

He walked across the terrace and, turning the flank of the house, passed under the sculptured lintel of the chapel. A smell of autumn rose from the cold paving, where the kneeling Thwartes elbowed each other on the narrow floor, and under the recumbent effigies the pillows almost mingled their stony fringes. How many there were, and how faithfully hand had joined hand in the endless work of enlarging and defending the family acres! Guy's glance travelled slowly down the double line, from the armoured effigy of the old fighting Thwarte who had built the chapel to the Thornycroft image of his own mother, draped in her marble slumber, just as the boy had seen her, lying with drawn lids, on the morning when his father's telegram had called him back from Eton. How many there were—and all these graves belonged to him, all were linked to the same soil and to one another in an old community of land and blood; together for all time, and kept warm by each other's nearness. And that far-off grave which also belonged to him—the one to which his father had alluded—how remote and lonely it was, off there under tropic skies, among other graves that were all strange to him!

He sat down and rested his face against the back of the

bench in front of him. The sight of his mother's grave had called up that of his young Brazilian wife, and he wanted to shut out for a moment all those crowding Thwartes, and stand again beside her distant headstone. What would life at Honourslove have been if he had brought Paquita home with him instead of leaving her among the dazzling white graves at Rio? He sat for a long time, thinking, remembering, trying to strip his mind of conventions and face the hard reality underneath. It was inconceivable to him now that, in the first months of his marriage, he had actually dreamed of severing all ties with home, and beginning life anew as a Brazilian mine-owner. He saw that what he had taken for a slowly matured decision had been no more than a passionate impulse; and its resemblance to his father's headlong experiments startled him as he looked back. His mad marriage had nearly deflected the line of his life—for a little pale face with ebony hair and curving black lashes, he would have sold his birth-right. And long before the black lashes had been drawn down over the quiet eyes, he had known that he had come to the end of that adventure. . . .

All his life, and especially since his mother's death, Guy Thwarte had been fighting against his admiration for his father, and telling himself that it was his duty to be as little like him as possible; yet more than once he had acted exactly as Sir Helmsley would have acted, or snatched himself back just in time. But in Brazil he had not been in time. . . .

"One brilliant man's enough in a family," he said to himself as he stood up and left the chapel.

Forgetting his projected visit to the stables, he turned back to the house and, crossing the hall, opened the door of his father's study. There he found Sir Helmsley seated at his easel, retouching a delicately drawn water-colour copy of the little Rossetti Madonna above his desk. Sir Helmsley, whose own work was incurably amateurish, excelled in the art of copying, or, rather, interpreting, the work of others; and his water-colour glowed with the deep brilliance of the original picture.

As his son entered he laid down his palette with an embarrassed laugh. "Well, what do you think of it—eh?"

"Beautiful. I'm glad you've not given up your painting."

"Eh—? Oh, well, I don't do much of it nowadays. But I'd promised this little thing to Miss Testvalley," the baronet stammered, reddening handsomely above his auburn beard.

Guy echoed, bewildered: "Miss Testvalley?"

Sir Helmsley coughed, and cleared his throat. "That governess, you know—or perhaps you don't. She was with the little new Duchess of Tintagel before her marriage: came here with her one day to see my Rossettis. She's Dante Gabriel's cousin; didn't I tell you? Remarkable woman—one of the few relations the poet is always willing to see. She persuaded him to sell me a first study of the *Bocca Baciata,* and I was doing this as a way of thanking her. She's with Augusta Glenloe's girls; I see her occasionally when I go over there."

Sir Helmsley imparted this information in a loud, almost challenging voice, as he always did when he had to communicate anything unexpected or difficult to account for. Explaining was a nuisance, and somewhat of a derogation. He resented anything that made it necessary, and always spoke as if his interlocutor ought to have known beforehand the answer to the questions he was putting.

After his bad fall in the hunting-field, the year before Guy's return from Brazil, the county had confidently expected that the lonely widower would make an end by marrying either his hospital nurse or the Gaiety girl who had brightened his solitude during his son's absence. One or the other of these conclusions to a career over-populated by the fair sex appeared inevitable in the case of a brilliant and unsteady widower. Coroneted heads had been frequently shaken over what seemed a foregone conclusion; and Guy had shared these fears. And behold, on his return, he found the nurse gone, the Gaiety girl expensively pensioned off, and the baronet, slightly lame, but with youth renewed by six months of enforced seclusion, apparently absorbed in a little

brown governess who wore violet poplin and heavy brooches of
Roman mosaic, but who (as Guy was soon to observe) had eyes
like torches, and masses of curly-edged dark hair which she was
beginning to braid less tightly, and to drag back less severely from
her broad forehead.

Guy stood looking curiously at his father. The latter's bluster
no longer disturbed him; but he was uncomfortably reminded of
certain occasions when Sir Helmsley, on the brink of an imprudent investment or an impossible marriage, had blushed and explained with the same volubility. Could this outbreak be caused
by one of the same reasons? But no! A middle-aged governess? It
was unthinkable. Sir Helmsley had always abhorred the edifying,
especially in petticoats; and with his strong well-knit figure, his
handsome auburn head, and a complexion clear enough for
blushes, he still seemed, in spite of his accident, built for more
alluring prey. His real interest, Guy concluded, was no doubt in
the Rossetti kinship, and all that it offered to his insatiable imagination. But it made the son wonder anew what other mischief
his inflammable parent had been up to during his own long absence. It would clearly be part of his business to look into his
father's sentimental history, and keep a sharp eye on his future.
With these thoughts in his mind, Guy stood smiling down pater-
nally on his father.

"Well, sir, it's all right," he said. "I've thought it over, and
I'll go to Longlands; when the time comes I'll stand for Lowdon."

His father returned the look with something filial and obedient in his glance. "My dear fellow, it's all right indeed. That's
what I've always expected of you."

Guy wandered out again, drawn back to the soil of Honourslove
as a sailor is drawn to the sea. He would have liked to go over
all its acres by himself, yard by yard, inch by inch, filling his eyes
with the soft slumbrous beauty, his hands with the feel of wrinkled tree-boles, the roughness of sodden autumnal turf, his nos-

trils with the wine-like smell of dead leaves. The place was swathed in folds of funereal mist shot with watery sunshine, and he thought of all the quiet women who had paced the stones of the terrace on autumn days, worked over the simple-garden and among the roses, or sat in the oak parlour at their accounts or their needle-work, speaking little, thinking much, dumb and nourishing as the heaps of faded leaves which mulched the soil for coming seasons.

The "little Duchess's" note had evoked no very clear memory when he first read it; but as he wandered down the glen through the fading heath and bracken he suddenly recalled their walk along the same path in its summer fragrance, and how they had stayed alone on the terrace when the rest of the party followed Sir Helmsley through the house. They had leaned side by side on the balustrade, he remembered, looking out over that dear scene, and speaking scarcely a word; and yet, when she had gone, he knew how near they had been. . . . He even remembered thinking, as his steamer put out from the dock at Liverpool, that on the way home, after he had done his job in Brazil, he would stop a few days in New York to see her. And then he had heard— with wonder and incredulity—the rumour of her ducal marriage; a rumour speedily confirmed by letters and newspapers from home.

That girl—and Tintagel! She had given Guy the momentary sense of being the finest instrument he had ever had in his hand; an instrument from which, when the time came, he might draw unearthly music. Not that he had ever seriously considered the possibility of trying his chance with her; but he had wanted to keep her image in his heart, as something once glimpsed, and giving him the measure of his dreams. And now it was poor little Tintagel who was to waken those melodies; if indeed he could!

Sir Helmsley had informed him of the engagement in one of his sprightly bulletins, with a flourish of commentary:

I flatter myself that I deserve your congratulations in that, unlike the rest of the world—*our* world—I view the match as refreshingly piquant. To think of a little ingénue taking on that *maîtresse femme* Blanche Tintagel! of a little Puritan moving into the temple of Antonio Correggio, whose very saints, whose Assumptions of the Virgin, are voluptuous! As for his classical subjects—you won't have forgotten that day in Parma when we looked at his Jupiter raping Io in the shape of a cloud and agreed that it may be the most erotic painting of the Christian era. . . .

For a few weeks the news had blackened Guy's horizon; but he was far away, he was engrossed in labours and pleasures so remote from his earlier life that the girl's pale image had become etherealized, and then had faded out of existence. He sat down on the balustrade of the terrace, in the corner where they had stood together, and, pulling out her little note, re-read it.

"The writing of a school-girl . . . and the language of dictation," he thought; and the idea vaguely annoyed him. "How on earth could she have married Tintagel? That girl! . . . One would think from the wording of her note that she'd never seen me before. . . . She might at least have reminded me that she'd been here. But perhaps she'd forgotten—as I had!" he ended with a laugh and a shrug. And he turned back slowly to the house, where the estate agent was awaiting him with bills and estimates, and long lists of repairs. Already Sir Helmsley had slipped that burden from his shoulders.

XXIII.

When Their Graces were in residence at Longlands, the Dowager did not often come up from the Dower-House by the gate. But she had the awful gift of omnipresence, of exercising her influence from a distance; so that while the old family friends and visitors at Longlands said, "It's wonderful, how tactful Blanche is—how she keeps out of the young people's way," every member of the household, from its master to the last boots and scullion and gardener's boy, knew that Her Grace's eye was on them all, and the machinery of the tremendous establishment still moving in obedience to the pace and pattern she had set.

But at Christmas the Dowager naturally could not remain aloof. If she had not participated in the Christmas festivities the county would have wondered, the servants have gossiped, the tradesmen have thought the end of the world had come.

"I hope you'll do your best to persuade my mother to come next week. You know she thinks you don't like her," Tintagel had said to his wife, a few days before Christmas.

"Oh, why?" Nan protested, blushing guiltily; and of course she had obediently persuaded, and the Duchess had responded by her usual dry jerk of acquiescence.

For the same reason, the new Duchess's family, and her American friends, had also to be invited; or at least so the Duke thought. The Dowager was not of the same mind; but thirty years of dealings with her son ("from his birth the most obstinate baby in the world") had taught her when to give way; and she did so now.

"It does seem odd, though, Ushant's wanting all those strange people here for Christmas," she confided to her friend Miss March, who had come up with her from the Dower-House, "for I understand the Americans make nothing of any of our religious festivals—do they?"

Miss March, who could not forget that she was the daughter of a clergyman of the Episcopal Church of America, protested gently, as she so often had before: "Oh, but, Duchess, that depends, you know; in our church the feasts and observances are exactly the same as in yours. . . ." But what, she reflected, have such people as the St. Georges to do with the Episcopal Church? They might be Seventh-Day Baptists, or even Mormons, for all she knew.

"Well, it's very odd," murmured the Duchess, who was no longer listening to her.

The two ladies had seated themselves after dinner on a wide Jacobean settee at one end of the "double-cube" saloon, the great room with the Thornhill ceiling and the Mortlake tapestries. The floor had been cleared of rugs and furniture—another shock this to the Dowager, but also accepted with her small stiff smile—and down the middle of the polished *parquet* spun a long line of young (and some more than middle-aged) dancers, led, of course, by Lady Dick Marable and her odd Brazilian brother, whose name the Dowager could never remember, but who looked so dreadfully like an Italian hair-dresser. (A girl who had been a close friend of the Dowager's youth had rent society asunder by breaking her engagement to a young officer in the Blues, and running away with her Italian hair-dresser; and when the Dowager's eyes had first rested on Teddy de Santos-Dios she had thought with a shudder: "Poor Florrie's man must have looked like that.")

Close in Lady Dick's wake (and obviously more interested in her than in his partner) came Miles Dawnly, piloting a bewil-

dered Brightlingsea girl. It was the custom to invite Dawnly wherever Conchita was invited; and even strait-laced hostesses, who
had to have Lady Dick because she "amused the men," were so
thankful not to be obliged to invite her husband that they were
glad enough to let Dawnly replace him. Everyone knew that he
was Lady Dick's chosen attendant, but everyone found it convenient to ignore the fact, especially as Dawnly's own standing, and
his fame as a dancer and a shot, had long since made him a
welcome guest.

The Dowager had always thought it a pity that a man with
such charming manners, and an assured political future, should
seem in no hurry to choose a wife; but when she saw that he had
taken for his partner a Marable rather than a Folyat, she observed
tartly to Miss March that she did not suppose Mr. Dawnly would
ever marry, and hoped Selina Brightlingsea had no illusions on
that point.

At the farther end of the great saloon, the odd little Italian
governess who used to be at Tintagel with the Duchess's younger
daughters, and was now "finishing" the Glenloe girls, sat at the
piano rattling off a noisy reel which she was said to have learned
in the States; and down the floor whirled the dancers, in pursuit
of Lady Richard and the Brazilian.

"Virginia reel, you say they call it? It's all so unusual," repeated the Dowager, lifting her long-handled eye-glass to study
the gyrations of the troop.

Yes; it certainly was unusual to see old Lord Brightlingsea
pirouetting heavily in the wake of his beautiful daughter-in-law
Lady Seadown, and Sir Helmsley Thwarte, incapacitated for pirouetting since his hunting-accident, standing near the piano,
clapping his hands and stamping his sound foot in time with Lady
Dick's Negro chant—they said it was Negro. All so very unusual,
especially when associated with Christmas . . . Usually that noisy
sort of singing was left to the waits, wasn't it? But under this new
rule the Dowager's enquiring eye-glass was really a window opening into an unknown world—a world in whose reality she could

not bring herself to believe. "Ushant might better have left me down at the Dower-House," she murmured with a strained smile to Miss March.

"Oh, Duchess, don't say that! See how they're all enjoying themselves," replied her friend, wondering, deep down under the old Mechlin which draped her bosom, whether Lord Brightlingsea, when the dance swept him close to her sofa, might not pause before her with his inimitable majesty, lift her to her feet, and carry her off into the reel, whose familiar rhythm she felt even now running up from her trim ankles. . . . But Lord Brightlingsea pounded past her unseeingly. . . . Certainly, as men grew older, mere youth seemed to cast a stronger spell over them; the fact had not escaped Miss March.

Lady Brightlingsea was approaching the Dowager's sofa, bearing down on her obliquely and hesitatingly, like a sailing-vessel trying to make a harbour-mouth on a windless day.

"Do come and sit with us, Selina dear," the Dowager welcomed her. "No, no, don't run away, Jacky. . . . Jacky," she explained, "has been telling me about this odd American dance, which seems to amuse them all so much."

"Oh, yes, do tell us," exclaimed Lady Brightlingsea, coming to anchor between the two. "It's called the Virginia reel, isn't it? I thought it was named after my daughter-in-law—Seadown's wife is called Virginia, you know. But she says no; she used to dance it as a child. It's an odd coincidence, isn't it?"

The Dowager was always irritated by Lady Brightlingsea's vagueness. She said, in her precise tone: "Oh, no, it's a very old dance. The Wild Indians taught it to the Americans, didn't they, Jacky?"

"Well, I'm sure it's wild enough," Lady Brightlingsea murmured, remembering the scantily clad savages in the great tapestry at Allfriars, and thankful that the dancers had not so completely unclothed themselves—though the *décolletage* of the young American ladies went some way in that direction.

Miss March roused herself to reply, with a certain impatience: "But no, Duchess; this dance is not Indian. The early English colonists brought it with them from England to Virginia—Virginia was one of the earliest colonies (called after the Virgin Queen, you know), and the Virginia reel is just an old English or Scottish dance."

The Dowager never greatly cared to have her statements corrected; and she particularly disliked its being done before Selina Brightlingsea, whose perpetual misapprehensions were a standing joke with everybody.

"I daresay there are two theories. I was certainly told it was a Wild Indian war-dance."

"It seems much more likely; such a very odd performance," Lady Brightlingsea acquiesced; but neither lady cared to hazard herself further on the unknown ground of American customs.

"It's like their *valse*—that's very odd too," the Dowager continued, after a silence during which she had tried in vain to think up a new topic.

"The *valse*? Oh, but surely the *valse* is familiar enough. My girls were all taught it as a matter of course—weren't yours? I can't think why it shocked our grandparents, can you?"

The Dowager narrowed her lips. "Not *our* version, certainly. But this American *valse*—'waltz,' I think they call it there—"

"Oh, is it different? I hadn't noticed, except that I don't think the young ladies carry themselves with quite as much dignity as ours."

"I should say not! How can they, when every two minutes they have to be prepared to be turned upside down by their partners?"

"*Upside down?*" echoed Lady Brightlingsea, in startled italics. "What in the world, Blanche, do you mean by *upside down?*"

"Well, I mean—not exactly, of course. But turned round. Surely you must have noticed? Suddenly whizzed around and made to dance backward. Jacky, what is it they call it in the States?"

"Reversing," said Miss March, between dry lips. She felt

suddenly weary of hearing her compatriots discussed and criticized and having to explain them; perhaps because she had had to do it too often.

"Ah—'reversing.' Such a strange word too. I don't think it's English. But the thing itself is so strange—suddenly pushing your partner backward. I can't help thinking it's a little indelicate."

The Dowager, with reviving interest, rejoined: "Don't you think these new fashions make all the dances seem—er—rather indelicate? When crinolines were worn, the movements were not as—as visible as now. These tight dresses, with the gathers up the middle of the front—of course one can't contend against the fashion. But one can at least not exaggerate it, as they appear to do in America."

"Yes—I'm afraid they exaggerate everything in America. . . . My dear," Lady Brightlingsea suddenly interrupted herself, "what in the world can they be going to do next?"

The two long rows facing each other (ladies on one side of the room, gentlemen opposite) had now broken up, and two by two, in dancing pairs, forming a sort of giant caterpillar, were spinning off down the double-cube saloon and all the length of the Waterloo room adjoining it, and the Raphael drawing-room beyond, in the direction of the classical sculpture gallery.

"Oh, my dear, where *can* they be going?" Lady Brightlingsea cried.

The three ladies, irresistibly drawn by the unusual sight, rose together and advanced to the middle of the Raphael drawing-room. From there they could see the wild train, headed by Lady Dick's rhythmic chant, sweeping ahead of them down the length of the sculpture gallery, back again to the domed marble hall which formed the axis of the house, and up the state staircase to the floor above.

"My dear—my dear Jacky!" gasped Lady Brightlingsea.

"They'll be going into the bedrooms next, I suppose," said the Dowager with a dry laugh.

But Miss March was beyond speech. She had remembered

that the fear of being late for dinner, and the agitation she always felt on great occasions, had caused her to leave on her dressing-table the duplicate set of fluffy curls which should have been locked up with her modest cosmetics. And in the course of this mad flight Lord Brightlingsea might penetrate to her bedroom, and one of those impious girls might cry out: "Oh, look at Jacky March's curls on her dressing-table!" She felt too faint to speak. . . .

Down the upper gallery spun the accclerated reel, song and laughter growing longer to the accompaniment of hurrying feet. Teddy de Santos-Dios had started "John Peel," and one hunting-song followed on another in rollicking chorus. Door after door was flung open, whirled through, and passed out of again, as the train pursued its turbulent way. Now and then a couple fell out, panting and laughing, to join the line again when it coiled back upon itself—but the Duchess and Guy Thwarte did not re-join it.

Annabel had sunk down on a bench at the door of the Correggio room. Guy Thwarte stood at her side, leaning against the wall and looking down at her. He thought how becomingly the dance had flushed her cheeks and tossed her hair. "Poor little thing! Fun and laughter are all she needs to make her lovely—but how is she ever to get them, at Longlands and Tintagel?" he thought.

The door of the Correggio room stood wide as the dance swept on, and he glanced in, and saw the candle-lit walls, and the sunset glow of the pictures. "By Jove! There are the Correggios!"

Annabel stood up. "You know them, I suppose?"

"Well, rather—but I'd forgotten they were in here."

"In my sitting-room. Come and look. They're so mysterious in this faint light."

He followed her, and stood before the pictures, his blood beating high, as it always did at the sight of beauty.

"It sounds funny," he murmured, "to call the Earthly Paradise a sitting-room."

"I thought so too. But it's always been the Duchess's sitting-room."

"Ah, yes. And that 'always been'—" He smiled and broke off, turning away from her to move slowly about from picture to picture. In the pale-amber candle-glow they seemed full of mystery, as though withdrawn into their own native world of sylvan loves and revels; and for a while he too was absorbed into that world, and almost unconscious of his companion's presence. When at last he turned, he saw that her face had lost the glow of the dance, and become small and wistful, as he had seen it on the day of his arrival at Longlands.

"You're right. They're even more magical than by daylight."

"Yes. I often come here when it's getting dark, and sit among them without making a sound. Perhaps some day, if I'm very patient, I'll tame them, and they'll come down to me. . . ."

Guy Thwarte stood looking at her. "Now, what on earth," he thought, "does Tintagel do when she says a thing like that to him?"

"They must make up to you for a great deal," he began imprudently, heedless of what he was saying.

"For a good deal—yes. But it's rather lonely sometimes, when the only things that seem real are one's dreams."

The young man flushed up, and made a movement toward her. Then he paused, and looked at the pictures with a vague laugh. She was only a child, he reminded himself—she didn't measure what she was saying.

"Oh, well, you'll go to *them,* some day, in their Italian palaces."

"I don't think so. Ushant doesn't care for travelling."

"How does he know? He's never been out of England," broke from Guy impatiently.

"That doesn't matter. He says all the other places are foreign. And he hates anything foreign. There are lots of things he's never done that he feels quite sure he'd hate."

Guy was silent. Again he seemed to himself to be eavesdropping—unintentionally leading her on to say more than she meant; and the idea troubled him.

He turned back to his study of the pictures. "Has it ever occurred to you," he began again after a pause, "that to enjoy them in their real beauty—"

"I ought to persuade Ushant to send them back where they belong?"

"I didn't mean anything so drastic. But did it never occur to you that if you had the courage to sweep away all those . . . those touching little—er . . . family mementos—" His gesture ranged across the closely covered walls, from illuminated views of Vesuvius in action to landscapes by the Dowager Duchess's great-aunts, funereal monuments worked in hair on faded silk, and photographs in heavy oak frames of ducal relatives, famous race-horses, bishops in lawn sleeves, and undergraduates grouped about sporting trophies.

Annabel coloured, but with amusement, not annoyance. "Yes; it did occur to me; and one day I smuggled in a ladder and took them all down—every one."

"By Jove, you did? It must have been glorious."

"Yes; that was the trouble. The Duchess—"

She broke off, and he interposed, with an ironic lift to the brows: "But you're the Duchess."

"Not the real one. You must have seen that already. I don't know my part yet, and I don't believe I ever shall. And my mother-in-law was so shocked that every single picture I'd taken down had to be put back the same day."

"Ah, that's natural too. We're built like that in this tight little island. We fight like tigers against change, and then one fine day accept it without arguing. You'll see: Ushant will come round, and then his mother will, because he has. It's only a question of time—and, luckily, you've plenty of that ahead of you." He looked at her as he spoke, conscious that he was not keeping the admiration out of his eyes, or the pity either, as he had meant to.

Her own eyes darkened, and she glanced away. "Yes, there's

plenty of time. Years and years of it." Her voice dragged on the word as if in imagination she were struggling through the long desert reaches of her own future.

"You don't complain of that, do you?"

"I don't know; I can't tell. I'm not as sure as Ushant how I shall feel about things I've never tried. But I've tried this—and I sometimes think I wasn't meant for it. . . ." She broke off, and he saw the tears in her eyes.

"My dear child—" he began; and then, half embarrassed: "For you *are* a child still, you know. Have you any idea how awfully young you are?"

As soon as he had spoken, he reflected that she was too young not to resent any allusion to her inexperience. She laughed. "Please don't send me back to the nursery! 'Little girls shouldn't ask questions. You'll understand better when you're grown up.' . . . How much longer am I to be talked to like that?"

"I'm afraid that's the most troublesome question of all. The truth is—" He hesitated. "I rather think growing up's largely a question of climate—of sunshine. . . . Perhaps our moral climate's too chilly for you young creatures from across the globe. After all, New York's in the latitude of Naples."

She gave him a perplexed look, and then smiled. "Oh, I know—those burning hot summers . . ."

"You want so much to go back to them?"

"Do I? I can't tell. . . . I don't believe so. . . . But somehow it seems as if this were wrong—my being here. . . . If you knew what I'd give to be able to try again . . . somewhere where I could be myself, you understand, not just an unsuccessful duchess."

"Yes; I do understand—"

"Annabel!" a voice called from the threshold, and Miss Test-valley stood before them, her small brown face full of discernment and resolution.

"My dear, the Duke's asking for you. Your guests are beginning to leave, and I must be off with Lady Glenloe and my girls." Miss Testvalley, with a nod and a smile at young Thwarte, had linked her arm through Annabel's. She paused a moment on the threshold. "Wasn't I right, Mr. Thwarte, to insist on your coming up with us to see the Correggios? I told the Duke it was my doing. They're wonderful by candle-light. But I'm afraid we ought not to have carried off our hostess from her duties."

Laughing and talking, the three descended together to the great hall, where the departing guests were assembled.

XXIV.

The house-party at Longlands was not to break up for another week; but the morning after the Christmas festivities such general lassitude prevailed that the long galleries and great drawing-rooms remained deserted till luncheon.

The Dowager Duchess had promised her son not to return to the Dower-House until the day after Boxing Day. By that time, it was presumed, the new Duchess would be sufficiently familiar with the part she had to play; but, meanwhile, a vigilant eye was certainly needed, if only to regulate the disorganized household service.

"These Americans appear to keep such strange hours; and they ask for such odd things to be sent to their rooms—such odd things to eat and drink. Things that Boulamine has never even heard of. It's just as well, I suppose, that I should be here to keep him and Mrs. Gillings and Manning from losing their heads," said the Dowager to her son, who had come to her sitting-room before joining the guns, who were setting out late on the morning after the dance (thereby again painfully dislocating the domestic routine).

The Duke made no direct answer to his mother's comment. "Of course you must stay," he said, in a sullen tone, and without looking at her.

The Duchess pursed up her lips. "There's nothing I wouldn't

do to oblige you, Ushant; but last night I really felt for a moment—well, rather out of place; and so, I think, did Selina Brightlingsea."

The Duke was gazing steadily at a spot on the wall above his mother's head. "We must move with the times," he remarked sententiously.

"Well—we were certainly doing that last night. Moving faster than the times, I should have thought. At least, almost all of us. I believe you didn't participate. But Annabel—"

"Annabel is very young," her son interrupted.

"Don't think that I forget that. It's quite natural that she should join in one of her native dances. . . . I understand they're very much given to these peculiar dances in the States."

"I don't know," said the Duke coldly.

"Only I should have preferred that, having once joined the dancers, she should have remained with them, instead of obliging people to go hunting all over the house for her and her partner— Guy Thwarte, wasn't it? I admit that hearing her name screamed up and down the passages, and in and out of the bedrooms . . . when she ought naturally to have been at her post in the Raphael room . . . where I have always stood when a party was breaking up . . ."

The Duke twisted his fingers nervously about his watch-chain. "Perhaps you could tell her," he suggested.

The Dowager's little eyes narrowed doubtfully. "Don't you think, Ushant, a word from *you*—?"

He glanced at his watch. "I must be off to join the guns. . . . No, decidedly—I'd rather you explained . . . made her understand. . . ."

His hand on the door, he turned back. "I want, just at present, to say nothing that could . . . could in any way put her off. . . ." The door closed, and his mother stood staring blankly after him. That chit—and he was afraid of—what did he call it?—"putting her off"? Was it possible that he did not know his rights? In the Duchess's day, the obligations of a wife—more especially the wife of a duke—had been as clear as the Ten Commandments. She must give her husband at least two sons, and if in fulfillment of this duty a dozen daughters came uninvited, must receive them with suitably maternal sentiments, and see that they were properly clothed and educated. The Duchess of Tintagel had considered herself lucky in having only eight daughters, but had grieved over Nature's inexorable resolve to grant her no second son.

"Ushant must have two sons—three, if possible. But his wife doesn't seem to understand her duties. Yet she has only to look into the prayer-book. . . . But I've never been able to find out to what denomination her family belong. Not Church people, evidently, or these tiresome explanations would be unnecessary. . . ."

After an interval of uneasy cogitation, the Dowager rang, and sent to enquire if her daughter-in-law could receive her. The reply was that the Duchess was still asleep (at midday—the Dowager, all her life, had been called at a quarter to seven!), but that as soon as she rang she should be given Her Grace's message.

The Dowager, with a sigh, turned back to her desk, which was piled, as usual, with a heavy correspondence. If only Ushant had listened to her, had chosen an English wife in his own class, there would probably have been two babies in the nursery by this time, and a third on the way. And none of the rowdy galloping in and out of people's bedrooms at two in the morning. Ah, if sons ever listened to their mothers . . .

The luncheon hour was approaching when there was a knock on the Dowager's door and Annabel entered. The older woman scrutinized her attentively. No—it was past understanding! If the girl had been a beauty one could, with a great effort of the imagination, have pictured Ushant's infatuation, his subjection; but this pale creature with brown hair and insignificant features, without height, or carriage, or even that look of authority given by inherited dignities even to the squat and the round—what right had she to such consideration? Yet it was clear that she was already getting the upper hand of her husband.

"My dear—do come in. Sit here; you'll be more comfortable. I hope," continued the Duchess with a significant smile, as she pushed forward a deep easy-chair, "that we shall soon have to be asking you to take care of yourself . . . not to commit any fresh imprudence—"

Annabel, ignoring the suggestion, pulled up a straight-backed chair, and seated herself opposite her mother-in-law. "I'm not at all tired," she declared.

"Not consciously, perhaps . . . but all that wild dancing last night—and in fact into the small hours—must have been very exhausting."

"Oh, I've had a good sleep since. It's nearly luncheon-time, isn't it?"

"Not quite. And I so seldom have a chance of saying a word to you alone that I . . . I want to tell you how much I hope, and Ushant hopes, that you won't run any more risks. I know it's not always easy to remember; but last night, for instance, from every point of view, it might have been better if you had remained at your post." The Dowager forced a stiff smile. "Duchesses, you know, are like soldiers; they must often be under arms while others are amusing themselves. And when your guests were leaving, Ushant was naturally—er—surprised at having to hunt over the house for you. . . ."

Annabel looked at her thoughtfully. "Did he ask you to tell me so?"

"No; but he thinks you don't realize how odd it must have seemed to your guests that, in the middle of a party, you should have taken Mr. Thwarte upstairs to your sitting-room—"

"But we didn't go on purpose. We were following the reel, and I dropped out because I was tired; and as Mr. Thwarte wanted to see the Correggios I took him in."

"That's the point, my dear. Guy Thwarte ought to have known better than to take you away from your guests and go up to your sitting-room with you after midnight. His doing so was—er—tactless, to say the least. I don't know what your customs are in the States, but in England—" The Dowager broke off, as if waiting for an interruption which did not come.

Annabel remained silent, and her mother-in-law continued with gathering firmness: "In England such behaviour might be rather severely judged."

Annabel's eyes widened, and she stood up with a slight smile. "I think I'm tired of trying to be English," she pronounced.

The Dowager rose also, drawing herself up to her full height. "Trying to be? But you *are* English. When you became my son's wife you acquired his nationality. Nothing can change that now."

"Nothing?"

"Nothing. Remember what you promised in the marriage service. 'To love and to obey—till death us do part.' Those are not words to be lightly spoken."

"No; but I think I spoke them lightly. I made a mistake."

"A mistake, my dear? What mistake?"

Annabel drew a quick breath. "Marrying Ushant," she said.

The Dowager received this with a gasp. "My dear Annabel—"

"I think it might be better if I left him; then he could marry somebody else, and have a lot of children. Wouldn't that be best?" Annabel continued hurriedly.

The Dowager, rigid with dismay, stood erect, her strong plump hands grasping the rim of her writing-table. Words of wrath and indignation, scornful annihilating phrases, rushed to her lips, but were checked by her son's warning. "I want to do nothing to put her off." If Ushant said that, he meant it; meant, poor misguided fellow, that he was still in love with this thankless girl, this barren upstart, and that his mother, though authorized to coax her back into the right path, was on no account to drive her there by threats or reproaches.

But the mother's heart spoke louder than she meant it to. "If you can talk of your own feelings in that way, even in jest, do you take no account of Ushant's?"

Annabel looked at her musingly. "I don't think Ushant has very strong feelings—about me, I mean."

The Dowager rejoined with some bitterness: "You have hardly encouraged him to, have you?"

"I don't know—I can't explain. . . . I've told Ushant that I don't think I want to be a mother of dukes."

"You should have thought of that before becoming the wife of one. According to English law, you are bound to obey your husband implicitly in . . . er . . . all such matters. . . . But, Annabel, we mustn't let our talk end in a dispute. My son would be very grieved if he thought I'd said anything to offend you—and I've not meant to. All I want is your happiness and his. In the first years of marriage things don't always go as smoothly as they might, and the advice of an older woman may be helpful. Marriage may not be all roses—especially at first; but I know Ushant's great wish is to see you happy and contented in the lot he has offered you—a lot, my dear, that most young women would envy," the Dowager concluded, lifting her head with an air of wounded majesty.

"Oh, I know; that's why I'm so sorry for my mistake."

"Your mistake? But there's been no mistake. Your taking Guy Thwarte up to your sitting-room was quite as much his fault as yours; and you need only show him, by a slightly more distant manner, that he is not to misinterpret it. I daresay less importance is attached to such things in your country—where there are no dukes, of course. . . ."

"No! That's why I'd better go back there," burst from Annabel.

The Dowager looked at her in incredulous wrath. Really, it was beyond her powers of self-control to listen smilingly to such impertinence—such blasphemy, she had almost called it. Ushant himself must stamp out this senseless rebellion. . . .

At that moment the luncheon-gong sent its pompous call down the corridors, and at the sound the Duchess, hurriedly composing her countenance, passed a shaking hand over her neatly crimped *bandeaux*. "The gong, my dear! You must not keep your guests waiting. . . . I'll follow you at once. . . ."

Annabel turned obediently to the door, and went down to join the assembled ladies and the few men who were not out with the guns.

Her heart was beating high after the agitation of her talk with her mother-in-law, but as she descended the wide shallow steps of the great staircase (up and down which it would have been a profanation to gallop, as one used to up and down the steep narrow stairs at home) she reflected that the Dowager, though extremely angry, and even scandalized, had instantly put an end to their discussion when she heard the summons to luncheon. Annabel remembered the endless wordy wrangles between her mother, her sister, and herself, and thought how little heed they would have paid to a luncheon-gong in the thick of one of their daily disputes. Here it was different: everything was done by rule, and according to tradition, and for the Duchess of Tintagel to keep her guests waiting for luncheon would have been an offence against the conventions almost as great as that of not being at her post when the company were leaving the night before. A year ago Annabel would have laughed at these rules and observances; now, though they chafed her no less, she was beginning to see the use of having one's whims and one's rages submitted to some kind of control. "It did no good to anybody to have us come down with red noses to a stone-cold lunch, and go upstairs afterward to sulk in our bedrooms," she thought, and she recalled how her father, when regaled with the history of these domestic disagreements, used to say with a laugh: "What a lot of nonsense it would knock out of you women to have to hoe a potato-field, or spend a week in Wall Street."

Yes; in spite of her anger, in spite of her desperate sense of being trapped, Annabel felt in a confused way that the business of living was perhaps conducted more wisely at Longlands—even though Longlands was the potato-field she was destined to hoe for life.

XXV.

That evening, before dinner, as Annabel sat over her dressing-room fire, she heard a low knock. She had half expected to see her husband appear, after a talk with his mother, and had steeled herself to a repetition of the morning's scene. But she had an idea that the Duchess might have taken her to task only because the Duke was reluctant to do so; she had already discovered that one of her mother-in-law's duties was the shouldering of any job her son wished to be rid of.

The knock, however, was too light to be a man's, and Annabel was not surprised to have it followed by a soft hesitating turn of the door-handle.

"Nan dear—not dressing yet, I hope?" It was Conchita Marable, her tawny hair loosely tossed back, her plump shoulders draped in a rosy dressing-gown festooned with swansdown. It was a long way from Conchita's quarters to the Duchess's, and Annabel was amused at the thought of the Dowager's dismay had she encountered, in the stately corridors of Longlands, a lady with tumbled auburn curls, red-heeled slippers, and a pink deshabille with a marked tendency to drop off the shoulders. A headless ghost would have been much less out of keeping with the traditions of the place.

Annabel greeted her visitor with a smile. Ever since Conchita's first appearance on the verandah of the Grand Union, Annabel's admiration for her had been based on a secret sympathy. Even then the dreamy indolent girl had been enveloped in a sort of warm haze unlike the cool dry light in which Nan's sister and the Elmsworths moved. And Lady Dick, if she had lost something of that early magic, and no longer seemed to Nan to be made of rarer stuff, had yet ripened into something more richly human than the others. A warm fruity fragrance, as of peaches in golden sawdust, breathed from her soft plumpness, the tawny spirals of her hair, the smile which had a way of flickering between her lashes without descending to her lips.

"Darling—you're all alone? Ushant's not lurking anywhere?" she questioned, peering about the room with an air of mystery.

Annabel shook her head. "No. He doesn't often come here before dinner."

"Then he's a very stupid man, my dear," Lady Dick rejoined, her smile resting approvingly on her hostess. "Nan, do you know how awfully lovely you're growing? I always used to tell Jinny and the Elmsworths that one of these days you'd beat us all; and I see the day's approaching. . . ."

Annabel laughed, and her friend drew back to inspect her critically. "If you'd only burn that alms-house dressing-gown, with the horrid row of horn buttons down the front, which looks as if your mother-in-law had chosen it—ah, she *did*? To discourage midnight escapades, I suppose? Darling, why don't you strike, and let me order your clothes for you—and especially your underclothes? It would be a lovely excuse for running over to Paris, and with your order in my pocket I could get the dressmakers to pay all my expenses, and could bring you back a French maid who'd do your hair so that it wouldn't look like a bun just out of the baking-pan. Oh, Nan—fancy having all you've got—the hair and the eyes, and the rank, and the power, and the money. . . ."

Annabel interrupted her. "Oh, but, Conchie, I haven't got much money."

Lady Dick's smiling face clouded, and her clear eyes grew dark. "Now why do you say that? Are you afraid of being asked to help an old friend in a tight place, and do you want to warn me off in advance?"

Annabel looked at her in surprise. "Oh, Conchita, what a beastly question! It doesn't sound a bit like you. . . . Do sit down by the fire. You're shaking all over—why, I believe you're crying!"

Annabel put an arm around her friend's shoulder, and drew her down into an armchair near the hearth, pulling up a low stool for herself, and leaning against Lady Dick's knee with low sounds of sympathy. "Tell me, Conchie darling—what's wrong?"

"Oh, my child, pretty nearly everything." Drawing out a scrap of lace and cambric, Lady Dick applied it to her beautiful eyes; but the tears continued to flow, and Annabel had to wait till they had ceased. Then Lady Dick, tossing back her tumbled curls, continued with a rainbow smile: "But what's the use? They're all things you wouldn't understand. What do you know about being head-over-ears in debt, and in love with one man while you're tied to another—tied tight in one of these awful English marriages, that strangle you in a noose when you try to pull away from them?"

A little shiver ran over Annabel. What indeed did she know of these things? And how much could she admit to Conchita— or, for that matter, to anyone—that she did know? Something sealed her lips, made it, for the moment, impossible even to murmur the sympathy she longed to speak out. She was benumbed, and could only remain silent, pressing Conchita's hands, and deafened by the reverberation of Conchita's last words: "These awful English marriages, that strangle you in a noose when you try to pull away from them." If only Conchita had not put that into words!

"Well, Nan—I suppose now I've horrified you past forgiveness," Lady Dick continued, breaking into a nervous laugh. "You never imagined things of that sort could happen to anybody you knew, did you? I suppose Miss Testvalley told you that only wicked queens in history-books had lovers. That's what they taught us at school. . . . In real life everything ended at the church door, and you just went on having babies and being happy ever after—eh?"

"Oh, Conchie, Conchie," Nan murmured, flinging her arms about her friend's neck. She felt suddenly years older than Conchita, and mistress of the bitter lore the latter fancied she was revealing to her. Since the tragic incident of the Linfry child's death, Annabel had never asked her husband for money, and he had never informed himself if her requirements exceeded the modest allowance traditionally allotted to Tintagel duchesses. It had always sufficed for his mother, and why suggest to his wife that her needs might be greater? The Duke had never departed from the rule inculcated by the Dowager on his coming of age: "In dealing with tenants and dependents, always avoid putting ideas into their heads"—which meant, in the Dowager's vocabulary, giving them a chance to state their needs or ventilate their grievances; and he had instinctively adopted the same system with his wife. "People will always think they want whatever you suggest they might want," his mother had often reminded him: an axiom which had not only saved him thousands of pounds, but protected him from the personal importunities which he disliked even more than the spending of money. He was always reluctant to be drawn into unforeseen expenditure, but he shrank still more from any emotional outlay, and was not sorry to be known (as he soon was) as a landlord who referred all letters to his agents, and resolutely declined personal interviews.

All this flashed through Annabel, but was swept away by Conchita's next words: "In love with one man, and married to another . . ." Yes; that was a terrible fate indeed . . . and yet, and yet . . . might one perhaps not feel less lonely with such a sin on one's conscience than in the blameless isolation of an uninhabited heart?

"Darling, can you tell me . . . anything more? Of course I

want to help you; but I must find out ways. I'm almost as much of a prisoner as you are, I fancy; perhaps more. Because Dick's away a good deal, isn't he?"

"Oh, yes, almost always; but his duns are not. The bills keep pouring in. What little money there is is mine, and of course those people know it. . . . But I'm stone-broke at present, and I don't know what I shall do if you can't help me out with a loan." She drew back, and looked at Nan beseechingly. "You don't know how I hate talking to you about such sordid things. . . . You seem so high above it all, so untouched by anything bad."

"But, Conchie, it's not bad to be unhappy—"

"No, darling; and goodness knows I'm unhappy enough. But I suppose it's wrong to try to console myself—in the way I have. You must think so, I know; but I can't live without affection, and Miles is so understanding, so tender. . . ."

Miles Dawnly, then . . . Two or three times Nan had wondered—had noticed things which seemed to bespeak a tender intimacy; but she had never been sure. . . . The blood rushed to her forehead. As she listened to Conchita she was secretly transposing her friend's words to her own use. "Oh, I know, I know, Conchie—"

Lady Dick lifted her head quickly, and looked straight into her friend's eyes. "You know—?"

"I mean, I can imagine . . . how hard it must be not to . . ."

There was a long silence. Annabel was conscious that Conchita was waiting for some word of solace—material or sentimental, or if possible both; but again a paralyzing constraint descended on her. In her girlhood no one had ever spoken to her of events or emotions below the surface of life, and she had not yet acquired words to express them. At last she broke out with sudden passion: "Conchie—it's all turned out a dreadful mistake, hasn't it?"

"A dreadful mistake—you mean my marriage?"

"I mean all our marriages. I don't believe we're any of us really made for this English life. At least I suppose not, for they seem to take so many things for granted here that shock us and make us miserable; and then they're horrified by things we do quite innocently—like that silly reel last night."

"Oh—you've been hearing about the reel, have you? I saw the old ladies putting their heads together on the sofa."

"If it's not that it's something else. I sometimes wonder—" She paused again, struggling for words. "Conchie, if we just packed up and went home to live, would they really be able to make us come back here, as my mother-in-law says? Perhaps I could cable to Father for our passage-money—"

She broke off, perceiving that her suggestion had aroused no response. Conchita threw herself back in her armchair, her eyes wide with an unfeigned astonishment. Suddenly she burst out laughing.

"You little darling! Is that your panacea? Go back to Saratoga and New York—to the Assemblies and the Charity balls? Do you really imagine you'd like that better?"

"I don't know. . . . Don't you, sometimes?"

"Never! Not for a single minute!" Lady Dick continued to gaze up laughingly at her friend. She seemed to have forgotten her personal troubles in the vision of this grotesque possibility. "Why, Nan, have you forgotten those dreary endless summers at the Grand Union, and the Opera boxes sent on off-nights by your father's business friends, and the hanging round, fishing for invitations to the Assemblies and knowing we'd never have a look-in at the Thursday Evening dances? . . . Oh, if we were to go over for a visit, just a few weeks' splash in New York or Newport, then every door would fly open, and the Eglintons and van der Luydens, and all the other old toadies, would be fighting for us, and fawning at our feet; and I don't say I shouldn't like that— for a while. But to be returned to our families as if we'd been sent to England 'on appro' and hadn't suited—no, thank you! And I wouldn't go for good and all on any terms—not for all the Astor diamonds! Why, you dear little goose, I'd rather starve and freeze here than go back to all the warm houses and the hot baths, and the emptiness of everything—people and places. And as for you, an English duchess, with everything the world can give heaped up at your feet—you may not know it now, you innocent infant, but you'd have enough of Madison Avenue and Seventh Regiment balls inside of a week—and of the best of New York and Newport before your first season was over. There—does the truth frighten you? If you don't believe me, ask Jacky March, or any of the poor little American old maids, or wives or widows, who've had a nibble at it, and have hung on at any price, because London's London, and London life the most exciting and interesting in the world, and once you've got the soot and the fog in your veins you simply can't live without them; and all the poor hangers-on and left-overs know it as well as we do."

Annabel received this in silence. Lady Dick's tirade filled her with a momentary scorn, followed by a prolonged searching of the heart. Her values, of course, were not Conchita's values; that she had always known. London society, of which she knew so little, had never had any attraction for her save as a splendid spectacle; and the part she was expected to play in that spectacle was a burden and not a delight. It was not the atmosphere of London but of England which had gradually filled her veins and penetrated to her heart. She thought of the thinness of the mental and moral air in her own home: the noisy quarrels about nothing, the paltry preoccupations, her mother's feverish interest in the fashions and follies of a society which had always ignored her. At least life in England had a background, layers and layers of rich deep background, of history, poetry, old traditional observances, beautiful houses, beautiful landscapes, beautiful ancient buildings, palaces, churches, cathedrals. Would it not be possible, in some mysterious way, to create for oneself a life out of all this richness, a life which should somehow make up for the poverty of one's personal lot? If only she could have talked of it with a friend . . . Laura Testvalley, for instance, of whom her need was so much greater now than it had ever been in the school-room. Could she not perhaps persuade Ushant to let her old governess come back to her—?

Her thoughts had wandered so far from Lady Dick and her

troubles that she was almost startled to hear her friend speak.

"Well, my dear, which do you think worse—having a lover, or owing a few hundred pounds? Between the two, I've shocked you hopelessly, haven't I? As much as even your mother-in-law could wish. The Dowager doesn't like me, you know. I'm afraid I'll never be asked to Longlands again." Lady Dick stood up with a laugh, pushing her curls back into their loosened coil. Her face looked pale and heavy.

"You haven't shocked me—only made me dreadfully sorry, because I don't know what I can do. . . ."

"Oh, well; don't lie awake over it, my dear," Lady Dick retorted with a touch of bitterness. "But isn't that the dressing-bell? I must hurry off and be laced into my dinner-gown. They don't like unpunctuality here, do they? And tea-gowns wouldn't be tolerated at dinner."

"Conchie—wait!" Annabel was trembling with the sense of having failed her friend and been unable to make her understand why. "Don't think I don't care—Oh, please, don't think that! The way we live makes it look as if there wasn't a whim I couldn't gratify; but Ushant doesn't give me much money, and I don't know how to ask for it."

Conchita turned back and gave her a long look. "The skin-flint! No, I suppose he wouldn't; and I suppose you haven't yet learned to manage him."

Annabel blushed more deeply. "I'm not clever at managing, I'm afraid. You must give me time to look about, to find out—" It had suddenly occurred to her, she hardly knew why, that Guy Thwarte was the one person she could take into her confidence in such a matter. Perhaps he would be able to tell her how to raise the money for her friend. She would pluck up her courage, and ask him the next day.

"Conchie, dear, by tomorrow evening I promise you . . ." she began; and found herself instantly gathered to her friend's bosom.

"Two hundred pounds would save my life, you darling—and five hundred make me a free woman. . . ."

Conchita loosened her embrace. The velvet glow suffused her face again, and she turned joyfully toward the door. But on the threshold she paused, and coming back laid her hands on Annabel's shoulders.

"Nan," she said, almost solemnly, "don't judge me, will you, till you find out for yourself what it's like."

"What what is like? What do you mean, Conchita?"

"Happiness, darling," Lady Dick whispered. She pressed a quick kiss on her friend's cheek; then, as the dressing-bell crashed out its final call, she picked up her rosy draperies and fled down the corridor.

XXVI.

The next morning Annabel, after a restless night, stood at her window watching the dark return of day. Dawn was trying to force a way through leaden mist: every detail, every connecting link, was muffled in fields of rain-cloud. That was England, she thought; not only the English scene but the English life was perptually muffled. The links between these people and their actions were mostly hidden from Annabel; their looks, their customs, their language had implications beyond her understanding.

Sometimes fleeting lights, remote and tender, shot through the fog; then the blanket of incomprehension closed in again. It was like that day in the ruins of Tintagel, the day when she and Ushant had met. . . . As she looked back on it, the scene of their meeting seemed symbolical: in a ruin and a fog. . . . Lovers ought to meet under limpid skies and branches dripping with sunlight, like the nymphs and heroes of Correggio. The "Earthly Paradise," Guy Thwarte had said. . . . The Garden of Eden, with which no other garden could compare—

> *Not that faire field*
> *Of Enna, where Proserpin gathring flowrs*
> *Herself a fairer flowre by gloomie Dis*

Was gatherd, which cost Ceres all that pain
To seek her through the world . . .

Pain had no place in the garden where Correggio's lovers
lived "in unreprovéd pleasures free. . . ." The thought that she
had even imagined Ushant as a lover—imagined him, any more
than his mother, *approving* of pleasure—made Annabel smile,
and she turned away from the window. . . . Those were dreams,
and the reality was: what? First that she must manage to get five
hundred pounds for Conchita; and, after that, must think about
her own future. She was glad she had something active and helpful to do before reverting once more to that dreary problem.

Through her restless night she had gone over and over every
possible plan for getting the five hundred pounds. The idea of
consulting Guy Thwarte had faded before the first hint of daylight. Of course he would offer to lend her the sum; and how
could she borrow from a friend money she saw no possibility of
repaying? And yet to whom else could she apply? The Dowager?
Her mind brushed past the absurd idea . . . and past that of her
sisters-in-law. How bewildered, how scandalized the poor things
would be! Annabel herself, she knew, was bewilderment enough
to them: a wife who bore no children, a duchess who did not yet
clearly understand the duties of a groom-of-the-chambers, or
know what the Chiltern Hundreds were! To all his people it was
as if Ushant had married a savage. . . .

There was her own family, of course; her sister, her friends
the Elmsworths. Annabel knew that in the dizzy up-and-down of
Wall Street, which ladies were not expected to understand, Mr.
Elmsworth was now "on top," as they called it. The cornering of
a heavy block of railway shares, though apparently necessary to
the development of another line, had temporarily hampered her
father and Mr. Closson, and Annabel was aware that Virginia
had already addressed several unavailing appeals to Colonel St.
George. Certainly, if he had cut down the girls' allowances it was
because the poor Colonel could not help himself; and it seemed

only fair that his first aid, whenever it came, should go to Virginia, whose husband's income had to be extracted from the heavily burdened Brightlingsea estate, rather than to the wife of one of England's wealthiest dukes.

One of England's wealthiest dukes! That was what Ushant was; and it was naturally to him that his wife should turn in any financial difficulty. But Annabel had never done so since the Linfry incident, and though she knew the sum she wanted was nothing to a man with Ushant's income, she was as frightened as though she had been going to beg for the half of his fortune.

Of "the girls," Lizzy and Mabel Elmsworth had married men who were rich though devoid of title. But Virginia and poor Conchita had long since become trained borrowers and beggars. Money—or rather the want of it—loomed before them at every turn, and they had mastered most of the arts of extracting it from reluctant husbands or parents. This London life necessitated so many expenditures unknown to the humdrum existence of Madison Avenue and the Grand Union Hotel: Court functions, Royal Ascot, the Cowes yachting season, the entertaining of royalties, the heavy cost of pheasant-shooting, deer-stalking, and hunting, above all (it was whispered) the high play and extravagant luxury prevailing in the inner set to which the lovely newcomers had been so warmly welcomed. You couldn't, Virginia had over and over again explained to Annabel, expect to keep your place in that jealously guarded set if you didn't dress up, live up, play up to its princely standards.

Virginia had spoken of a privilege which she, loveliest of the newcomers, had not yet enjoyed. Two pregnancies had prevented her from going into society; next, the Prince of Wales had gone to India for many months; lastly, her father-in-law's uncle Lord John Brightlingsea had died. Lord John, known as the only man in England more absent-minded than his nephew, had still enjoyed excellent health on the day when he forgot to breathe. Family mourning had drastically curtailed activity at Allfriars; and in town, though Conchita nonchalantly abbreviated the observance

of secluded grief, Virginia had behaved with meticulous, if pee-
vish, decorum. In December, she had at last been able to accept
an invitation to Marlborough House. But when Nan asked about
the event during the Christmas house-party at Longlands, Jinny
had said bitingly, "The *Princess* of Wales received us. *He* was
elsewhere." Nan's puzzled "What difference does that make?"
had incurred the scathing look her sister had so often bestowed
on her in their childhood. "You—little—goose!" Virginia had
said, between her teeth.

Annabel wanted nothing of what her sister and her sister's
friends were fighting for; their needs did not stir her imagination;
she was inattentive to their hints, and they soon learned that,
beyond occasionally letting them charge a dress, or a few yards
of lace, to her account, she could give them little aid.

It was Conchita's appeal which first roused her sympathy.
"You don't know what it is," Lady Dick had said, "to be in love
with one man and tied to another": and instantly the barriers of
Nan's indifference had broken down. It was wrong—it was no
doubt dreadfully wrong—but it was human, it was understand-
able, it made her frozen heart thaw in soft participation. "It must
be less wicked to love the wrong person than not to love anybody
at all," she thought, considering her own desolate plight. . . .

But such thoughts were pure self-indulgence; her immediate
business was the finding of the five hundred pounds to lift Conchita's weight of debt.

When there was a big shooting-party at Longlands, every
hour of the Duke's day was disposed of in advance, and Nan
regarded this as a compensation for the boredom of the occasion.
She was resolved never again to expose herself to the risks of those
solitary months at Tintagel, with an Ushant at leisure to dissect
his grievances as he did his clocks. After much reflection, she
scribbled a note to him: "Please let me know after breakfast when
I can see you"—and to her surprise, when the party rose from
the sumptuous repast which always fortified the guns at Longlands, the Duke followed her into the east drawing-room, where

the ladies were accustomed to assemble in the mornings with their needle-work and correspondence.

"If you'll come to my study for a moment, Annabel."

"Now—?" she stammered, not expecting so prompt a response.

The Duke consulted his watch. "I have a quarter of an hour before we start." She hesitated, and then, reflecting that she might have a better chance of success if there were no time to prolong the discussion, rose and followed him.

The Duke's study at Longlands had been created by a predecessor imbued with loftier ideas of his station, and the glories befitting it, than the present Duke could muster. In size, and splendour of ornament, it seemed singularly out of scale with the nervous little man pacing its stately floor; but it had always been "the Duke's study," and must therefore go on being so till the end of time.

Ushant had seated himself behind his monumental desk, as if to borrow from it the authority he did not always know how to assert unaided. His wife stood before him without speaking. He lifted his head, and forced one of the difficult smiles he had inherited from his mother. "Yes—?"

"Oh, Ushant—I don't know how to begin; and this room always frightens me. It looks as if people came here only when you sent for them to be sentenced."

The Duke met this with a look of genuine bewilderment. Could it be, the look implied, that his wife imagined there was some link between the peerage and the magistracy? "Well, my dear—?"

"Oh, you wouldn't understand. . . . But what I've actually come for is to ask you to let me have five hundred pounds."

There, it was out—about as lightly as if she had hurled a rock at him through one of the tall windows! He frowned and looked down, picking up an emblazoned paper-cutter to examine it.

"Five hundred pounds?" he repeated slowly.

"Yes."

"Do I understand that you are asking me for that sum?"

"Yes."

There was another heavy silence, during which she strained her eyes to detect any change in his guarded face. There was none.

"Five hundred pounds?"

"Oh, please, Ushant—yes!"

"Now—at once?"

"At once," she faltered, feeling that each syllable of his slow interrogatory was draining away a drop of her courage.

The Duke again attempted a smile. "It's a large sum—a very large sum. Has your dress-maker led you on rather farther than your means would justify?"

Nan reddened. Her dress-maker! She wondered if Ushant had ever noticed her clothes? But might he not be offering her the very pretext she needed? She hated having to use one, but since she could think of no other way of getting what she wanted, she resolved to surmount her scruples.

"Well, you see, I've never known exactly what my means were . . . but I do want this money. . . ."

"Never known what your means were? Surely it's all clearly enough written down in your marriage contract."

"Yes; but sometimes one is tempted to spend a trifle more. . . ."

"You must have been taught very little about the value of money to call five hundred pounds a trifle."

Annabel broke into a laugh. "You're teaching me a lot about it now."

The Duke's temples grew red under his straw-coloured hair, and she saw that her stroke had gone home.

"It's my duty to do so," he remarked drily. Then his tone altered, and he said on a conciliatory note: "I hope you'll bear the lesson in mind; but, of course, if you've incurred this debt it must be paid."

"Oh, Ushant—"

He raised his hand to check her gratitude. "Naturally . . . If you'll please tell these people to send me their bill." He rose stiffly, with another glance at his watch. "I said a quarter of an hour—and I'm afraid it's nearly up."

Nan stood crestfallen between her husband and the door. "But you don't understand. . . ." (She wondered whether it was not a mistake to say that to him so often?) "I mean," she hurriedly corrected herself, "it's really no use your bothering. . . . If you'll just make out the cheque to me, I'll . . ."

The Duke stopped short. "Ah—" he said slowly. "Then it's *not* to pay your dress-maker that you want it?"

Nan's quick colour flew to her forehead. "Well, no—it's not. I—I want it for . . . my private charities. . . ."

"Your private charities? Is your allowance not paid regularly? All your private expenditures are supposed to be included in it. My mother was always satisfied with that arrangement."

"Yes; but did your mother never have unexpected calls—? Sometimes one has to help in an emergency. . . ."

The two faced each other in a difficult silence. At length the Duke straightened himself, and said with an attempt at ease: "I'm willing to admit that emergencies may arise; but if you ask me to advance five hundred pounds at a moment's notice, it's only fair that I should be told why you need it."

Their eyes met, and a flame of resistance leapt into Nan's. "I've told you it's for a *private* charity."

"My dear, there should be nothing private between husband and wife."

She laughed impatiently. "Are you trying to say you won't give me the money?"

"I'm saying quite the contrary. I'm ready to give it if you'll tell me what you want it for."

"Ushant—it's a long time since I've asked you a favour, and you can't go on forever ordering me about like a child."

The Duke took a few steps across the room; then he turned

back. His complexion had faded to its usual sandy pallor, and his lips twitched a little. "Perhaps, my dear, you forget how long it is since *I* have asked for a favour. I'm afraid you must make your choice. If I'm not, as you call it, to order you about like a child, you may force me to order you about as a wife." The words came out slowly, haltingly, as if they had cost him a struggle. Nan had noticed before now that anger was too big a garment for him; it always hung on him in uneasy folds. "And now my time is up. I can't keep the guns waiting any longer," he concluded abruptly, turning toward the door.

Annabel stood silent; she could find nothing else to say. She had failed, as she had foreseen she would, for lack of the arts by which cleverer women gain their ends. "You can't force me. . . . No one can force me . . ." she cried out suddenly, hardly knowing what she said; but her husband had already crossed the threshold, and she wondered whether the closing of the door had not drowned her words.

The big house was full of the rumour of the departing sportsmen. Gradually the sounds died out, and the hush of boredom and inactivity fell from the carved and gilded walls. Annabel stood where the Duke had left her. Now she went out into the long vaulted passage on which the study opened. The passage was empty, and so was the great domed and pillared hall beyond. Under such lowering skies the ladies would remain grouped about the fire in the east drawing-room, trying to cheat the empty hours with gossip and embroidery and letter-writing. It was not a day for them to join the sportsmen, even had their host encouraged this new-fangled habit; but it was well known that the Duke, who had no great taste for sport, and practised it only as one of the duties of his station, did not find the task lightened by feminine companionship.

In the lobby of one of the side entrances, Annabel found an old garden hat and cloak. She put them on and went out. It would have been impossible for her, just then, to join the bored but placid group in the east drawing-room. The great house had become like a sepulchre to her; under its ponderous cornices and cupolas she felt herself reduced to a corpse-like immobility. It was only in the open that she became herself again—a stormy self, reckless and rebellious. "Perhaps," she thought, "if Ushant had ever lived in smaller houses he would have understood me better." Was it because all the great people secretly felt as Ushant did—oppressed, weighed down under a dead burden of pomp and precedent—that they built these gigantic palaces to give themselves the illusion of being giants?

Now, out of doors, under the lowering skies, she could breathe and even begin to think. But, for the moment, all her straining thoughts were arrested by the same insurmountable barrier: she was the Duchess of Tintagel, and knew no way of becoming anyone else. . . .

She walked across the gardens opening out from the west wing, and slowly mounted the wooded hillside beyond. It was beginning to rain, and she must find a refuge somewhere—a solitude in which she could fight out this battle between herself and her fate. The slope she was climbing was somewhat derisively crowned by an octagonal temple of Love, with rain-streaked walls of peeling stucco. On the summit of the dome the neglected god spanned his bow unheeded, and underneath it a door swinging loose on broken hinges gave admittance to a room stored with the remnants of derelict croquet-sets and disabled shuttlecocks and grace-rings. It was evidently many a day since the lords of Longlands had visited the divinity who is supposed to rule the world.

Nan, certain of being undisturbed in this retreat, often came there with a book or writing-materials; but she had not intruded on its mouldy solitude since the beginning of winter.

As she entered, a chill fell on her; but she sat down at the stone table in the centre of the dilapidated mosaic floor, and rested her chin on her arms. "I must think it all out," she said aloud, and, closing her eyes, she tried to lose herself in an inner world of self-examination.

But think out what? Does a life-prisoner behind iron bars take the trouble to think out his future? What a waste of time, what a cruel expenditure of hope . . . Once more she felt herself sinking into the depths of childish despair—one of those old be-numbing despairs without past or future which used to blot out the skies when her father scolded her or Miss Testvalley looked disapproving. Her face dropped into her hands, and she broke into sobs of misery.

The sobs murmured themselves out; but for a long time she continued to sit motionless, her face hidden, with a child's reluc-tance to look out again on a world which has wounded it. Her back was turned to the door, and she was so sunk in her distress that she was unconscious of not being alone until she felt a touch on her shoulder, and heard a man's voice: "Duchess—are you ill? What's happened?"

She turned, and saw Guy Thwarte bending over her. "What is it—what has made you cry?" he continued in the compassion-ate tone of a grown person speaking to a frightened child.

Nan jumped up, her wet handkerchief crumpled against her eyes. She felt a sudden anger at this intrusion. "Where did you come from? Why aren't you out with the guns?" she stammered.

"I was to have been, but a message came from Lowdon to say that Sir Hercules is worse, and Ushant has asked me to pre-pare some notes in case the election comes on sooner than we expected. So I wandered up the hill to clear my ideas a little."

Nan stood looking at him with a growing sense of resent-ment. Hitherto his presence had roused only friendly emotions; his nearness had even seemed a vague protection against the un-known and the inimical. But in her present mood that nearness seemed a deliberate intrusion—as though he had forced himself upon her out of some unworthy curiosity, had seized the chance to come upon her unawares.

"Won't you tell me why you are crying?" he insisted gently.

Her childish anger flamed. "I'm not crying," she retorted, hurriedly pushing her handkerchief into her pocket. "And I don't know why you should follow me here. You must see that I want to be alone."

The young man drew back, surprised. He too, since the distant day of their first talk at Honourslove, had felt between them the existence of a mysterious understanding which every subsequent meeting had renewed, though in actual words so little had passed between them. He had imagined that Annabel was glad he should feel this; and her sudden rebuff was like a blow. But her distress was so evident that he did not feel obliged to take her words literally.

"I had no idea of following you," he answered. "I didn't even know you were here; but since I find you in such distress, how can I help asking if there's nothing I can do?"

"No, no, there's nothing!" she cried, humiliated that this man of all others should surprise her in her childish wretchedness. "Well, yes, I *am* crying . . . now. . . . You can see I am, I suppose?" She groped for the handkerchief. "But if anybody could do anything for me, do you suppose I'd be sitting here and just bearing it? It's because there's nothing . . . nothing . . . anyone can do, that I've come here to get away from people, to get away from everything. . . . Can't you understand that?" she ended passionately.

"I can understand your feeling so—yes. I've often thought you must." She gave him a startled look, and her face crimsoned. "But can't you see," he pursued, "that it's hard on a friend—a man who's ventured to think himself your friend—to be told, when he sees you in trouble, that he's not wanted, that he can be of no use, that even his sympathy's unwelcome?"

Annabel continued to look at him with resentful eyes. But already the mere sound of his voice was lessening the weight of her loneliness, and she answered more gently: "You're very kind—"

"Oh, *kind*!" he echoed impatiently.

"You've always been kind to me. I wish you hadn't been away for so long. I used to think that if only I could have asked you about things . . ."

"But—but if you've really thought that, why do you want to drive me away now that I *am* here?" He went up to her with outstretched hands; but she shook her head.

"Because I'm not the Annabel you used to know. I'm a strange woman, strange even to myself, who goes by my name. I suppose in time I'll get to know her, and learn how to live with her."

The angry child had been replaced by a sad but self-controlled woman, who appeared to Guy infinitely farther away and more inaccessible than the other. He had wanted to take the child in his arms and comfort her with kisses; but this newcomer seemed to warn him to be circumspect, and after a pause he rejoined, with a smile: "And can't I be of any use, even to the strange woman?"

Her voice softened. "Well, yes; you can. You are of use. . . . Thinking of you as a friend does help me. . . . It often has. . . ." She went up to him and put her hand in his. "Please believe that. But don't ask me anything more; don't even say anything more now, if you really want to help me."

He held her hand without attempting to disregard either her look or her words. Through the loud beat of his blood a whisper warned him that the delicate balance of their friendship hung on his obedience.

"I want it above all things, but I'll wait," he said, and lifted the hand to his lips.

XXVII.

Like Annabel, the Dowager had known restless hours since their conversation on Boxing Day; but reflection had persuaded her that her daughter-in-law's undisciplined, seditious talk was not to be taken seriously. The absurdity of the idea that any woman, let alone a little American parvenue, could envisage leaving a ducal marriage proved that Annabel had only wanted to annoy. She was doubtless ashamed of herself by now. The best course would be to treat her as if their talk had not taken place. As for reporting it to Ushant . . . that would be undesirable, for the present at least. Having settled this to her satisfaction, the Dowager felt entitled to a little personal pleasure.

As long as she ruled at Longlands, she had found her chief relaxation from ducal drudgery in visiting the immense collection of rare and costly exotic plants in the Duke's famous conservatories. But when she retired to the dower-house, and the sole command of the one small glass-house attached to her new dwelling, she realized the insipidity of inspecting plants in the company of a severe and suspicious head gardener compared with the joys of planting, transplanting, pruning, fertilizing, writing out labels, pressing down the earth about outspread roots, and compelling an obedient underling to do in her own way what she could not manage alone. The Dowager, to whom life had always presented itself in terms of duty, to whom even the closest human relations had come draped in that pale garb, had found her only liberation in gardening, and since amateur horticulture was beginning to be regarded in the highest circles not only as an elegant distraction but almost as one of a great lady's tasks, she had immersed herself in it with a guilty fervour, still doubting if anything so delightful could be quite blameless.

Her son, aware of this passion, which equalled his own for dismembering clocks, was in the habit of going straight to the conservatory when he visited her; and there he found her on the morning after his strange conversation with his wife.

The Dowager was always gratified by his visits, which were necessarily rare during the shooting-parties; but it would have pleased her better had he not come at the exact moment when, gauntleted and aproned, she was transferring some new gloxinia seedlings from one pan to another.

She laid down her implements, scratched a few words in a notebook at her elbow, and dusted the soil from her big gloves.

"Ah, Ushant—" She broke off, struck by his unusual pallor, and the state of his hair. "My dear, you don't look well. Is anything wrong?" she asked in the tone of one long accustomed to being told every morning of some new wrongness in the course of things.

The Duke stood looking down at the long shelf, the heaps of upturned soil and the scattered labels. It occurred to him that, for ladies, horticulture might prove a safe and agreeable pastime.

"Have you ever tried to interest Annabel in this kind of thing?" he asked abruptly. "I'm afraid I'm too ignorant to do it myself—but I sometimes think she would be happier if she had some innocent amusement like gardening. Needle-work doesn't seem to appeal to her."

The Dowager's upper lip lengthened. "I've not had much chance of discussing her tastes with her; but of course, if you wish me to . . . Do you think, for instance, she might learn to care for grafting?"

It was inconceivable to the Duke that anyone should care

for grafting; but, not wishing to betray his complete ignorance of the subject, he effected a diversion by proposing a change of scene. "Perhaps we could talk more comfortably in the drawing-room," he suggested.

His mother laid down her tools. She was used to interruptions, and did not dare to confess how trying it was to be asked to abandon her seedlings at that critical stage. She also weakly regretted having to leave the pleasant temperature of the conservatory for an icy drawing-room in which the fire was never lit till the lamps were brought. Such economies were necessary to a dowager with several daughters but whose meagre allowances were always having to be supplemented; but the Duchess, who was almost as hardened to cold as her son, led the way to the drawing-room without apology.

"I'm sorry," she said, as she seated herself near the lifeless hearth, "that you think dear Annabel lacks amusements."

The Duke stood before the chimney, his hands thrust despondently in his pockets. "Oh—I don't say that. But I suppose she's been used to other kinds of amusement in the States: skating, you know, and dancing—they seem to do a lot of dancing over there; and even in England I suppose young ladies expect more variety and excitement nowadays than they had in your time."

The Dowager, who had taken up her alms-house knitting, dropped a sigh into its harsh folds.

"Certainly in my time they didn't expect much—luckily, for they wouldn't have got it."

The Duke made no reply, but moved uneasily back and forth across the room, as his way was when his mind was troubled.

"Won't you sit down, Ushant?"

"Thanks. No." He returned to his station on the hearth-rug.

"You're not joining the guns?" his mother asked.

"No. Seadown will replace me. The fact is," the Duke continued in an embarrassed tone, "I wanted a few minutes of quiet talk with you."

He paused again, and his mother sat silent, automatically

counting her stitches, though her whole mind was centred on his words. She was sure some pressing difficulty had brought him to her, but she knew that any visible sign of curiosity, or even sympathy, might check his confidence.

"I—I have had a very—er—embarrassing experience with Annabel," he began; and the Dowager lifted her head quickly, but without interrupting the movement of her needles.

The Duke coughed and cleared his throat. ("At the last minute," his mother thought, "he's wondering whether he might not better have held his tongue.") She knitted on.

"A—a really incomprehensible experience." He threw himself into the chair opposite hers. "And completely unexpected. Yesterday morning, just as I was leaving the house, Annabel asked me for a large sum of money—a very large sum. For five hundred pounds."

"Five hundred pounds?" The needles dropped from the Dowager's petrified fingers.

Her son gave a dry laugh. "It seems to me a considerable amount."

The Dowager was thinking hurriedly: "That chit! *I* shouldn't have dared to ask him for a quarter of that amount—much less his father. . . ." Aloud she said: "But what does she want it for?"

"That's the point. She refuses to tell me."

"Refuses—?" the Dowager gasped.

"Er—yes. First she hinted it was for her dress-maker, but, on being pressed, she owned it was not."

"Ah—and then?"

"Well—then . . . I told her I'd pay the debt if she'd incurred it; but only if she would tell me to whom the money was owing."

"Of course. Very proper."

"So I thought; but she said I'd no right to cross-examine her—"

"Ushant! She called it that?"

"Something of the sort. And as the guns were waiting, I said that was my final answer—and there the matter ended."

The Dowager's face quivered with an excitement she had no means of expressing. This woman—he'd offered her five hundred pounds! and she'd refused it. . . .

"It could hardly have ended otherwise," she approved, thinking of the many occasions when a gift of five hundred pounds from the late Duke would have eased her daily load of maternal anxieties.

Her son made no reply, and as he began to move uneasily about the room, it occurred to her that what he wanted was not her approval but her dissent. Yet how could she appear to encourage such open rebellion? "You certainly did right," she repeated.

"Ah, there I'm not sure," the Duke muttered.

"Not sure—?"

"Nothing's gained, I'm afraid, by taking that tone with Annabel." He reddened uncomfortably, and turned his head away from his mother's scrutiny.

"You mean you think you were too lenient?"

"Lord, no—just the contrary. I . . . oh, well, you wouldn't understand. These American girls are brought up differently from our young women. You'd probably say they were spoilt. . . ."

"I should," the Dowager assented drily.

"Well—perhaps. Though in a country where there's no primogeniture I suppose it's natural that daughters should be more indulged. At any rate, I . . . I thought it all over during the day—I thought of nothing else, in fact—and after she'd gone down to dinner yesterday evening I slipped into her room and put an envelope with the money on her dressing-table."

"Oh, Ushant—how generous, how noble!"

The Duchess's hard little eyes filled with sudden tears. Her mind was torn between wrath at her daughter-in-law's incredible exactions, and the thought of what such generosity on her own husband's part might have meant to her, with those eight girls to provide for. But Annabel had no daughters—and no sons—and the Dowager's heart had hardened again before her eyes were dry.

Would there be no limit to Ushant's weakness, she wondered?

"You're the best judge, of course, in any question between your wife and yourself; but I hope Annabel will never forget what she owes you."

The Duke gave a short laugh. "She's forgotten it already."

"Ushant—!"

He crimsoned unhappily and again averted his face from his mother's eyes. He felt a nervous impulse to possess himself of the clock on the mantel-shelf and take it to pieces; but he turned his back on the temptation. "I'm sorry to bother you with these wretched details . . . but . . . perhaps one woman can understand another where a man would fail. . . ."

"Yes—?"

"Well, you see, Annabel has been rather nervous and uncertain lately; I've had to be patient. But I thought—I thought that when she found she'd gained her point about the money . . . she . . . er . . . would wish to show her gratitude. . . ."

"Naturally."

"So, when the men left the smoking-room last night, I went up to her room. It was not particularly late, and she had not undressed. I went in, and she did thank me . . . well, very prettily. . . . But when I . . . when I proposed to stay, she refused, refused absolutely—"

The Dowager's lips twitched. "Refused? On what ground?"

"That she hadn't understood that I'd been driving a bargain with her. The scene was extremely painful," the Duke stammered.

"Yes; I understand." The Dowager paused, and then added abruptly: "So she handed back the envelope—?"

Her son hung his head. "No; there was no question of that."

"Ah—her pride didn't prevent her accepting the bribe, though she refused to stick to the bargain?"

"I can't say there was an actual bargain; but—well, it was something like that. . . ."

The Dowager sat silent, her needles motionless in her hands. This, she thought, was one of the strangest hours of her life, and not the least strange part of it was the light reflected back on her own past, and on the weary nights when she had not dared to lock her door. . . .

"And then—?"

"Then—well, the end of it was that she said she wanted to go away."

"Go away?" Could it be that, after all, Annabel had spoken to her husband in what the Duchess had hoped was a passing fit of hysteria?

"She wants to go off somewhere—she doesn't care where—"

Again the memory of her own past thrust itself between the Duchess and her wrath against her daughter-in-law. Ah, if she had ever dared to ask the late Duke to let her off—to let her go away for a few days, she didn't care where! Even now she trembled inwardly at the thought of what his answer would have been. . . .

"—alone with her old governess. You know; the little Italian woman who's with Augusta Glenloe and came over the other night with the party from Champions."

"You forget." If the Dowager had been speaking to anyone but her son, she would have said it impatiently. "The woman was governess to your sisters." And, she might have added, the recipient of a rare burst of confidence on her own part. She had once mentioned to the governess, apropos of the already scandalous reputation of young Lord Seadown, that the only worry *her* son had given herself and the late Duke was that at school he had neglected the classics, not for cricket (a preference her husband would have condoned), but for mechanics, in fact, for . . . clocks, his fetish for which he had never divulged to his father and which he supposed was unknown to him.

"Well, she seems to be the only person Annabel cares for, or who, at any rate, has any influence over her."

The Duchess, still thinking, pursed her lips. "I have wondered who planted that notion of an Anglican nunnery in Almina's head. One naturally suspects Italians of being Papists, and both Selina Brightlingsea and I made sure Testvalley was *not;* but how could we know that she was High Church?" The Duchess turned her mind from her foolish but duteous youngest daughter to the unguessable inconveniences and embarrassments crammed into a Pandora's box, thus far kept firmly under lid, which the perverse behaviour of her daughter-in-law might let loose. "Do you think her influence over Annabel is good?" she asked at length.

"I've always supposed it was. She's very much attached to Annabel. But how can I ask Augusta Glenloe to lend me her girls' governess to go—I don't know where—with my wife?"

"It's out of the question, of course. Besides, a duchess of Tintagel can hardly wander about the world in that way. But perhaps—if you're sure it's wise to yield to this . . . this fancy of Annabel's . . ."

"Yes, I am," the Duke interrupted uncomfortably.

"Then why not ask Augusta Glenloe to invite her to Champions for a few weeks? I could easily explain . . . putting it on the ground of Annabel's health. Augusta will be glad to do what she can. . . ."

The Duke heaved a deep sigh, at once of depression and relief. It was clear that he wished to put an end to the talk and escape as quickly as possible from the questions in his mother's eyes.

"It might be a good idea."

"Very well. Shall I write?"

The Duke agreed that she might—but of course without giving the least hint. . . .

Oh, of course; naturally the Dowager understood that. Augusta would accept her explanation without seeing anything unusual in it. . . . It wasn't easy to surprise Augusta.

The Duke, with a vague mutter of thanks, turned to the door; and his mother, following him, laid her hand on his arm. "You've been very long-suffering, Ushant; I hope you'll have your reward."

He stammered something inaudible, and went out of the

room. The Dowager, left alone, sat down by the hearth and bent over her scattered knitting. She had forgotten even her haste to get back to the gloxinias. Her son's halting confidences had stirred in her a storm of unaccustomed emotion, and memories of her own past crowded about her like mocking ghosts. But the Dowager did not believe in ghosts, and her grim realism made short work of the phantoms. "There's only one way for an English duchess to behave—and the wretched girl has never learnt it. . . ." Smoothing out her knitting, she restored it to the basket reserved for pauper industries; then she stood up and tied on her gardening-apron. There were still a great many seedlings to transplant, and after that the new curate was coming to discuss arrangements for the next Mothers' Meeting . . . and then—

"There's always something to be done next. . . . I daresay that's the trouble with Annabel—she's never assumed her responsibilities. Once one does, there's no time left for trifles." The Dowager, half way across the room, stopped abruptly. "But what in the world can she want with those five hundred pounds? Certainly not to pay her dress-maker—that was a stupid excuse," she reflected; for even to her untrained eye it was evident that Annabel, unlike her sister and her American friends, had never dressed with the elegance her rank demanded. Yet for what else could she need this money—unless indeed (the Dowager shuddered at the thought) to help some young man out of a scrape? The idea was horrible; but the Dowager had heard it whispered that such cases had been known, even in their own circle; and suddenly she remembered the unaccountable incident of her daughter-in-law's taking Guy Thwarte upstairs to her sitting-room in the course of that crazy reel. . . .

XXVIII.

At Champions, the Glenloe place in Gloucestershire, a broad-faced amiable brick house with regular windows and a pillared porch replaced the ancestral towers which had been destroyed by fire some thirty years earlier and now, in ivy-draped ruin, invited the young and romantic to mourn with them by moonlight.

The family did not mourn; least of all Lady Glenloe, to whom airy passages and plain square rooms seemed infinitely preferable to rat-infested moats and turrets, a troublesome over-crowded muniment-room, and the famous family-portraits that were continually having to be cleaned and re-backed; and who, in rehearsing the saga of the fire, always concluded with a sigh of satisfaction: "Luckily they saved the stuffed birds."

It was doubtful if the other members of the family had ever noticed anything about the house but the temperature of the rooms, and the relative comfort of the armchairs. Certainly Lady Glenloe had done nothing to extend their observations. She herself had accomplished the unusual feat of having only two daughters and four sons; and this achievement, and the fact that Lord Glenloe had lived for years on a ranch in Canada, and came to England but briefly and rarely, had obliged his wife to be a frequent traveller, going from the soldier sons in Canada and India to the gold-miner in South Africa and the Embassy attaché at St. Petersburg, and returning home via the Northwest and the marital ranch.

Such travels, infrequent in Lady Glenloe's day, had opened her eyes to matters undreamed of by most ladies of the aristocracy, and she had brought back from her wanderings a mind tanned and toughened like her complexion by the healthy hardships of the road. Her two daughters, though left at home, and kept in due subordination, had caught a whiff of the gales that whistled through her mental rigging, and the talk at Champions was full of easy allusions to Thibet, Salt Lake City, Tsarskoë, or Delhi, as to all of which Lady Glenloe could furnish statistical items, and facts on plant and bird distribution. In this atmosphere Miss Testvalley breathed more freely than in her other educational prisons, and when she appeared on the station platform to welcome the young Duchess, the latter, though absorbed in her own troubles, instantly noticed the change in her governess. At Longlands, during the Christmas revels, there had been no time or opportunity for observation, much less for private talk; but now Miss Testvalley took possession of Annabel as a matter of course.

"My dear, you won't mind there being no one but me to meet you? The girls and their brothers from Petersburg and Ottawa are out with the guns, and Lady Glenloe sent you all sorts of excuses, but she had an important parish-meeting—something to do with alms-house sanitation—and she thought you'd probably be tired by the journey, and rather glad to rest quietly till dinner."

Yes—Annabel was very glad. She suspected that the informal arrival had been planned with Lady Glenloe's connivance, and it made her feel like a girl again to be springing up the stairs on Miss Testvalley's arm, with no groom-of-the-chambers bowing her onward, or housekeeper curtseying in advance. "Everything's pot-luck at Champions." Lady Glenloe had a way of saying it that made pot-luck sound far more appetizing than elaborate preparations; and Annabel's spirits rose with every step.

She had left Longlands with a heavy mind. After a scene of tearful gratitude, Lady Dick, her money in her pocket, had fled to London by the first train, ostensibly to deal with her more pressing creditors; and for another week Annabel had continued to fulfill her duties as hostess to the shooting-party. She had wanted to say a word in private to Guy Thwarte, to excuse herself for her childish outbreak when he had surprised her in the temple; but the day after Conchita's departure he too had gone, called to Honourslove on some local business, and leaving with a promise to the Duke that he would return for the Lowdon election.

Without her two friends, Annabel felt herself more than ever alone. She knew that the Duke, according to his lights, had behaved generously to her; and she would have liked to feel properly grateful. But she was conscious only of a bewildered resentment. She was sure she had done right in helping Conchita Marable, and she could not understand why an act of friendship should have to be expiated like a crime, and in a way so painful to her pride.

She felt that she and her husband would never be able to reach an understanding, and, this being so, it did not greatly matter which of the two was at fault. "I guess it was our parents, really, for making us so different," was her final summing up to Laura Testvalley, in the course of that first unbosoming.

The astringent quality of Miss Testvalley's sympathy had always acted on Annabel like a tonic. Miss Testvalley was not one to weep with you, but to show you briskly why there was no cause for weeping. Now, however, she remained silent for a long while after listening to her pupil's story; and when she spoke, it was with a new softness. "My poor Nan, life makes ugly faces at us sometimes, I know."

Annabel threw herself on the brown cashmere bosom which had so often been her refuge. "Of course you know, you darling old Val. I think there's nothing in the world you don't know." And her tears broke out in a releasing shower.

Miss Testvalley let them flow; apparently she had no bracing epigram at hand. But when Nan had dried her eyes, and tossed back her hair, the governess remarked quietly: "I'd like you to try a change of air first; then we'll talk this all over. There's a good deal of fresh air in this house, and I want you to ventilate your bewildered little head."

Annabel looked at her with a certain surprise. Though Miss Testvalley was often kind, she was seldom tender, and Nan had a sudden intuition of new forces stirring under the breast-plate of brown cashmere. She looked again, more attentively, and then said: "Val, your hair's grown ever so much thicker; and you do it in a new way."

"I— Do I?" For the first time since Annabel had known her, Miss Testvalley's brown complexion turned to a rich crimson. The colour darted up, flamed, and faded, all in a second or two; but it left the governess's keen little face suffused with a soft inner light like—why, yes, Nan perceived with a start, like that velvety glow on Conchita's delicate cheek. For a moment, neither of the women spoke; but some quick current of understanding seemed to flash between them.

Miss Testvalley laughed. "Oh, my hair . . . you think? Yes; I have been trying a new hair-lotion—one of those wonderful French things. You didn't know I was such a vain old goose? Well, the truth is, Lady Churt was staying here (you know she's a cousin); and after she left, one of the girls found a bottle of this stuff in her room, and just for fun we—that is, I . . . Well, there's my silly secret. . . ." She laughed again, and tried to flatten her upstanding ripples with a pedantic hand. But the ripples sprang up defiantly, and so did her colour. Nan kept an intent gaze on her.

"You look ten years younger; you look *young*, I mean, Val dear," she corrected herself with a smile.

"Well, that's the way I want you to look, my child. No; don't ring for your maid—not yet! First let me look through your dresses and tell you what to wear this evening. You know, dear, you've never thought enough about the little things; and one fine day, if one doesn't, they may suddenly grow into tremendously big ones." She lowered her fine lids. "That's the reason I'm letting my hair wave a little more. Not too much, you think? . . . Tell me, Nan, is your maid clever about hair?"

Nan shook her head. "I don't believe she is. My mother-in-law found her for me," she confessed, remembering Conchita's ironic comment on the horn buttons of her dressing-gown. . . . "Lady Churt?—Is that the Lady Churt Jinny and Lizzy and Mabel once told us about?"

"The same. She stopped here on her way from one house-party to another. To tell the truth, Lady Glenloe was a bit un-happy. That old scandal with Lord Seadown hasn't been forgotten, and neither Lady Glenloe nor I was sure about letting Kitty and Cora meet her. But she couldn't very well be refused when she wrote to invite herself; and it was a simple family din-ner, none of the sons was here, even; and nothing was said that the girls shouldn't have heard. They saw nothing remarkable about her except, as I say, her wonderful French paints and pow-ders and lotions!"

Presently Lady Glenloe appeared, brisk and brown, in rough tweed and shabby furs. She was as insensible to heat and cold as she was to most of the finer shades of sensation, and her dress always conformed to the calendar, without taking account of such unimportant trifles as latitudes.

"Ah, I'm glad you've got a good fire. They tell me it's very cold this evening. So delighted you've come, my dear; you must need a change and a rest after a series of those big Longlands parties. I've always wondered how your mother-in-law stood the strain. . . . Here you'll find only the family—we don't go in for any ceremony at Champions—but I hope you'll like being with my girls. . . . By the way, dinner may be a trifle late; you won't mind? The fact is, Sir Helmsley Thwarte sent a note this morning to ask if he might come and dine, and bring his son, who's at Honourslove. You know Sir Helmsley, of course? And Guy—he's been with you at Longlands, hasn't he? We must all drive over to Honourslove. . . . Sir Helmsley's a most friendly neighbour; we see him here very often, don't we, Miss Testvalley?"

The governess's head was bent to the grate, from which a coal had fallen. "When Mr. Thwarte's there, Sir Helmsley naturally likes to take him about, I suppose," she murmured to the tongs.

"Ah, just so!—Guy ought to marry," Lady Glenloe announced. "I must get some young people to meet him the next time he comes. . . . You know that there was an unfortunate marriage at Rio—but, luckily, the young woman died . . . leaving him a fortune, I believe. Ah, I must send word at once to the cook that Sir Helmsley likes his beef rather underdone. . . . Sir Helmsley's very particular about his food. . . . But now I'll leave you to rest, my dear. And don't make yourself too fine. We're used to pot-luck at Champions."

Annabel, left alone, stood pondering before her glass. She was to see Guy Thwarte that evening—and Miss Testvalley had reproached her for not thinking enough about the details of her dress and hair. Hair-dressing had always been a much-discussed affair among the St. George ladies, but something winged and impatient in Nan resisted the slow torture of adjusting puffs and curls. Regarding herself as the least noticeable in a group where youthful beauty carried its torch so high, and convinced that, wherever they went, the other girls would always be the centre of attention, Nan had never thought it worth while to waste much time on her inconspicuous person. The Duke had not married her for her beauty—how could she imagine it, when he might have chosen Virginia? Indeed, he had mentioned, in the course of his odd wooing, that beautiful women always frightened him, and that the qualities he especially valued in Nan were her gentleness and her inexperience—"And certainly I was inexperienced enough," she meditated, as she stood before the mirror; "but I'm afraid he hasn't found me particularly gentle."

She continued to study her reflection critically, wondering whether Miss Testvalley was right, and she owed it to herself to dress her hair more becomingly, and wear her jewels as if she hadn't merely hired them for a fancy-ball. (The comparison was Miss Testvalley's.) She could imagine taking an interest in her hair, even studying the effect of a flower or a ribbon skilfully placed; but she knew she could never feel at ease under the weight of the Tintagel heirlooms. Luckily, the principal pieces, ponderous coronets and tiaras, massive necklaces and bracelets hung with stones like rocs' eggs, were locked up in a London bank, and would probably not be imposed upon her except at Drawing-rooms or receptions for foreign sovereigns; yet even the less ceremonious ornaments, which Virginia or Conchita would have carried off with such an air, seemed too imposing for her slight presence.

But now, for the first time, she felt a desire to assert herself, to live up to her opportunities. "After all, I'm Annabel Tintagel, and as I can't help myself I might as well try to make the best of it." Perhaps Miss Testvalley was right. Already she seemed to breathe more freely, to feel a new air in her lungs. It was her first escape from the long oppression of Tintagel and Longlands, and the solemn London house; and freed from the restrictions they imposed, and under the same roof with the only two friends who truly understood her, she felt her spirits rising. "I know I'm always too glad or too sad—like that girl in the German play that Miss Testvalley read to me," she said to herself, and wondered whether Guy Thwarte knew Clärchen's song, and would think her conceited if she told him she had always felt that a little bit of herself was Clärchen. "There are so many people in me," she thought; but tonight the puzzling idea of her multiplicity cheered instead of bewildering her. . . . "There can't be too many happy Nans," she thought with a smile, as she drew on her long gloves.

Her maid had had to take her hair down twice before each coil and ripple was placed to the best advantage of her small head, and in proper relation to the diamond briar-rose on the shoulder of her coral-pink *poult-de-soie*.

When she entered the drawing-room she found it empty; but

the next moment Guy Thwarte appeared, and she went up to him impulsively.

"Oh, I'm so glad you're here. I've been wanting to tell you how sorry I am to have behaved so stupidly the day you found me in the temple—" "of Love," she had been about to add; but the absurdity of the designation checked her. She reddened and went on: "I wanted to write and tell you; but I couldn't. I'm not good at letters."

Guy was looking at her, visibly surprised at the change in her appearance, and the warm animation of her voice. "This is better than writing," he rejoined, with a smile. "I'm glad to see you so changed—looking so . . . so much happier. . . ."

("Already?" she reflected guiltily, realizing that she had been away from Longlands only a few hours!)

"Yes, I am happier. Miss Testvalley says I'm always going up and down. . . . And I wanted to tell you—do you remember Clärchen's song?" she began in an eager voice, feeling her tongue loosened and her heart at ease with him again.

Lady Glenloe's ringing accents interrupted them. "My dear Duchess! You've been looking for us? I'm so sorry. I had carried everybody off to my son's study to see this extraordinary new thing—this telephone, as they call it. I brought it back with me the other day from the States. It's a curious toy; but to you, of course, it's no novelty. In America they're already talking from one town to another—yes, actually! Mine goes only as far as the lodge, but I'm urging Sir Helmsley Thwarte to put one in at Honourslove, so that we can have a good gossip together over the crops and the weather. . . . But he says he's afraid it will unchain all the bores in the county. . . . Sir Helmsley, I think you know the Duchess? I'm going to persuade her to put in a telephone at Longlands. . . . We English are so backward. They have them in all the principal hotels in New York; and when I was in St. Petersburg last winter they were actually talking of having one between the Imperial Palace and Tsarskoë—"

The old butler appeared, to announce dinner, and the procession formed itself, headed by Annabel on the arm of the son from the Petersburg Embassy.

"Yes, at Tsarskoë I've seen the Empress talking over it herself. She uses it to communicate with the nurseries," the diplomatist explained impressively; and Nan wondered why they were all so worked up over an object already regarded as a domestic utensil in America. But it was all a part of the novelty and excitement of being at Champions, and she thought with a smile how much less exhilarating the subjects of conversation of a Longlands dinner would have been.

XXIX.

The Champions party chose a mild day of February for the drive to Honourslove. The diplomatic son conducted the Duchess, his mother and Miss Testvalley followed in the wagonette, and the others followed in various vehicles piloted by sons and daughters of the house. For two hours they drove through the tawny winter landscape bounded by hills veiled in blue mist, traversing villages clustered about silver-gray manor-houses, and a little market-town with a High Street bordered by the wool-merchants' stately dwellings, and guarded by a sturdy church-tower. The dark green of rhododendron plantations made autumn linger under the bare woods; on house-fronts sheltered from the wind, the naked jasmine was already starred with gold. This merging of the seasons, so unlike the harsh break between summer and winter in America, had often touched Nan's imagination; but she had never felt as now the mild loveliness of certain winter days in England. It all seemed part of the unreality of her sensations, and as the carriage turned in at the gates of Honourslove, she recalled her only other visit there, when she and Guy Thwarte had stood alone on the terrace before the house, and found not a word to say. Poor Nan St. George—so tongue-tied and bewildered by the surge of her feelings; why had no one taught her the words for them? As the carriage drew up before the door, she seemed to see the pitiful figure of herself at eighteen flit by like a ghost; but in a moment it vanished in the warm air of the present.

The day was so soft that Lady Glenloe insisted on a turn through the gardens before luncheon; and, as usual when a famous country-house is visited, the guests found themselves following the prescribed itinerary, saying the proper things about the view from the terrace, descending the steep path to the mossy glen of the Love, and returning by the walled gardens and the chapel.

Their host, heading the party with the Duchess and Lady Glenloe, had begun his habitual and slightly ironic summary of the family history. Lady Glenloe lent it an inattentive ear; but Annabel hung on his words, and, always quick to discover an appreciative listener, he soon dropped his bantering note to unfold the romantic tale of the old house. Annabel felt that he understood her questions, and sympathized with her curiosity, and as they turned away from the chapel he said, with his quick smile: "I see Miss Testvalley was right, Duchess—she always is. She told me you were the only foreigner she'd ever known who cared for the real deep-down England, rather than the sham one of the London drawing-rooms."

Nan flushed with pride; it still made her as happy to be praised by Miss Testvalley as when the little brown governess had sniffed appreciatively at the posy her pupil had brought her on her first evening at Saratoga.

"I'm afraid I shall always feel strange in London drawing-rooms," Nan answered; "but that hidden-away life of England, the old houses and their histories, and all the far-back things the old people hand on to their grandchildren—they seem so natural and home-like. And Miss Testvalley, who's a foreigner too, has shown me better than anybody how to appreciate them."

"Ah—that's it. We English are spoilt; we've ceased to feel the beauty, to listen to the voices. But you and she come to it with fresh eyes and fresh imaginations—you happen to be blessed with both. I wish more of our Englishwomen felt it all as you do. After luncheon you must go through the old house, and let it talk to you. You hadn't enough time for it when you came before. My son, who knows it all even better than I do, will show it to you. . . ."

"I remember a painting by Holbein—a young man in Tudor dress, with a sensitive face."

"Ah! Yes, the portrait of Brereton Thwarte . . . Poor chap, he has his niche in history. He was one of the men accused of being Queen Anne Boleyn's lovers. He was beheaded before her eyes, before *she* was executed."

"You spoke the other day about Clärchen's song—the evening my father and I drove over to dine at Champions," Guy Thwarte said suddenly.

He and Annabel, at the day's end, had drifted out again to the wide terrace. They had visited the old house, room by room, lingering long over each picture—the Cavalier Thwarte, and the Holbein—each piece of rare old furniture or tapestry, and already the winter afternoon was fading out in crimson distances overhung by twilight. In the hall Lady Glenloe had collected her party for departure.

"Oh, Clärchen? Yes—when my spirits were always jumping up and down Miss Testvalley used to call me Clärchen, just to tease me."

"And doesn't she, any longer? I mean, don't your spirits jump up and down any more?"

"Well, I'm afraid they do sometimes. Miss Testvalley says things are never as bad as I think, or as good as I expect—but I'd rather have the bad hours than not believe in the good ones, wouldn't you? What really frightens me is not caring for anything any more. Don't you think that's worse?"

"That's the worst, certainly. But it's never going to happen to you, Duchess."

Her face lit up. "Oh, do you think so? I'm not sure. Things seem to last so long—as if in the end they were bound to wear people out. Sometimes life seems like a match between oneself and one's gaolers. The gaolers, of course, are one's mistakes; and the question is, who'll hold out longest? When I think of that,

life, instead of being too long, seems as short as a winter day. . . .
Oh, look, the lights already, over there in the valley . . . This
day's over. And suddenly you find you've missed your chance.
You've been beaten. . . ."

"No, no; for there'll be other days soon. And other chances.
Goethe was a very young man when he wrote Clärchen's song.
The next time I come to Champions I'll bring *Faust* with me, and
show you some of the things life taught him."

"Oh, are you coming back to Champions? When? Before I
leave?" she asked eagerly; and he answered: "I'll come whenever
Lady Glenloe asks me."

Again he saw her face suffused with one of its Clärchen-like
illuminations and added, rather hastily: "The fact is, I've got to
hang about here on account of the possible bye-election at Lowdon. Ushant may have told you—"

The illumination faded. "He never tells me anything about
politics. He thinks women oughtn't to meddle with such things."

Guy laughed. "Well, I rather believe he's right. But, meanwhile, here I am, waiting rather aimlessly until *I'm* called upon
to meddle. . . . And as soon as Champions wants me I'll come."

In Sir Helmsley's study, he and Miss Testvalley were standing
together before Sir Helmsley's copy of the little Rossetti Madonna. The ladies of the party had been carried off to collect their
wraps, and their host had seized the opportunity to present his
water-colour to Miss Testvalley. "If you think it's not too
bad—"

Miss Testvalley's colour rose becomingly. "It's perfect, Sir
Helmsley. If you'll allow me, I'll show it to Dante Gabriel the
next time I go to see the poor fellow." She bent appreciatively
over the sketch. "And you'll let me take it off now?"

"No, I want to have it framed first. But Guy will bring it to
you. I understand he's going to Champions in a day or two for a
longish visit."

Miss Testvalley made no reply, and her host, who was beginning to know her face well, saw that she was keeping back many comments.

"You're not surprised?" he suggested.

"I—I don't know."

Sir Helmsley laughed. "Perhaps we shall all know soon. But, meanwhile, let's be a little indiscreet. Which of the daughters do you put your money on?"

Miss Testvalley carefully replaced the water-colour on its easel. "The . . . the daughters?"

"Corisande or Kitty . . . Why, you must have noticed. The better pleased Lady Glenloe is, the more off-hand her manner becomes. And just now I heard her suggesting to my son to come back to Champions as soon as he could, if he thought he could stand a boring family-party."

"Ah—yes." Miss Testvalley remained lost in contemplation of her water-colour. "And you think Lady Glenloe approves?"

"Intensely, judging from her indifferent manner." Sir Helmsley stroked his short beard reflectively. "And I do too. Whichever of the young ladies it is, *cela sera de tout repos.* Cora's eyes are very small, but her nose is straighter than Kitty's. And that's the kind of thing I want for Guy: something safe and unexciting. Now that he's managed to scrape together a little money—the first time a Thwarte has ever done it by the work of his hands or his brain—I dread his falling a victim to some unscrupulous woman."

"Yes," Miss Testvalley acquiesced, a faint glint of irony in her fine eyes. "I can imagine how anxious you must be."

"Oh, desperately; as anxious as the mother of a flirtatious daughter—"

"I understand that."

"And you make no comment?"

"I make no comment."

"Because you think in this particular case I'm mistaken?"

"I don't know."

Sir Helmsley glanced through the window at the darkening terrace. "Well, here he is now. And a lady with him. Shall we toss a penny on which it is—Corisande or Kitty? Oh—no! Why, it's the little Duchess, I believe. . . ."

Miss Testvalley still remained silent.

"Another of your pupils!" Sir Helmsley continued, with a teasing laugh. He paused, and added tentatively: "And perhaps the most interesting, eh?"

"Perhaps."

"Because she's the most intelligent—or the most unhappy?"

Miss Testvalley looked up quickly. "Why do you suggest that she's unhappy?"

"Oh," he rejoined with a slight shrug, "because you're so incurably philanthropic that I should say your swans would often turn out to be lame ducks."

"Perhaps they do. At any rate, she's the pupil I was fondest of, and should most wish to guard against unhappiness."

"Ah—" murmured Sir Helmsley, on a half-questioning note.

"But Lady Glenloe must be ready to start; I'd better go and call the Duchess," Miss Testvalley added, moving toward the door. There was a sound of voices in the hall, and among them Lady Glenloe's, calling out: "Cora, Kitty—has anyone seen the Duchess? Oh, Mr. Thwarte, we're looking for the Duchess, and I see you've been giving her a last glimpse of your wonderful view. . . ."

"Not the last, I hope," said Guy, smiling, as he came forward with Annabel.

"The last for today, at any rate; we must be off at once on our long drive. Mr. Thwarte, I count on you for next Saturday. Sir Helmsley, can't we persuade you to come too?"

The drive back to Champions passed like a dream. To secure herself against disturbance, Nan had slipped her hand into Miss Testvalley's, and let her head droop on the governess's shoulder.

She heard one of the Glenloe girls whisper, "The Duchess is asleep," and a conniving silence seemed to enfold her. But she had no wish to sleep; her wide-open eyes looked out into the falling night, caught the glint of lights flashing past in the High Street, lost themselves in the long intervals of dusk between the villages, and plunged into deepening night as the low glimmer of the west went out. In her heart was a deep delicious peace such as she had never known before. In this great lonely desert of life stretching out before her she had a friend—a friend who understood not only all she said, but everything she could not say. At the end of the long road on which the regular rap of the horses' feet was beating out the hours, she saw him standing, waiting for her, watching for her through the night.

XXX.

Sir Helmsley Thwarte might cavil at Corisande's eyes and Kitty's nose, but the eyes of both Glenloe sisters were bright china-blue and the noses pert, and both sisters had pink cheeks and smooth light-brown hair. At seventeen and eighteen, they were on terms of equable friendship which made Nan reflect sadly on her worship of Jinny and the patronizing bossiness Jinny had given in return. "And they're *happy*!" she marvelled. "When I compare them with Ushant's sisters! who are older, of course . . ."

Corisande and Kitty were closeted with a dress-maker. Annabel, Miss Testvalley, and Guy Thwarte sat in the morning-room, where divans and armchairs deeply soft in cushions and bright with chintz cheerfully flouted the demands of elegance, and priceless Ming vases exhaled the fragrant potpourri of home-grown roses.

Guy, on horseback, and Sir Helmsley (whose injury rendered the saddle impossible) in a light and narrow cabriolet, could make the journey from Honourslove cross-country along lanes that tunnelled through overarching hedges, and wide smooth grassy rides, and stubbly old rights-of-way through fields, in half the time it took carriages and wagons obliged to follow the roundabout road that linked a dozen villages; and the father and son frequently called at Champions.

"The Duke's sisters were not very happy at Kitty and Cora's age, either; that is when I had them," Miss Testvalley said. "But

Kitty and Cora are very young for their age, mere children. The Duke's sisters were never children. They leapt from infancy to wearing long dresses and putting their hair up."

"Almina says she yearns to enter a convent and it's because of you."

"Ah?" Miss Testvalley raised finely interrogative eyebrows. "Lady Almina may have been more impressed than I realized when I mentioned that my cousin Maria Rossetti had found great joy as a nun."

"Well, *I* would hate lying on a cold stone floor all night and wearing haircloth to lacerate my flesh, but if Almina wants it why shouldn't she be allowed? The Dowager says it's High Church mummery. She is very proud of being Low. But what in the world difference does it make?"

Guy laughed. "I don't think the Church of England goes in for haircloth nowadays." But he turned to Miss Testvalley, as to a higher authority.

The governess hesitated. When a dreamy young Annabel was being prepared for marriage, etiquette had been put forward as more momentous than the Thirty-nine Articles of a Church to which she was hastily introduced.—Miss Testvalley said only: "It makes *all* the difference to some people. My cousin Christina Rossetti refused two suitors, men she liked—or loved, I've never known—because they were too Low."

She rose promptly, as if glad to be freed from a vexing subject, when Sir Helmsley entered and announced:

"Lady Glenloe informs me, firstly, that Kitty and Corisande are about to be released; secondly, that she would be delighted to ride with you now, Duchess; and, thirdly, that you, Miss Testvalley, have expressed a willingness to show me the work that's being done—under your supervision, I collect?—on the new glass-house."

Annabel, who found the very mention of theology boring, simply wanted people to have food, shelter, and a doctor for a sick child.

The Duke had forbidden her to deal personally with his tenants, hence the catastrophe which had ruined their marriage: for more and more she felt that it was ruined.

At Champions, she soon learned, on the first hint of illness in the village Lady Glenloe set off in her pony-cart, clutching a battered leather bag known to contain mystic elixirs, with a terrine of calf's-foot jelly at her feet. Whereas at Longlands . . . The Dowager Duchess knit things for a "poor basket." Annabel had seen her at her work of charity, her hard little eyes snapping as the needles clicked at the orders of her stubby little fingers. The Dowager chose gray yarn, and a green like . . . like the slime on a pond, Nan had once decided, searching for comparisons. She inflicted ugliness, even if it was useful ugliness, on people she disapproved of, like the poor . . . and like *me,* Nan thought, suddenly seeing the horn-buttoned dressing-gown in a new light, as a form of punishment.

In the Champions library, Nan found in a collection of *Travels in Eastern Europe* the legend of St. Elizabeth of Hungary, whose heathen husband, the King, forbade her to feed the poor on pain of death. The Queen stole out of the palace one morning carrying a basket of loaves of bread. He saw her and demanded that she show him what she had. When she removed the cloth that covered them, the loaves had been turned into roses.

Was the King subsequently converted? The version of the legend Nan had happened on did not say. When *she* had tried to help the poor against the Duke's command, God had worked no miracle. He had punished her by killing her unborn child. That, she knew, was what Ushant's mother believed: and probably Ushant as well, though Ushant had never said so.

The stuffed birds rescued from the fire in the old Champions shared the new glossy-oak library with trophies of post-conflagration Glenloe travels. On the book-shelves, Voyages and

Explorations jostled witch-masks, scrimshaw-work, and *guislas*, and a corner of the Feraghan rug was occupied by an enormous and handsome globe of the world which, unlike its counterpart at Allfriars, had lost some of its varnish as the result of much fingering by intending travellers with itineraries to plot.

When Guy came to call, he often found Annabel curled in a window-seat in the pleasant sunny room, reading.

In Lemprière's *Classical Dictionary Condensed*, she had encountered an unattractive husband of an earlier day than the King of Hungary. "As the place of Pluto's residence was obscure and gloomy," she read, "all the goddesses refused to marry him; but he determined to obtain by force what was denied to his solicitations." Visiting Sicily after an earthquake caused by his brother Neptune, he saw Proserpine, daughter of his sister Ceres and his brother Jupiter, gathering flowers in the field of Enna. "He became enamoured of her," Annabel learned, "and immediately carried her away to the underworld. Proserpine called upon her attendants for help, but in vain; and she became the wife of her ravisher and the queen of hell." ("Poor Queen," thought Annabel, seeing in her mind's eye the slight young girl in the Naxos fragment.) "Pluto sat on a throne of sulphur. . . . The dog Cerberus watched at his feet, the harpies hovered around him. Proserpine sat on his left, and near to her stood the Eumenides, with their heads covered with snakes."

Nan went on to a history of the Crimean War. Did he know, she asked Guy Thwarte, that Miss Testvalley's cousin Eliza Polidori had worked with Miss Nightingale? . . . And had he read the report on the slums of London?

Guy said reluctantly: "England is in my blood, I can't criticize England without criticizing myself. But when I came home I saw that many people are as poor as the wretched creatures I saw in Brazil. Or almost."

His brows lowered as he thought of Brazil, and of Paquita: six weeks out of a convent when they married; poignantly sweet, innocent, and incurious. He had adored her. She had been happy with him; that, he knew. But would she have remained happy if she had lived? When he made his precipitate return to England (his father said the Thwarte motto should be, not "I follow my duty," but "I follow my impulse"), a well-wisher had let him know that he was believed to have left Brazil a rich man thanks to his late wife. The truth was that, when he learned that his father-in-law was systematically working to death the enslaved men, women, and children who mined his ore, he had cut all financial ties with Don Carlos. Paquita had died before she knew of the breach. How would she have felt if her father had demanded that she take sides? Would she have understood, at all?

One day, Guy, having ridden over from Honourslove alone, found the library empty. Her Grace, he was told, had said that she was going for a long walk, perhaps as far as Chipping, and not to hold luncheon back. He was standing, hands in pockets, at a window, frowning over nothing, when the girls came in. The girls were always coming in.—Well, it was their house! And they were perfectly nice girls . . . nice children.

Corisande had a book to return. "Kitty!" Lady Glenloe called from the doorway. "I want you, my dear." With a "Yes, Mamma," Kitty departed.

Lady Glenloe's collie-like driving of an eligible young man into a pen with a marriageable daughter gave Miss Testvalley private amusement. More experienced in girls than many mothers, the governess could have told Lady Glenloe that Kitty and Cora, petted since birth by the four indulgent older brothers who came and went, were too immature to dream about Guy Thwarte, who was at least thirty. Furthermore, Miss Testvalley had an un-amused, disquieting sense that Guy Thwarte's heart was not whole.

Guy guessed his father's motive in suggesting so often that they visit Champions. He had no intention of proposing marriage either to Corisande or to Catharine, but to say so might precipitate one of Sir Helmsley's all-too-well-known volcanic eruptions of rage; Guy affected stolid ignorance of the paternal wishes, hoping that they might lose themselves in the sands. . . . The visits served a half-forgotten purpose of his own. He had felt it his duty to ascertain whether his father had taken a freakish fancy to the "little brown governess." Impossible to judge during the Christmas festivities at Longlands, but at Champions Guy's surveillance had a twofold result. He saw that his father took Miss Testvalley aside, paid her "attentions"—but in order, evidently, to leave the field free for his son to court her pupils . . . *one* of her pupils. Guy also saw that Miss Testvalley, with her brilliant eyes and her quick intelligence, would not have been a ridiculous object of infatuation. He hoped she would not be misled by his father's gallantry. . . . Her eyes were splendid. . . . Still, the Duchess's sweeter, dark-fringed eyes, so often sad, were more captivating. . . . What was it she'd said about being the captive of her mistakes? . . . Hardly aware of the line his thoughts were taking, Guy wished the little Duchess were here now. . . .

However, the Duchess was not here, and Cora *was*; and, with a show of avuncular interest, Guy asked Cora what the book was.

"Browning." Cora handed it to him politely. "Miss Testvalley had us read selections."

"And which poems do you like best?"

"Kitty likes the Cavalier Tunes; *I*," Cora said, "prefer mediaeval wickedness. . . . Mr. Thwarte, oh, do please excuse me, but it's almost time for our history lesson."

Leafing through the volume after Corisande's skirts had whisked through the door, Guy caught the title "My Last Duchess."

> That's my last Duchess painted on the wall,
> Looking as if she were alive. . . .

The Duke of Ferrara was showing a guest the art treasures in his palazzo:

> *She had*
> *A heart—how shall I say?—too soon made glad,*
> *Too easily impressed; she liked whate'er*
> *She looked on, and her looks went everywhere.*
> *Sir, 't was all one! My favour at her breast,*
> *The dropping of the daylight in the West,*
> *The bough of cherries some officious fool*
> *Broke in the orchard for her, the white mule*
> *She rode with round the terrace—all and each*
> *Would draw from her alike the approving speech,*
> *Or blush, at least. She thanked men,—good! but thanked*
> *Somehow—I know not how—as if she ranked*
> *My gift of a nine-hundred-years-old name*
> *With anybody's gift.*
>
> . . . .
>
> *Oh sir, she smiled, no doubt,*
> *Whene'er I passed her; but who passed without*
> *Much the same smile? This grew; I gave commands;*
> *Then all smiles stopped together.*

At Longlands, last Christmas, Guy had seen a housemaid with a dust-mop grin and make a bob as Annabel darted at her from out of nowhere and cried, "Polly, you're over the mumps? Wasn't it *beastly*? My sister and I had it once—" When, from somewhere, the Duke had appeared, he could not be said to have frowned, but his impassive gaze had wiped all expression from Annabel's face.

The stodgy, nondescript, petty Duke of Tintagel would not, like Browning's villain, do away with his wife for promiscuous friendliness, but he could stifle her spirit. "And I'm damned if he's not doing it," Guy fumed: and then berated himself. The plight of Annabel Tintagel was no more his affair here than it had been at Longlands. He traced Lady Glenloe to a room where two semp-stresses were gathering yards of frothy pale-blue stuff into flounces, and told her that he feared that business would prevent him from coming for some time. Expressing her regret, Lady Glenloe smiled to herself: "He knows that Corisande and Kitty are going away."

XXXI.

They were going to be bridesmaids to their cousin Victoria Bingham of Over Bacton in Norfolk. Creation of their gowns had disrupted lessons for weeks, and their journey had been under prolonged discussion with General Sir John Bingham, the cousin's father, who, viewing it as part of a complex military operation, felt duty-bound to provide plans for meeting contingencies ranging from a railway collision to the abduction of the bridesmaids by a gang of London criminals. The correspondence, soldierly on Sir John's side, was increasingly impatient on that of the bridesmaids' mother.

Miss Testvalley was to conduct her pupils to London, to an hotel where a Bingham convoy would take them over. (*She* would not go on; the mediaeval seams of the manor-house would be dangerously stretched by the horde of close relations who had to be put up.) But the hotel was as yet undecided on.

When at last Lady Glenloe threw up her hands and declared that it was easier to get from St. Petersburg to Tashkent than in and out of London, and the Duchess, after hesitation, suggested diffidently, "Would you . . . if I . . . Suppose I went to London too? We could all stay at Folyat House overnight," the girls held their breath; and when their mother gratefully returned, "My dear Annabel, how kind!," they hugged each other for joy.

The Duchess said happily: "I'll write to Folyat House to tell them to have things ready . . . and I'll write to Longlands to let the Duke know."

Perhaps, Annabel thought, bringing bright young company to the great morose mansion in Portman Square would break the dark spell it exercised over its mistress. . . . At any rate, she would be acting as Duchess in an unexceptionable undertaking. Ushant might even be pleased.

Gritty smoke from the locomotive billowed past the compartment window as the train bustled toward London. Cinders rained on the scorched grass along the rails; beyond, visible between gusts of smoke, raying out from a distant focus of rounded hills, sped pastures, sheep, fields, hedges, neatly demarcated woods, yellow-gray stone farm-buildings, and huddled hamlets. Now and then the train hooted and puffed to a stop at little stations where Corisande and Kitty pushed the window down and craned to watch two or three passengers descend and board. It was the first time they had been away from home by themselves—or *would* be by themselves when they left Miss Testvalley. (It didn't count that they would be accompanied by a maid, assigned to them *ad hoc* by their mother, who was travelling two carriages forward, second class, with the Duchess's maid, Mabbit, and their luggage.)

As they came out of a long roaring tunnel, Kitty sighed: "Oh, Duchess, if only you could come to the wedding too!"

"I have something exciting to look forward to myself," said the Duchess. "Miss Testvalley is taking me to meet Mr. Dante Gabriel Rossetti."

"Oh, what is he like?" Corisande asked Miss Testvalley. "He is the only famous artist we know about from somebody who knows them."

"Knows *him*, Cora!" Miss Testvalley wrinkled her brow, considering. "From what critics who understand such matters say, I believe he will have a place in history as a poet and painter. But, apart from that, people—even writers and artists greater than he is—see him as a king. A leader! There's something about him. . . . Even now that he's old and very ill, they'd give their lives for him. . . . I felt like that myself, from the time I was a little girl."

And then glancing out the window, she said briskly: "We're coming into London. Collect your odds and ends, girls!"

It was dark when Folyat House loomed high and stately in Portman Square, light shining from its long rows of windows and torches flaming at the grand portal. Footmen jumped down from the barouche which had met the travellers at Paddington, opened its escutcheoned doors, and helped them out. Other footmen led them up steps and into an oval colonnaded lobby. The Glenloe girls' eyes widened as the groom-of-the-chambers, attended by yet other footmen, conducted them into a great rectangular hall three storeys high which offered the vista of another hall through an arch at the opposite end. The girls were led up a marble-and-wrought-iron staircase which swept up along two sides of the great hall, past embrasures containing marble statues, to a balustraded balcony, its pilastered arches two storeys high, and on to their rooms.

"I've said we'll dine early," the Duchess told her guests. "I'll knock on your doors at seven and we'll go down together."

Dinner was laid on the longest table the Glenloes had ever seen. "Oh, bother," the Duchess murmured. "I ought to have said the breakfast-room. . . . We'll be miles apart." After biting her lip for a moment, she told the butler: "We shall all sit together at the head, Ogilvy"; and when *couverts* and candelabra had been moved and she and her friends had taken their places, she indicated a pyramid of ferns and gardenias that mounted two feet high in front of her, saying: "And move that, please, so that we can see each other."

Kitty and Cora, seated at the Duchess's left, opposite Miss Testvalley, watched by the mutes with powdered hair, knee breeches, and silk stockings who stood motionless along the walls, dared not look up from the plates into which other mutes were ladling turtle soup.

The Duchess turned to Miss Testvalley. "Since this is the prelude to a special occasion, don't you think Corisande and Catharine might take some wine?"

Corisande and Catharine, eyeing their governess hopefully, saw a fierce mock-scowl form on her mobile brown face and melt into an infectious smile as she replied: "I certainly do! Especially as Kitty and Cora face several days of festivities when wine will pour like water. But you *will* be prudent, won't you, girls? A little water in the wine, do you think, tonight—*and* at the Binghams'?"

"Do you know," the Duchess said to her younger guests, dimpling, "Miss Testvalley let me drink wine for the first time when *I* was a bridesmaid too. It was at Lady Richard Marable's wedding, in New York; and something so funny happened just around then. There was a ball—an Assembly ball, rather like the ones in country towns here; only in New York it's a little like being presented at Court, because there isn't any Court, and the White House isn't the same thing; so if you weren't invited it *did* hurt—"

What with hot soup and watered Chablis, Kitty and Cora were no longer intimidated by their surroundings.

"Oh, Duchess, did you suffer?" Kitty asked pityingly.

"Oh, I wasn't even out yet. But some other girls felt awfully bad. Well, two of the ones who weren't invited went to the ball even so—by pretending they were the sisters of a English lord! Someone got them tickets, using the English girls' names."

"Highly reprehensible," Miss Testvalley interposed, as the Glenloes gasped.

"The New York papers," the Duchess continued, "said how beautiful and elegant and lively and what wonderful dancers English girls were, compared with Americans.—But that's not all," she went on, over the sisters' squeals of laughter. "Can you imagine, the papers *here* copied the New York articles—giving the names of the real English girls!—who'd never left home, of course, and were totally, absolutely *dumbfounded*! In fact, they still are, I happen to know. . . . No, I can't tell you their names. As Miss Testvalley says, it was an unforgiveable masquerade."

Dover sole had followed soup. Miss Testvalley carried on the Duchess's chatter—neither her present pupils nor her former one had ever seen her so animated; so keyed up, even—with anecdotes that lasted through veal, beef, partridge, salad, syllabub, cheese, fruit, and a savoury, to which the two youngest diners, though the others flagged, did full justice.

"Once upon a time," she said, "Dante Gabriel Rossetti had a menagerie. It was supposedly in his back garden, which is a good size, but the animals actually had the freedom of the house—and sometimes of the neighbours' gardens, I'm afraid. He had . . . Let me think. He had peacocks . . . he had gazelles and armadillos and kangaroos, a raccoon—the raccoon ate one of his manuscripts. He had a wombat . . . I believe a sloth . . . but what he really wanted was an elephant. . . ."

"Oh, why?"

"He wanted the elephant to clean the windows."

From behind Miss Testvalley came a deeper sound than the trills of laughter at the table. One of the statues lined against the wall stood tensed, his eyes squeezed shut and his cheeks puffed out, as though he were trying to control a fit of hiccups. Glancing over at him, the Glenloes saw that the Duchess also looked, but quickly averted her eyes.

"Cora, we are in London, and tomorrow we'll be in Norfolk," Kitty told her sister, as they snuggled in bed, "and the day after we'll be in the wedding."

They had been escorted to separate rooms, but as soon as

their maid departed Kitty had run out of hers and jumped into bed with Cora.

"I can't sleep, can you?"

"Oh, no . . . Did you notice how the Duchess pretended not to hear that man laugh, so he wouldn't be punished?"

"Oh, yes," Kitty said reverently, "the Duchess is my ideal!"

"Then I suppose she can't be mine too, so I don't know who my ideal is—Yes, I do. The Princess of Wales. Ah . . . lex . . . ahn . . . dra . . . Such a beautiful name . . ."

"Ummm."

"Are you awake? I can't sleep either. . . ."

Miss Testvalley, peeking in, heard, unsurprised, the breathing of two sleepers, and made her way, with guidance by servants, to the Duchess's narrow, high-ceilinged boudoir and on through a tapestried bedroom to a pretty octagonal room walled with mirrors. There sat Annabel, in a dressing-gown that was far from pretty, having her thick brown-gold curls brushed into ruliness by a prim-visaged woman whom the governess knew to be her maid.

"Come in," Nan cried. "Thank you, Mabbit, good night.— Oh, Val, what fun, thanks to you! And tomorrow, after all these years, I'll meet Mr. Rossetti! I can't believe it."

"It's possible too that we may meet . . . That is, Sir Helmsley Thwarte may come with us. He wants to see that replica of his Madonna and show Dante Gabriel a copy he's made, and he may be in town on business. . . . Annabel, I must explain that Dante Gabriel is vague about money. His problems—" Miss Testvalley paused, eyeing Annabel's innocently receptive face. Why tell her that Dante Gabriel was addicted to chloral mixed with whisky? "He is ill, you see, and he sometimes asks for, for . . . financial help. I hope and pray he won't importune you—or Sir Helmsley." She was afraid that Nan would wonder at her jerky babbling, but Nan only asked:

"Do you think that Mr. Guy Thwarte will come too?"

Next morning, an important person in black bombazine with a tall footman and a chubby buttons in her wake identified herself as the Bingham Nanny and supervised the transfer of the Glenloe party into the Bingham carriage. Shortly afterward, Sir Helmsley Thwarte, unaccompanied by his son, arrived at Folyat House in a hansom-cab into which, vigorously, and limping only slightly, he helped the two ladies, telling the driver: "Chelsea. Tudor House, Cheyne Walk.—It *is*, in fact, Tudor," he observed to Nan as they bowled along. "You like historical associations, Duchess; did you know that Henry the Eighth's sixth wife, Catherine Parr, lived there after his death?—Am I not right, Miss Testvalley?" Stroking his fine auburn beard, the baronet turned deferentially to the governess, but she had her head at the window, watching for what proved to be a bow-fronted ivy-grown brick house separated from the walk and the river-bank by a little neglected-looking garden.

Rossetti, seated by an ornate fireplace, apologized with an expansive and courtly gesture for not rising, and murmured: "Laura, *cara*! . . . Enchanté, Duchess! . . . Sir Helmsley!" He looked far more ill than when Sir Helmsley had seen him last. His pallor was accentuated by the black circles around his deep-set, dark, liquid eyes, but the eyes had all their old magnetism.

After careful scrutiny, pulling at the long drooping moustache that made him resemble at first glance a Chinese mandarin rather than an Anglo-Italian painter-poet, he pronounced Sir Helmsley's water-colour exquisite. "I wonder if it wasn't *I* who copied *you*, Sir Helmsley!"

"But why," the baronet asked him, "have you not painted Miss Testvalley?"

"Ah, but only Goya could do justice to those incandescent eyes!" Rossetti answered.

"Precisely the painter I have always thought of for her!" Sir Helmsley accepted the statement as an accolade; he could have had no more gratifying confirmation of his artist's sensibility. "As Petrarch is the poet! *'Costei, ch'è tra le donne un sole, In me, movendo de' beglio ochi i rai, Cria d'amor penseri. . . .'* "

Rossetti, raising his heavy brows, looked, blandly quizzical, from his old patron to Miss Testvalley; who blushed darkly and asked her cousin, in haste, "And for the Duchess?"

"For that naïve grace"—Rossetti was as prompt as magisterial in his reply—"those soft eyes, that eloquent play of expression—Romney! Without a doubt, Romney."

Leaving Miss Testvalley to chat with her cousin, Sir Helmsley and the Duchess walked about the high shadowy parlour, looking at Rossetti's drawing of the austere profiles of his sister Christina and their mother and other works by him and and his Brethren, and investigated the ancient room that was now a studio, with its smell of turpentine, recalling to the baronet his own Paris *atelier* in *les beaux jours d'autrefois* and of—he sniffed uncertainly—some sort of exotic incense. After he returned to the others, the Duchess lingered, turning over canvasses here and there. She re-joined the older people with a look of puzzlement.

When the three visitors had taken leave of the great Pre-Raphaelite, the Duchess strolled down the little garden path and crossed the walk to the edge of the Thames. Sir Helmsley gently detained Miss Testvalley. Tapping the re-wrapped water-colour he held pressed under his left arm, his voice urgent, he said: "My dear Laura, in offering you this trifle I beg you to accept the poor copier with it. You must know that I hope you will consent to be my wife."

Miss Testvalley's lids fell over the eyes which only Goya could have painted, and she crimsoned almost painfully; but after a moment she looked her suitor straight in the face. "And you must know my regard for you, Sir Helmsley; but it is a very serious step—for each of us; and not to be taken on impulse."

"You have regard for me!—Then," Sir Helmsley pressed, "then you do not say no?"

"Oh, no," Laura Testvalley replied, "I do not say no—"

"Then you say yes!" Without more ado, his handsome worn face shining, Sir Helmsley seized her hand and kissed it lingeringly; and as he relinquished it said: "You have made me very happy."

Meanwhile Nan stood gazing at the Thames and across at the Battersea shore through a gauzy mist that shimmered green and gold in the pale late-winter sunlight. A string of barges glided by, outstripped by a rowing-boat. . . . The unresting, changeable river had frolicked past the bungalow at Runnymede some miles ago. Around the next bend, it would surge grandly, mightily, past the Houses of Parliament, where Ushant sat in the Lords and where Guy Thwarte would sit (for of course he would win the election) in the Commons.

She heard Miss Testvalley call her name, and turned back.

When Sir Helmsley had escorted them to Folyat House and gone on (to business, he said, with his solicitor), Annabel led the governess up into her boudoir, where, remembering, she cried: "Val, you won't believe it! There were some canvasses standing on edge, and when I tipped them over to see, they were Sir Helmsley's Madonna—at least *ten* Madonnas, all identical!"

Miss Testvalley seemed abstracted, as if shaking herself free from some pleasant musing. "Thank heaven *you're* the one who saw them! People want replicas, and Dante Gabriel . . . for years he has been too busy or too ill to do them, and so he pays other painters, poor ones, or students, to rough out copies for him to finish. I *had* heard that sometimes all he contributes is his signature, but I didn't know that he was running a factory!" Miss Testvalley cast her speaking eyes up to the puce-and-gold ceiling. "And what's more, he asks for payment for paintings he may not begin for years. Thank heaven too that he didn't ask Sir Helmsley—or you—for money!"

Nan said eagerly: "But he's not mercenary. . . . And when his wife died, isn't it true that he buried his poems with her?"

Miss Testvalley hesitated. "Yes . . . he had his poems buried with poor Lizzy Siddal, but later he . . . he lost his vein, he needed to publish, and he had her body exhumed.—No, no," she said quickly as Nan's mouth opened in horror, "that was human nature; he found he couldn't bear to annihilate his work. . . . The thing is that he hadn't the courage to retrieve the manuscripts himself, he made someone else do it for him. . . . Annabel," Miss Testvalley said with some severity, "you are romantic by nature, which is excellent, but romanticism should include recognition of facts."

As Nan, at the other end of the sofa on which they had installed themselves, frowned thoughtfully, Miss Testvalley rose briskly, her face again subtly a-glow. "However, my dear, just now, like a sundial, I can think only of happy hours! You're returning to Champions at once? I'll see you there when I bring Corisande and Kitty back. Meanwhile, I'll be with Miss March for a day or so."

Nan, too, stood up, smiling. "Yes. The carriage will be at the door whenever you say, Val dear."

"Thank you, Annabel!" Miss Testvalley was pleased out of all proportion to the service itself (though her arrival in a ducal barouche in view of all Curzon Street would provide Jacky March with an innocent thrill). During the last few days she had noted several indications that her favourite pupil was learning to make modest use of her prerogative as Duchess. And whatever happened—in her unwonted mood of joy, Miss Testvalley did not analyze a "whatever" that betrayed her underlying uneasiness as to Annabel's situation—whatever happened, it could do Annabel nothing but good to learn to assert herself.

"Afterward," she continued, "I'll go on to my family for a bit. But I think I shall *not* tell them about this latest performance of D.G.R.'s. *Arrivederci,* Annabel!"

XXXII.

When Annabel opened the library door, Lady Glenloe looked up from a large atlas open on the table before her and came, arms open and wind-burnt face beaming, to welcome her back to Champions as a third daughter.

After demanding and receiving a report of the evening at Folyat House and the departure of the bridesmaids for Norfolk, she sat down with a nod of satisfaction and a sigh of frustration. "My dear, Ralph writes that he has been posted to 'Noru.' In India, I fancy, but I can't find it on the map. Where in the world can it be?"

"Noru, Nohru . . . ?" Obligingly, Nan turned and began to search the big globe.

"You say Sir Helmsley was there when you visited Miss Testvalley's cousin?" Lady Glenloe, pleased with events, vouchsafed a confidence. "Of course, you've seen that I hope his son will marry one of my girls."

Bent over the globe, Nan put her hand to her heart as if she had been stabbed.

"And I'm sure that Sir Helmsley hopes so too. You've noticed how he takes Miss Testvalley off to chat so that Guy can be alone with Corisande or Catharine? Tell me, have you noticed any signs of preference?—on Guy's part, that is?" Lady Glenloe cocked a cheerful head expectantly.

As the countries of the world rolled past in varnished yellows, pale greens, and pinks—as the small world that was herself was suddenly decentralized—Nan drew on a courage she hadn't known was in her.

"No." She turned to Lady Glenloe. "No. They are both dears."

"Is Your Grace ill?" Mabbit, who was arranging gloves in a drawer, looked up with a frown and a tone of repressed annoyance, as of one improperly interrupted in performance of a duty, when Nan took refuge in her room.

"No," Nan said, without looking at her. "You may go."

"Yes," she moaned, throwing herself on her bed when Mabbit had left. "Yes, I am ill. I am in love. I never knew. . . . And what am I to do . . . ? I didn't know. . . ."

"You are pale," Lady Glenloe said compunctiously, when Nan came down to dinner. "I ought not to have allowed you to go to London and back in such a short time, especially since the Dowager said you were run-down and needed change of air. Fortunately, I have a special decoction that may help."

So her mother-in-law had engineered the invitation to Champions. But it didn't matter. Nan submitted to a dose of *alakar* ("which they use in the Caucasus; Piers says it accounts for their longevity, along with that curious curd *yahoor*"), grateful to be supplied with a plausible cover for heartache.

Incurable heartache; for there was no remedy. Alone at last in her canopied bed, the fierce Nan St. George who had cried out that she would kill a beastly governess revived, like a free-spirited dryad breaking from long captivity in a granite boulder—to savage *herself*. How could she, who used to make believe she was

Yseult and Guinevere and Nicolette and mooned over Rossetti's "fleshly" verse, how could— First she'd imagined that she was in love when she wasn't, letting the magic of Camelot enshroud the Duke's dull lovelessness in Celtic mist. Then she had *really* fallen in love: and not known. She had delighted in the Correggios, even looked at them with Guy Thwarte, but stupidly had seen only their sunny joyousness, not their passion. She had let her love grow, nourished it, and not known.

She had heard a laughing aside of Conchita's, "Guy Thwarte's no longer a detrimental," and had paid no heed. But how could she have failed to understand that he would be pursued? No; not merely pursued, she had to face the worst—the obvious—that he would of course, for every reason, *want* to marry? "Oh," she moaned, shaken by waves of anguish, not knowing to whom she might be pleading, "don't let me be jealous of them. . . . It would be contemptible. . . ."

But Annabel, who had never been in love and had never been jealous, *was* jealous, and it was that cruellest of passions, striking like lightning, that showed her that she was in love. . . . Contemptible or not, she could not be here when *they* came home and Guy resumed his visits. (Visits, but to which one?) She could not stay. But neither could she go back to Longlands. . . .

Her pillow wet with tears, the Duchess of Tintagel tossed and turned all night.

"Do you know, I think Nan's coming to stay next week!"

Mrs. Hector Robinson laid down the letter she had been perusing and glanced across the funereal architecture of the British breakfast-table at her husband, who, plunged in *The Times,* sat in the armchair facing her. He looked up with the natural resentment of the Briton disturbed by an untutored female in his morning encounter with the news. "Nan—?" he echoed interrogatively.

Lizzy Robinson laughed—and her laugh was a brilliant affair, which lit up the late-winter darkness of the solemn pseudo-Gothic breakfast-room at Belfield.

"Well, Annabel, then; Annabel Duchess—"

"The—not the Duchess of Tintagel?"

Mr. Robinson had instantly discarded *The Times*. He sat gazing incredulously at the face of his wife, on which the afterglow of her laugh still enchantingly lingered. Certainly, he thought, he had married one of the most beautiful women in England. And now his father was dead, and Belfield and the big London house, and the Scottish shooting-lodge, and the Lancashire mills which fed them all—all for the last year had been his. Everything he had put his hand to had succeeded. But he had never pictured the Duchess of Tintagel at a Belfield house-party, and the vision made him a little dizzy.

"The—Duchess—of—Tintagel." Still amused, his wife mimicked him. "Has there never been a duchess at Belfield before?"

Mr. Robinson stiffened slightly. "Not *this* Duchess. I understood the Tintagels paid no visits."

"Ushant doesn't, certainly—luckily for us! But I suppose he can't keep his wife actually chained up, can he, with all these new laws, and the police prying in everywhere? At any rate, she's been at Lady Glenloe's for the last month; and now she wants to know if she can come here."

Mr. Robinson's stare had the fixity of a muscular contraction. "She's written to ask—?"

His wife tossed the letter across the monuments in Sheffield plate. "There—if you don't believe me."

He read the short note with a hurriedly assumed air of detachment. "Dear me—who else is coming? Shall we be able to fit her in, do you think?" The detachment was almost too perfect, and Lizzy felt like exclaiming: "Oh, come, my dear, don't overdo it!" But she never gave her husband such hints except when it was absolutely necessary.

"Shall I write that she may come?" she asked, with an air of wifely compliance.

Mr. Robinson coughed—in order that his response should not be too eager. "That's for you to decide, my dear. I don't see why not; if she can put up with a rather dull hunting-crowd," he said, suddenly viewing his other guests from a new angle. "Let me see—there's old Dashleigh—I'm afraid he *is* a bore—and Hubert Clyde, and Colonel Beagles, and of course Sir Blasker Tripp for Lady Dick Marable—eh?" He smiled suggestively. "And Guy Thwarte; is the Duchess likely to object to Guy Thwarte?"

Lizzy Robinson's smile deepened. "Oh, no; I gather she won't in the least object to him."

"Why—what do you mean? You don't—"

In his surprise and agitation, Mr. Robinson abandoned all further thought of *The Times*.

"Well—it occurs to me that she may conceivably have known he was coming here next week. I know he's been at Champions a good deal during the month she's been spending there. And I— Well, I should certainly have risked asking him to meet her, if he hadn't already been on your list."

Mr. Robinson looked at his wife's smile, and slowly responded to it. He had always thought he had a prompt mind, as quick as any at the uptake; but there were times when this American girl left him breathless, and even a little frightened. Her social intuitions were uncannily swift; and in his rare moments of leisure from politics and the mills he sometimes asked himself if, with such gifts of divination, she might not some day be building a new future for herself. But there was a solid British baby upstairs in the nursery, and Mr. Robinson was richer than anybody she was likely to come across, except old Blasker Tripp, who of course belonged to Conchita Marable. And she certainly seemed happy, and absorbed in furthering their joint career. . . . But his chief reason for feeling safe was the fact that her standard of values was identical with his own. Strangely enough, this lovely alien who had been swept into his life on a brief gust of passion, proved to have a respect as profound as his for the concrete re-

alities, and his sturdy unawareness of everything which could not
be expressed in terms of bank-accounts or political and social
expediency. It was as if he had married Titania, and she had
brought with her a vanload of ponderous mahogany furniture
exactly matching what he had grown up with at Belfield. And he
knew she had an eye for a peerage.

"Yes; but, meanwhile . . ." He picked up *The Times,* and
began to smooth it out with deliberation, as though seeking a
pretext for not carrying on the conversation.

"Well, Hector—?" his wife began impatiently. "I suppose I
shall have to answer this." She had recovered Annabel's letter.

Her husband still hesitated. "My dear—I should be only too
happy to see the Duchess here. . . . But . . ." The more he reflected,
the bigger grew the But suddenly looming before him. "Have you
any way of knowing if—er—the Duke approves?"

Lizzy again sounded her gay laugh. "Approves of Nan's
coming here?"

Her husband nodded gravely, and as she watched him her
own face grew attentive. She had learned that Hector's ideas were
almost always worth considering.

"You mean . . . he may not like her inviting herself here?"

"Her doing so is certainly unconventional."

"But she's been staying alone at Champions for a month."

Mr. Robinson was still dubious. "Lady Glenloe's a relative.
And besides, her visit to Champions is none of our business. But
if you have any reason to think—"

His wife interrupted him. "What I think is that Nan's dying
of boredom, and longing for a change; and if the Duke let her go
to Champions, where she was among strangers, I don't see how
he can object to her coming here, to an old friend from her own
country. And Mabel will be here too! I'd like to see him refuse
to let her stay with me," cried Lizzy in what her husband called
her "Hail Columbia voice."

Mr. Robinson's frown relaxed. Lizzy so often found the right
note. This was probably another instance of the advantage, for

an ambitious man, of marrying someone by nationality and up-
bringing entirely detached from his own social problems. He now
regarded as a valuable asset the breezy independence of his wife's
attitude, which at first had alarmed him. "It's one of the reasons
of their popularity," he reflected. There was no doubt that London society was getting tired of pretences and compliances, of
conformity and uniformity. The free and easy Americanism of this
little band of invaders had taken the world of fashion by storm,
and Hector Robinson was too alert not to have noted the renovation of the social atmosphere. "Wherever the men are amused,
fashion is bound to follow," was one of Lizzy's axioms; and certainly, from their future sovereign to his most newly knighted
subject, the men were amused in Mayfair's American drawing-
rooms.

At Champions, after another unhappy night, Nan had Mabbit
help her into her riding-habit and went wanly down into the
breakfast-room, where she put on a bright face and asked Lady
Glenloe if she might have Comet, the old chestnut gelding she had
used when they had ridden before. "I'd like the exercise," she
said.

"Of course, of course! The air will do you good. I knew the
alakar would help," Lady Glenloe said, pleased. "Llewellyn can
go with you."

"Oh, thanks," Annabel said quickly, "but I don't need a
groom. I won't go far; I thought I'd just wander about."

Llewellyn, a short wiry man whose dark face revealed his
Celtic origin, had a lad lead Comet out of his stall, fetch a side-
saddle, and tack him up. As he helped Annabel to mount, he
nodded toward a long black head looking over another stall door.
"I'll not be a minute, Your Grace—"

"No," Nan said firmly, "I won't need you. I'm not going
far . . . and I won't run Comet at a fence," she added with a half-
smile, understanding the focus of the head groom's concern.

Comet was a notorious sluggard, but Llewellyn was grumpily protective of every horse in the stables. "Don't worry about him."

On a childhood holiday on a farm in New York State she and Jinny had tucked up their pinafores and ridden a broad-backed Shetland pony astride, to their mother's horror; in New York they had taken riding lessons at Dickel's Riding Academy, and in London they had ridden a few times in Hyde Park. But after her marriage Ushant had discouraged Nan's riding, even before her miscarriage. She knew that Llewellyn—and Lady Glenloe, and the girls—had, rightly, no opinion of her as a horsewoman. But she could stay on a lazy old mount, at a walk, and she needed to be alone. Until she could escape . . . She had written inviting herself to Lizzy's. . . .

Patting the indifferent Comet on the neck, she walked him sedately through the yard and the paddock into the park, where she let him have his way, a dragging way that suited her inner desolation. The whispers of approaching spring, the tender green shoots of crocuses in the reviving grass—nothing drew her from her sad reflections until, approaching the principal entrance to the park, she heard fast hoof-beats in the lane outside the wall. A moment later Guy Thwarte, on a roan mare, trotted in between the old escutcheoned stone posts of a gate that was always kept open.

Nan's heart seemed to turn over inside her, and her hands on the reins became tight fists as she halted.

Guy, equally startled, reined in so abruptly that his horse reared a little. As he pulled it in he raised his hat.

"Duchess! . . . I thought you were in London."

"It's only me," Annabel stammered, her heart beating almost to suffocation. "They won't . . . Kitty and Cora won't be back till next week. . . . I'm sorry," she finished as Guy frowned at her.

"Cora, Kitty, what do you mean?" he demanded.

"Well, of course, you've come to see them . . . one of them. . . ." Nan tried to keep her voice steady and was grateful for Comet's calming lethargy beneath her.

Guy looked at the forlorn white face under the jaunty riding-hat, at the violet smudges beneath the great dark eyes which looked away from him.

"What on earth?" He made a wide gesture with his crop. "What—? I stopped coming because—"

"Yes, I know—we know," Nan said hastily—she couldn't bear to hear *him* say it—"but they are still away."

"For God's sake!" Guy sounded desperately angry. "Do you mean—? Can you—? I stopped coming because of you. How could I think of anyone else when I know you? How could I care—?" As Nan stared at him with a white intensity, he said roughly: "I can't have you, and it's impossible having to see you—"

He broke off as Llewellyn came up from behind Nan at an easy trot and touched his cap to both of them.

"Your Grace, her ladyship says as I must ride with you." The groom's bold black eyes went back and forth between the Duchess and the flushed and agitated young man beside her.

"Please make my apologies to Lady Glenloe," Guy said to Nan. "I can't come to luncheon after all, because I have to go to Lowdon." With a last long stern look at her, he raised his hat again and trotted out of the park.

"If that fellow hadn't come, I'd have taken her in my arms. And she'd never have forgiven me." Guy cantered on with no destination in mind. "It is intolerable. . . . As my father says, Tintagel is our Duke. I am the Duke's candidate for Lowdon." He trotted through a somnolent hamlet and left it at a reckless gallop. "If I win, it will be thanks to his interest. I shall be 'his man in the Commons,' with endless meetings and visits, dinners at Longlands and Folyat House. And Annabel at his side. . . ."

He must immediately tell the committee that he was withdrawing, so that they could look for a new candidate.

But he'd still be living in the Duke's fief.

Impossible. England would be impossible. He must go to London and make arrangements—at once.

The next morning, Guy was in Leadenhall Street, weaving his way through a crowd of City workers toward the office of his old engineering firm.

BOOK FOUR

XXXIII.

Three middle-aged ladies sat in the jungle warmth of a centrally heated drawing-room, decorated in the French Empire style, in a mansion in Fifth Avenue, New York City, while outside the windows a heavy snowfall whitened the leafless branches of the trees in the Central Park.

Mrs. Elmsworth (whose mansion it was), Mrs. St. George, and Mrs. Closson had long since taken for granted their acceptance, in varying degrees, by the best New York society as mothers of daughters who had married, severally, a duke, an earl who would become a marquis, a courtesy lord who was the earl's brother, a prominent young British statesman widely regarded as a future prime minister, and an American multi-millionaire who was a benefactor of causes dear to van der Luyden, Parmore, and Eglinton hearts.

Three summers ago at Runnymede, when Mrs. St. George and Mrs. Elmsworth had come downstairs in the bungalow to learn that while they dozed the afternoon away Virginia had become Lord Seadown's fiancée, they were told by Mabel and Conchita and, tearfully, by Virginia herself, how Lizzy had sacrificed herself to Virginia's advantage. Mrs. Elmsworth had not been resentful; and Mrs. St. George, knowing that *she* would not have been so generous, had salved her conscience, when they returned to New York, by pushing and pulling Mrs. Elmsworth up a few steps of the great staircase that mounted to the Parmores, Eglintons, and van der Luydens. A relatively lowly station seemed appropriate to a woman who tended to be red of face and short of breath because of overly rigid whaleboning. Mrs. Elmsworth's coarseness was also betrayed by her cheerful unawareness that she—and Mrs. Closson—were being condescended to by their old friend.

Neither Mrs. Elmsworth nor Mrs. Closson, however, was possessed by the almost religious zeal that had driven Mrs. St. George to fight for entry into the circle of Knickerbocker families whom she revered as "aristocracy" superior to any in the Old World. Mrs. St. George had emerged from the battle victorious, and feared a shift in fortune no more than she feared that the storm outside, fast becoming a blizzard, would blow in the windows of Mrs. Elmsworth's salon.

But—vanity of vanities!—"Now that we're here," she and Mrs. Elmsworth sometimes said, echoing the Preacher, "what good is it?" and Mrs. Closson, amiably echoing her two friends, would sigh: "What good?" When Colonel St. George observed after a van der Luyden dinner: "Well, my dear, as the French say, the price of moving in high society is eternal boredom," his wife blamed it on his liking the vulgar company of race-goers and card-players, and . . . those women. (On today's visit at Mrs. Elmsworth's, Mrs. St. George's round featureless face under its fair tower of sculpted curls, crimps, and plaits was ornamented right and left by a pair of large emerald ear-drops which the Colonel had handed her on his return from a business trip to New Orleans.) Yet she had to admit to herself now and then that the big dinners, "*soirées*," balls, and weddings to which they were invited *were* all much of a muchness and, unless you had a daughter to settle in life, presented no challenge.

Of course, in her right mind Mrs. St. George knew that it was thrilling to be bored in the society of van der Luydens, Eglintons, and Parmores. A pistol shot makes no sound if nobody hears it. Her eminence was brilliant less in itself than because of the thousands on thousands of women who read of it, and envied. Mrs. St. George held little stock in imagination. Annabel's "suppose that's" and "if only's" had always irked her. But she pictured with a soaring fancy, and a freedom from geographical pedantry that rivalled Lady Brightlingsea's, those women in their multitudes, from Manhattan on through the Middle West—Montana, Illinois, and the great wheat-fields of Utah—to the Pacific Coast. To know that they would see her name in the proper paragraphs in society columns and read, in interviews by society reporters, her views on benefit concerts and divorce, and her descriptions of the home-life of her daughter the Duchess—for nothing in life, or indeed in the afterlife, would Mrs. St. George have relinquished all that.

Moreover, there *was* a challenge! A revelation had come to Mrs. St. George one morning on the road to the Parmores' such that she cried, in the poet's spirit if not his precise words: "Say not the struggle naught availeth!" In twenty years or so, Jinny's two sons would be of marriageable age; and Jinny'd have others. And surely *some* day Annabel would begin to produce heirs. Without going so far as to advocate the infant betrothals of the wicked European past, Mrs. St. George envisaged an array of noble grandsons in England who would be a compelling attraction to American mothers of baby girls who would duly reach eighteen and come out. Already, if far-seeing prospective grandmothers, her contemporaries, were cultivating her acquaintance, it could only be with match-making in mind; and she could look forward to a place in their very tabernacle, at those *inteem* dinners she was always hearing of, to which *she* was not invited, she was sure, only because the guests were all members of the family.

Meanwhile, since the present grandeur of Mrs. Elmsworth, Mrs. St. George, and Mrs. Closson savoured sweetest when set against the past they had shared in Saratoga and New York City, and against deeper, murkier pasts known only partially to each other, the three matrons often met on slight or no pretext. The theme of today's convocation, though, was not trivial. They were talking about the recently widowed Mabel Whittaker, *née* Elmsworth.

Caleb Whittaker, the Steel King, a man so inordinately rich as to be invulnerable to the "market" that affected Elmsworths, Clossons, and St. Georges, had been a hero of industry and a celebrated patron of the arts for many years. But his apotheosis had come with his marriage late in life to the young and beautiful Miss Mabel Elmsworth, after which funds that had nourished the cultural life of Magnesia, Illinois, were extended to support the art and music of New York, New York. It was known that Mr. Whittaker's wife had guided the extension of his beneficence to New York, and in particular that she had inspired his gift to the newly founded, though not yet opened, Metropolitan Museum of his Meissoniers, Winterhalters, and Bouguereaus.

The Steel King's vast remaining private collection, now his widow's, included Old Masters (Titians, Raphaels, Correggios); sculptures (Berninis, Clodions, Houdons, classical pieces); prints (Rembrandts and Dürers). . . . New York looked forward to a Golden Age of donation and patronage. But last week, after gracious farewells to her fellow-devotees of the arts, Mabel had departed for Europe with her infant daughter, Rosabel Whittaker, and it was to discuss this move that her mother had convened Mesdames St. George and Closson.

Mrs. St. George felt obscurely that Mabel was taking unfair advantage—was, as the Colonel might have said, jumping the gun—in transporting her baby in its very cradle from New York to the scene of international action. But Mrs. Elmsworth exuded maternal pride, not grandmotherly calculation.

"I never realized Mabel was so cultured till I saw these!" Mrs. Elmsworth retrieved the morocco-bound portfolio of newspaper cuttings, compiled by her social secretary, which her guests had been examining. "If I do say so myself, I always made a point of her and Lizzy not getting eye-wrinkles by reading too much. But from a child she was quick to get the gist of a thing—music, art, whatever. People said she married Mr. Whittaker for his money, but it was for the chance to *do* things. . . . Fashion, too, she always had an eye. She promised me she'll tell me about those terrible new narrow gowns."

This was a grievance to which Mrs. St. George could respond. "It was bad enough when we had to stop wearing crinolines, but now! Jinny says the bustle is gone forever, she wouldn't be seen dead in one. And when I asked how they can get enough petticoats under such tight skirts she said . . . she said: 'We don't. We wear long drawers instead.'—*Pantalettes,* you understand!" Mrs. St. George gestured at a large framed drawing of the Empress Josephine, placed by Mrs. Elmsworth's decorator between two gilt-eagle wall-sconces as a final touch to his Empire interior. It was typical of Mrs. Elmsworth, thought Mrs. St. George, to display a portrait of someone with such a reputation as a . . . a . . . Well, Napoleon must have had some good reason to end their marriage! . . . In a voice a-tremble with indignation, Mrs. St. George declared: "It's getting to be almost as bad as in *those* days, when they wore those loose flimsy dresses with nothing whatever underneath, to judge by pictures."

"It depends on the figure, of course." Mrs. St. George's moral fervour had gone over the head of the more pragmatic Mrs. Closson, who continued: "I guess Conchita's going to be like me, full-figured, but your girls, and Lizzy, have the shape. And Mabel looked to me as slim as before the baby."

"And—ain't she pretty?" Mrs. Elmsworth patted a recent photograph of Mabel. "While Lizzy was there it didn't show so much, but now!"

"Very pretty," Mrs. St. George conceded. Mrs. Closson nodded happily. Reclining on an Empire sofa, layered in satin overskirts and petticoats of silk, wrapped in a feather cape dyed peacock-blue—an obelisk on the banks of the Hudson—she was as indolently good-natured as ever. She rejoiced in the triumphs of the other "girls" as in Conchita's, and would have been a perfectly happy woman but that now and then the unpromising situation of her son by Mr. de Santos-Dios set her casting, as in some great fish-pond full of golden carp just beyond her range of vision, for "ideas." Last month she had, yet once again, asked Conchita if there surely didn't have to be some girl in Nan's family, since there wasn't any in *hers,* who Teddy and his guitar could settle down with.

(Conchita, giggling, had shown the letter to Nan, who had said gravely: "Tell your mother that at Longlands we have twenty-five balconies overlooking gardens where Teddy could serenade, but no suitable serenadees." Nan had, in fact, invited Teddy to Longlands for Christmas, but Conchita had been obliged to report to their mother that no young lady had conceived a passion for him.)

Mrs. Elmsworth's latest news of Mabel gave Mrs. Closson a new thought. "Now that Mabel's staying at Lizzy's house— that's in London, ain't it?—do you suppose Teddy could go to visit? He might meet some nice girl there, better than in the country. He wouldn't have to travel."

Mrs. St. George could not deny that, since Conchita was related by marriage to Jinny and Nan, her mother was a St. George connection; but when Mrs. Closson, her person swathed in luxuriant furs to almost globular effect, had descended to her carriage, Mrs. St. George, waiting for her own conveyance, followed what was now a ritual conclusion to meetings of the three friends. "I am more certain than ever," she darkly confided to Mrs. Elmsworth, "that Mrs. Closson . . . Mrs. de Santos-Dios . . . is a *divorcée*— something we have never had in *my* family, or the Colonel's!"

XXXIV.

Belfield was not, as Mrs. Closson supposed, in London, but it was so close that Mr. Robinson had no need to keep the house in Vincent Square open, or maintain a *pied à terre* in Westminster, for nights when the House sat into the small hours. An eighteenth-century-Gothic structure slowly accumulating moss and ivy, capacious enough for the entertainment of many people, it lacked land; but guests so inclined could keep their horses in the Robinsons' stables and enjoy the hunting country on which the Belfield gardens abutted, as did those of nearby Bainton, a house the Prince of Wales was known to visit.

With Mabel's arrival at Belfield after her ocean crossing and Nan's arrival from the Cotswolds, the five girls who had met in Saratoga almost six years ago were together for the first time since Virginia's wedding.

All but one of them were mothers. The infant Rosabel Whittaker and her cousin Aeneas Robinson were here in the house. Conchita's son (conceived, though the few who knew had forgotten, in Saratoga) and Jinny's two were in their nurseries at home. But Annabel, who was responsible for a dynasty, had miscarried of an heir by her own fault and, though only she and her husband, and his mother, knew it, was refusing to cooperate in producing a new one. When Mabel, delighted to be with her friends again and eager to catch up with their stories, asked what it felt like to be called "Your Grace," Nan answered ruefully: "I often feel . . . graceless. I've been slow to learn the rules."

It was five o'clock, and they were at tea in the drawing-room. Nan was still in travelling dress. The others wore loose graceful tea-gowns of coral, peach, vermilion, and, Mabel's, necessarily black—but black with a difference; confected with a thousand tiny pleats and delicate ruchings and bands of ethereal jet-dark lace, it set off a clear face enlivened by a smile that was no longer toothy.

"After all this time, girls—!" Lizzy flourished the silver tea-pot at her guests, who responded by raising their teacups. "And it's the last time we'll be alone together," she told them. "The others will be here before dinner."

"Who else is coming?" Virginia was languidly playing with an amethyst bracelet.

"I think you know them all. The Dashleighs, the Clydes, Horace Beagles . . . and Sir Blasker Tripp," Lizzy ended with a demure side-glance at Conchita, who merely complained: "I thought Guy Thwarte was coming?"

"He was." Lizzy's circling gaze took in Nan, but Nan had turned to place her cup and saucer on the table beside her. "However, I had a note from him this morning, 'regretting.' . . . Some political crisis, I dare say."

"Who is Guy Thwarte?" asked Mabel.

"A charmer, darling," Conchita informed her, "who doesn't try to be one.—But I'm positively *stricken* that he won't be here, Lizzy! He's a widower"—Conchita turned to Mabel again—"who doesn't seem eager to change his status."

"He may be afraid of Mabel." Virginia's rosy lips curved in a teasing smile.

"More likely of Conchita's fatal beauty," Mabel laughed.

"But of course *all* the men are afraid of me." Conchita lazily stretched her arms in their long floating sleeves behind her head. "Actually, I suspect it's you he dreams of, Lizzy."

"I doubt it." Lizzy sent an arch smile in Annabel's direction. "It was when he learned Nan was coming that he begged off. *I* think he cherishes a guilty passion for little Nan and doesn't dare trust himself in her company."

"Ah, you've guessed the truth!" Nan took it up merrily, screwing her features into the funny face she used to produce to make the other girls laugh. They laughed now, and Lizzy said gaily, "So, that secret's out! But now"—she glanced out the window—"here's someone driving up. . . . We'll all meet at dinner."

The older girls—slight differences in age seemed to matter again; Nan caught herself thinking: "the big girls"—wafted from the room like butterflies, pastels and black.

Nan followed more slowly. While she submitted herself to Mabbit's ministrations, she tried to understand why Guy had, according to Lizzy, changed his mind about coming to Belfield when he learned that she would be there.

Was she only imagining that he loved her? No. Since their meeting in the park three days ago she had known beyond doubt that he did. She had hugged the knowledge to her day and night—knowing that she ought not to, but, in her wretchedness, clinging to it as she'd once clung to a tree in a hurricane, trying to clasp her short childish arms around the trunk so as not to be blown off her feet. . . . And because he loved her he was keeping away from her. Realizing that loving her was impossible, he didn't want to see her only among other people, having to guard every word, every look. . . . he didn't want to compromise her.

And perhaps, a sore heart admonished her, he also—naturally—didn't want to compromise himself . . . his whole future.

Of course, he didn't know that his love was returned! If Llewellyn the Welsh groom hadn't come up, so exultant at having won his point about attending her and Comet, she'd have said something that would have shown Guy that she felt as he did. . . . But once she had emerged from a dazzle of amazement and senseless joy, she had resolved that Guy should not learn that she loved him. No one must ever know that they loved each other.

"In a fairy story," she thought, kneeling at her Perpendicular bedroom window and contemplating through its casement, not perilous seas, but dun fields drably extending toward a gray horizon, "I would say, 'You are the only man I've ever loved,' and we'd fly away together. But it can't be so."

When she first met Guy he had been on the eve of self-imposed exile in order to save Honourslove. He had saved Honourslove, and now he must not lose it, lose the whole immemorial fabric of friendships and alliances—Folyats, Marables, and Glenloes, the county—the *country*; Parliament. Nan did not esteem herself highly enough to suppose that he would relinquish his birth-right for her; but, had he wanted to, she would not have let him. He would carry on with his life, even if for one impulsive moment he'd thought he could not. And *she* would strive to carry on being a duchess. But how could she bear seeing him only at Longlands, at Folyat House . . . with Ushant? And how could he not marry? . . . But she would *have* to endure it. "*You must, therefore you can*," Miss Testvalley would have said.

That first night at Belfield she dreamed that she was at Longlands, looking at the sad girl in the Naxos bas-relief, and then suddenly *was* that girl, walking through a field of weeds and outworn flowers toward a black hole into which she automatically began to lower herself, carefully gathering in the folds of her simple Grecian chiton, to return to the Duke. The next instant the free tunic was a tight-laced Worth gown with puffed sleeves and flounces. "This is only a dream," Nan reasoned, immediately; "she's younger than I am, and besides, I can't speak Greek." She woke abruptly.

But Proserpine, Queen of Hades, would return to earth, and crops and flowers would grow again. Annabel Tintagal was living in the unmythological world of railways and gaslight—and the telephone—in the reign of Queen Victoria.

Annabel, convinced that she was still the stupidest and most awkward of the five girls now reunited at Belfield, was nevertheless one of the greatest noblewomen in the United Kingdom. It was thanks to her presence, Hector Robinson pointed out to Lizzy, that their house-party was invited *en masse* to Bainton for the afternoon by neighbours hitherto oblivious of the Robinsons' existence.

Mr. Robinson was detained in town by a meeting and arrived at Bainton House late. So mild was the day that he found everyone outside on a wide stone terrace. He looked about for his Belfield contingent and saw them grouped as if posing for a *tableau vivant.*

Glorious Lizzy. Merely *Mrs.* Robinson, but that would change. Mabel. Softer than in the past, Mabel was handsome and sparkling without being showy, poised without being cold; a modest womanly owner of steel mills and railways. Conchita was more bewitching than ever, Virginia more beautiful. But Virginia's sister—Mr. Robinson still felt not quite right in calling a duchess "Annabel"—lovely Annabel seemed pensive, even sad. With a bow to her and his other guests—Beagles; the Dashleighs and the Clydes; and Sir Blasker Tripp with his out-of-fashion Dundreary whiskers—he took Lizzy's arm in his.

As he did so, the company, as if the wind were cutting a swathe through a stand of wheat, undulated in deeper bows and deep curtsies, opening the way for a bearded man, heavy but erect and of great presence, who slowly came within view of the Belfield party.

H.R.H. the Prince of Wales! And at his side, her left arm prettily crossing a bosom on which diamonds glittered amid the frills of a Valenciennes fichu, the fingers of her left hand playing on his left sleeve—fringe, tip-tilted nose, powder and rouge—it was Lady Churt! Mr. Robinson's mind flew back to the day at the Runnymede bungalow when Lady Churt and his Lizzy had settled Virginia's fate. The same cast of characters—no; Annabel had been in Cornwall then, meeting the Duke of Tintagel.

The Prince of Wales halted—staring, Mr. Robinson thought for one giddy moment, at *him,* the Honourable Hector Robinson,

M.P. . . . But no—at the glowing dark-haired Mrs. Robinson. It was the look of a satyr in a frock-coat, Hector thought, and to his own subsequent astonishment he took a savage grip on the tense arm of his wife: which relaxed as the princely survey of the field swept on and the princely eyes dilated at the sight of the blonde divinity that was Virginia Lady Seadown.

Lady Churt tapped the Prince with a feathery fan, daintily, to recall his attention. Unnoticing, he glanced at a groom-in-waiting, evidently experienced in preparing the battue, who discreetly brought Lady Seadown forward. Her obeisance had the kinetic grace of . . . a Venus—clothed, of course. . . . Mr. Robinson abandoned the quest for comparisons and merely watched as the Prince took Virginia's hand and raised her to her feet. After some words inaudible to bystanders, who had respectfully backed away, and with a bow to Virginia, who curtsied again, the Prince turned back toward the house.

Planted where H.R.H. had left her, her fetching tragic-comic mask fixed in a grimace, Lady Churt took the arm of the groom-in-waiting and, as if continuing a conversation, declared in penetrating tones:

"Yes, an American. But they behave so oddly. Like pirates. You know the Duchess of Tintagel, who's one of them, squeezed eight hundred pounds out of the wretched Duke. She *said* it was for someone who was being blackmailed on account of her, but everyone knows it was *she* who was being blackmailed. It seems she'd had someone in her bedroom on Christmas Eve: Sir Helmsley Thwarte's son, Guy."

Breathless, Hector Robinson watched the unfolding of this new act in the drama he had seen open at Runnymede. Nan's great brown eyes widened and she went red and then ash-white, almost reeling under such an assault by a woman who was a total stranger to her. Virginia blazed at Lady Churt: "You know the Duchess is my sister!" Conchita put her arm around Nan; Lizzy, on Nan's other side, took her hand; and Mabel told Lady Churt distinctly: "*This* is the Duchess of Tintagel!"

As the invaders closed ranks, Lady Churt raised a lorgnette to examine Nan from head to foot and then, shrugging, again addressed the company at large. "How shamingly idiotic of me. But how could one possibly guess that *she* was a duchess?"

"Darling, of course you couldn't."

Lady Churt swung to face Conchita, who let her eyes travel over her old friend's face, from scowling forehead to mascara-ed lashes to painted mouth taut with hatred, before continuing: "*No one* could, Idina darling, because she is so young and fresh— unlike poor old scare-crows like you and me."

"We must leave," Mr. Robinson muttered.

"Not till the Prince goes," his wife admonished him *sotto voce.*

While they waited, Conchita whispered to Nan, "I didn't tell anyone about the five hundred, only Miles, but I haven't seen him for ages, he was becoming a bore. . . ."

"Could there be something in what Lady Churt said, not just servants' gossip, do you think?" Mr. Robinson, worried, asked Lizzy when, after a dinner at which conversation had avoided the one topic of burning interest to all present, final good nights had been said and they were beside the hearth in their bedroom. "If so, you must urge Annabel to be sensible."

But Lizzy's private speculations over the Bainton incident had been taking her in a different, and bolder, direction. She shook her small regal head decisively. "If she's in love with Guy Thwarte . . . if there's trouble between her and the Duke . . . If she wants to leave the Duke we should encourage it . . . but not be seen to do so."

"Leave the Duke?—Leave—?" Hector gabbled, half rising.

With an abstracted "Nan was always one to do the unexpected," Lizzy pondered possibilities. "If Nan went off with Guy

Thwarte, the Duke might want *not* to divorce her, to prevent her re-marrying; but he'd have to, because he must have an heir, and to have an heir he would have to re-marry."

"And so—?"

"So, we have here, at Belfield, not only Annabel but the perfect next Duchess."

As soon as Hector was with her, he flamed with admiration. "Ah! Lizzy, you are a strategist! . . . It—just—might—be done." He laughed. "After all, Mabel is the widow of a King."

"And wouldn't it," his wife asked gently, "be a nicer way to manoeuvre for a peerage through my sister than through . . . the Heir to the Throne?" She eyed him curiously. "Did you really suppose I would . . . ?"

But Mr. Robinson's surge of husbandly supremacy at Bainton House had left its mark. "Did you really suppose," he countered, "that I would let you?" And Lizzy dropped her eyes, then held out a hand, which he took to his lips.

XXXV.

Nan had left the drawing-room early. Virginia, whom she'd expected to insist on catechizing her, had been too absorbed in conversation with the Dashleighs—notoriously the most boring couple in all South Kensington—to look in Nan's direction even once. Nan understood. Jinny repented her grand gesture of solidarity, and wished to be seen as dissociating herself from a compromised sister. Conchita had caught Nan up at the door, saying, "I'll come up; you mustn't care about Idina Churt," but Nan had begged, "Tomorrow, Conchie; I'm dreadfully tired," and had been thankful when Conchita, with a reluctant nod, returned to the bewhiskered, faithfully and hopefully attentive Sir Blasker Tripp.

That afternoon, Annabel had undergone the greatest shock of her life. Her honour and integrity had been savagely attacked, and her deepest privacy violated. A love which she had only the other day acknowledged to herself, and the enraptured discovery that she was loved in return, had been blared out, hideously deformed, before a crowd. . . . As Annabel sat at her dressing-table having her hair brushed, she set her teeth so as not to betray her torment to Mabbit. Her eyes were fixed on the whitely face in the glass, but what she saw was the exquisite, cunningly made up, clever, malignant visage of Lady Churt.

When at last she fell asleep she knew she was lost, somewhere out of doors. She saw her mother looking for her and ran to her, arms out, wailing; but Ceres said, "Don't touch me, darling, your hands are dirty," and Nan found herself on the verge of a black sulphurous crevice that suddenly gashed open a field of poppies. She woke in time to save herself from falling in.

How could she spend the rest of her life in the shades? Why, she might live to be fifty. Or older.

At breakfast, while Mr. Robinson absorbed his *Times,* Sir Blasker looked up from the *Morning Post* and boomingly announced to those at table—Jinny, Mabel, and Conchita had not yet come down: "So, it's not just a rumour: Thwarte *is* withdrawing his candidature."

Hector gave a jerk to the outspread paper that shielded him from view. Lizzy glanced at Nan, whose unguarded face revealed only surprise—and not happy surprise. "She didn't know," Lizzy thought, passing her the toast-rack with a reproachful "You're not eating a thing."

"Who but that fool Tripp," Hector growled in Lizzy's ear when they left the table, "would have had the blasted stupidity to bring that name up, after yesterday? I hope," he told his wife accusingly, "you haven't asked him to stay on!"

Nan went out into the fresh air of the dormant garden and walked up a path edged by box and holly to a bench overlooking the fields she had seen from her room. Far to the right, half obscured by a grove of oaks, lay Bainton House.

Her smooth brow wrinkling, she tried to understand the news that Sir Blasker had reported. Why had Guy resigned his candidacy? Nan realized by now that Lady Churt had not fabricated her lies out of thin air; they must have been a wanton distortion of rumours already going about. Guy must have thought that the scandal would make him a drawback to his party, and removed his name for that reason. "How can he not be angry with me?" she asked herself, sick at heart.

That might be why he had declined the invitation to Belfield.

When she went indoors, Lizzy handed her a note. "It's just come. From the Duke, I think. His carriage is outside."

"My dear Annabel," the Duke had written, "I am at Folyat House and wish you to join me here. The carriage which conveys this message will bring you into town. Yr affectionate husband, T."

The Duchess passed the note to her hostess, saying: "I should be back by mid-afternoon." Her only preparation was to put on, without even looking in the mirror, the hat and jacket that Mabbit fetched, and pick up her purse.

The carriage drew up before Folyat House. The groom-of-the-chambers conveyed Annabel through the oval lobby and rectangular hall and along the wide vaulted corridor issuing from the hall, past the high doors to the gallery where she had shyly presided at dinners for ambassadors, ministers, and minor royalty, and the private dining-room where she and Miss Testvalley and the Glenloe girls had laughed about an elephant, to the Duke's study.

The Duke did not come at once. Nan walked back and forth in a ceremonious room almost as large as the study at Longlands, darkened by mahogany panelling and a purple carpet, its glazed book-cases faintly reflecting the feeble light that penetrated stiffly curtained windows. Seeing a dishevelled image in the mirror above the fireplace with its unlit coals, she took off her hat to pat her hair, but threw it on to a chair when her husband entered. He came to her soberly and kissed her on the cheek.

"It is time—" The Duke interrupted himself to motion Nan to a seat, and placed himself in a chair facing hers before resuming: "It is time that you return where you belong, and do what you ought to do. If your absence continues people may begin to talk."

"People *are* talking." Nan blurted it out. In her disarray she had neither considered in advance what the Duke might say to her nor prepared replies: nor, indeed, thought of a need for preparation—or for discretion. "And I'm sorry; but, Ushant, I have done nothing dishonourable. The five hundred pounds were for a friend, but *not* for Mr. Thwarte; for someone I knew I *must* try to help."

She saw that, if the Duke had come more prepared than she, it was not for those words. Fingering his sandy moustache in obvious bewilderment, he replied: "I do not accuse you . . . do not suspect you of . . . dishonourable conduct. I do not—I am not reviving the subject of the money. But my mother has been upset to learn that you left Champions, for people whom we do not know, without asking my permission."

"I didn't know I needed—" Nan began again: "My sister was there"—and halted. She longed for some recognition by him, even if it took the form of accusing her of serious wrong-doing, that there were difficulties in their marriage that went deeper than his mother's displeasure over what was at most a peccadillo. "Ushant, it's more than that. . . . If I could explain . . ."

"Explain what?" he asked coldly.

Nan looked helplessly at his closed, colourless face. "He always keeps his gloves on," she thought; "he can't bear to touch anything important directly. He can't talk about his own heart.— If I could make you understand . . ." But . . . how could she "explain" the long-accumulated misery that was filling her nights with dreams of death and hell? She gave a protracted painful sigh. "I do nothing but disappoint you; I realize that more and more. I don't justify myself . . . but I am not right for you; you need a different kind of wife. . . ."

The Duke moved his head from side to side, as if trying to shake off a gnat. "It is not a question of a 'kind' of wife. You are my wife. That is the fact, and it is all that matters. . . ." As Nan merely looked at him without speaking, he rose and went to stand with his back to the hearth.

Nan had come to a decision. She rose too. "Ushant, you need, you *deserve* a wife whom you can love and . . . respect; and who loves you. I—don't, and I want to leave you." As he looked at her open-mouthed, she continued, making a great effort: "I must tell you that I love—someone else."

The Duke's face tightened, but he made no sound.

"But he doesn't know it, and he won't. There has been no misconduct. . . . And there won't be. . . . That's not why I'm leaving; it's because I'm so unhappy about the way you and I live. . . . Ushant, I don't even know where I'll go. . . ."

If this announcement of intention had the elements of a cry for help, the Duke did not treat it as such. He said collectedly: "This is all nonsense, one of your fantasies. You appear to think that it's for you to decide what to do—'where to go'—! But it's not. You are bound to do what I say, and I shall see to it that you do."

Annabel looked at a man who had taken her to him passionately on their wedding-night, had been exultant when he learned that she was with child—a child he could not let her forget she had killed. His present remoteness chilled her, yet he *had* loved her; and everything about him spoke unhappiness. Perhaps it did hurt him to know that she loved someone else. . . . Unexpectedly sorry, she put both hands flat to his breast. "I've outlived fantasy. I don't expect happiness. Even now, if I could think you wanted me to stay with you because you miss me . . . love me . . ." Earnestly, intently, Annabel tried to see into his eyes and read his heart.

The Duke returned a stare as unblinking as hers, but his eyes, pewter-gray, clouded and opaque, gave no spark of response, of awareness that something of import was going on. . . . Without repelling her, he backed away from her hands.

"It's not a matter for you to argue about, or appeal . . . for you to decide," he said hoarsely. "You are to come back to Longlands with me now, and you are to live as my wife. You have no choice but to obey. . . . If I have to force you to, I will."

"Ushant—goodbye." Nan turned toward the door.

"You are not to leave this house!" The Duke strode past her, opened the door, called out, in the direction of the great hall, "Don't let anyone leave the house!," and slammed the door shut.

"You can't keep me from going!" The old Nan St. George the Duke had never known flashed at him with such fury that Annabel expected him to seize her by the arm and hold her there, but he crossed to the massive desk beyond the fireplace and pulled the bell-rope.

Nan walked out of the room. Far to her left, moving shapes were silhouetted against the daylight entering the lobby. The footmen had gathered there. Guards. To them, she must be in darkness. She pushed at a green baize door farther along the corridor.

It opened on a narrow passage. On her right was the half-open door, labelled "The Clerk of the Kitchen," of an office with a table and papers. A bell rang in the passageway ahead, the Duke repeating his summons, and a door ahead opened toward her. She stepped into the office and pressed herself back against the wall as Ogilvy, the butler, hurried by and, approaching the baize door, slowed to assume a more dignified gait.

Darting out of the office, Nan hastened past a stairway leading to depths from which a smell of fresh bread wafted, past closed doors, to a doorless pantry where a young man in livery with his sleeves rolled up, polishing silver, saw her and let a porringer slip to the floor.

"I want to go out—is this the way?" she asked.

"Yes . . . yes, Your Grace," he said, and led her down a cross-passage to a door, which he held open for her.

"Aren't you Arthur, from Longlands?" Nan asked, "and weren't you in the dining-room the night when my friends stayed here?"

"Yes, Your Grace."

"Well, thank you, Arthur," Nan said with the sketch of a smile. "And goodbye."

("She spoke sweetly," Arthur Bliss was to say in the months that followed, telling and re-telling the story as the scandal rocked England, "and she smiled at me. A sweet lass she were, even though she were a harlot.")

Nan was in a narrow cobblestoned mews, among pails of water and bundles of hay. At one end, the horses unharnessed from the carriage in which she had been driven from Belfield were being rubbed down, blocking the exit. Taking the other direction, she passed under a high narrow arch into a street, turned a corner, a series of corners, found herself in Oxford Street, and knew that she was safe from recognition. Her progress in the shuffling throng of women shoppers on the pavement was scarcely slower than that of the congested street-traffic of cabs, carriages, and horsemen. Passing a brewer's wagon drawn by two huge Percherons, redolent of hops, she came up with a black-moustachioed organ-grinder who was singing to the metallic tinkle of his barrel:

"Nita, Jua-au-au-nita, ask thy soul if we must part!"

To that tune, seven carefree young people and a poodle with an orange bow had met her governess in the dusty heat of the Saratoga railway station—where everything had begun. Feeling in her purse, Nan found a sixpence and gave it to the musician's monkey.

"Nita, Jua-au-au-nita, thou hast won—my—heart!"

At last, feeling safe from pursuit, Nan paused to get her bearings. She turned into North Audley Street, and, automatically following paths which had become familiar when she and Jinny and their mother lived in town before Jinny's marriage, walked back into her former life. At the tiny house in Curzon Street, pink geraniums still at its windows, her knock was answered by a new beruffled maid no less amazed to see a lady arrive on foot, hatless, than Arthur Bliss had been to see her leave; and when the maid asked, "Whom shall I announce?," Nan replied without thinking: "Annabel St. George."

In her daintily appointed drawing-room Miss Jacky March started from her chair, and Miss Laura Testvalley, already on her feet, exclaimed, "Annabel!"

"I have left the Duke," Nan said. "I have left my husband. . . ."

Miss March dropped back onto her chair. A strange expression crossed her delicate faded face—indefinable, but not of amazement only.

"When did this happen, Annabel?" Miss Testvalley asked quietly.

"Just now. He is in town, at Folyat House; I have just told him. I came here because I thought Miss March might know where I could reach you. . . ."

Miss March's countenance now revealed what was unmistakeably anxiety. " 'Wee, sleekit, cow'rin', tim'rous beastie, O, what a panic's in thy breastie,' " thought Miss Testvalley, eyeing her friend not ungently. Taking Nan by the arm, she said to her: "How lucky, you haven't needed to ask Miss March, after all! and she knows nothing whatever of all this.—Jacky dear, I was about to leave, so I'll just take Annabel along."

Miss Testvalley led a passive, almost inert, runaway Duchess into Hyde Park to a couple of chairs set under a plane tree, and asked bluntly: "Have you left because of Mr. Thwarte?"

"No. That is, in a way." Nan told her governess about Lady Churt's attack at Bainton House.

Miss Testvalley listened raptly, and more than one expression crossed her vivid face; but at the end she said only, quietly: "Ah, that unfortunate visit to the Correggio room."

"I am afraid he has given up his candidacy, because of that lie, but . . . Val, that's the end of it. Even if he wanted anything to do with me, after all this, I—I don't want to hurt him any more."

Looking at the changed face of the cheerful girl she had said goodbye to after the visit to Cheyne Walk, Miss Testvalley sighed. "Annabel, have you come here from Belfield? You need a place where you can be by yourself for a while—away from your sister and the other girls—and from Mr. Thwarte," she said with a mild emphasis that made Nan drop her eyes, "and where, my dear, you will not embarrass your hosts. Some place respectable but obscure. I think . . . yes, I think you would be well advised to collect your things from Belfield and go to my family, in Denmark Hill. Only it would be best not to say where you are going. I can't stay till you go to Belfield and back—I must meet Kitty and Cora, to take them home—but when I fetch my bag at my family's I shall tell them to expect you, and they will be happy to put you up." Miss Testvalley gave Nan the address. "I'll write, and I'll come back to town and talk with you at the first possible moment.—Now I must be off; I'll take a hansom, and Belfield is close enough for you to take one too."

As they walked toward Hyde Park Corner, Miss Testvalley stopped in her tracks. "Have you any money?"

Nan looked in her purse. "Masses. And when I was at Champions, Ushant forwarded a letter from my father saying he's deposited money for me at his London bank. It's a huge amount."

(It was far and away the largest of the sums the Colonel had sent, irregularly, to his daughters. He was on to "something big," he had told Nan in his cheerily dashed-off note, and this was for her private, "secret," purposes. If only she'd had it earlier, she realized, she needn't have asked Ushant for money for Conchita. She suddenly felt a craving for her father, for him to engulf her in his bear-hug and promise with a grandiose wave of his cheroot that he would "take care of things.")

At the Hyde Park Corner stand, Nan insisted that the governess take the first cab and waved as it set off—then swayed where she stood. She had had no lunch, no breakfast, and next to nothing at dinner last night, a dinner aeons distant. She bought and devoured, standing, two large buns, with a cup of strong India-tea, before setting off in a cab herself.

The arrival of the Duchess of Tintagel in a hackney-cab caused a sensation at Belfield among the servants who witnessed it. When she asked where she would find Mrs. Robinson, she was reminded: "Your Grace, it's the time when the mistress goes up to see Master Aeneas." She had forgotten Lizzy's schedule of motherhood. At the foot of the last flight of stairs to the crenellated turret that housed the day-nursery, she drew her skirts back to make room for a buxom nanny preceding two young nursemaids, one carrying Lizzy's boy, and the other Mabel's girl, down to perambulation in fresh air. In the nursery, its Gothic walls papered with bright pictures of kittens and jack-in-the-boxes, Lizzy, Mabel, Virginia, and Conchita were laughing about something, two of them on a sofa and two on small chairs at a small table.

Seeing Nan's face, all four fell silent.

"I have left the Duke."

A stunned silence was broken by a shriek: "Nan St. George! Are you crazy? You—you—why, you just wait till I tell—" Virginia stopped, but Nan knew how the sentence would have ended: "—till I tell Mother."

Conchita hugged Nan and murmured: "But, darling, you don't need to leave your husband to be happy." Mabel cocked her head, puzzled but alert; Lizzy frowned and pursed her lips.

Virginia recovered from her regression to childhood. Her blue eyes blazing in a face crimson with a fiercer rage than yesterday's, she lashed out: "How can you do this to us? We all stood up for you against Lady Churt!—And was it true, what she said, after all?"

Nan shook her head wearily. "No, it wasn't, Jinny. But I *must* leave Ushant, and I had to tell all of you."

She went down to her room, rang, and, when her maid appeared, asked: "Will you please pack some things I'll need for two or three days? And then I'm not going to need you, and I think you'll want to go to Longlands."

Mabbit, stiff with injured pride, asked, "Haven't I satisfied Your Grace?"

"Oh, yes," Nan said in eager reassurance, "you have, and I thank you; only from now on I shan't have a maid. And at Longlands they'll be glad—"

Having knocked, Lizzy came quietly in. Nan told Mabbit: "Mrs. Robinson will see that you get to Longlands safely—won't you, Lizzy?"

"Certainly, if necessary," Lizzy said formally, "but, as you may know, Mabbit, my sister, Mrs. Whittaker, needs a personal maid; hers is ill. Could you stay on with her?"

"Very kind I'm sure, ma'am." Mabbit looked down her nose. "But I have always been in the service of the Family."

"Yes, of course; but if you could bear to help out for just a little while? Mrs. Whittaker would be more than grateful—"

"Well . . ." Grudgingly, Mabbit nodded.

("You've installed an agent of the Dowager Duchess in our house," Mr. Robinson protested, when he heard of this arrangement. "She'll store up everything she sees and hears and report to Longlands."—"We'll be able to decide what the Dowager gets," retorted Lizzy. "Mabbit's description of Mrs. Whittaker as a model young widow in every way may arouse interest.")

When Mabbit had left, Lizzy perched on a chaise-longue, her face softening, and said gently: "Nan, I didn't say, but I . . . I want to help—"

"Oh, Lizzy!" Surprised—she had not expected Lizzy, who managed life so competently, to feel concern for a woman who'd made so poor a use of greater opportunities—Nan knelt beside the chaise-longue and took Lizzy's hands in hers. "You're generous, but—well, Jinny and Conchita are secure, but you and Mr. Robinson . . . I am already damaging someone's career, I don't want to compromise the two of you."

Lizzy gripped Nan's hands while her fine blue eyes searched

Nan's face. "Nan, tell me. . . ." Lizzy hesitated. "Do you really, truly, want to leave the Duke? Have you thought carefully?"

"Yes." Nan met Lizzy's question with equal gravity: "I can't go on. I'm too unhappy with him. Ushant needs a different sort of wife entirely. He wants to do right, but he thinks he has to be perfect, and so he has this mountain of perfection bearing him down. . . . Lizzy, he is *scared stiff* of his mother! Any of you would have been a better wife to him than I. He needs someone"—Nan had a flash of illumination—"*someone like Mabel!*—who would help him stand up for himself, and please the Dowager at the same time. And Mabel is so rich, maybe the richest woman in the world, it said in the papers! She'd be on equal terms in a way.—Well, almost," Nan emended with a crooked smile, thinking of the Dowager's expectations.

Lizzy embraced Nan to hide a mounting blush.

"We might as well have taken her into our confidence," she told her husband when they went up to bed. "She suggested Mabel, herself. I am ashamed."

Mr. Robinson, who intended to become a statesman, not a mere politician, had trained himself to see all sides of a situation. He rubbed his chin thoughtfully. "It would be unwise to write Guy Thwarte off. Sir Helmsley's not what you'd call a good life. That high colour—those wheezing fits—an apoplexy could carry him off any day, and then it'll be Sir Guy and Lady Thwarte; and with a duchess who wasn't hostile to Annabel . . . Let us suppose—" Assuming his parliamentary posture (unconsciously modelled on Napoleon's well-known attitude), Hector began to tick points off with a finger as he did when presenting a bill in the House: "Let us suppose that the Duke marries Mabel and has a son and then dies . . . is killed in a shooting accident, say—he's said to be a careless gun—leaving Mabel as guardian of his heir. Sir Guy and Lady Thwarte return to Honourslove. Mabel's influence makes them accepted by the county. In time, her son the new

Duke marries a daughter of theirs. . . ." Hector halted, belatedly aware of Lizzy's icy stare.

"I never knew," she said tartly, "that you were so imaginative."

Nan had told Lizzy that she would take a valise with things for a few days to London, by train. Lizzy could send the rest of her belongings to the left luggage at St. Pancras.

"But where will you go, in London, Nan? Will you be all right?" Lizzy asked as they waited at the door for the fly to come round from the stables. The others were at tea. Nan had told Lizzy that she would leave quietly; she'd write to Virginia later.

Unused to deception, Nan answered, "To Miss Testvalley's family in Denmark Hill" before she remembered that Miss Testvalley had counselled secrecy. "But, please, Lizzy, don't tell anyone."

The fly carried the Duchess to the local station. From St. Pancras she took a cab to the Testavaglia house in Denmark Hill.

XXXVI.

When the Duke of Tintagel was informed that the Duchess had left Folyat House by a door into the mews, he said, "Very well," and told his informant he might go. He dined alone that night without uttering a word.

The Dowager Duchess had carefully grafted pride of rank and reverence for custom on a nature already cautious, humourless, and self-distrustful, but neither nature nor scientific improvements had rendered her son capable of violence. He could endure; could resist, dig his heels in; he could insist, and (as he had just proved) could even threaten if convinced that his cause was just. But he knew he could not employ physical force. Annabel's religious duty to produce as many children as he saw fit was also a legal obligation. He could have the police find her, wherever she had gone (to one of her American friends, probably), and hale her back. But, the abhorrent public show aside, if when she was restored to him she remained recalcitrant, was he to break her door down, or order his servants to do so? Impossible. And once he had entered her room? The Duke tried to imagine. . . . "Perhaps, if I were angry enough," he thought, "but . . . how many times?" He *must* have a son. He must have more than one son. But his mother, conscientious though she was, had produced six girls before *he* was born. . . . In trying to keep Annabel at Folyat House—actually shouting to his servants to bar the door—he had gone as far as he could.

The event itself, the stupefying fact that she had run away from his house—and by a mean egress, with his stable-boys as witnesses—and the strain of preserving an impassive exterior delayed his full consideration of his scene with Annabel. No sooner had he realized that jealousy might be appropriate than, a self-disciplined man, he had deferred indulgence of the emotion. Only when he had retired to his grand gloomy bedchamber and dismissed his valet did he allow himself to dwell on her saying that she "loved" another man. He had believed what she said about there being no misconduct: that the man didn't know. Yet it came back to him that she had lied about the five hundred pounds being for a charity. There also came back to him his mother's face on Boxing Day, when she spoke of Annabel's indiscretion in the Correggio room, and the day after, when he told her that Annabel was refusing him his rights.

Now he saw that jealousy was uncalled for. It was a case of theft. Annabel had withheld something that belonged to him. A thief had taken it (or meant to) from her—that is to say, from him. It was not that he had failed as a husband. Annabel's affections, flighty to begin with, had been alienated by Another.

The brooding Duke interpreted his misfortunes in the perspective of a very personal *Weltanschauung*. He viewed the God of the Church of England as a master Clock-maker who had designed an eternal machine which He kept wound up and which needed no repair save when damaged by Nihilists or Republicans. (Or, the Duke now added to the list of trouble-makers, contumacious wives.) Too modest to aspire practically to more than tending to common clocks, in this realm of secret pleasure the Duke had always had his dreams. At Eton he had passionately followed reports of the construction and triumphant public début of Big Ben, and he had gone on to examine foreign achievements. That clock in Munich with its mechanically gesticulating figures of a king and queen and musicians had, almost, tempted him to travel, as the Colosseum and the Alps had not. Without going abroad, he had conceived of an even finer wonder-works: At the first stroke of noon, doors would open on a platform onto which a throng of wooden figures, shining with gilt and the brightest possible red, green, orange, and violet, would step in order. A king and queen would bow to each other, a mitred bishop would raise his crook, a soldier aim a gun, a blacksmith strike an anvil . . . each figure performing its divinely appointed, divinely timed, role.

The microcosm of human society which the Duke had an ineluctable obligation to govern fell short of his ideal. The Duchess failed to curtsey to the Duke, or turned up in the slot belonging to the milkmaid . . . or the key in her back unwound crazily and her springs flew apart.

It was typical of her that she had gone out into the street bare-headed! How (the Duke asked the world defensively) could he have been expected to know that she wasn't simply going to her room, when she left her hat in his study?

But while the Duke did not underrate Annabel's imperfections, he admitted to himself that he had been inept. He had wanted a young maiden whose foot, under his careful schooling, would grow to fit the glass slipper. It might have been wiser to seek a woman whose feet were full-grown, whose record of performance could be analyzed like that of a race-horse. . . . But such thoughts, irresistibly as the defective apparatus in the wooden Annabel's spine, sent him whizzing back to his distaste for marrying a woman who wanted to marry a duke. . . . He had longed for an Impossible She who would appreciate his position—and not want him because of it.

Next morning he walked down through St. James's to his club. His intention was to avoid the unseen glances of his servants—he knew there were glances!—and hear nothing that would remind him of his wife, but he had forgotten that the matter ramified beyond his household. His was a Tory club. Thwarte of Honourslove—whom Annabel had mentioned and not mentioned—had withdrawn from the Lowdon bye-election, citing "personal reasons"; and no fewer than three members, among them the venerable Lord St. Alfont, the Duke's godfather, alluded to a rumour that Thwarte was about to leave the country. Before the Duke went home, he wrote a letter and rang for a servant to deliver it to Chancery Lane.

At eleven the next morning, Mr. Cyril Dinsmore of Dinsmore, Fortescue, and Ford conducted the Duke to the heart of a labyrinth of darkish rooms stacked with deed-boxes and trusted that His Grace and the Duchess were well; he regretted not having had the pleasure of seeing Her Grace since the wedding. He blinked three times in rapid succession when the Duke said heavily: "The marriage must end. She has left me. By the door to the mews, in full view of my servants."

Mr. Dinsmore, whose wizened mien suggested a diet of ink and parchment, was the grandfather of four young children with whom he played lawn-cricket every week-end when weather allowed. "Poor boy," he thought, "so that's why he came here instead of summoning me. But that charming girl!—*Poor boy?!* You're a dead stick, sir!"—"An informal separation," he offered, "not infrequently eventuates in reconciliation."

The Duke's lips stiffened. "Impossible. The marriage must end."

"Your Grace envisages divorce? On what grounds? Desertion? Adultery?"

"She has told me that she is . . . attached to someone but that there has been no misconduct. I believe she is truthful. I believe . . ." With stronger conviction, the Duke said: "For two years she has refused to . . . perpetuate the ducal line."

Sighing, Mr. Dinsmore (of such stuff are eminently successful family-solicitors made) quelched sentimental considerations, deftly put questions, and quickly perceived that the answers formed a not-unfamiliar pattern.

The Duchess had asked for money for a person whom she refused to identify but who she stated, unasked, was not Mr. Guy Thwarte. She stated that she wished to leave the conjugal abode but not because of a man whom she admitted to "loving" but did not name. Mr. Thwarte had abruptly cancelled his political plans and was reportedly leaving England and his family estate.

Having ascertained these facts, Mr. Dinsmore deliberated for a few moments before he gave an opinion. "Certainly, refusal to perform what a learned jurist has termed"—he coughed—" 'the most obvious duty of a wife' is cause for divorce, as is desertion. If there is adultery, the co-respondent could be jailed and sued for damages. If the parties are taken *in flagrante delicto*—"

The Duke's face puckered. "I prefer," he said fastidiously, "to avoid the sensational."

"Your Grace is too young to remember when the Duchess of Newcastle left the conjugal abode—with a foreigner of lower class, a Mr. . . . Opdebeck." Mr. Dinsmore clucked at the uncouth name. "After a hue and cry over the Continent, they were caught, although they were using an alias. . . . *There* was sensation for you! And the press, Duke, is far more licentious today."

"I only want it over with," the Duke said bleakly, "as soon and as quietly as possible. I do not want anyone fined or gaoled or, or . . . I am not vindictive. I only want—*never to see her again*." He turned a proud cold face to his adviser while his fingers moved as if twisting some minute object. "I must be at Longlands for the County Assizes, and I wish to have a plan decided before . . ."

Silently supplying "my mother knows," Mr. Dinsmore proposed: "If so, Your Grace, let us review the possibilities."

Since Annabel's unexpected visit, Miss Jacky March had quivered through gradations of amazement, horror, and, yes, something like exultation! at behaviour so unlike her own. She felt drawn to a compatriot who would demonstrate that *one* American scorned the greatest marriage in the United Kingdom! (Other than Royal, Miss March corrected herself, scrupulously; but, of course, Royal marriages were inviolable.) She could not jeopardize the network of noble friendships that was her very life; could do little to help, and nothing openly; yet there were tiny practical details which dear Laura, so intellectual, might not have thought of.

Miss March had heard the Dowager Duchess congratulate herself on having found for her "perfect daughter-in-law" a lady's-maid who was loyal to the Family. She opened a quaint *papier-mâché* box, looked through its contents, murmured, "Yes, they would do," and procured a sheet of note-paper. A conscientious frown crinkled her delicate withering face as she began a letter pointing out to "My dear Laura" that, obviously, Annabel must have a maid who was loyal to *her*:

> . . . Alas, a woman willing to serve a lady in A.'s *peculiar* situation would probably present a "character" from an actress *or worse!!* However, I know of two respectable women who might consent to serve A. I attach details. <u>My name should not appear in this connection.</u>
>
> Some might think my wish to help A. impious; but my dear Father, who was revered by his parishioners in South Braintree, and *indeed throughout Eastern Massachusetts,* held views on the position of married women which he used to say were "un-*orthodox* but not un-*Christian*"! Neither woman has experience in hair-dressing, but that, you will agree, is of small importance in these quite <u>extra-ordinary</u> circumstances!! I <u>rely!! on your not mentioning my name!!!</u> Ever your affect. friend, J.M.

When Miss Testvalley delivered Corisande and Catharine, fatiguingly rapturous over their experiences as bridesmaids in Norfolk, to Champions, Lady Glenloe was not there. She had left a note explaining that Lady Brightlingsea had implored her to come to Allfriars, as Lord Brightlingsea was seriously ill. Seadown and Lord Richard were coming to see their father, but she needed Lady Glenloe's company and support.

Miss Testvalley read the note with acute interest. Her mind flew to poor silly Jacky March, a letter from whom lay beside Lady Glenloe's, and who must not first learn of the absent-minded peer's fatal illness by seeing his name among the Deaths in her morning paper. "My dear," she wrote, "I have sad news which I wish I could give you in person, knowing how grieved you will be to hear. . . ." She was sure, in a P.S., that A. would be grateful for the kind suggestion as to a lady's-maid communicated by an unknown friend.

Dear Jacky had the crotchety innocence of an American spinster; no—Miss Testvalley quickly enlarged her generalization— the innocence of an American. Unlike the English, she always assumed the best. "Whereas nothing evil under the sun can astonish me. . . . Not," Miss Testvalley—who was alone in the sitting-room—muttered with a fine Italian shrug, "that I am exactly English, spinster or no." Jacky lived in a choice cranny of the world of fashion; she got on well with Lady Churt; she helped make matches that were often, at best, convenient, with the innocence of an ostrich. Apparently it hadn't entered her head that Annabel might be guiltily in love with someone. (The Reverend Mr. March's broad-mindedness presumably had not extended to adultery.) Or if it *had* entered her head, Jacky supposed that Annabel enjoyed the same rarefied sentiment that she herself entertained for Lord Brightlingsea. Miss Testvalley had decided long ago that only ignorance of passion had enabled Miss March to spaniel at heel the very people who had insulted her. That, and—but was it cause or effect?—a deranged sense of reality. A phrenologist palping that busy little head under its curls true and false would certainly be struck by the development of Miss March's bump of self-delusion.

The still more engrossing news awaiting Miss Testvalley at Champions was that Sir Helmsley Thwarte at Honourslove had

had another fall and was back on crutches, poor gentleman. After a moment's disappointment and concern, she felt an ashamed relief that she would not, immediately, have to discuss his son with him while concealing what she had learned from Annabel.

On the day after her return, she received a basket of yellow roses from the Honourslove conservatory and a basket of blushful grapes from the grapery, with a note eloquently expressing Sir Helmsley's vexation that he could not bear the jolting of a carriage even when his destination was his Laura—for whose comforting presence he longed, for reasons *trop complexes et pénibles* to confide to a letter. Miss Testvalley composedly asked the man who had brought the offerings to thank Sir Helmsley on behalf of the young ladies and herself and extend their kindest wishes for his rapid recovery.

Later in the day, following a conversation with the Honourslove messenger, who had partaken of a meal below-stairs, the housekeeper approached Miss Testvalley in the hall with avid speculation in her eyes: "They do say Sir Helmsley's that beside himself because Mr. Guy won't be in the Parliament. Right wild, he is!" Folding her arms over an imposing black wool bosom, the woman paused, in evident expectation of a good long talk. With a nod and a non-committal "Oh?" Miss Testvalley went past her into the library.

Refusing to gossip about the Family helped preserve a self-respect often bruised by disdain or thoughtless discourtesy from above. Having had more than her fair share of "the spurns that patient merit of the unworthy takes" (not that she was always patient!), Miss Testvalley sometimes reminded herself that the cultured Greeks to whom Roman citizens used to entrust their sons' education had the legal status of slaves. That was a sour consolation. She found healthier recompense in the play of her nimble irreverent mind over the absurdities of the great. But she would not chatter about them—even if she antagonized domestics already hostile toward a person who put on airs, though her *clothes* were *mended*!

Like all the county, Laura Testvalley knew about Sir Helmsley Thwarte's near-criminal thriftlessness. (She had discovered the falsity of the rumour that his son too was feckless and had married for money.) She had heard of Sir Helmsley's legendary uncontrollable fits of rage, ugly and even dangerous; and she knew from personal observation that he was vain (but what man was not?).

Against all that, Sir Helmsley, besides being charming in his hard-bitten way, was cultivated. Refined by bodily suffering, he had come to delight in the company of a woman who read Petrarch and to identify her, playfully, with Petrarch's Laura: far more interesting, he maintained, than Dante's Beatrice; and who had inspired a real, human love, not a tepid idealization! The governess felt an astonished gratitude that he found her attractive as a woman. This was how Daphne, who was metamorphosed into a tree—in fact, into a laurel, Laura thought with a little laugh—might have felt had she found herself changing back from wood into soft sensuous female flesh. As for Sir Helmsley's offering a middle-aged Cinderella the unimaginable solace of shelter and protection . . . offering an end to the fear and loneliness that clutched her by the throat at midnight . . .

Miss Testvalley—Sir Helmsley chose to call her Miss Testavaglia, in honour of her illustrious antecedents—was too familiar with disappointment to dare succumb to hope. There were obstacles to the match of which, almost certainly, Sir Helmsley had as yet no suspicion. For he believed that his son was still fancy free.

What *was* certain was that her post at Champions was nearing its end, though whether she would go on to become the lady of a baronet, or vanish into a struggle for subsistence unarmed by references from great ladies, was in the lap of gods whom Miss Testvalley knew to be capricious. Anticipating the day when she would leave her pupils for good, she firmly brought them back from weeks of frivolity to school-work; and while Cora and Kitty, amenable if not all that studious, plodded through assignments in French and the history of art, she drew up a Reading List which she presented to them in a session held not in the school-room, with its homely vestiges of the nursery, but in the library. They were books by authors, some of whom they already knew, which they *should* know and would be *glad* they knew as time passed. "Shakespeare, Mr. Matthew Arnold, Mr. Browning. Hamilton's *History of Philosophy*. Lord Macaulay's *Lays of Ancient Rome*. Lord Bacon's *Essays*. Read *Jane Eyre* (though some disapprove of it). Coppée's *Elements of Logic*. Homer in Pope's translation." As the two pairs of china-blue eyes fixed upon her grew rounder and bluer, the governess ended, smiling: "And I hope you'll read Manzoni's *Triumph of Liberty* and some poems of Leopardi's, which I have translated, though not so well as they deserve; I've re-copied them, to place in this library for you."

"But, Miss Testvalley," Cora gasped, in panic, "there must be at least a hundred books! How long a time do we have to read them in?"

"Oh, years! As long as you like. Only don't think of them as lessons, but as great books which will enlarge your experience. As Lord Bacon says, 'Reading maketh a full man'—or woman! You will be happier, more resourceful for knowing them."

"How many years," Kitty asked, "did it take the Duchess to read them?"

XXXVII.

"If Her Grace isn't there, ask where she can be reached."

Guy Thwarte sealed an envelope and gave it to his manservant Spaulding in the hushed writing-room of his club, where he had been putting up while in London.

He had been occupied by meetings with his colleagues, with City bankers, with representatives of the King of the Hellenes; with manufacturers of steel rails and directors of railway companies who might have old rolling-stock to sell. Immersion in work saved him from thinking of Annabel. But whenever he lifted his head from papers, her face, dimpling or wet with tears, a rainbow face, was there; and her soft voice, with its lingering American intonations, was a strain of music always at the back of his head.

Guy did not regret his hasty decision to leave England. He knew from experience that work would deaden memory. New work, a new country—and a new language. He had been assured that in Greece everybody who was anybody spoke fluent French or English; but he wanted to talk with nobodies, as he had talked Portuguese with workmen in Brazil, and would have learned the local Indian dialect if he had remained. A knack for languages had made his teachers direct him into the diplomatic, where he had found that only French mattered. Now a little white-haired man with the archaic profile and the archaic grimace, Mr. Demosthenes Goussias, was giving him a few lessons in modern Greek (the Greek of Eton being incomprehensible to present-day Hellenes).

He knew he wouldn't go on forever repeating Byron's "*Zoe mou, sas agapo (Annabel, sas agapo)*" like a love-dazed automaton. But in the meantime he had before him Annabel's pale, shocked expression and tragic eyes when he had burst upon her in the park at Champions. He couldn't go away without seeing her. He would ask forgiveness for his boorish outburst, tell her that he was going away, wish her happiness, and leave.

As Guy pondered his future, the club porter brought him a letter from his father angrily demanding an explanation of his absence from Honourslove and informing him that Lady Glenloe had said that her girls would soon be home and that the Duchess had left Champions to stay with people called Robinson, at Belfield, near London.

Annabel at Belfield?!—Guy would have been there himself if he hadn't written telling Mrs. Robinson that he couldn't come, on the truthful pretext of business. They would have been under the same roof. . . . Probably better that he hadn't gone . . . he might not have kept to his resolution. . . . Was she still there?— He couldn't very well go now, himself. . . . Besides, he didn't want to see her for the last time in a crush. . . .

Spaulding took Guy's note for delivery by hand to Annabel at Belfield, where the servant at the door said that Her Grace had left for London; and subsequently took it to Folyat House, where a footman stated that Her Grace was not at home, but then, looking behind him, whispered to his confrère that Her Grace weren't at Longlands neither: a dereliction of duty which Spaulding, although he gave his master only the gist of the reply, recognized as symptomatic of grave domestic upheaval. In the Thwarte establishment too there was disturbance. Spaulding had wondered at Mr. Thwarte's strange decision not to run for Lowdon (he had looked forward to being the private gentleman of an M.P.); and when he heard of the move to heathen parts he decided, after mulling it over, to tell his employer that he would prefer to stay in England and trusted he might hope for a favourable reference.

Guy in person went twice to a house in Mayfair where Lady Seadown was not at home. On his third enquiry at Lady Richard Marable's, two streets away, he was told that Lady Richard *had* returned to town, and as he mounted the narrow red-carpeted stairs Conchita rushed down to meet him.

"Where? If only I knew!"—Conchita talked over her shoulder as she led him up into her little L-shaped drawing-room, where he shook his head at the offer of a chair and stood tensely as she continued: "How could that woman tell such lies!" Seeing Guy's blank face, Conchita cried, "You don't know about Bainton House?" She pushed him down on to a sofa and sat beside him: "H.R.H. was there, and Idina Churt said, in the loudest possible voice—and you know her quietest voice is a *shriek*—she told everyone present that Nan had wheedled eight hundred pounds out of the Duke to give to you—"

As Guy's mouth dropped, Conchita sobbed, "Idina Churt is a dangerous woman; they ought to have someone walk in front of her waving a red lantern to warn people. It was *me* Nan lent money to—five hundred pounds, not eight!—money I desperately needed, but I wish now I hadn't asked for. She's my dearest friend, ever since Saratoga, my best friend."

Guy got up, at once taut and befuddled. "Please, Lady Richard, I can make no sense. . . . Why in God's name would this Lady Churt want to harm Annabel?"

"Why, to get at Jinny! Seadown threw her over to marry Jinny! Didn't you know?" Conchita demanded. "Darling, everyone knew! And just now— You see, we were all at Belfield, and we were invited over to Bainton, and H.R.H. was there. He saw Jinny, and everyone could see he was absolutely bowled over.

He'd had Idina hanging on his arm, but he simply forgot that she existed. So, you see, it was the *second time* Jinny had a triumph over Idina. . . ."

Guy passed a hand over his forehead.

"So, Idina screamed out that Nan got the money from the Duke to pay you because you had been in Nan's bedroom at Christmas—"

Guy's bewilderment became horror. He looked aghast at Conchita, wondering if she were mad, or *he*, as she hurtled on with her story.

"—Then, when we were back at Belfield, Nan had a command from Ushant to come to Folyat House, though I don't think he knew about Bainton; the Marlborough House set is not his style. So she went, and then she came back to Belfield—in a hansom, darling!—and told us she had left Ushant."

"*What—?*" Guy almost shouted.

Conchita paused, as if only now aware of her visitor's special interest in the story she was telling. When she resumed it was with a significant smile. "Yes! She'd run away from him! Then, only no one knew but Lizzy, because we were all at tea, she went off bag and baggage, except that actually she only took a little valise. She even left her jewel-case behind, her maid said."

"But where"—Guy asked between his teeth—"did she go?"

Conchita sadly shook her pretty auburn head.

His visit to Conchita Marable left Guy in a turmoil of emotions. He was agonized in Annabel's behalf. That she—shy, a stranger to smart society, transparently candid and vulnerable—should have been exposed to an attack that would have been scarifying even for a blasée woman of the world—!

But . . . she had *left Ushant*! And if she truly meant to be free of her magnificent, burdensome marriage he would no longer be prohibited from telling her how he felt. They might be able to share a future. . . .

Had she *really* left Ushant, though? Or was Lady Dick, in her exuberant way, exaggerating? Or had she left him only because of a quarrel they might both want to patch up, to avoid a scandal beside which the Bainton House incident would be as nothing? . . . "Moreover, she may think that I talked—lied—about the Correggio room," Guy thought wretchedly as he walked down Park Lane.

His mind was still a battle-ground for hope and fear when he walked up Holborn next day in a dismal smoking rain.

Guy had removed his legal affairs from the family firm when his father's inroads on the fortune left him by his mother created a conflict of interest and a chaos which only a fresh mind could reduce to order. The solicitor whose fresh mind he had called on, Anthony Grant-Johnston, had been at Eton with him. Both had entered the Foreign Office, both had left it for less prestigious but more satisfying careers. Grant-Johnston—stockier now, but his round freckled face still framed by ginger curls—was negotiating, with the solicitor of the engineering firm, the details of Guy's new post.

"They want you to find out whether it's feasible to build a railway in Greece. The study may take several months, and I collect that the feasibility is doubtful?"

"Ten years ago the Americans linked the Atlantic and Pacific oceans by completing the Union Pacific. In Greece, ten years ago, Piraeus, the port of Athens, was linked with Athens—seven miles away." Guy recited these facts as by rote, scowling at the wall over Tony's head. "Nothing has happened since. The question is, can the line be extended to Larissa?" Guy stood up and, shoving his hands into his pockets, paced the short distance from his chair to a window overlooking Chancery Lane, gray with drizzle, and back.

"Quite." Tony looked at his client askance. "Next, there is construction in India which I gather may go on *ad infinitum*. Besides paying"—Tony read off particulars from a file of papers on his desk—"they propose to make you a partner, sharing general profits. It's a handsome offer; shall I tell them you agree?" When Guy failed to respond, he asked: "Difficulties?"

"Not with their terms." Guy stalked across the room to admire the view of Chancery Lane again, and turned. "I had better tell you."

"Pray do." Tony leaned back in his chair and clasped his hands behind his head. "Pray do."

Guy sat down again. "A lady whom I know—" he began; and stopped.

At school, of course, one had not talked about personal matters. Parents, sisters and brothers, girls one might know, were never mentioned. When Guy went back to school after his mother's funeral he had spoken to no one about it, not even to Tony, a friend; nor had the code of reticence been violated on the occasions, widely separated, when they had met since. Guy was aware that he was crossing a boundary when he went on:

"This lady has left her husband. So I have been told by a friend of hers."

Guy gave what he took to be the tenor of Conchita's disorganized story. "If she actually *has* left him," he told Tony emphatically at the end, "it's not on account of me. She thinks of me only as a friend. But if the—if her husband should want to divorce her, this scandal connecting our names might make things far worse for her—and *everything the Churt woman said was a damned lie!*" Guy realized that he was shouting almost with his father's ungoverned vehemence. "Tony," he said more calmly, "I can't have her made a spectacle of. She's only a girl, and a foreigner, with no family here—that is, no men of her family—to look after her. Not that I suppose her husband would want publicity, either. He is a peer, in fact a duke, and he has an aversion to being talked about."

"No matter what any of you might *wish,* I don't see how an open scandal could be avoided." Tony's mind was almost visibly running down the short list of extant dukes with foreign wives.

"She is utterly innocent.—I daresay," Guy brought out pessimistically, "it's not easy for a solicitor to believe that possible."

"Believe?!" Tony's good-natured face clouded. "I *know*! Not as a lawyer, as a brother." He picked up the dossier before him and smote the table with it. "My sister's husband was a brute. He put her through hell. She left him and . . . she was indiscreet, nothing more! But he set detectives on her, and their evidence was accepted in court. *She* was the guilty party." Tony threw the papers down and looked levelly at Guy. "I stayed with her for a time. I'd left the F.O., partly on her account, and I was reading for exams at her place in Runnymede. There was a cottage near by which Lady Churt—that same Lady Churt—had let to some jolly American girls." Tony's mouth twisted. "I went over once or twice, but their duenna made it clear to me that I would not be allowed to bring my sister."

With the awkwardness of a new intimacy, Guy only said, slowly: "I had no idea. . . . It's a beastly world. . . ." He drew a long breath. "Well, then you know who the lady is. . . . She's only twenty-three—if that. How can I go off leaving her in God knows what kind of mess?"

Tony was cool again. "If you want to help her, don't be seen with her. For one thing, remember that in these cases there is always the possibility of a reconciliation; all the more reason to be discreet." Seeing that this idea did not rejoice Guy, he drummed his fingers on his desk. "She thinks of you as 'a friend.' But you—?"

Guy found a relief in saying frankly: "If she has left the Duke I shall ask her to marry me. But she's thought of me *only* as a friend, and now she may blame me for her being named in that canard. And she may be right to blame me." He sprang up and again stalked to the window and back, thinking of the Correggio-room incident and what gossip had made of it. "Only—if you knew her, you'd know it's impossible to associate her with anything sordid. She is—crystalline." His fists on the edge of Tony's desk, Guy said desperately: "I *must* see her."

Tony looked up at him with an unencouraging face. "Obviously, that canard may make the Duke and his people believe he has stronger grounds than desertion—he had the right to detain her in his house, you know. They may allege adultery. The truth doesn't matter—Be she as pure as snow, she shall not escape calumny." He persisted over Guy's growl of protest: "If you see her, don't let people know. I'll try to find out what's happening. Be prepared for detectives. For melodrama. Don't be seen together."

Tony stood up and clapped his friend on the shoulder.

"Seen together!" Guy laughed shortly. "I don't even know where she is."

The evening was clear and windless; starry, with a full moon, and chilly. People crossing Westminster Bridge walked hurriedly, while Guy, leaning on the parapet, repeated to himself: "I don't even know where she is."

Ships, towers, domes . . . the view was as fair by moonlight as at dawn. " 'Dull would he be of soul who could pass by a sight so touching in its majesty. . . .' Then I *am* dull of soul," the young man thought, "for all I can think of is Annabel Tintagel." Would he see her to say goodbye forever, or would he prevail on her to come with him?

Uncertainty and suspense were new to him. Whereas his father might be said to leap to confusions, actions Guy took equally without forethought usually turned out to be as sensible as if consciously based on "*usage et raison.*" He had changed his profession without soul-searching; but it had been the logical course if Honourslove was to be saved. There had, of course, been Paquita—But this was different. His new move was a means of escape; and although his mind had been assuring him that it would "work," his heart contended that any happiness he could know would depend on Annabel's being . . . at least not *un*happy. If he went away knowing that she was miserable in her marriage . . .

How had it come about that she meant more to him than anything else in life? He hadn't intended, hadn't expected, it. When he returned from Brazil he had felt the old attraction; but she was both an unattainable duchess and a "poor little thing" whom he wanted to protect—and his protectiveness included protecting her from caring too much for him. . . . How fatuous! He had supposed that *he* ran no danger of affection's turning into passionate love. Older and more experienced, he could control the situation! . . . Then, at some indeterminable moment *entre chien et loup,* he was in love as violently as if she were a *femme fatale* and he a callow youth; as deeply as if Paquita and the other women he had loved were only a prelude. A phrase came to him: "Twice or thrice had I loved thee, before I knew thy face or name."

Guy felt as if he were wallowing in the trough of the waves: not the mild ripples of the moonlit Thames, but the mountainous breakers of an ocean sea.

He would try to do whatever was best for her. But—he must *see* her.

He had tried Lady Seadown's house again; although lights and the music of a pianoforte indicated life upstairs, she was still not at home. She might be sheltering her sister from a man with whom she was being falsely linked.

A police-boat issued from under the arch beneath him. Police! Guy thought of Tony's warning and trembled for Annabel. . . . But if Tintagel had found her, rather than sue for divorce he might have sequestered her in some remote Folyat tenement as suppressive as an oubliette. . . .

Such ideas could enter the head of an engineer only by way of a fevered imagination. Fevered, but suddenly cold, Guy pulled his collar up and left the bridge as Big Ben began to chime the hour. The last stroke of seven sounded as he entered Palace Yard and asked for the Honourable Hector Robinson, who joined him promptly, his ruddy face eager, in the busy lobby of the House.

"I hope this is to say you've changed your mind about Lowdon, Thwarte? The Party needs you."

"Decent of you to say so." Guy shook hands. "But I'm leaving the country, to be away for some time. I ought to see the Duchess of Tintagel, on business of my father's" (a lie Guy had decided on), "or get a letter to her, before I go. I think she's been staying with you; would you know where she can be reached?"

"She's not at Folyat House?" Hector began hypocritically. He had always resented a man born into the ancient gentry, a man with a casual self-assurance that came, unfairly, of "birth." Since learning of Thwarte's withdrawal from candidacy (though supported by a duke!), Hector had also felt a wondering contempt for a man who could knowingly ruin his own career. And there was a rumour in the House that Thwarte was going abroad (South Africa some said)—a rumour Mr. Robinson could now tell his colleagues was confirmed! Mr. Robinson knew as never before the intoxication of being an insider in the inmost centre of the capital of the world.

Lizzy's plan called for Guy's learning where Nan was. ("Unless they meet, nothing will happen," she had argued; "if he went abroad without seeing her, it might all fizzle out. She might go back to the Duke; or he might charge desertion, which takes ages.") But Lizzy didn't wish to be known as the person who revealed Nan's whereabouts. When the message came that Guy's man had a letter to deliver to the Duchess, Virginia had been in the room, and therefore Lizzy had told her servant simply to say that the Duchess was no longer at Belfield. Hector could safely give the information now. But, seeing Thwarte's drawn face, he spoke out of sudden fellow-feeling, as well as calculation, when he went on: "If not, I rather think she's gone to a former governess, Miss, ah . . ."

"Testvalley. Miss Testvalley. Where?"

"In Denmark Hill. I don't know the number."

"Thanks, Robinson." Guy wrung Hector's hand.

"He *is* leaving England!—though he didn't say where he's going. Somebody said tonight, Turkey. And the whisper is that Tintagel is taking steps. . . ."

"Imagine," Lizzy murmured, "of the whole lot of us, little Nan in a scandal! It's ironical."

Hector had come home at ten, and sat in his study amid piles of White Papers and ranks of Hansards with a whisky and soda at his elbow and Lizzy across the hearth. All their guests except Mabel had left.

"And scandal mostly false," Lizzy added.

"Mostly?" Hector's tone made it a challenge. "Is there any truth whatever—?"

Lizzy politicly treated the question as a simple request for information. "Nan is certainly in love with Guy Thwarte, but I don't think there's anything 'going on.' And I don't think she's run away from the Duke because she expects to marry Guy. But no one is going to believe it's all innocent, with gossip spreading as it is. . . . Mabel says that Mabbit, when she was packing Nan's things to send on, told her, sanctimoniously, she was 'sure there was nothing in what the head groom at Champions said about Her Grace's having an assignation with Mr. Thwarte in the park one morning.' "

Hector made a sound of disgust.

"We're all at the mercy of our lady's-maids," Lizzy said philosophically; "though how Mabbit could talk that way about Nan, who couldn't have been sweeter to her . . . ! Mabel loathes her."

"Why keep her?" There were times when Hector wished to dissociate himself from his wife's machinations.

"The stakes are high," Lizzy reminded him.

"But just how do you bring Mabel and the Duke together?"

Lizzy chose to overlook the personal pronoun. "You remember that funny little Jacky March? She's close to Lady Brightlingsea and friendly with the Dowager. Mabel's going to call on her, naturally; she introduced us to London, you know. Mabel has a beautiful bit of antique silver she bought at an auction, to give her. Paul Revere work; it seems he was an ancestor of Miss

March's." Hector's blank face revealed an abysmal ignorance of the ancestral silversmith's name, but Lizzy went on without breaking step to enlighten him. "Her *forte* is 'facilitating social contacts,' especially match-making. The Runnymede bungalow was her idea. She will naturally mention Mabel to the Dowager Duchess. That comes first."

"But if Miss March helped bring Annabel's marriage about, will she want to work for the cause of another candidate for duchess?" Parliamentary figures of speech were second nature to Hector.

"She had nothing to do with that! If anyone helped there—helped the Duke, I mean, not Nan; it was the Duke who wanted Nan, not *vice versa*—it was Miss Testvalley.—You know, I'm almost positive that Miss March and Lady Brightlingsea had intended *me* for Seadown, not Jinny. Miss March and I," Lizzy added pensively, "understand each other."

Hector abstained from comment. "Second?"

"Lord Brightlingsea's very ill. They say it's a matter of months." As Hector's good-looking face lighted up on receipt of a new item of news, Lizzy continued: "The Duke, his nephew, will stay at Allfriars with the new Marquis and the new Marchioness—Seadown and Virginia."

"Marchioness thanks to you."

"And now it's her turn to help us."

"But look here!" Hector felt obliged to point out flaws in feminine reasoning. "The Duke won't want anything to do with Annabel's sister."

"Virginia will make it plain that she disowns Annabel—as, believe me, she does; she is seething!—and sides with the Folyat-Marable family. Among the guests at Allfriars will be one of her oldest friends, Mrs. Whittaker, who's godmother to the little new Lord Seadown and therefore part of the family."

"Ah!" A reminder of reverence for motherhood and the Church. "I hadn't thought of that," Hector handsomely acknowledged.

"Jinny will also make sure that our dear old Miss March is

there. She'll be in widow's weeds, the same as Lady B., I don't doubt, for Lord B., who jilted her!" Lizzy laughed with rich amusement at the foible. "I'm told she thinks of Seadown as her son, so I suppose Jinny's her daughter-in-law! She and Jinny will make Mabel known to the Dowager—and thus to the Duke!"

XXXVIII.

In Denmark Hill, London, S.E., Annabel Folyat or Tintagel, calling herself St. George, was hidden away as securely as if she had donned the cap of invisibility. Nobody knew where she was except Lizzy, who wouldn't tell anyone, and, of course, Miss Testvalley, who had written to say that she could not leave Champions because Lady Glenloe was at Allfriars with Lady Brightlingsea, as Lord Brightlingsea was very ill.

Miss Testvalley had made no reference to the Thwartes of Honourslove. When she came to London, Nan would ask her to let Guy Thwarte know where she was, even if, as she sensed, Miss Testvalley disapproved of her seeing him. Then he could come or not come as he chose. Nan feared that he was angry because the scandal had caused him to give up his candidacy, yet she believed that he would want to see her again—once. And she would assure him that there'd be no further scandal to harm his career, for she'd be across the Atlantic. . . . At that point, every time she rehearsed a self-sacrificing farewell speech, Nan would break off and go for a walk through the streets of Camberwell and Peckham to clear her head and whip up her heroism—and return to the Testavaglias' house having achieved very imperfect success.

It was a modest brick house set close to the pavement in a suburban street of comfortable mansions environed by spacious gardens and inhabited by wealthy tradesmen. The family had owned it, Nan knew from Miss Testvalley, since their early days as refugees, thanks to a political sympathizer, black sheep of a wine-merchant's flock (but *not* the wine-merchant whose son Mr. John Ruskin, also of Denmark Hill, had become the apostle of Dante Gabriel and the Pre-Raphaelite Brotherhood). The rebel son had sold the leasehold to old Gennaro Testavaglia, then young and fiery Gennaro Testavaglia, for the nominal sum of twenty guineas. But the rebel had been tamed, had served a term as Lord Mayor and received his knighthood; and for many years Miss Testvalley's family had had no protector except (though she did not say so) Laura Testavaglia.

Annabel was a refugee in a household which her mother would have decried as "low-class." At the round table that had rubbed threadbare circles on the cheap Turkey carpet in the dining-room, Gennaro and his two old sisters, benign and silent, breakfasted on coffee and thick pieces of bread, unbuttered; their other meals consisted of soup and what they called "pasta," manufactured daily by the old cook and *bonne à tout faire* Serafina, accompanied by red wine that Serafina bought by the jug. But the same table, its surface not always innocent of tomato sauce, also served for Gennaro's halting and vague work on a study of Petrarch; and the walls, like those in all the other rooms, were lined with books in several languages and hung with lithographic portraits of Risorgimento patriots, and faded broadside manifestos of creeds no longer seditious. For the first time, Annabel was among people who cared—*had* cared—more for ideas than for possessions; and she divined a nobility of the spirit loftier than the *noblesse* derived from Norman blood.

Old Testavaglia, his black eyes dimmer than in his portrait, evinced no curiosity as to Fifth Avenue or Wall Street in talking with Nan (whom Laura had introduced as an American). He requested information as to the state of the serfs emancipated by President Lincoln and the recent work of la Signora Harrietta Stowe. Once or twice, his eyes glittering strangely as eras coalesced, he spoke to Nan not only of Garibaldi and Mazzini but of Voltaire and Washington and the Marchese di Lafayetta, and once even of Brutus, in a conspiratorial whisper, tugging an invisible cloak up to cover his lower face, and looking over his shoulder from under an imaginary slouched hat.

Conversation was confined to meal-times, between which the Testavaglias dozed, read, or slowly wrote; except when Nan, too restless to read, went to the kitchen, where Serafina vouchsafed copious information as to her children and their children and her nephew who had died whose widow, Anna, a cousin from Firenze, was staying with her. The sad-faced Anna, dressed like a Londoner—whereas Serafina dressed exactly as she had in her village in Calabria—told Nan that she wanted to return to Italy. "But I am waiting till I will have more money from the restaurant which I work, I am at the *cassa*. . . . One gains more in London, but I would better go." Anna's black eyes suddenly glistened with tears. "Italy is more beautiful, and my family will be glad. I have the *nostalgia* of Italia; I am . . . what is the word?"

"You are 'homesick,' " Nan answered, wondering whether *she* could work at a restaurant *cassa*, envying Anna a family whom she would gladden by returning home.

At night, despondently gazing from her bedroom window at roofs and treetops and stars, Annabel thought of the New York hotels she and Jinny had grown up in. Of Saratoga. Conchita's wedding. The steamer, and the low undistinguished New York skyline receding as her heart leapt toward the storied beauty she would find in England. And of the myriad changes wrought by a single journey.

Now a return crossing was ordained. For she couldn't stay in England. That she would be an embarrassment to everyone she knew was irrelevant. She *could not* stay on never seeing Guy. Reading, one day, of his engagement to a suitable girl. . . . How could Miss March have elected to remain, not only seeing her false fiancé but actually cultivating the friendship of his wife? Nan had once warmly sympathized with an elderly lady whose love had been greater than her pride; but she now thought that Miss March's love must have been of a weedy, sickly variety.

New York (where else could Nan go?) was a blur of gor-

geous private houses like the one her parents had built in Fifth
Avenue, and which her mother had described minutely in letters
to both daughters; of tasteless public buildings, wretched slums,
unhandsome inharmonious streets, noise, confusion; above all, a
city where she would have no friends. The people she and Jinny
had known, and those their mother now knew, were all in the
business of getting married or being married and having children
or getting their children married. She would no longer be a *jeune
fille à marier,* but a divorced woman, unfit for the society whence
she came, and obliged to earn a living.

"For I can't let Father support me as a reward for my making
a failure of my life," she thought as she went into the sitting-
room with pen and paper.

The room was furnished in a style which her mother's and
Mrs. Elmsworth's decorator might have dubbed "Second-hand
Utilitarian," and it was icy cold. "Even so," Annabel thought,
"it's England, and I'd rather be here." Sighing, she began a letter
to her governess. "Please thank your anonymous friend for her
suggestion," she wrote:

> But I shan't have a servant—let alone a lady's-maid! I
> must find a way to support myself, in America. I can't
> let my father support me—why should he? I count on
> your advice when you come. I thought I might be able
> to teach small children, just to read and write, or per-
> haps work in a settlement-house, or an orphanage. I
> believe they sometimes give their staff room and board.

"It will be very exciting," Nan went on with a great sob, "to
be in a different place and be able to do something to help people.
I hope to see you soon. Please give my love to Kitty and Cora."

Nan knew that she wasn't qualified to be a governess. Denmark Hill had given her a new appreciation of the Marias, Elizas,
Christinas, Francescas, Lauras (but there was only one Laura!)
who acquired learning (even Greek, some of them) from their

fathers and brothers, and then taught the daughters of the aristocracy, in order to support the idealistic Republican men of the tribe.

Nan gave way to helpless, solitary mirth at the vision of her mother—or Lizzy's, or Conchita's—sending "the girls" out to support the Colonel or Mr. Elmsworth or Mr. Closson. Or Teddy de Santos-Dios!

The hilarity did not last. She thought about the precariousness of Miss Testvalley's penurious and uncomplaining life, with the result that she posted a note asking Virginia to meet her the next day between eleven and twelve at . . . She had thought of a park or a museum, but fixed on St. Paul's, which she and Jinny had visited as tourists, as being far from Mayfair in every sense; and at eleven the next morning she walked slowly about the vast domed cathedral, where the music of an organist practising sounded grandly, stopped, and soared again in sublime new chords.

Tired, and too strained to yield herself to the music, Nan sat down, put her head in her hands, and wished she could turn to Jinny, not necessarily for sympathy, but for intimate talk. They had grown away from each other; yet somehow life didn't dissolve bonds between sisters, only made the bonds more tortuous even than they had been when they seemed simple. She and Jinny had played together and slept together; had fought with each other, but had also shared some of their thoughts. Once, when she was about nine, Jinny had confided in her a strange memory from when she was little, maybe two or three, of being in a kitchen and watching Mother at a stove, stirring something in a pot. Did Nan think it could be true? They had considered the question solemnly and decided that Jinny had had a funny kind of dream. Neither girl had ever mentioned it to the other since.

Rising, Nan saw Jinny coming toward her, veiled, but recognizable by her graceful shape and elegant gliding walk.

As they sat down, Virginia raised the veil and demanded in a tone between a low voice and a loud whisper: "Nan, how could you do this to me?"

This was not what Nan had hoped for; the old fierce anger welled up. "I didn't 'do' anything to you!" she said hotly. But as Virginia frowned, Nan controlled herself and said quietly: "I can't stay with Ushant. I'm going away; it will be best for you, won't it, if I just vanish quietly?"

"It can't be 'quiet,' and *he* doesn't like scandals." As Nan frowned, puzzled, Jinny, without explaining, asked defiantly: "And what about Guy Thwarte?"

"There's *nothing* about Mr. Thwarte!"

"Do you realize people are saying that Ushant is going to divorce you?"

"He ought to. Not because of Mr. Thwarte; but because I've deserted him."

"Nan, you're crazy," Jinny said beneath her breath. "I came here—at the risk of being seen with you—because I thought you might say you want to go back to him."

"No. I asked you to come because I want you to do something for Miss Testvalley."

"What? *Who?*" Jinny's eyes, blue even in the dimness of the nave, widened. "Why?"

"She'll need to find a new post. She had nothing to do with my leaving Ushant; I think she disapproves. But everyone will think she's behind me. I don't think she'll be at Champions much longer. And who will give her letters of recommendation now? My mother-in-law? *Yours?* Lady Glenloe?"

Nan bit her tongue. She was afraid that Jinny would ask why Lady Glenloe should be angry, and didn't want to reveal Lady Glenloe's hopes for her daughters (or, rather, for one of them). But Jinny didn't ask, and Nan went on quickly: "*You* can help her. She lived in our family for three years. It's thanks to her that we came to England—that you'll soon be the new Lady Brightlingsea, the première Marchioness. *Do* write a letter she can show at the agency she goes to. You know she's a perfectly splendid teacher!"

"I wouldn't know how to." Jinny had never been much of a one with a pen.

"Say 'pleased to recommend . . . long acquaintance . . .' Well, I've written it out." Nan handed Jinny a sheet of paper. "Write something like that, and be sure to show that you are Virginia Marable, Countess Seadown. Do you promise?"

"I'll . . . try," Virginia said sulkily. "I'll see. Only, if you're right about people blaming her, they'd be furious if they found out. Nan, I have to go, I'm supposed to be . . ." She stood up.

Nan, rising with her, forgot her grievance in a rush of sadness and affection. "Jinny, we may not see each other again for years and years." With a sore heart, she put her arms around her sister, who kissed her cheek. "Goodbye, Nan; I really must go." Virginia carefully lowered her veil and walked to the door. Then, suddenly, she turned.

"Jinny?" Nan went to her eagerly.

"If you go to New York," Jinny said simply, "Mother will kill you."

From the porch, Nan watched her descend the great flight of stairs and gracefully mount the step of a waiting hansom. Only on her way back to Denmark Hill did she realize that her sister had given her no promise.

"She never lets me forget that I'm younger and more ignorant," Nan fumed as she jounced about in a stuffy, crowded eastbound omnibus. "I always think I'm the youngest person in the room . . . in the bus. Ushant thought I was a malleable child, but I invited it. I let myself fall in love with Guy by making believe that he was an 'older' man, and I encouraged him to think that I was a little girl. But I am twenty-three years old; I am a married woman who has had a miscarriage; I am going to be divorced; and I am in love with a man I can't marry . . . who won't want to marry me."

"In fact, *I* am a detrimental now. And I'm tired," Nan muttered that evening, eyeing with disgust the baby-face in the mirror as she brushed crossly at her hopelessly tangled curls, "of being an ingénue."

She would write to Ushant and to her father, and she would try to arrange her future—once she had seen Guy. She must tell him that she was going to America, and say goodbye in a civilized, modern, nineteenth-century way.

XXXIX.

Guy Thwarte asked the old woman who came to the door garbed in Mediterranean black if the Duchess of Tintagel could receive him.

"*Duchessa?*" A stare and a headshake.

Was Robinson wrong? Guy wondered. "Is there not a young lady, a friend of Miss Testvalley's, *una giovane donna*—?"

"Ah." The wrinkled face lightened. "Annabella, *la ragazza. Sì, sì, vieni, vieni. . . .*" Serafina crooked a finger and led him in.

Nan, at the sitting-room window, had recognized Guy's tall figure and firm stride as he came down the street; had seen him go to the house opposite, where someone opened the door and, after a moment, pointed at the Testavaglia house. She was glad of this brief warning, which allowed her to recover some presence of mind. She had at last prepared a speech, and when Guy entered she was able to begin it. "I'm so glad you've come, so that I can say goodbye properly; we've been such friends. . . ." She kept her head high.

Guy stood and looked at a *ragazza,* her tawny curls coiled carelessly at the nape of her neck, whose huge dark eyes met his gaze steadily even though a fierce blush mounted to her cheeks. "No one would believe," he said, "that we have never even kissed," and took her in his arms. In their eager, long first kiss, Nan trembled with pleasure; and as Guy's lips moved from her mouth to her closed eyes she gasped, clinging to him, "Oh, I do love you. . . ." She was dazed, yet aware of her every pulse-beat, and of every breath of the body so close to hers. She ran her hands over the strong shoulders beneath the smooth broadcloth as Guy muttered against her cheek:

"I could not ask you . . . I knew you didn't care about Longlands and all that . . . but how could I ask you to give it up? Ushant was never the man for you, but I couldn't let you lose . . . I love you more than anything in the world, and now— Is it true that you have left him?"

"I have left him, yes. I ought never to have married him."

"You were too young to know. Now you must marry me."

Nan, still in Guy's arms, and with her arms about him, half lost in a fiery sweetness, could still say: "No!—I'm not too young now to know what *you* would lose if we married. I know what you *have* lost." She pressed his head closer to hers, stroking his thick fair hair. "You can't give up Parliament."

"That's done," Guy said firmly. "And so is this—I am leaving England."

Nan pulled back and looked into his face, astounded. "What?"

"I'm going abroad, to work. To Greece. I leave within a fortnight. The only question is, will you come with me?"

"I don't understand." Nan stared.

"I couldn't go on seeing you and him together. . . . When I saw you in the park at Champions and knew I'd have swept you from your saddle if the groom hadn't interrupted, I decided I couldn't go on in London—or anywhere else in England."

"Even then? Was *that* why? I thought you had quit the election because you'd heard those rumours—those lies! But *have* you heard them?"

"Only yesterday. Lady Richard told me. I was trying to find you. She told me that you'd left the Duke, but she didn't know where you were. Finally, Hector Robinson told me."

"Well," Nan said, "you must not go away. *I* am going back

to America. Do you think I would let you sacrifice Honourslove? I know what it is to you!"

Guy took her by the shoulders and looked down into her flushed determined face. "I *would* give it up for you—I was going to—but now I hope I shan't need to. Do you remember when we talked about that Cavalier poem, on the terrace, years ago? 'I could not love thee, dear, so much, Loved I not honour more'? In the last few weeks—you can't think how insane I've been—it's turned itself round in my head: 'I could not love Honourslove so much, Loved I not Annabel more.' It's monstrous poetically; but everything I care about in Honourslove is *in you* too. If you were with me, I'd have it with me. Whereas if I were there without you, knowing you were with him, and unhappy—"

"Oh . . ." Nan sighed from the sheer joy, however short-lived it must be, of knowing that her deepest feelings were shared. "And all that I care about is in you. I've been so lonely—a stranger even to myself for so long. . . . It's like coming out of cold and darkness into the sunlight . . . like coming to life. . . ."

"Like a flower unfolding." Guy touched her soft cheek. "You *are* a flower, Annabel . . . a rose coming to bloom."

"Not a rose, with the colour of my petals." Nan dimpled. "A tiger-lily, more like. . . ." But a sense of the brevity of their time together came over her. "Dear Guy," she said sadly, "it's sweet loving each other, the sweetest thing I've ever known, but we can't go on, we—"

Glancing about the small, poorly furnished room, Guy led her to a horsehair sofa and sat down beside her. "Does Ushant understand that you're definitely leaving him?"

Annabel hesitated. It was important to tell Guy exactly what had happened. "Yes. He said he would make me go back to Longlands with him by force if he had to. He said he would force me to . . . act as his wife. He said I had no choice but to obey him."

Accustomed to Ushant's phlegmatism, Annabel hadn't expected the fury Guy displayed; he jumped up, swearing under his breath; then came back and gripped her hands in his. "But, my God, Annabel—"

Annabel swallowed. "I haven't—been his wife since I lost my baby. I said no, and when he tried to stop me I ran away by a door to the mews. . . . It was a *very* definite departure, not to say vulgar. Now he will divorce me for deserting him."

"When he hears about that Churt woman's lies he will try to divorce you for more than desertion. For . . . infidelity."

"I told him I was in love with someone else; I didn't say who. I told him there'd been no wrong-doing, that the man didn't even know; that nothing would come of it. . . . I'm sure he knew I was telling the truth."

"His lawyers will advise him to act as if you hadn't been truthful."

"I have thought of that—oh, I've thought! . . . And you would be named; you'd be involved."

"Darling Annabel," Guy said, "we're both involved, and, except for the insult to you, I welcome anything that will set you free."

There was a new tenseness in him. Nan looked at him, gravely questioning.

"If you had simply left Ushant," he said slowly, "—not that 'simply' is the word—I'd have begged you to marry me, and have kept on begging. If you had said yes, we'd have stayed apart, waiting till you were free. But things have changed, thanks to Lady Churt. Ushant will probably sue for divorce, citing me. And I'm afraid . . . How can I leave you alone, to face the horrors alone, either here or in America? If you will come with me, I . . . I will hold you in respect."

Nan shook her head vehemently. "You can extricate yourself and live as you ought to, but not with me as a drag. Does your father know about this? He will be very angry—"

"I've written to say that I'm going abroad to work on a railway project. Now that I've found you—at last!—I'll go down and face him, and if you'll allow me, I'll tell him about us as well—" Over Nan's attempted expostulation, Guy persisted: "We can't let him, any more than Ushant, decide the whole rest of our lives. . . . You will come with me, Annabel?"

Nan tried to muster her failing resolution. "I want so much to be with you that I can't see things clearly; I need to think, I've never thought of anyone but myself, now I'm thinking of you too, and I have to be sure. . . . I must wait till Miss Testvalley comes."

"Miss Testvalley?" Guy was obviously taken aback. Perhaps, Nan thought anxiously, he was hurt, or displeased, that another person's opinion was so important; she hastened to explain. "You see, I told her that I had *not* left Ushant because of you, and I wrote to her saying that I'm going to America and asking advice about earning money. . . . She won't try to influence me; she's wise but she's . . . well, detached, even when she's fond of people. . . ."

Nan fell silent. Guy was unquestionably frowning, yet not angry—or not angry with *her*.

"Annabel," he said, taking her hands in his, "I would never deny you independent thoughts—other advisers."

It hovered between them, the image of the Duke, whose attitudes Guy evoked by their opposite. It was so palpable that words weren't necessary to tell him that she understood. It was enough to exchange a long, deep look in a silence broken only when Guy said, drolly: "That is, of course, so long as the advisers advise you to marry me. . . . Annabel"—he was serious again— "you know, it hardly makes sense for you to go to America and me to go to Greece when what we want is to be together. Heroics won't do!"

Nan started to smile. "The truth is," she confessed, "I've been bracing myself so hard to cope with an unhappy ending that I can hardly imagine anything else. . . . I'm still afraid to hope."

"I'll go to Honourslove tomorrow. I'll tell my father that I love you and won't rest till you say you'll marry me.—No!" Guy jumped up, pulling Nan with him. "No, I'll go today!—I want to see my solicitor—I shall just manage the train." He stroked Nan's face. "Darling, your cheeks are hollow . . . and you're thin; you've gone through a frightful time. But that's going to change." He held Nan as if he'd never let her go, then broke away, with an "If I leave now I'll see you again all the sooner." He seized the hat he had dropped on a table and went out. From the window, Nan watched him turn at the gate and wave, then hurry up the street.

"Application of the law," Grant-Johnston stated, "is inconsistent, absurd—and unequal, which may be to your advantage."

As Guy looked a question, his friend's candid freckled face creased in a smile that was in large part cynical. "It's easier for a man to get a divorce than for a woman, for a nobleman to get a divorce than for a commoner . . . and I daresay for a duke than for a marquess, an earl, a viscount, or a mere baron. A husband can hire detectives to spy on his wife and the co-respondent, and bribe servants to bear witness. On the other hand . . . the Lords heard a case—you were abroad, or you'd have seen it in the papers—in which the husband had petitioned for divorce; the wife had sent him a letter saying she had left him for another man and then gone to Australia."

"And?"

"The Lords deferred issuing the decree until they were sure that the lady had been served notice of the lawsuit. . . . So a letter of confession sometimes serves; and if a duke wants a divorce but doesn't care about revenge—"

"But, of course, the spouses can't say they both want the divorce?"

Tony, who had been leaning back, teetering on his chair, sat up so abruptly that the front legs hit the floor with a thud. "Don't *breathe* the idea! There's covert agreement all the time—everybody knows it—but the worst thing that can happen is for a judge to suspect 'collusion, condonation, or connivance.' Though, there again, I wonder. . . . With a duke the court might turn a blind eye."

"It's barbaric."

"At best. But"—Tony wagged a cautionary finger—"assume the worst. If you do persuade her to . . . to . . . to . . . to accept your protection until you can marry, assume that you'll both be followed. That is, the Duchess will be if they find out where she is. She may think the Duke wouldn't 'do' that, but his lawyers would. We're a cutthroat crew.—What are your plans, if she agrees?"

"I would have her cross the Channel; to Boulogne, I think. I'd follow as soon as these papers are taken care of, and we would go to Greece from France."

"Have your man travel to Folkestone with your luggage and get it aboard the Channel steamer."

"He doesn't want to stay with me, understandably; but he's a good sort. I can trust him to do that."

"You will travel separately, as for a short business-trip, with one bag and a ticket to Paris. At Boulogne have your luggage put in the *consigne*. You won't take the train to Paris, but go to a hotel. Not hers. From there on, you make your own arrangements.—Yes." Tony understood Guy's look. "There's a regular *modus operandi*. Just the same, old man, this case has its points." Tony's eyes unmistakably glinted. "How often does an American girl want to leave an English duke? It's bound to interest not only us lawyers but the public."

"Forgive me," Guy said, "if I don't share your professional excitement."

Sir Helmsley received his son without preliminaries. "What's this! You're not standing for Lowdon! Now you say you're 'leaving'? Leaving England, leaving Honourslove? I trusted you!" Gasping, Sir Helmsley continued: "I—I have kept Honourslove for you,

I trusted you to carry on—it's eight centuries—to tend to the estate . . . to merit your birth-right!"

He lowered his eyes as his son looked at him.

"The estate is in good running-order," Guy said. "There shouldn't be any extraordinary expenses, but I'll continue to help if needed. But there's more, sir, and I know you will . . . Please sit down, sir; I know that this will be a blow." As his father subsided tensely into a chair, Guy said rapidly, rattling it out: "I expect to be named as co-respondent in a divorce suit by the Duke of Tintagel."

Sir Helmsley gripped the arms of his chair. It was many seconds before he had taken in what his son had said; then, white hot with fury, he shouted, "What—? Are you mad?" With difficulty, he stood up on his crutches. "Nothing like this has ever happened— Do you realize that he can put you in gaol—you and little Miss Mouse too—and it would serve you right, both of you. . . . The scandal, the—"

"She has left Tintagel, but not because of me. Even he won't say that." Guy, trying to remember that compassion was due, kept himself from meeting explosion with explosion, and waited for a lull. When it came, Sir Helmsley, breathing more slowly, demanded: "Don't you know he can sue you for damages? He can ruin you for life!"

"He has had no grounds. Father, I didn't decide to go abroad again so as to take her with me. She knew nothing about it. But I hope that she will marry me as soon as she is free—"

"And where are you hiding her now; where are you keeping her?" Imprudently letting one crutch go in order to shake a fist at his son, Sir Helmsley staggered, but recovered his balance. "I suppose she's in some squalid, vile hotel where they'll trap her—and you with her?"

"She is staying with Mi——" Involuntarily, Guy's eyes went from his father to the little Rossetti painting for an instant as he suppressed the "Miss" he had almost, in his extreme agitation, uttered. "She's in safe keeping, she is *not* with me, but I regard her as under my protection; she—"

"She, she, she—! And what about *me*? Look at what you're doing to *me*!" Sir Helmsley, shaking with bitterness, subsided, panting; then rose in a new crescendo. "You! You would desert; you would have Honourslove go to a child by an—an—an American? A woman with no scruples? one of those damned pirates?" A purple vein in his forehead throbbing, Sir Helmsley Thwarte cried: "Why should I care to preserve the place?" and in a shrill, insensate, infantile fury screamed: "Damn you, I . . . I . . . I'll sell the Holbein!"

XL.

At two in the morning, Miss Testvalley, tired to the bone after a cold, crawling journey from the Champions way station to Paddington and an endless wait for a hansom to take her across London, let herself into the sleeping house in Denmark Hill, hours late. She lit one of the candles on the table in the entry and crept noiselessly up to her old room, to find a nosegay of purple and red anemones in a copper jug which she recognized as pilfered from the kitchen. It acted as a cordial. "So affectionate, and so eager for love," she thought, opening her valise and removing the few objects needful for the night. "I warned the Duke that she was young and impressionable. But I didn't warn *her* properly." Miss Testvalley pulled a long nightgown over her head. "I shouldn't have left her to her own childish free choice. She was seduced by the Celtic gloaming of Tintagel. As I was by the greatness of the match. . . . I see that now. *And* I let her read too much pseudo-mediaeval poetry."

Murmuring, "Only *pour le sport*—why not?" Miss Testvalley took a volume of D. G. Rossetti's poems from a shelf, rested it on its spine, shut her eyes, and let it fall open. "Yes, quite so," she thought, reading the poem thus revealed. "But is it meant for her, or for me?"

"*Mrs. Robinson* approved of your leaving the Duke!?" Miss Testvalley widened her eyes at Annabel.

After a late breakfast, as soon as Miss Testvalley could gently extricate herself from old Gennaro, who happily patted her hand while the old sisters smiled and nodded, and Serafina spooned honey on to her bread, she had taken Nan into the sitting-room for a review of all that had been happening at Champions, at Belfield, and here in Denmark Hill since they had said goodbye at Hyde Park Corner.

"I was surprised too," Nan replied in the same key of amazement; "so much so that, without thinking, I'm afraid, I told her I was coming here."

Miss Testvalley considered. "Discretion seemed advisable, but if Mrs. Robinson was sympathetic she won't have told the Duke—or anyone else—where you are."

"It was Mr. Robinson who told Mr.—who told Guy where to find me."

Nan pronounced the Christian name with a self-conscious, bashful, expectant look at her governess, who, sitting upright in a high-backed cushionless armchair, remarked tonelessly, "I imagine that the Duke would welcome you back."

"I don't think he would." Nan perched on a footstool. "He was more than angry, he was . . . *outraged*; I understand that word now. He'd gone *beyond* rage. By now he'll be erasing me from his life.—And I wouldn't go back to him even if I didn't love someone else."

Miss Testvalley scrutinized her gravely. "Tell me about Mr. Thwarte."

Nan eagerly welcomed her first mention of the name. "As you know, I'd made up my mind to go back to America. But now I find that *he* is leaving England, on *my* account."

"Leaving—!" Miss Testvalley sat back, astounded. This was completely unexpected. She kept herself from asking: "Does his father know?"

"He wants me to go with him," Nan continued in a rush, "and marry him as soon as Ushant divorces me—"

Miss Testvalley's mouth fell open. "To go with—before you are married?"

"To *be* with him, not to *live* with him." An eloquent facial expression, and a deep blush, rather than her words, made Nan's distinction clear. "But I'm afraid it would be ruinous for him. I said I must talk with you. I don't want to be irrational, or selfish."

But as she invoked reason and selflessness, Annabel's great dark-fringed eyes pleaded for encouragement to follow her heart; she had a bloom, a radiance, the governess had not seen since her marriage, and there was a new vibrancy in her voice as she said, "He's here!" almost before a knock on the door sounded and Serafina let the visitor in.

Guy too had changed since Miss Testvalley's last sight of him. His face was thinner, almost grim; and vertical lines were etched on either side of his mouth. But his eyes brightened and softened as they went instinctively to Nan before he turned and bowed to the older lady.

"I hope that Sir Helmsley is making a good recovery?" Miss Testvalley asked at the same moment that Nan asked: "Is your father very angry?"

"Thank you, yes—yes, to both questions," Guy said unsmilingly.

He had no idea, the governess saw, that *her* enquiry had been inspired by anything other than courtesy. He took a seat near her throne-like chair, across from the footstool from which Annabel informed him: "I was about to tell—" She turned to Miss Testvalley. "Oh, Val, don't think I don't know that you may suffer for sheltering me, but I hope I can help—"

"No!" Miss Testvalley, raising a prohibitive hand, achieved her most clipped, most authoritative tone. "I shall manage beautifully; there are more offers than I can accept, quite without regard to such employers as you know of. And in any case, Annabel, I would not allow *my* concerns to affect your future.

Wherever that may lie," she added, looking deliberately, but uncertainly, at Guy, who might well be reluctant to admit a third person to this discussion.

However, Guy addressed her with alacrity. "Annabel may have told you that I have a job in Greece? And after that, work in India. The pay is decent—or indecent; in those poor countries we'd be rich. I also have some money of my own. I can undertake to support Annabel!"

"He might be some young bank-clerk asking a parent for a daughter's hand in marriage," Miss Testvalley thought, with a strange sense of *déjà vécu*. She had once interrogated Lord Richard Marable as to his feeling for Conchita Closson. (Well, the feeling had been as true as his nature allowed; no truer, though consecrated and legalized, than in his brief clandestine pursuit and conquest of the family governess.) Later, the Duke of Tintagel had sought her help in his wooing of Annabel St. George. And now, in the dissolving of the Duke's marriage, she was again being treated as Annabel's quasi-mother.

"But"—she silently told the tall, lean, fair young man, so like and so unlike his father—"I may be *your* *step*mother."

As she phrased the thought, however, the "may be" tentatively modulated to "might be" . . . and, tremblingly, to "might have been." Just as her frail cockle-shell of a bark spoke the unhoped-for tiny island of Ithaca, a thunderhead was forming over it, and winds beyond her power to resist were sweeping it out to sea toward Scylla and Charybdis and the Symplegades. . . .

"Greece!" Though she wasn't happy, Miss Testvalley smiled a little. "Mr. Thwarte, when she was sixteen Annabel said that if she loved a man—I believe that at that period he had to be a poet—she would leave her marble halls and follow him to the Isles of Greece. We didn't know then that she *would* live in marble halls. A cousin of mine," she added, parenthetically, out of genealogical habit, "was Lord Byron's doctor."

"Since Byron's time, few Westerners have gone to Greece,

and they've gone mostly in comfort, on private yachts." Guy became his own devil's advocate. "I don't want to mislead Annabel. It's a rugged country. I've been talking with people. It's as rough"—he turned to Nan—"as your Wild West. Few roads, no railways—hence my job—almost no doctors; it's still in a way under Turkish rule. Either you'd stay in Athens while I explored, or you'd ride a donkey and we'd sleep in villages and live on goat cheese and olives."

Nan's eyes were shining. "It must be as beautiful as ever!"

Seeing an answering light in Guy Thwarte's eyes, Miss Testvalley coughed. "It may be a long time," she said pointedly, "before you are free to marry. If Annabel goes to Greece now—?" She looked from one to the other.

"Miss Testvalley," Guy said emphatically, "I'm not proposing it out of sheer selfishness. Think!"—he leaned forward, fists on his knees—"Think! If she stays here, defendant in a law suit, what life will she have?—even if Ushant does *not* want her to be persecuted. And in America, journalists—not only American but English, French—would swoop on her like harpies—"

With a shake of the head, Nan interrupted him. "From what I've heard," she said wryly, "I could go to one of the new American territories.—In the Wild West!" she threw at Guy, half-smiling, "for a few days and *buy* a divorce. But I married Ushant in the Church of England. The Dowager says I should have thought before I made vows, and she's right. It's only fair to let Ushant divorce me according to the same rules."

"He will have to anyway," Miss Testvalley put in, "to be free to re-marry."

Nan nodded. "In any case, until we are both free, I—I want to keep my word to him. But I'll write now and tell him that I am going away and . . . hope to be with someone else."

"To serve as the 'confession' one hears of?" Miss Testvalley suggested.

"I had not thought of it as a confession," Nan said loftily.

Just as she was ceasing to be a duchess, thought her governess, Nan was beginning to display something of a duchess's hauteur. Then she realized that Nan was trying to express something that manifestly did not come easily.

"I wouldn't feel immoral living with Guy, even before we could marry. I *would* feel immoral if I went back to Ushant, not loving him and having to . . . produce sons for him." Nan addressed the speech to her governess, and the colour mounted to the roots of her tawny hair; but when she had finished she looked directly at Guy, who, with a "No matter how long, I will wait," got up and kissed her hands.

All at once Miss Testvalley felt depressed and jaded. They *would* go off together; this discussion was farcical. And it was unlikely that they would keep a sword between them during the months of waiting. And why should they? The social deterrent would no longer affect Annabel, who'd already have lost her reputation. Still, she had to state the obvious, to make sure Annabel knew.

"Mr. Thwarte," she said bluntly, "Annabel thinks that she may do you harm, but she will lose more than you ever could. The arduousness of life in Greece is irrelevant, as are marble halls. Wherever you go, you, as a man, will be accepted. She will be ostracized—even after you marry—by Europeans and the few Americans you'll meet. And by 'respectable' natives. You have lived abroad; do you agree with what I say?"

"I d-do." In his sincerity, Guy stuttered. "I have thought about it. I shall have to associate with Europeans, especially in India. But I will never c-c-consort, never have any but the unavoidable business contacts, with anyone, anywhere, where Annabel isn't honoured." He stood up, energetic and buoyant, as if re-invigorated by Annabel's mettlesome flouting of convention, and said roundly: "Miss Testvalley! If Annabel were to be unhappy, or I to be unhappy *for* her, we wouldn't stay! We'd go to Canada, or Australia—New Zealand—where life is different. I'm a working man. A civil engineer. I care no more than Annabel does about society."

Guy's self-assurance spoke in the high poise of his head, the direct gaze of his gray eyes; and it was a bold assurance new in kind in Miss Testvalley's experience of the privileged classes, deriving as it did from personal achievement in the ungentle world where ability mattered. "I can build railways," he continued, "and they want railways all over the world. We can travel. Annabel wants to help poor people and teach children. She'll find more work than she can ever do. What can I say, Miss Testvalley, except that, that—I pledge Annabel my life."

"It's true love," Miss Testvalley thought. "I believe he will be loyal." Her heart was gripped, as in a vise, by a pang of yearning; she shut her eyes a moment for the pain. Nevertheless her immediate comment was dry: "You would at least escape the great obstacle to casual elopers—boredom." She had in mind various couples she knew of who had "bolted" dramatically to Biarritz or Monte-Carlo expecting that thenceforth life would be an endless holiday. . . . More kindly, she said to Guy: "You will understand my concern. Annabel is an idealist; she can easily be taken advantage of in this rough world."

"Ah, but I've become a realist," Nan protested, while Guy demanded: "Miss Testvalley, won't you trust me?"

Miss Testvalley blazed at them. "Oh, you are both impetuous, too impetuous! The trouble is that I too am a romantic! Last night I tried the *sortes Virgilianae* with Dante Gabriel's poems, and the book opened to:

> *"Look in my face: my name is Might-have-been;*
> *I am also called No-more, Too-late, Farewell. . . .*

"You see, *I* would act! I would seize the moment! That's why," she lied, "I'm always glad to take off to some new post, some new country. But I do not feel entitled to be adventurous with *other* people's lives; and what you're doing will affect other people . . . your families, their friendships. . . ."

"Val!" Nan clasped her hands in her lap as she bent forward.

"I think the only person I have a serious obligation to is Ushant, and he won't truly be hurt, only in his sense of correctness. I've thought and thought about it all." She spoke like a good pupil expecting praise. But the teacher said nothing, and her stillness, rather than any expression, roused Nan's alarm. "There's something else, Val, isn't there? Have I another responsi— There's something you're not telling me!"

In her stillness, Miss Testvalley had made a decision. What she chose to say, however, was tangential. "When all this comes out, you realize, no one will be allowed to mention your name in front of Kitty and Corisande."

Nan flinched. "Of course," she said slowly, "I'll be a Fallen Woman. . . ."

Nan's visceral jealousy of the two girls had vanished as quickly as it had smitten her, and she again thought of them fondly; the more fondly (naturally) because she knew how much they admired her. She was so jolted by Miss Testvalley's unsparing reminder that she failed to realize that *this* particular consequence of an elopement hardly accounted for the governess's somber mien; but Guy asked quietly:

"Miss Testvalley, is there more that we should know?— Some obligation?—Is there someone else who will suffer besides Ushant and"—he halted, but then went on firmly—"my father?"

Miss Testvalley looked into the friendly, worried eyes that were searching hers. Did he know, did he guess? She couldn't tell. But if he did, what difference would it make? Leadenly, she said: "Obligation? Yes. What you're doing lays a heavy obligation on you to be happy with each other." Both young people were caught by her tone. But martyrdom was not in her combative nature. Drawing a deep breath, she summoned an encouraging smile. "And I am sure that you will be!—Besides, you are not going into exile forever. Mr. Thwarte, you will inherit Honourslove. Your son will inherit Honourslove, and at some time you'll return home. People forget. They forget even the unforgettable. . . . So," she went on briskly, "I take it that you will not contest a charge of . . . of infidelity, but will avoid the possible danger of actual arrest. Just what are your plans?"

"I'd like Annabel to go to Boulogne," said Guy, who had sat back in relief. "To the Hôtel de Boulogne et de l'Univers. It's a quiet family place. I should be able to join her soon afterwards, and from there we'd go to Brest or Bayonne, and then by sea to the Piraeus."

Miss Testvalley nodded. "I can go to Boulogne with Annabel."

"I'm capable of going by myself," Nan protested; but Guy and the governess simultaneously said "No!" and the latter went on: "A young lady of fashion travelling alone would attract curiosity. It's not inconceivable that detectives are watching the ports."

"Dear Val," the new Annabel exclaimed, "all the more reason for you not to be with me!—And I see a way to manage," she pursued. "Serafina's niece wants to go back to Italy. I'm sure she'd go with me and stay with me in Boulogne. I can pay her more than she'd get in her restaurant, and her fare on to Florence besides. And *she* wouldn't be accused of being a—an accomplice, or whatever."

"She must travel in your compartment," the governess, yielding, insisted, "and have a room next to yours in the hotel, as if you were mother and daughter."

Slowly, Nan shook her head. An Italian country-woman. A stranger . . . A sense of guilt too deep for conscious recognition kept her from saying it aloud to Miss Testvalley, but she thought: "*You* are my mother."

XLI.

Conchita was already in St. Paul's, waiting. She kissed Nan and cried: "Oh, are you really going to America? Jinny says you are. But how ghastly!"

"I thought I was. And don't tell people otherwise; it's important!"

"I won't, truly." Conchita was relieved. "But where are you going, then?"

"To Greece . . . with Guy Thwarte."

Conchita's amethyst eyes shone. "Nan, how lovely . . . And Ushant?"

"When I meant to go to America, I supposed he would divorce me for desertion, but now—"

"But now it will be adultery," Conchita cried happily, "and that's a thousand times faster; you and Guy Thwarte can be married sooner. So can the Duke. I wonder whom he'll pick? Or be picked by . . . ! Darling, I *am* glad. At first I couldn't see why you needed to *leave* the Duke, but it will be heavenly for you two to be together all the time, not just snatching half-hours."

"Jinny's mad at me."

"Well, she would be," Conchita said matter-of-factly; "besides, remember H.R.H. doesn't like his friends, or their families, to be in the public eye."

"H.R.— Oh, I see," Nan said slowly. "So. Conchita, will

you do something for me? I asked Jinny, but I don't think she will. I am worried about Miss Testvalley. Will you help her find a new post?"

"But I'll do it for *her*! You know I've always liked her a lot, and I can see that she can't produce credentials from your mother-in-law—or mine! I'll try—I'll find people who want a governess and persuade them! Give me her address. I'll tell them she had nothing to do with your bolting.—Oh, Nan," Conchita exclaimed as Nan wrote down the details. "Could we ever have dreamed—? Think of the Grand Union Hotel—! For you to be a duchess, and then not want to be! It's like Cinderella running away from Prince Charming and going off with the raggle-taggle-gypsies-O! Or, no, it's like her finding that he was an impostor, and going off with the *true* Prince Charming. . . ." Conchita's voice changed. "But, Nan, will you write to me?"

Tears were running down Conchita's dusky cheeks.

"Ah, don't, Conchie; of course I'll write, and you'll write to me, and we'll meet again, I simply know it! Conchie, don't," Nan begged, "or you'll make me!"

Upstairs in her room that evening, Miss Testvalley carefully placed her candle on the table beside the jug of anemones. She found some paper, and took up her pen.

"My dear Sir Helmsley . . ."

She clenched her fists so tight that her nails cut into her palms. Where next? A textile magnate's family in Yorkshire? A broker's in Purley? Or New York again? Saratoga? With no respectable references . . . She dismissed the idea of help, through Annabel, from any of "the girls."

He might never suspect. But more probably her role *would* come out. Things usually did. In any case, could she live a lie? "*Noblesse oblige,*" she muttered without joy, almost without pride, and began a letter which she ended—

... with deep regret that our union must be impossible. You will understand when I tell you that, although I deeply grieve for your disappointment, and deplore the many unhappy consequences of this unexpected event, my regard for your son, and my affection and regard for my former pupil Annabel Tintagel, remain unchanged, and that in the interest of what I believe to be their deserved true happiness I could not wish them to live their lives apart.

Sincerely, Laura Testavaglia

"He will not even answer," Laura muttered as she dribbled molten wax on to her envelope and impressed it with her Testavaglia signet ring: *Tar ublia chi bien eima.*

"It's all hypothetical. It's fanciful. It's playing a game."

Mr. Robinson faced his wife, unobstructed either by his paper (there was no Sunday *Times*) or by the monumental apparatus of the Belfield breakfast-room. A notable success in Lizzy's undermining of his stubborn British orthodoxy had been her persuading him that cozy breakfasts in her little boudoir, on a round table by the window spread with crisp white linen, before he had doffed his dressing-gown, were not wickedly Continental and had special charm, even if he felt obliged later to sally below for blood pudding and kippers.

But this morning, despite the cheerful sunlight on his one side and cheerful firelight on his other, and an enjoyment of comfort that was also a virtuous concession to a wife's wish, Hector Robinson, usually sanguine, experienced an unwonted disenchantment. There were intrigues enough in Whitehall. He wished they could be banished from the home.

Thwarte's readiness to leave his ancestral estate (it was now said that he was going to South Africa) was imbecilic. As for Annabel—! Yet she was intelligent, as well as delightfully lovely.

"Are you *quite* sure," he had asked Lizzy, "that Annabel doesn't want to change her mind?" "Can you possibly think—?" Lizzy had begun, but had abandoned rhetoric to answer quietly: "Believe me, if Nan had liked duchessdom, none of this would be taking place. We'd none of us take something from her that she wasn't ready to lose."

But it was a long road from Annabel's rumoured elopement to Tintagel's marrying a second wife of Lizzy's choice. Out of delicacy, Hector had not discussed the programme with Mabel herself, and he had shied away from asking Lizzy directly: Did her sister even endorse the plan? Did she really expect it to work? On this fine Sunday morning, he allowed himself to grumble.

"It's all hypothetical," he repeated testily. "Not only is there no assurance that the Duke will be interested; the probabilities are almost infinitely against it. One can't simply decide that two people are going to marry each other—"

He was about to expatiate when Mabel, by previous invitation, came into the room. Relieved of the black she punctiliously wore in public, wrapped in a rose-coloured peignoir—fresh, clear-eyed, and glowing with health and good humour—she helped herself to coffee and smiled at Hector.

"Of course it's all uncertain—absolutely!—and I'm so glad you realize it. Goodness, remember, I've never even met the Duke." Mabel buttered a bit of toast and spread marmalade. "That is, I know he came to Runnymede once, but I can't remember what he looked like, let alone know what he really is, as a person." She nibbled at the toast. "How can I know that he would suit me?"

As her brother-in-law swallowed his tea the wrong way and choked, Mabel continued earnestly: "You know, Hector, in the last few months, since Mr. Whittaker died, I've been forced to be, well, I hope not cynical, but—I have had to think very carefully about the motives of men who—and there already are some!—who want to marry me. Money becomes a frightful burden. I *do not* want to be married for my money. And I wouldn't want the Duke of Tintagel to have false hopes."

After Mabel, two pieces of toast and marmalade later, had drifted from the room, Lizzy observed quietly: "You see the note to strike."

"Yes," Mr. Robinson muttered, "I see. But," he posited, unconsciously throwing out his chest—if Lizzy had her "Hail Columbia" moments, he had his "Rule Britannia" strain—"Tintagel *is* a duke! It is all very improbable. There are other rich women, and other, ah, entrepreneurs, eager to make arrangements. We have not one fact—no firm advantage—nothing solid."

"There's one advantage solid as marble. What does the Naxos throne mean to you?"

"Nothing. Oh, ah—" Mr. Robinson had a highly trained memory. "Didn't one of the obituary notices your mother sent us mention that Whittaker had a very important classical sculpture in his collection?"

"Part of one. By an act of providence."

"How so?"

"Mab says the other part of the sculpture is at Longlands. And Nan told me that the Duke loathes having a fragment. He considers it demeaning, like having one shoe. . . . So, Mabel will ask if she might be allowed to view the throne. Whereupon she— with me, or you and me, to chaperone—is invited to Longlands to see it. Or she might stay alone, decorously, at the Dower-House. She has a drawing of her part of the throne. The Duke will ask if he may call on her to look at it. By that time, of course, she'll have taken a house in Belgravia.—Did I tell you that she's looking at one in Eaton Place?"

"And she'll offer to sell?" But Hector blushed at his crudity even before Lizzy's impatient "Certainly not! She will offer to restore her part to its proper place at Longlands as a gesture in keeping with her late husband's international spirit. And so on, and so on . . . I admit that it isn't quite a Q.E.D., but the odds are high.—And as for selling," Lizzy added sedately, "from what Mab says, it's unlikely that the Duke could afford it."

Mr. Robinson sat motionless, fixedly gazing at the tea-cup —the dagger, as it were—in the air before him, held by his forgetful hand. His mind rapidly reviewed the plunder, pillage, sack, and rapine of his native land throughout the course of history. First, the Romans had come. Then the Angles, Jutes, and Saxons. Then the Danes terrorized England for three centuries. Norman pirates took the country over in 1066. Five centuries later Turks raided the Thames and took prisoners to sell in the Libyan slave-market. . . . But never had there been any phenomenon to match this, this—he recalled an article—this "invasion of England by American women and their chiefs of commissariat, the silent American men. . . ." "What a gang of buccaneers you are!" he breathed to his wife.

"Buccaneers," Lizzy reminded him gently, "were not notorious for paying fortunes for what they took."

The post which brought Sir Helmsley Thwarte Laura's letter, evoking the emotions she had foreseen, also contained a request from D. G. Rossetti for a loan of thirty guineas which provided more fuel for the baronet's wrath and grief.—"Damnation! Hell! Damnation!" He'd suspected—*he'd known for certain!*—that Guy had begun to say that that . . . that *woman*—that false woman—was sheltering that girl. . . . *"Damnation!"* This catastrophe was the work of Italian—Italian—Sir Helmsley shook a crutch at his little Rossetti and barely refrained from knocking it into the fire with the two letters—"Damnation!—Italian *banditti,* and American—American *pirates!"*

"My dear love." Guy held Nan tight, in the cramped entrance hall of the house in Denmark Hill from which she, Miss Testvalley, and Serafina's niece were about to set forth in the hansom waiting outside the door. "Darling, be brave. We'll meet at the Hôtel de Boulogne et de l'Univers."

Nan, her arms about his neck, smiled up at him. "With such a name, how can we fail to reach the Isles of Greece?"

"And then the Vale of Kashmir."

"I . . ." Nan broke off.

"What—?"

Nan choked. If she told him again how happy she was she'd begin to cry. "Will you do something for me?" she asked instead, and, when Guy had murmured "Anything," said to him: "Please bring a side-saddle for my donkey. I doubt if they sell them in Athens."

In the grimy chill of Charing Cross Station, passengers for Paris and Milano via Folkestone–Boulogne, and those seeing them off, milled about the boat-train. English gentlemen in travelling-caps and valets carrying tartan travelling-rugs, French bourgeois couples muffled to the ears in prevision of *courants d'air* in their carriage, vociferous Italian *contadini* laden with victuals for a two-days' journey, London porters shouting, "Mind your step, please," jostled in a medley of embraces and waving hands and high-pitched *bon voyage*'s, *arrivederci*'s, and goodbyes. Serafina's niece Anna, a cloak encompassing her sturdy bustled form, dwarfed Miss Testvalley in a new dolman, Nan's parting gift, and Nan in a slim ulster and small neat hat and veil. When a porter had found her compartment, Nan boarded and dropped her hand-bag; then, while Anna disposed their travelling-oddments, jumped down onto the platform and with bursting heart threw her arms around Miss Testvalley and hugged her tighter and tighter. "Oh, Val . . . How can I ever . . . ?" Weeping, as the guard blew his whistle for the third time, she let go of the governess, lunged at the steps of the carriage, and climbed aboard. A second later, she leaned from the open window of the compartment and waved, in tears and smiles, as with a deep laborious chug, chug the train began to move.

Miss Testvalley watched it vanish in the outer reaches of the yards to click across the Thames and gain momentum as it made for the Channel. Then she turned and slowly walked back down the long platform. Giving up her platform ticket at the barrier, she crossed the great hall with its acrid smell of coal-smoke and its echoes of farewell sobs and mournful locomotive-whistles. At the exit to the Strand, she drew herself erect, put her hand up to push back the hair that was escaping beneath her hat brim but fluffed it out instead, and aimed her furled umbrella upward.

With a weary flick of his whip, a cabman set his horse clomping toward her in recognition of a signal. Another observer might have seen a female warrior raising a sword to lead the remnants of an army to battle.

Afterword

Edith Wharton had written some 89,000 words of *The Buccaneers* when she died in 1937. Her literary executor, Gaillard Lapsley, had the incomplete manuscript published in New York the following year. It was a draft which Wharton wrote with great spontaneity and brio, departing in some important ways from the "Synopsis" she had drawn up, setting forth the main lines of the novel. Lapsley made "certain verbal emendations required by sense or consistency," and a few other changes have been made here, when it seemed that Wharton would have revised to avoid being repetitive, and when she referred to race in terms offensive to modern readers; her original language can be found in the 1938 edition. The passages I have interpolated in the original text serve to reconcile discrepancies in the narrative or prepare for later developments.

Marion Mainwaring
April 1993

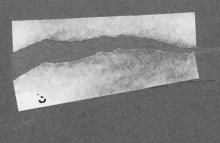